HIDDEN BY THE
LAW

More Seth Hannen stories to come

HIDDEN BY THE
LAW

A SETH HANNEN NOVEL BY
SIMON BOWDEN

OBELUS
PUBLISHING

OBELUS PUBLISHING

First Published in Great Britain in 2021 by Obelus Publishing

1 3 5 7 9 10 8 6 4 2

First Edition

A CIP catalogue record of this book is available from the British Library.

ISBN	978 1 8384501 3 7	Hardcover
	978 1 8384501 1 3	Paperback
	978 1 8384501 2 0	eBook

Cover design by Obelus Publishing

Typeset in Bembo by Obelus Publishing

Printed by Amazon

Obelus Publishing

Simon Bowden trading as Obelus Publishing (Imprint)

www.obeluspublishing.com

For Elizabeth, who supports all of my endeavours

The police are the public and the public are the police

Sir Robert Peel

PROLOGUE

1978

'Gracious God, surround us and all who mourn this day with your continuing compassion. Do not let grief overwhelm your children, or turn them against you…'

Seth was just six years old when he attended his first funeral. He listened to the vicar reading the prayers, his eyes clamped tightly shut, and his forehead wrinkled. He tried his hardest not to shed a tear, struggling desperately to close it all out. His jaw was locked rigid with stress, and his teeth were grinding.

'Seth, boys don't cry. They are tough – come on, be a man like me,' his father would tell him.

He often cried, and every time he would think to himself; *it can't be true that only girls cry.* But on that day, he was not going to shed a single tear, no way, not with his father there.

Seth stood in his slightly oversized black suit, holding his mother's hand. He was desperately waiting for his father to walk over and kiss him on the forehead and then tell him everything would be okay; his dad always made everything okay. Of course, that was not going to happen. His father was dead.

Now the family was smaller by one, just Seth, his mother, and his older sister Leah. Life had changed beyond all recognition.

By the time of the funeral, his father had been gone for three weeks. The detective had spoken to Seth twice, but at six years old, it was hard for him to understand everything that was going on, let alone comprehend why someone would want to kill his dad.

Until Edward's death, the Hannen family was like any other. They lived an unassuming existence with nothing worth stealing and seemingly nothing particularly exciting happening in their lives. Their home was an average house in Burnham, near Slough, and they kept themselves to themselves. Kathleen, Seth's mother, worked as a typist at the local police station, almost directly opposite their home on Stomp Road. His father, Edward, was a former Royal Navy diver who had finished his military career and joined the Civil Service, having applied unsuccessfully to be a police officer – he was not quite tall enough to meet the height requirements of the day.

On a warm September afternoon, Edward had returned from work in London early. He had planned to surprise Kathleen on her birthday when she came home after picking Seth up from school. He disturbed a burglar and tried to tackle him, chasing him into the kitchen. As the resultant struggle ensued, the burglar snatched a kitchen knife and sank the blade into Edward's abdomen, severing his aorta and proving fatal. He died on the kitchen floor before Kathleen and Seth found him. The police had never solved Edward's murder.

In time, the only inheritance waiting for Seth was his father's watch, issued to him by the Royal Navy, and the proceeds of a small investment that his father had made, due to pay out when Seth was older. No other legacy awaited him. But one thing was for sure, Seth was going to live out his father's dream – he would grow up tall and become a policeman and do some good in the world.

PART ONE

BRIGHT FUTURE AHEAD
1992

CHAPTER 1

Double-Bubble

Thursday the 18th of June 1992 looked like a typical day, but it wore a disguise for some people, hiding its true identity from its victims. For those few individuals, the 18th of June had decided to be a bastard. The spinning wheel of fate had chosen Seth Hannen to be one of them.

Seth's mind woke up first, before the rest of his body, pushing the same initial thought into his head that he had woken up to every morning since he was just six years old. The image of his father's coffin in the church, the vicar, stood the other side of it, leading the service. As Seth, the boy, shut his eyes tight to block out his father's death, Seth, the man, opened his eyes to a brand-new day.

He looked across at the digital clock beside his bed. The glowing red numbers of the display beamed the time back at him.

05:07

Still half asleep, he let his eyelids slide shut again, allowing himself to drift back into a light sleep.

Seth joined the Thames Valley Police in September 1990 at the age of only eighteen. He had completed his initial training at Ashford Police Training Centre before being posted to Maidenhead Police Station and had now almost completed his two-year probationary period.

Having joined so young, he was on a lower pay scale than his older colleagues. Anyone joining at the age of twenty-two or older went straight to the post-probation pay point and earned more money from the start. Seth had to wait a little longer before he would receive a half-decent pay rise.

Despite living in the free accommodation in the single officers' quarters above the police station, he spent his money fast, so he needed his flexible friend the Access Card to get him by.

Seth's room was a mere three-metre square box, with a built-in wardrobe, a desk, a bedside table and of course, a bed. There was no room for anything personal whatsoever. The curtains were a thin dreary brown coloured material that added to the room's gloominess. At night, they failed to keep out the light from the police vehicles in the back yard. The window was a single glazed aluminium framed piece of glass that allowed any noise from the back yard to invade the tiny room. Despite the reasonably grim accommodation, Seth was happy, he had started on the career that his father had wanted before his life was abruptly cut short.

Thud, thud, thud, Seth woke with a jolt. *What the fuck?* He thought as he looked again at the digital clock, the red glowing numbers still shining like beacons.

06:09

'You'd better not be pissing me around, Rivett,' shouted Seth, assuming that his next-door neighbour was playing an early morning prank, in the knowledge that Seth had probably sneaked a woman onto the male floor of single quarters.

'Get your arse out of bed, Constable Hannen,' came the slightly lisped reply.

Sergeant Ian Jones, known as Jonesy, was looking for two officers to work overtime at short notice. Working on a rest day with less than eight days' notice was paid at double time.

'What's up, sarge?' asked Seth, still in his bed.

'Today's your lucky day, mate, double-bubble, rest-day less-than-eight, and you're off to Royal Ascot. Get yourself to the skipper's office in fifteen minutes sharp,' shouted Jonesy.

Jonesy held his head close to Seth's door, suspecting that he may have someone else in the room with him. If he found out that he did, then he would withdraw the offer of working a rest-day on overtime for sure.

Happy Birthday to me! Thought Seth to himself, as he turned to the young woman police constable, with who he had shared his single bed the night before.

'Shhh! He's not gone yet,' Seth placed a finger up to Jackie's lips.

They had been out for a few drinks on Wednesday night, then gone back to single quarters, and one thing had led to another.

Jackie's accommodation was on the next floor up from Seth's, where the 'wopsy's' rooms were. Men were not allowed up there, and vice versa. If Seth got caught with her in his room, he would be in deep shit. If he were not still in his probation period, it would not be so bad, but he still had three months to go until he was confirmed in post. Messing it up now would not be a good idea.

Thud, thud, thud, Jonesy had moved to the next room. Seth heard the same routine called out as Jonesy woke up Constable Mark Rivett, only this time, as he walked off, he added a last request.

'Oh, and Constable Rivett, you can bring me a hot cup of

coffee and a chocolate digestive to show me your gratitude, mate!'

Seth scurried off to the communal bathroom for a shower, before returning to his room. He quickly pulled on his uniform, a clean pair of black woollen trousers, a freshly ironed light blue shirt, with epaulettes already fastened to the shoulders. He did the buttons up at lightning speed, then snapped the black clip-on tie to the collar. Then he slid his peg into the long pocket in his trousers, pushing the leather thong under his belt to make it easy for him to pull the truncheon out quickly if he needed to. Then the cuff pouch - clipped shut, polished boots on and tied tight. He grabbed his tunic and helmet, and he was ready to rock 'n' roll.

Seth leant down and gave Jackie a hug.

'I've got my key, stay here long enough for the night-turn blokes to get into their rooms, then you'd better get back upstairs, lock up and pop the spare key under the door, will you? If it's left unlocked, someone will either play a prank or nick some of my uniform.'

'Okay, that's fine, but are we alright, Seth?' I feel a bit weird about last night,' she replied.

'We're good, Jax… and it was good!' he smiled cheekily then opened the door a little before poking his head out to check that the coast was clear, so nobody would see her in the room as he left, then he was gone.

Seth looked good in his uniform; at just over six foot, he carried his athletic figure well, always walking tall and proud. He had regulation, short dark brown hair and was always cleanly shaven (beards or moustaches had to be grown whilst on leave, and only after a supervisor had granted permission). His appearance was youthful and boyish, making him look like a very young cop indeed, often bringing about comments like 'the police are getting younger these days,' from witnesses he took statements from and old ladies in the street.

Seth walked into the skipper's office on the ground floor carrying his helmet by its strap to see Mark already there chatting to Jonesy, who was happily munching on a chocolate digestive and sipping coffee from a big white mug with 'SKIPPER' written across it in bold blue writing.

'You took your time Hannen,' exclaimed Jonesy through a mouthful of biscuit, a couple of crumbs leaving his mouth as he spoke.

'Sorry, sarge, I was just—'

'Just getting your bird out of your room, eh.' Jonesy interjected, laughing through his digestive. 'Good job I didn't see her!'

Seth felt himself blush a little.

'Right, you two owe me big time, two of the blokes working Royal Ascot have thrown a sickie, and you'll be working together in the Old Paddock. The bus leaves in ten minutes; don't miss it, for fuck's sake,' said Jonesy, nodding his head towards his office door.

'Cheers, sarge, thanks for the overtime,' said Seth.

'You're welcome, mate,' replied Jonesy, smiling.

Jonesy was a fair skipper, and he had heard that Seth may be having some financial problems.

That was it, briefing over. Seth and Mark wrote their start time on the duty sheet, and Jonesy countersigned it. Then they walked out to the back yard, giving each other a wry smile at the thought of at least ten hours of work on double pay.

'This is perfect timing, Mark, I really need the cash. My mum called a couple of weeks ago. My credit card is well over the limit, and I've had a letter at home threatening a County Court Judgement if I don't clear it,' said Seth.

'Well, that'll scupper you passing your probation, matey, the job won't take a forgiving stance, Seth, you'll be out on your ear in a shot,' replied Mark.

'I know, if I can hold them off for three more months, so I can get through my probation first, then I'll be home and dry. The pay rise will help a lot.'

They jumped onto the almost full single decker bus about to take officers to Ascot for the event briefing.

* * *

The bus parked up on the main road directly outside Ascot Police Station. Everyone filed off and walked into the back yard, where they joined other cops that had been drafted in from across the whole police force area. Over three hundred officers had crammed into the small enclosure behind the police station, waiting to be briefed by the police event commander.

'Listen-in, everyone. I'm Superintendent Richard Lewington, and I'm in command of the Royal Ascot Races' policing operation. So far this week, we've enjoyed little in the way of trouble, just the odd drunken fight in the pubs later in the evening. Make sure you've read your operation orders and had your specific briefing from your serial supervisors.

'Oh, and I know I don't need to tell you not to accept any alcoholic beverages from well-wishing racegoers, at their car park picnics, after the racing. Anyone that does will have me to answer to. Have a good day, and don't let me down.'

Superintendent Lewington spoke with an authoritative voice that made it clear he was very much in charge.

Seth and Mark were called over to a smaller group of officers, where an inspector gave them their specific deployments for the day.

After the briefing, they headed out of the police station, turning left onto the High Street, before descending the steps to the tunnel that would take them under the main road. It brought them up inside the racecourse, just a few metres away from the Old Paddock enclosure, which is where the more well-off clientele would spend the day quaffing champagne, accompanied with perhaps strawberries and cream.

'I'm literally only here for the money,' announced Seth. 'To be honest, I hate events, I'd much rather be investigating a car theft, you know a Cosworth or something, that kind of work I don't mind. This stuff should be the work of security firms. They really don't need police officers here, not over three hundred of us anyway.'

'Look, if we're working together all day, less moaning would be a good idea, stop telling me about your money troubles, will you. We're getting paid double-bubble, and we're in the posh end. There'll be totty for sure, that should help make it an enjoyable day,' said Mark.

Mark was pretty laid back about the whole thing, he enjoyed policing events, and had aspirations of running the Operations Team one day. He wanted to plan the policing of occasions like Royal Ascot Races, State visits, and Henley Regatta.

It was not long before groups of women were asking Seth and Mark for photograph opportunities. Men in uniform, especially tall young ones, were a hit at this kind of event. *As long as the blokes don't get too pissed and Seth stops moaning, the day should be a good one,* thought Mark.

'Excuse me officers, could we get a picture with you? Would that be okay?'

The two cops looked over to see three exceptionally well-dressed young women, one wearing a pink hat, in the shape of the Rolls Royce driven by Parker and Lady Penelope in Thunderbirds, and the other two wearing blue dresses, and hats like Scott and Virgil would wear during an international rescue.

'Well now… this is more like it,' said Seth, winking at Mark, as his spirits began to lift.

They lined up against the white railing that separated the racehorses from the spectators. Two of the women put their arms around the cop's waists, while the third took a photograph with her Olympus thirty-five-millimetre camera, then she swapped places with the Lady Penelope lookalike for a second picture. After the mini photo-shoot, Seth and Mark began to walk away, to do a circuit of the enclosure before the arrival of the Queen and the other royals.

'So, my name's Paula', called the woman in the pink dress, as Seth and Mark walked off.

Seth turned around just as she caught hold of his left hand with her right.

'Wow… my luck's in!' Seth mouthed to his colleague.

'Please don't go yet,' she said, giving him a huge grin. 'Could we meet later, once you finish your official duties maybe… or perhaps I could call you?'

'You go on, mate. I'll meet you at meal break,' said Seth to Mark, giving him another wink.

Paula was in her mid-twenties at most, she was slim with long auburn hair, with eyes that matched perfectly. Despite the somewhat silly hat, she looked terrific in her figure-hugging dress. Seth took out his notebook from his tunic pocket, not the buff-coloured official police one that he would record evidence in, but the other little black notebook that he carried and used to make non-evidential notes.

'I'd love to meet you sometime. I'd better take your number though, I live in police single quarters right now, and if you call the phone in there, God only knows who you'll get on the other end,' he said, handing her his notebook and pen.

Paula wrote her details and then kissed the page to leave a lipstick print.

Paula 0628 776549
Please call me – soon!

Seth had no idea of the significance of this fleeting encounter. His decision to stay and have a short flirtatious liaison with Paula rather than stick with his patrol partner would bring about immense changes in his life.

Time for a sneaky coffee back at the nick, thought Seth, as he headed for the gates that led back out and onto the High Street. He decided to walk along the footpath, jump the barrier and cross over the road, rather than use the tunnel. *It should be quieter now. Pretty much everyone's inside the course waiting to see the Queen arrive,* he thought to himself as he lengthened his stride. He felt a warm feeling inside about his meeting with Paula, the day was not turning out so bad after all.

As Seth jumped the temporary barrier between the pavement and the road, he noticed a shiny black Aston Martin Vantage parked near the staff entrance to the racecourse. The car was stationary in the road, blocking its side of the carriageway and causing chaos. It was early for anyone to be leaving the course, it was more likely that the driver was looking for a missed car park entrance, or the car may even have been stolen after it had been parked by its owner. *Maybe I'll get a crime arrest after all,* he thought. Arresting someone in a stolen Aston Martin could give Seth a leg up to a CID attachment after his probation. He stepped into the road and headed towards the Aston, quickly jumping back into the barrier as an old green Ford Capri sped past, narrowly missing him. Seth failed to get the registration number as the car shot down Ascot High Street and away. After he had brushed himself down, he walked over to the driver's door of the Aston. His luck was in, the car's door window was completely open. Seth put his hand in and grabbed the ignition key, pulling it out before the driver had any idea what was happening.

'Is this your car, sir, mind if we have a chat?' asked Seth.

'Yes, officer, it's my fuckin' car; I'm sat in it aren't I, who

21

else's would it be, eh?' replied Laurence Fowler, in a slight East London accent.

Seth immediately smelt alcohol; this was not going to be the arrest that he had hoped for. *Where is Rivett when I need him? This would be right up his street.*

Seth had no idea that he was talking to one of organised crime's most successful entrepreneurs. He moved his hand towards his personal radio's parrot mic, clipped to the lapel of his tunic. Just as he was about to press the button to call for a colleague to attend with a breathalyser, Fowler reached out of the car window and firmly pulled Seth's arm away from the radio.

'What do you think you're—'

Seth was interrupted by Fowler.

'I'm sorry, officer, but you look... well, you look like a reasonable copper, mate. I've had a tad too much bubbly, I admit that, but nothin' has happened, you've not even seen me driving. Drunk in charge is the best you'll get, and I promise you, I have the best lawyers that money can buy. You're wasting your time,' said Fowler, with a slight air of arrogance.

'I've got no choice, have I, sir? I'm duty-bound,' replied Seth.

While Seth was in no mood for a drink-drive case, he really had no option but to deal with the man in the car. Ignoring it would be a disciplinary offence that would end his career before he had even finished his probation if anybody found out.

'Look, I live less than three miles from here, losing my licence would affect more than just me, officer. My family and my business, they'd all be up the swanny, just take me home, and I'll get a taxi back up here later, then everyone's happy.'

Fowler was doing his best to influence Seth, who had already started to hesitate. 'If you drive me back to my house in my car, then I'll get you a lift back up here, nobody needs to know anything, and nobody would be hurt, plus I'd have learned my lesson, officer, good and proper.'

'I can't do that, sir, you know that,' replied Seth.

Fowler kept working on Seth. He was not begging and did not seem to be stressed in any way whatsoever.

His attitude surprised Seth, drink-drivers had begged and even cried before, trying to get him to let them off. But Fowler had a way about him, he was grooming Seth to do as he asked, bringing about an almost spell-like response from him.

'Come on, I'll make it worth your while, a small token of my appreciation, a little extra cash in your pocket, no questions asked,' said Fowler, as he started to reel Seth in.

As Seth moved his hand back towards his radio's transmit button, he wavered, just for a second. If he drove this guy back to his house, he could lose his job. But if he was unable to clear his debt, he would lose his job anyway. It seemed like a fifty-fifty gamble. *If I don't get caught driving him home, I may have extra cash to put towards my credit card. That could keep them off my back a little longer, or at least buy enough time to get my probation signed off.* As his mind finished thinking through the risk and the potential reward, he made his decision. There were well over three hundred officers there, and more on their way for the busy part of the day, *I won't be missed for half an hour.*

'Fuck it, move over, quickly,' Seth opened the driver's door, threw his police helmet into the rear seat and got into the car.

'I knew you were a good copper. You won't regret this. You've done me a great favour. No chance we could pick my wife up, is there? I was supposed to park the car and join her for the fuckin' gee-gees, we may as well both just go home now,' said Fowler, half-joking.

'No, there's bloody not, where am I going?' replied Seth, snapping at Fowler, the stress now building in his body.

Fowler had managed to talk a police officer around, and not for the first time. Seth, on the other hand, had just made a colossal mistake, one that would turn his day and his world upside down.

CHAPTER 2

Worlds Collide

Earlier that day, the wheels of fate had chosen another victim to be dealt a bastard of a day. Indiscriminate in its choice, Sharon McCrory had lived a life already defined by a childhood stricken with poor parenting, poverty, and drugs. She had already been dealt plenty of bastard days, but despite that, she had been chosen again.

Sharon woke up trembling, partly from being cold but mainly due to withdrawal symptoms from her last hit. She had fallen asleep after injecting the heroin that she shared with her dealer Matt before they had engrossed themselves in dispassionate sex. Sharon had passed out partway through, leaving him to finish off without her engagement. Afterwards he rested a while before returning for a second helping.

Matt left her sprawled naked on the mattress, laying on her back with her legs splayed. Sharon woke up in the middle of the night and pulled her knickers back on. She decided to have one more hit and then go back to sleep. So, she injected another shot of heroin and then passed out again, missing the opportunity to put any more clothes on.

Sharon needed a quick fix every morning before she could even try and start the day. She reached to the side of her filthy mattress, which lay directly on the dirty carpeted floor of her bedroom, and started rummaging through the pile of stuff beside her bed. Crumpled aluminium foil, used needles, empty condom packets, soiled underwear, and dirty spoons. She was hunting to locate the hypodermic she was sure she had left ready for the morning.

Putting the used syringe to one side, she pulled herself up on the mattress and swung herself around. Her arms and legs looked like pincushions from the repeated drug abuse. Sharon tidied the pile of drug paraphernalia and laid out her works in the order she needed to use them.

Still shaking, she lit a candle and then melted some wax onto an old jam jar lid. Then she stuck the base of the candle to it with the molten wax before it turned solid again. Next, in another jar lid, she mixed some water, lemon juice, and heroin – or brown as she called it – before transferring the mixture to a teaspoon, almost filling it to the brim with her brew. She held the spoon over the flame from the candle, watching as the liquid absorbed the brown powder and turned to a beautiful translucent bronze liquor.

Sharon's hands permanently shook, so she could no longer draw the mixture into the syringe directly from the spoon. If she tried, she would lose most of it to the carpet. Instead, she soaked the warm nectar up with a cigarette filter before pushing the hypodermic needle into it and then drawing the liquid heroin into the syringe. Then she grabbed an old stocking, already tied in a loop, and pushed it up her arm before sliding the handle of a wooden spoon between her skin and the nylon. She twisted it tight, turning the spoon full circle four or five times, then she wedged the end of the handle into the crook of her elbow, preventing the tourniquet from loosening.

The veins on her forearm filled with trapped blood, slowly ballooning to the surface in small lumps, some quickly let the blood go and dropped back into her flesh. Repeated injecting had ravaged her arms and legs, resulting in the subsequent slow breakdown of her veins. The process of finding a good one took longer these days, and she would soon have to move to her groin or in-between her toes, then the soft skin in the corner of her eyes would be the final resort.

Sharon picked the hypodermic back up and plunged the dirty needle into an engorged vein, pushing the plunger into the syringe and letting out a sigh of relief as the liquid fire hurried furiously into her body.

She lay back on her mattress as the heat subsided and the rush began. A foggy euphoria filled her head as her mouth dried out, and her skin started to feel warm and flushed all over her body. She felt alive again. Her shaking lessened, and her arms and legs began to feel heavy, as if her blood was being magnetically pulled downward, trying to take her limbs through the mattress and to the floor.

She lay still for ten minutes as her consciousness drifted between being hyper-alert, hearing every little sound, to being hedonistically drowsy, her mental capacity suffering a temporary paralysis. As she drifted, the bronze medicine allowed her to be temporarily free of the psychological pain that disturbed her mind.

The effects stayed with her for only forty-five minutes, her mind and body being far too familiar with the consequences of her dependence. *That's better, bring on the day,* she thought, as she glanced at the wall clock laying on the floor next to her pile of drug paraphernalia and last night's flaccid used condoms. *Fucking hell, it's only half-past eleven, I'm awake early today,* she thought as she got up to get dressed.

As a result of her addiction, Sharon was well known to the local police and social services. She had been arrested several times for possession as well as burglary. Her mates had given her the label of 'Shmack', which she liked. She was happy to hear her nickname called out in the street. Shmack was only twenty-three, but the years of drug abuse and poor diet had advanced the ageing process.

Sharon grew up in Slough, on the Manor Park housing estate, known locally as The Manor. She had been a drug addict since she was fourteen. Her family was a mess; she was the youngest of four sisters, all from different fathers, and there was no man in the house to provide a male role model. The sisters had no idea who their fathers were, and their mother was not able to give any clues as to who they might be.

Schooling was haphazard, as her mother had been on heroin for years and was often not there to enforce any kind of daily routine, frequently waking up hours after the children had already woken. They just stayed in their rooms or went out to play in the street rather than go to school.

Sharon's life revolved around heroin. Her mum used, her sisters used, and they all dealt for local pushers to help make enough money to buy more of it. Still, this was often not enough to feed their appetite for the drug, so petty crime and occasional prostitution tarnished their lives. Sharon would steal or sell anything to get the money she needed to fuel the habit that controlled her life. She stole from her mother and her boyfriends, as well as shops and other people's houses. When things were really tough, she would sell her body to anyone that would pay for sex or allow her dealer to sleep with her in return for a single deal-bag of heroin.

★   ★   ★

Sharon walked out of her council flat. She was unable to secure the door, as the lock was still missing from the last police raid a week or so ago, so she pulled it shut and wedged an old biro pen under the door to keep it closed. Then, she ran down the stairs and out into the street. The sunshine felt good as it warmed her pallid skin. She wore a white sports shell jacket, blue tracksuit bottoms, and old trainers. Her appearance was dishevelled, her messy hair scraped back from her pale face, and her body was unwashed. *Ascot week, easy pickings,* she thought to herself as she walked to the road to await her lift.

A green Ford Capri pulled up just a couple of minutes after she arrived at the corner of the road. She jumped into the car and gave the driver a kiss on the cheek.

'Drop me off in the posh bit of Ascot somewhere,' she said.

She had gotten a lift from her dealer, Matt Hopkins, who knew that a few thefts or burglaries would bring money his way once she had sold the stuff on.

Matt liked to think he was a racing driver and drove his car dangerously. They sped from Slough through Windsor and eventually into Ascot, only slowing when they hit the last of the traffic entering the racecourse car parks. The High Street was clear, so Matt put his foot down again. As he flew past the racecourse, a copper launched himself over the barrier and walked out into the road. Matt didn't notice him until the last second and narrowly missed hitting him. If he had not had to drive around a black sports car, the copper would have been up and on the bonnet.

'Bloody hell, Shmack, that was close. Eh.'

'What was?' she replied, not even noticing what had almost happened.

On he drove out towards the high-class houses that would offer good rewards for Sharon's efforts.

The Capri's tyres screeched as Matt turned the car around in the entrance to Coronation Road, coming to a halt across the junction.

'This alright for you, babe?' asked Matt.

'Yeah, proper rich,' replied Sharon.

The houses here were sparsely spaced, with lots of trees and foliage to use as cover if the police should come by or if she was disturbed breaking into a house or stealing from a car.

Sharon jumped out of the car, slamming the door behind her.

'Thanks, babe,' she called to Matt as she walked away.

Then she ran across the road, looking back and waving at her dealer. The rear wheels of the Capri spun as he drove off. There was no point hanging around and being seen in an area that would suffer burglaries and thefts. Besides, Matt had a load of cocaine wraps to sell to well-off users on their way to or from the races.

Fucking nutter, thought Sharon as he drove away, swerving across the road and out of sight.

Sharon pulled out a cocktail reefer that she had rolled earlier. She would make up several joints to get her through the day; they were made from a mixture of cannabis and tobacco, then laced with heroin. Smoking these allowed her to feed her habit in public without raising too much suspicion. Even the cops would think it was only weed, and at worst, she would get a warning for Class B drug possession and just get moved on. She put the joint between her lips, fired up her lighter and sucked in the sweet breath of a dragon.

As Sharon stood on the corner of Coronation Road, drawing in her fix and taking a few minutes to ready herself for the day ahead, Seth was setting off from the racecourse in the Aston Martin with Larry Fowler.

★ ★ ★

'Directions give me directions, we need to be off the High Street before someone sees me,' demanded Seth, as he put the ignition key in and turned the engine over.

The Aston's engine rumbled into life, *shit, this is not exactly inconspicuous, a bloody Aston Martin for God's sake,* Seth's mind started to race. He felt the stress bubbling inside his head, his jaw tightening as he ground his teeth together. *I'll just drive to the nick and deal with the drunk in charge, it's not too late to not screw my whole life up.* It was as if his unconscious brain was talking to his conscious one, trying its hardest to get him to reverse his decision or at least change its direction.

'Drive to the mini-roundabout, then take a right towards the railway station. My name's Laurence, by the way, but you can call me Larry,' said Fowler, in much more of a calm voice than Seth thought he was entitled to have right now.

Seth's adrenalin was pumping, he felt as if the car was driving itself, and that he was watching it in a movie. He passed the railway station and kept going, pretty sure that he had not been seen by any of his colleagues, but what if a member of the public saw something and called it in! His mind raced in parallel with the car. He already regretted the decision he had made.

Seth followed the road out of town, constantly on the lookout for other cops that might notice him. He saw two officers walking along the pavement back towards the racecourse; they were deep in conversation, eager to have an early meal break, before it started getting busy later in the afternoon. Seth was pretty sure they had not noticed him.

'Put your foot down, copper, be my guest; it's not every day you get to drive a fuckin' Aston Martin,' said Larry, smirking slightly as he observed Seth's obvious unease.

'You're fine, I'll just take it nice and easy if that's okay,' said Seth.

'Go on, you know you want to, it's a v-eight for fuck's sake, give it some welly son.'

Larry was goading Seth now.

'To be honest, I don't care if it's an Aston Martin or a fucking

Lada, just let me drive you home and then get back to Ascot,' replied Seth.

As the Aston rounded a bend, an old green Ford Capri, the one Seth had seen on the High Street, came into view heading in his direction. *Shit, he's on my side of the road.* Seth swerved to the left as the cars passed side by side, narrowly missing each other, the Capri sounding its horn as it flew past.

'That was fag-paper close, copper, what's your name, James fuckin' Hunt? At least do me the courtesy of sharing your name cunt-stable four-zero-seven-six,' said Larry, reading Seth's number from his shoulder and enjoying the fact that Seth looked so awkward and stressed.

'It's Seth, Seth Hannen.'

'Seth, that's a great name. Seth the Sleuth.'

Larry was poking fun at him, speaking in a sarcastic tone, trying to elicit a fiery response. It worked. Seth snapped and barked at Larry.

'Just bloody direct me will you, where am I going?' he shouted, pushing down hard on the accelerator pedal.

Larry laughed; Seth's response was what he had expected.

'Take a right into Coronation Road, my gaff 's down there, you can't miss it, it's fuckin' huge,' said Larry, feeling pleased that he had riled the young officer.

'Here, this one…?' asked Seth, with an air of panic in his voice. He was approaching the turn way too fast.

That was the moment when Sharon saw the flashy black car racing down the road. *Wow, that's better than a shitty old Capri,* she thought as she watched its sleek lines approaching, about to speed past. Except suddenly, it changed direction, heading directly toward her.

Seth was already on top of Coronation Road. He had not yet completed a police officer's driving course and was far from the best driver on the road. He turned the steering wheel, frantically trying to make the turn, but he overcooked it. The car started to slide, refusing to go into the corner. He took his foot off the accelerator, moving it quickly to the brake and pushing down hard, not realising that all he was doing was maintaining the slide and direction of the car. He felt the brakes bite, followed immediately by the wheels locking up and losing their grip on the tarmac. Quickly turning the steering wheel even further, he tried to get the car to make the turn, but it was already in a hopeless skid heading towards a wooden gate just inside the junction.

'Shit, shit, shit, this can't be happening,' Seth's thoughts came out of his mouth as panic-stricken words.

'Don't fuck up my motor, copper,' came Larry's reply. 'Seth, don't fuck this up, get it round the corner, you fuck-wit.'

Larry's voice failed to reach Seth; his ears had shut down. His face was locked onto the woman standing on the narrow pavement, directly ahead of the car. Everything slowed in Seth's brain, he could see her in perfect detail, about thirty years old, short at just over five feet tall, wearing a white shell suit jacket, blue tracksuit bottoms, and a pair of old grubby trainers. She looked unkempt and messy; her hair scraped back from her pasty face. Sharon was staring directly at Seth, transfixed and rooted to the spot.

As the car careered towards her, she opened her mouth and screamed, the sweet reefer falling to the ground. She was screaming in harmony with the tyres screeching on the tarmac. Seth heard nothing, the adrenalin now at fever pitch, his heart pumping like a steam engine. The woman's face reminded him of a famous painting.

'Fuck, you cock,' shouted Larry.

The car failed to stop. It just kept sliding towards Sharon.

She was still screaming, the driver looked as frightened as she was. *Fucking hell, it's a copper, what the—*

Her thought was cut short as the Aston ploughed into her, catapulting her up into the air and over the car, she landed on the tarmac behind it with a thud, then everything turned black.

Seth switched off the ignition, and all was quiet, his mind tried to make sense of what had just happened.

The road was not busy, and nobody appeared to have seen the accident. Seth sat still in the driver's seat, his heart thudding against the wall of his chest.

Larry was out of the passenger door in a flash. He grabbed the woman by both legs and started to drag her around the car and out of the road.

'Any chance of a bit of fuckin' help then, Seth?' called Larry, glaring at Seth through the car window.

Seth did not answer, he was frozen to the Aston's seat and unable to think straight.

Larry spoke through the window as he dragged her along the pavement and onto the grass verge. 'She's fuckin' dead, that's for sure.'

He pulled Sharon's body into the overgrown grass and nettles behind the Coronation Road sign. Then he bent the foliage over her body to conceal it from view as best he could.

'Wake up, copper, and move the car, get it off the grass and park it neatly,' he shouted to Seth.

Seth gave no response. He sat with his eyes closed and his head in his hands.

'Move the fuckin' car, copper,' said Larry, now bellowing at Seth.

Seth snapped out of his trance.

'Okay, okay… give me a moment.'

He put the car into reverse, moved it back off the pavement, changed gear and then pulled forward, parking it tight and parallel to the kerb, the rear end facing Sharon.

'That's better, I'll be with you in a tick,' said Larry, not at all fazed by the fact that the woman was dead.

'She's a smackhead, a druggy for sure,' called Larry, as he walked away from her body. 'She won't be missed by anyone important. It's fine, you'll be okay, copper. Now let's get me home, I'll sort this shit-storm out later.'

Larry walked around the car, glaring at Seth through the windscreen as he passed the front of the Aston. The front bumper had suffered a dent, and the left spotlight mounting had been bent backwards, pushing the light into the grille.

'You payin' for the damage then, eh, Seth?' said Larry, as he got back into the passenger seat. 'Fuckin' drive, my house is halfway down this road on the left, big black oak gates, gravel driveway.'

Larry sounded more pissed off than concerned at what had just happened.

Seth drove on tentatively, moving at a strikingly slow speed, his mind trying to keep him from leaving the scene of the accident.

'That one, turn in there and for fuck's sake wait for the gates to open first, don't crash the fuckin' car again… try not to kill anyone else, Seth, mate!'

CHAPTER 3

Kuredu

Larry lived at Kuredu with his wife Sandra and their twin boys Michael and Sean, who attended a local Ascot school. Sandra did not work, choosing a life of leisure financed by Larry's business enterprises. The family enjoyed a quiet private existence in Coronation Road, South Ascot, where the houses were far enough apart to allow no real neighbourly activities. That suited Larry, things needed to be quiet.

Seth pulled onto the driveway of the enormous house, which was probably built in the late eighteen-hundreds, it sat back from the road in a substantial garden.

'Park it round the side, make sure the front end is close up to the hedge,' said Larry, pointing out the direction to Seth.

Seth drove the car carefully up to the tall, neatly trimmed hedge, which separated the driveway from the garden and pool area to the side of the house.

The two men got out of the car, and Seth passed the keys to Larry.

'Don't forget your tit, Seth, wakey-wakey, mate,' chirped Larry, as he closed the passenger door.

'What…?' Seth had no idea what he meant.

'Your bloody helmet, mate,' said Larry, growling at Seth.

He led Seth from the parked Aston and into the house

through the side door, which Larry and Sandra used as the main way in and out of the property. As they walked along the hallway, they passed a large modern kitchen, then three more large rooms before reaching the main staircase in the entrance hall, then through a pair of large double doors and finally into a huge sitting room. It was furnished mainly with expensive antiques, and the walls were adorned with large oil paintings. There was a large portrait of Larry hanging above the mantlepiece.

'Ciggy, Seth, you could probably use one after that?' asked Larry.

'Yeah, go on then, what the hell,' Seth was still not thinking straight, unable to rid the image of the dead woman from his mind.

Larry pulled out an open packet of Kent cigarettes from his inside pocket.

'Microlite filters, Seth, healthy little buggers these are,' he said, flipping the lid open with his thumb as he offered Seth the packet.

'Thanks,' said Seth, as he tugged a cigarette out and placed it between his lips.

Larry flicked open an old beaten-up metal lighter and spun the knurled wheel to ignite the flame. He lit his own cigarette first, sucking in the smoke and appreciating the initial hit of nicotine, then he offered the flame to Seth.

'Have a seat, I need to make a phone call, I'll be with you in a tick,' said Larry, as he picked up the handset of the old black Bakelite telephone that sat neatly on top of an antique mahogany bureau.

Holding the receiver to his ear, Larry dialled a number that he clearly knew by heart.

Seth started to tune in, he needed to get back with it. He had more than his job at risk now, the rest of his life could be very different from what he had anticipated, depending on how all this turned out. The number was definitely not local, Seth heard the telephone dial turn nine or ten times, enough for there to have been an area code first.

Larry was calling Scotch, one of his trusted fixers who had worked for him since he was a teenager. Scotch had grafted his way from being a small-time drug dealer and opportunistic burglar to a big-time crook, running a section of Larry's local setup. He dealt with things for Larry when they got complicated, or 'sticky' as Larry would say. He was also the mastermind behind any burglaries of good quality houses that Larry wanted doing over, often taking the job on himself, for no other reason than the adrenalin rush.

'Scotch, it's Larry, there's been a spot of bother, mate, it's all got a bit fuckin' sticky, and I need your assistance,' said Larry, as he looked at Seth out of the corner of his eyes.

He turned toward the fireplace, cupping the mouthpiece with his left hand and lowering his voice so that Seth could not make out what was being said. Larry spoke quietly into the telephone, issuing instructions.

'Get yourself up to Coronation Road, the Ascot end, there's a woman's body in the undergrowth behind the road sign at the junction. I need it gone, before it starts fuckin' smelling and a bloody dog walker finds it, or some drunken race-goer takes a piss on the way home and finds her. Get rid of her, and do a proper job, make sure nobody sees you, and no one finds the body,' said Larry.

'It'll be easier to do when it's dark, Larry, the middle of the day is a bit bloody risky,' replied Scotch.

'It's Ascot week! The place will be swarming after six tonight, someone will find the body for sure.' Larry raised his voice before correcting his volume back to a quieter level so that Seth was unable to hear him. 'No, do it now... I want it gone.'

Larry hated his decisions being questioned by any of his people, to him it felt like an assault on his authority.

'Got it, Larry, leave it with me, I'm on it,' replied Scotch.

'Oh, and I need a car to the Ascot end of Coronation Road PDQ, my new friend, Seth, needs a lift back to Ascot; he's Old Bill, but he's alright, he's cushty,' said Larry.

Scotch started to reply, but Larry had already put the phone down and walked over to Seth.

'What to do with you, that's the fuckin' question now,' he said as he stood in front of Seth, who was still sat on the sofa.

'Well, I can't bloody report it can I? I'm not sure how I'd explain giving a drink-driver a lift home in his own car, accidentally killing a woman on the way, and then watching as he hid her body.' exclaimed Seth.

'Not if you want to keep your bloody job, mate, and stay out of prison, where of course they love cops,' Larry quipped back at him.

Seth took a deep breath, very aware of the situation that he found himself in. He had crossed the line the moment he agreed to drive Larry home from the races, and God, he regretted that decision now. He had no idea what to say to Larry, or how to even the keel and put anything right – for either of them.

Larry knew he had the upper hand. The young copper sitting in front of him looked like a rabbit in the headlights, scared with nowhere to run. He was putty in Larry's hands. Nevertheless, he could not risk the chance that Seth would become overrun with guilt and tell the police anything about what had happened, either formally or to one of his mates.

Seth, my man, I'll be honest. I have no place for another cop in my organisation right now. I don't need you in my pocket. I also don't want you on my back, and I certainly don't need to worry about you being a problem in the future. So, what do I do?' said Larry, in a menacing tone.

Seth felt himself tensing up. He was unable to use any of the myriad of police powers bestowed upon him. Arresting Larry and fighting his way back to the police station would only result in him getting arrested himself. The whole Complaints and Discipline Department machine would swing into action and get to the bottom of what had happened. At that moment, Seth thought that his only way out might be to bolt for the door and run.

Larry walked across the room to a painting of a racehorse, which he pulled from the wall. It opened up on hinges to reveal a high-security safe hidden behind it. He turned the knob back and forth before opening the thick metal door. Seth watched as best he could, his view partially blocked from being sat down. Larry rummaged in the safe, taking out what was clearly an automatic pistol, holding it by the barrel and placing it on the table below the painting. Then he pulled out a large hardback book, put the pistol back in, closed the safe and spun the knob to lock it. As he pushed the painting back to the wall, Larry turned to speak to Seth, relaxing his tone of voice a little, recognising that the boy-of-a-cop looked more than anxious.

'Well then, Seth, whatever we do, you need to be back before you're missed and before my lovely wife gets in from her little Royal Ascot jaunt. I had just dropped her off when you came along and ruined our day. Scotch is sorting out a car to take you back.'

'Okay, Larry, I won't say a word, I promise. It's really not worth my while, is it?' Seth failed to prevent his voice from trembling.

'I appreciate that, Seth, but I do need to make sure that you're compensated for the shit I've given you today, it would only be right and proper of me, don't you think?' Larry was insincere in his tone.

He tapped ash into the glass ashtray that sat on the arm of the sofa next to Seth, who followed suit with his nearly spent cigarette.

'Just a lift back will be fine, I really don't need anything else that will get me neck-deep in shit,' replied Seth, stubbing out his cigarette.

'In case you hadn't noticed, you're already neck-deep in fuckin' shit, Seth. Now, how much can I give you to ensure you stay schtum about all this?'

Seth's mind immediately returned to the phone call from his mother, and the Access Card problem. *A CCJ will be the least of my problems after today, if anyone finds out about this little lot.*

'I owe just over three-grand to my credit card company,' he replied, looking at Larry, the embarrassment unmistakeable in his expression.

'Okay, I can get that sorted for you, and then I reckon we'll be quits, don't you? If I do that for you, then you have to guarantee me that you'll never breathe a word of what happened today to anyone, not a soul, not even your fuckin' grandmother, am I clear? Do you understand me?' said Larry.

'Yes, yes, as if I would, I just need to forget today, forget the whole thing and get back to my life and my job.'

Seth watched as Larry walked over to a low burled wood cabinet. It had six lead crystal glasses neatly lined up on top, next to a decanter full of whisky. He turned two glasses upright, then pulled the stopper out of the decanter before pouring a considerable measure of whisky into each glass and picked them up and walked back towards Seth. Larry walked with a confident gait, which looked all the more impressive while wearing a morning suit. His yellow single-breasted waistcoat was stretched tight across his middle, showing glimpses of the blue shirt and the red houndstooth tie between its buttons. Larry offered Seth one of the glasses of whisky.

'Get that down you, boy, a bit of Dutch courage to get you through the rest of the day, I think you might just need it, mate,' said Larry, as he placed the glass on a small table beside the sofa, then he ran his fingers through his thick blonde hair.

'I'm not allowed to drink on duty, am I, Larry,' replied Seth, holding the palm of his hand up and shrugging his shoulders.

'Don't take the moral high ground with me now, Seth, you're not really in a position to say anything, mate. How many rules have you broken already today, how many crimes have you committed, Mr Policeman?' Larry was intentionally manipulating Seth's nervous trepidation, ensuring that Seth saw him as the solution to his problems.

Seth briefly looked down at the whisky, then he picked up the glass, lifted it to his lips and knocked it back in one gulp.

'Another one then?' asked Larry.

'No, that hit the spot. I'm more of a gin man, to be honest,' replied Seth.

'I'll need your bank details. Don't worry, the transfer will be legit. It'll come from one of my companies, it won't raise a concern to anyone. Write down your account number and sort code, and I'll get it arranged.'

Larry handed a lined yellow notepad to Seth, with a pen clipped into the red binding rings at the top.

Seth wrote down his account number and sort code.

'It's just in my name, Mr Seth Hannen,' he said, as he passed the pad back.

Larry tore off the page before opening the book that he had taken from the safe. He flicked through the pages of notes and placed the piece of yellow paper between two clean pages.

'Now, have another ciggy, and then you'd better fuck off back to work. Walk up to the corner of Coronation Road, where you killed that woman, a car will pick you up and take you back to Ascot, they'll drop you wherever you want.'

Seth did not need reminding that he had killed someone. It was still at the very forefront of his mind, her screaming face etched into his brain in freeze-frame. He accepted the second cigarette and smoked it in silence as Larry walked around the room, occasionally looking out of the window towards the gates at the end of the drive.

'Come on, get that ciggy finished,' said Larry, conscious of his wife's possible return.

Seth walked out of the house the way he had come in, closely followed by Larry just two paces behind him. They walked down the gravel driveway towards the gate, which was still open. Larry stopped short and called out to Seth as he walked into the road.

'Seth...' he waited a moment for him to stop and look back. 'You're not a bad man, shit happens... you just have to deal with it, so that it doesn't get any worse than it already is or let it hang around in your life for too fuckin' long.'

Larry certainly sounded like a man who had dealt with lots of shit in the past. 'You're only a victim as long as you allow yourself to be one. Once you let it go from your head, then you're no longer that fuckin' victim. Don't allow yourself be a victim, Seth.'

The gates started to close behind Seth as he turned right to head back towards the scene of the accident to get picked up. He looked back one more time to see Larry standing behind the gates, looking at him through the thick wooden bars.

'Seth...' called Larry in a loud voice. 'You're a bent copper now, don't ever forget that. The only person you can talk to about today is God.'

★ ★ ★

While Seth had been with Larry, Scotch had gotten to work

quickly. He wondered what had happened to leave a woman dead so close to Larry's house. After Larry hung up the call, Scotch put his Nokia 101 into his back pocket and pulled on a pair of dark grey overalls, then he grabbed his van keys and set off out of his front door.

'Zeus, with me, boy,' he shouted at his bulky Rottweiler.

I've been picked up by the cops plenty of times, but me picking up a cop, after picking up a body, that takes the biscuit! he thought to himself as he opened his up-and-over garage door. He went inside and grabbed a long blue crowbar and a collapsible red and white workman's road barrier and threw them into the back of his white Ford Escort van with Zeus, and they set off.

Scotch pulled up at the entrance to Coronation Road, parked the van and got out to check the undergrowth behind the road sign. Sure enough, there lay the body of the woman that Larry had told him about. *Shit, it's Shmack.* He recognised her lifeless face looking back at him, peering up from the grass and nettles. The leaves had blood on them, and he could see what looked like blood on the pavement. He opened the van's rear doors, pulled out the red and white barrier and set it up on the corner of Coronation Road to obscure the view from passing traffic, then he slammed the doors shut and moved the van. He pulled the bulky Nokia back out of his jeans and tapped in the phone number for his drug runner, Matt, who answered quickly.

'Yeah, it's Matt.'

'Mate, where the fuck are you, can you get to Ascot?' asked Scotch.

'Yeah, mate, I'm not that far away. I'm in Sunninghill, just sorting something out. I can be there in five, why the rush?' Matt could hear the urgency in Scotch's voice.

'Get your arse to the Ascot end of Coronation Road.

Shmack's fucking dead, and I need to move her.'

Silence.

'Matt, you there?'

'Yeah, mate... sorry, I only dropped her there less than an hour ago. I don't understand.'

'Just get your arse here now. There's no time,' said Scotch.

'Alright, I'm on my way, see you in a bit.'

Scotch walked back to his van and opened the rear doors. Zeus was laid out on the floor of the van panting in the heat. *It's going to be your unlucky fucking day, you fat slobbery shit of a friend*, he thought.

The Capri pulled up on the other side of the road sign to Scotch's van, just into Coronation Road. Matt jumped out, clearly flustered.

'What the fuck happened, Scotch? This is really bad shit,' said Matt.

'I have no frigging idea, mate. I got a call from Big-Gun. He needs this clearing up, and fast,' replied Scotch, using Larry's nickname.

Scotch was careful not to mention that Larry lived half a mile from the junction. Larry ruled the roost but appreciated privacy from the low-level foot soldiers under his command.

Scotch looked around to make sure nobody was about to stumble upon them.

'Open your boot, we need to make this snappy.'

Scotch took hold of Sharon's legs. 'Hurry up, grab her bloody arms, let's get this done,' he said, barking at Matt.

Matt opened the boot of his car, then took hold of Sharon's arms. As they lifted Shmack from the undergrowth, her legs crunched as the breaks in her shin bones ground against each other.

They shuffled awkwardly to the Capri, hoisting her into the boot. Matt slammed it shut before jumping into the driver seat and pulling the door closed, then he leaned out of the window and looked back towards Scotch.

'Where shall I dump her?' he asked, still looking shell shocked.

'That, my friend, is no longer my problem, just make sure she isn't found, and if you get any help, choose carefully. People talk, mate, make it clear this is direct from Big-Gun. This needs to stay schtum.'

'Alright, understood, mate,' replied Matt. He knew not to do anything to cross Big-Gun.

He put his foot to the floor, and the rear end of the Capri slid across the road as he drove off.

Scotch walked back to his van and took out the long blue crowbar.

'Here, Zeus, come,' he called his dog out of the van.

Zeus jumped out and sat at Scotch's feet, looking at him dutifully. Scotch looked at his dog as he lifted the crowbar high in the air, pausing for a moment before bringing it down with as much force as he could muster. It connected the dog's head with a crack as his skull gave way. Zeus immediately let out a high-pitched whimper, and then nothing. Death was almost instant. Scotch took a deep breath and then dragged Zeus's body behind the road sign, making sure it covered the spot that had been occupied by Shmack just a few moments earlier. He threw the crowbar and the collapsible barrier back into the van, closed the doors and got in the driver's seat. Then he slid a compact disc into the CD player and drove around the block to calm his nerves.

★ ★ ★

Seth walked to the end of the road. As he approached the junction, he saw the Coronation Road sign, and his stomach churned. He remembered the woman's face again, ghostly white with her mouth wide open – screaming. He stopped and threw up, vomiting whisky into the hedgerow. *I just need to be sure she's actually dead. What if she's alive? I can't leave her there to die if she's alive.*

As he approached the sign, Seth heard screeching tyres as a white van pulled up alongside him. The windows were down, and he could hear what sounded like a dog howling from inside.

'Seamus the Dog, Pink Floyd, mate, I'm guessing you're Larry's copper pal, Seth… get in,' called Scotch.

Before going to the van, he walked up to the sign, leaned over and looked into the undergrowth, immediately taking a startled step back. In the woman's place was the body of a dog. The black and tan Rottweiler lay in the bent and twisted grass, not breathing. Seth leant over, extending his arm to touch the animal. It was lifeless but still warm. *That's what Larry was arranging on the phone.*

Seth got into the passenger seat, holding his helmet in his lap, and looked out of the window. *How is this place so quiet?* He thought as the van pulled away.

Scotch drove Seth back to Ascot, neither of them speaking during the short journey. He drove the van into Car Park 6 of the racecourse, waving at the attendant as if he knew him.

'Out you get, copper.' he said to Seth. 'Sorry I'm not that fucking talkative, mate. I lost my dog, Zeus, today, he was only four, but shit happens, eh?'

Seth gave no reply, he just got out and walked away, still dazed by the events he had just been through. He walked along Ascot High Street and into the back yard of the police station, trying his best to appear as normal as possible, but very aware that his demeanour must look like that of a man in shock.

'Where've you been?' asked Rivett nonchalantly, as he sipped on a mug of coffee and smoked a cigarette. 'I had to cover for you with the guvnor, he came to thank us for working on a rest-day. I said you'd popped down the High Street to post some letters, first thing I thought of!'

'Thanks, Mark, appreciate it. I couldn't get away from Paula the Thunderbird. She's lovely; I'm going to call her later and arrange to take her out for lunch next weekend,' said Seth, forcing the words from his mouth.

'Good for you, now let's get back to work and don't let the guvnor smell your breath,' replied Mark.

They put their helmets on and walked out of the back yard, heading towards the racecourse to finish their tour of duty.

Seth's mind was anywhere than at work and he remained quiet for the rest of the day, Larry and the woman still at the forefront of his mind.

★ ★ ★

As they walked back towards the police station to get on the bus that would take them back to Maidenhead, a black Aston Martin slowly drove past with the windows down.

'That's had a bit of a bump – that'll be expensive,' said Mark, referring to the damage to the front end.

Driving the car was a man in his forties, with a woman of a similar age in the passenger seat. Larry Fowler called out as he drove past.

'You're looking good there, Cunt-stable Hannen!'

CHAPTER 4

In the Money

'Hello, Rebecca, how are you?'

It was about the same time as Matt and Scotch were dealing with Sharon that Larry made the phone call to Rebecca Langford, portfolio manager at Eatmon LLP, a large financial investment company in Victoria Street, London. Larry had bought a small stake in the company a couple of years earlier, used it to clean up his dirty money, and then invest in making more of it. His stake in the company was the latest addition to several other companies owned by Larry. They were all legitimate and served well to launder his money for him, allowing him to spend what he wanted without fear of alerting the authorities.

Larry had embedded Rebecca into Eatmon as his contact point and investment manager. She had worked hard for her first company, which Larry had initially used for his investments. But when he started to turn over big business-sized profits, Larry needed to have his money buried deeper in a larger organisation. By the time Rebecca moved to Eatmon, Larry had managed to get some of his wealthy friends to invest their money with Rebecca as well. She took Larry and these other clients with her to Eatmon, making quite an impression and establishing an early reputation as a trusted and effective fund manager. By having someone he trusted inside Eatmon running his financial affairs, Larry ensured that everything ran smoothly. The rest of Eatmon would not catch onto the fact that they were money laundering.

Rebecca had no problem cleaning up his cash, as long as it resulted in her becoming richer. Larry's financial matters were not really much different from any other big fish who had investments at Eatmon. She knew that Larry had presided over some very dodgy deals and was partial to less than gentlemanly ways of earning his income. But she had no idea of the true extent to which she was aiding and abetting criminal activity.

Over the years, Rebecca had learnt that money did strange things to people, clouding their judgement and bending their personal ethics. Greed would often become their driving force, taking over like an aggressive cancer.

'I'm fine, Larry… funny that you should call. I need to speak to you,' said Rebecca.

'If you're about to tell me that you're leaving to set up your own business, then you can fuck off on Monday, don't worry about giving me any notice or anything like that,' he said.

Larry half-joked, but he knew it would not be long before Rebecca would want to branch out on her own. Larry had eyes and ears everywhere, and he knew that she may be getting to that point in her career.

'How did you—' Rebecca was unable to finish her sentence.

'Not now, Rebecca, I need to send some fuckin' cash to a mate. It's urgent, but it must look legit. I can't afford it to be questioned by anyone. Can we do that quickly?' he asked.

'Yes, I can get a transfer in place. I just need his bank details and what funding stream you want me to use. And why do you have to swear so much? I don't like it.'

'Honestly, Rebecca, I don't give a flying shit about what you fuckin' like or which funding stream is used. Just use the one that costs me the least in capital gains tax or whatever other robbing tactics the taxman is using at the moment on liquidated investments. Whatever is cheapest and quickest.'

'Okay, let me have the details, and I'll get it sorted this afternoon. It'll clear in a couple of days. How much are we talking about, Larry?' replied Rebecca.

'I'm just deciding on the exact amount, but I want to send him a few grand. I'll fax everything over to you in a moment.' Larry moved the conversation on to Rebecca while he started writing out the memo. 'So, were you going to tell me that you're leaving Eatmon? I'd be keen to know your plans. I value your work for me, Rebecca, and I don't want to lose your services,' said Larry.

'Well...the thing is that I've found premises near St. James Park, so not that far from here—' Rebecca started gingerly and was quickly cut off by Larry.

'Rebecca, cut to the chase, will you, I don't have all bloody week. Are you fuckin' off or not?'

'Yes, I'd like to start my own business, Langford Investment Management. I've spoken to most of my clients, and so far, they are all willing to come with me. I have a significant investment figure available to me now. I'd like to take you and your money with me as well. I'm sure I can make it work harder for you and improve your returns,' said Rebecca. She was unsure how Larry would respond.

'Well, I—'

Rebecca interrupted Larry this time.

'You don't need to decide now, not today, just think about it. I need to set the company up first,' said Rebecca.

She was concerned that Larry was about to decline her offer.

'Rebecca, don't fuckin' interrupt me. I was thinking, for God's sake,' blustered Larry. 'Okay, go and set up your own business with my blessing. Once you're ready, I'll move my entire investment portfolio over to you. In the meantime, I'll send six hundred big ones as an investment kick-starter. I still need your financial expertise, and I trust you, Rebecca.'

'I don't know what to say, Larry, that's very kind of you. I'll get onto the transfer this afternoon; it'll all be taken care of.'

'Ta, Rebecca, thanks,' said Larry, then he put down the phone and fed the memo he had written into the fax machine.

The fax machine in Rebecca's office hummed as it woke up, printing out a copy of Larry's handwritten note. She pulled the message off and read it. Then she turned to a wicker tray at the corner of her desk, picked up a sealed letter and paused for a moment, taking time to think, before turning to her side and feeding it into a shredder.

★ ★ ★

Following his encounter with Seth, Larry became somewhat fascinated, watching his police career from afar. Something about Seth resonated with him, he was unsure quite what it was, but it sparked an interest that he could not switch off. Larry found himself needing to know what Seth was up to. He kept an eye on the local newspapers for reports about cases and investigations that Seth was involved in, cutting out the clippings and keeping them in a wooden cigar box in his safe. He would also get his contacts in the police to update him regularly. As Larry kept an eye on Seth from afar, he began to have ideas of recruiting him, but that would need to wait.

Like Rebecca and so many others, Seth had no idea that he was the subject of Larry's prying eyes. Larry was a master of the game, in it for the long haul. He always had something or someone up his sleeve, or in his pocket.

★ ★ ★

Seth was now back in his small, rather dull characterless room in single quarters, the events of the day repeatedly replaying in his mind like a bad movie. He sat on the edge of his bed, burying his head in his hands. The day was up there with the very worst of them, a bastard of a day indeed.

Having worked his Thursday rest-day, he would be back on late shifts from Friday afternoon and over the weekend. *I'm not sure I can face it,* he thought to himself. Every time he closed his eyes, all he could see was the face of the screaming woman, staring directly into his eyes. *I've got to come clean. I can't live with this. I killed someone today.*

Seth sat on his bed, going around the problem in his head, in a state of permanent indecision. One minute he would decide to live with the memory of what happened and the resultant guilt. The next minute, he would decide on coming clean and living with the consequences that would inevitably follow if he did. Neither option was appealing. Either would have an impact of enormous magnitude, one that he would have to live with for the rest of his life.

Seth decided to call in sick, in no frame of mind to go back out on the streets over a busy summer weekend. He pulled out his black notebook to pen a sick note, flipping it open to see Paula's message with her lipstick kiss. A glimpse of a smile began to move across his face as he tore the page out and pinned it to his notice board above the built-in desk, *one for next weekend, something to look forward to,* he thought to himself. Then he picked up a black biro and wrote the note for Jonesy.

> Sarge, I'm really sorry, but I'm reporting sick.
> Should be back for late-shifts next week.
> Please let my patrol sergeant know.
> Thanks, PC 4076 Seth Hannen

Seth tore the page out, folded it in half and then wrote 'Sgt

Jones - Urgent' before taking it down to the ground floor and leaving it on top of the station sergeant's in-tray.

After returning to his room, he pulled the ineffective drab curtains shut, hurriedly undressed and then climbed into bed, burying his head in his pillow. Then he drifted off to sleep, willing himself to wake up to the realisation that the whole day had been an awful dream.

★ ★ ★

It seemed to take an age, but Monday's rest-day eventually arrived. Seth had spent three whole days in bed, only leaving his room to use the toilet or make a snack in the communal kitchen.

He woke, grinding his teeth to the memory that greeted him every day, the one of his father's funeral. The image quickly faded and was replaced with a new waking nightmare; the woman's screaming face. His subconscious knew what had happened, reminding him of the grim reality. Seth sat up in bed and took deep breaths. *Time for some fresh air and some decent food,* he thought to himself.

After a much-needed shower, he pulled on a clean pair of Levi's jeans and a plain t-shirt, not bothering with socks, instead just wearing his size eleven Adidas Sambas on bare feet.

He left the nick and walked into Maidenhead town centre without stopping to talk to anyone, hoping not to bump into Jackie. That would be embarrassing. He managed to conceal his awkwardness well the other morning but would not manage to hide it now. Despite his indiscretion with Jackie, one-night stands were not really Seth's thing. He was a flirt and enjoyed women's company but rarely ended up in bed with them.

Seth slid his debit card into the ATM at Barclays bank. He needed cash for a good lunch and a solitary thinking session at The Bear public house. He punched in his PIN, which matched his shoulder number. Knowing money was tight, he decided to check the balance before taking any money from his account. The amount flashed up on the screen. *Holy shit!* Seth had expected to be getting close to his overdraft limit of three hundred pounds, but the figure on the screen looked nothing like anything he had ever seen in his account before.

> ACCOUNT BALANCE: 79713.60
> AVAILABLE FUNDS :   43.60

Thursday's events had certainly been real, and Larry had meant what he said about sending Seth a payment for his troubles, but eighty-grand, that was ridiculous! The Access Card balance and the demands to pay back overdue payments now paled into insignificance. The numbers on the screen made Seth feel nauseous. They represented a grave error in judgement, one that had cost an innocent woman her life. The guilt returned, as did her face.

Seth punched more numbers into the machine, taking out twenty-five pounds to cover lunch and leave something in his pocket for later. He stuffed the notes into his wallet. His mind was sprinting from thought to thought, eventually stopping to speak to him, offering three options; *report the money and the accident, then lose your job... give it away to charity and face a CCJ from the credit card company... or keep it and move on...* He was unable to decide, changing his mind by the second. I need to call Mum.

Eighty thousand pounds had been paid into Seth's account by bank transfer on Thursday afternoon by a small private investment company partly owned by Laurence Fowler.

Fearful of being overheard, Seth decided not to go back to the station and use the shared phone in the common room at single quarters. Instead, he walked up Maidenhead High Street to the red telephone box outside the post office and stepped inside. He pulled a British Telecom phonecard from his wallet and slid it into the slot, the balance flashing up on the tiny display. After dialling the number, he held the handset to his ear and waited.

'Hello, Burnham six-five-treble-three.'

Kathleen had answered the phone. It felt so good to hear his mum's voice; it was instantly calming.

'Hi, Mum, it's me; how are you?'

'I'm very well, thanks, Seth. I've been waiting for you to call back. I tried to call you on your birthday, but the policeman who answered the phone said you were working. What's up, my love?'

Kathleen was intuitive, and she knew her son well and could tell that there was something on his mind. Seth and Kathleen had never failed to speak on a birthday before. They had become extremely close, especially after Edward's death. That closeness had developed further when Leah, Seth's sister, had moved to the other side of the world.

'Mum, I've not had a good week. Things aren't going so well for me at the moment. I just need a chat,' said Seth, building himself up to telling her the whole story. She would offer wise words and help him decide what to do.

'Well, Seth, I'm not sure exactly what's going on, but if it's money trouble again, I'm sorry, but there's another letter here from the Access Card people. I opened it because I'm really worried about you, Seth. They are going to take you to court unless you pay by the end of next week; it's gone up to three thousand, four hundred and something now.' Kathleen was not able to hide the concern in her voice.

'I think that's the least of my problems, Mum; work has been bad, I've managed to get myself into trouble, and I don't know what to do to get out of it.'

'Seth, whatever it is, it's never as bad as you think,' said

56

Kathleen. She could never have imagined the mess her son was in.

'Mum, while I don't know what to do, I don't think I can tell you what's happened. I'm stuck in a corner,' said Seth, not able to bring himself to tell her.

'Just look at it from outside your head. Your father used to say that you should always ask yourself three things. Will anyone be hurt? What will the effect on me and my family be? And am I doing this for me or for someone else? Just take his approach, and I'm sure it'll all be fine,' she said.

Seth was silent for a moment, still fighting his demons.

'You're right, thanks, Mum. I knew you'd help.'

They chatted a little longer, before wishing each other well. Seth promised to pop in and see her on his next long weekend off. Then they hung up, and Seth walked out of the phone box. He knew exactly what he had to do.

Once he arrived at the counter in the bank, he pulled out a crumpled credit card invoice from his wallet.

'Can I borrow a pen, please? The one on the counter's missing.'

Seth filled out the payment box, writing in three thousand five hundred pounds, and then wrote a cheque for the same amount. He handed the cheque and the credit card bill, with the payment slip still attached, to the man behind the window.

'Can I just check that the pending balance in my account will clear before this cheque does?' asked Seth.

There was a short silence while the cashier checked the computer. Seth was almost hoping the money was not actually there.

'Yes, Mr Hannen, the pending figure will clear today and will be available tomorrow, and this payment will go through the day after that. Would you like me to process the payment?'

Seth paused momentarily. *This really is the point of no*

return, but if I come clean, that woman won't come back to life. I can't change what happened. I just get hurt, and Mum gets hurt, knowing what I've done. Coming clean would only be for me and my conscience, nobody else.

The cashier pressed Seth for a decision.

'Mr Hannen, would you like me to process the payment or not?'

'Yes... yes, please.'

Decision made, *thanks, Mum.*

The cashier tore off the payment slip, stamped the top half of the invoice, and then passed it back. *Job done!* Thought Seth as he walked out of the bank and headed towards The Bear. Although still carrying the guilt of the woman's death, he felt that a weight had lifted from his shoulders. He could now move on – no more debt.

After a good lunch and a beer, he walked back towards the police station with only his thoughts for company.

Everything happens for a reason. Larry was wrong. I was a bent copper, but not anymore. From this moment on, I won't be. I get to decide that. Shit does happen and you do have to deal with it so that it doesn't get any worse than it already is or hang around in your life for too long. The only difference is that I don't even need to tell God!

CHAPTER 5

Big-Gun

Laurence Fowler was born in East London in November 1947. He was a self-made multi-millionaire by the time he was thirty-five years old and had used criminality to accomplish it. Nobody got in his way. He ran a substantial business empire that masked his extensive criminal enterprise. He liked to have a finger in every pie, and he relished the thought of being an entrepreneur, taking calculated risks and usually winning against the odds to build more out of less.

Larry had not always lived the high life on the outskirts of leafy Ascot, his background was very different. He suffered a rough upbringing, which undoubtedly influenced the kind of man he turned out to be. If his childhood had not been so tortuous, he would have been a legitimate businessman, which is how he saw himself, rather than a master criminal. Larry had the brains for big business, combined with the motivation and greed of a criminal mind.

In 1956, Larry's parents, Frank and Pam, moved from Newham in London to Slough. They were provided with a house on the Britwell estate, one of several post-war London County Council expansions. Frank and Pam had agreed to turn over a new leaf, aiming to leave a dysfunctional family life well behind them in Newham and bring Larry up in a pleasant environment. That was at least Pam's priority, if not really Franks.

The Fowlers were among the first tenants that arrived on the then-modern housing development. They brought very little with them aside from essential furniture, clothing and their East London accents. The Britwell offered them the chance of a fresh start, away from the stresses of London and the entrenched hold of the hierarchical criminal life that Frank had led. He was a petty criminal, low in the pecking order, easily led and a soft target for other villains.

By day Frank worked as an engineer for a company on the Slough Trading Estate, while Larry's mother was a traditional stay at home mum. By night Frank was a heavy drinker and quickly returned to being a small-time criminal, dealing in stolen and counterfeit goods. His dodgy dealings operated mainly from a pub called the Good Companions on the Stoke Road, where he would drink – a lot – and pick up loose women and prostitutes.

It was not long after moving to Slough that Larry's parents started arguing and fighting again. The rows began as minor quibbles but soon escalated to the extreme drink-driven violence and cruel assaults that had been part of the family's daily routine in London. Larry often lay in bed, listening to his father beating his mother until she begged for the punches to stop. Once they did, she would lie in a heap on the floor as her blood filled the bruises with colour. Larry would clean her up, carefully bathing and disinfecting her wounds, and then cuddle up to her.

Within a year of moving, Pam had also reverted to type. She was trapped in a loveless marriage filled with anger, cruelty, and violence. She could not afford to leave, financially or emotionally, preferring to try and hold everything together in the belief that a family unit was still better for young Larry. Better a dysfunctional home than a broken one.

Pam would fall in and out of love quickly and frequently. She would meet her newest man for liaisons in nearby Stoke Park, or perhaps for a walk along the cinder track that connected the Britwell with the neighbouring Manor Park estate. Often the men she courted were married, resulting in undignified sexual encounters in dark parks, the back seats of cars, or sometimes at home in the sitting room while Frank was at work and Larry at school. Her promiscuity was as much a self-harming mechanism as it was an escape from Frank. She did her very best to keep everything discreet but often failed hopelessly. That failure would result in either a beating from Frank or an angry encounter with another man's wife.

Of course, Frank would sleep around as well, but he saw it as the male prerogative. It was okay for him to be unfaithful to Pam, but never the other way around. She was, after all, his possession, and in his mind, it was her infidelity that gave him the right to seek his pleasures elsewhere. He would pay local women for sex; they often needed the money to finance their drug habit.

Frank was less discreet than Pam with his improprieties; he would often come home drunk, with a woman on his arm, and have sex in his own home while his wife and son listened from their beds upstairs. For Pam, this was better than him coming home after a skinful and beating her. For Larry, it was better than listening to his mother being beaten to within an inch of her life. The fresh start had failed to fix their ingrained family problems, all of which stemmed from Frank, his drinking and his violent tendencies. The dysfunctionality had returned with a vengeance and in its fullest form.

Young Larry watched as his mother became more and more entrenched in her abusive relationship with Frank. With each ferocious episode, she became more accepting of it being normal, the violence embedding itself inside her. As Frank's beatings got worse, Pam's behaviour escalated too; they were stuck in a whirlpool of domestic abuse.

He may have been young, but Larry understood that his mother's immoral behaviour was driven by his father's drinking and ferocity, and that she needed an escape. He loathed what he witnessed and grew to despise his father, hoping that one day his mum would scoop him up and they would leave.

★ ★ ★

Late on Christmas Eve in 1957, a ten-year-old Larry lay in bed, still believing in Father Christmas and eagerly awaiting the arrival of a pile of gifts that he would open as soon as he could get away with it.

Larry was still awake at eleven-thirty when he heard his father come home. Frank sounded drunk, laughing with a woman he had with him - not Larry's mum. They went into the sitting room. His father was speaking bolshily, and the woman sounded half-drunk, giggling childishly whenever she spoke. Soon he was listening to the sound of his father grunting as the pair had sex on the sofa.

At just after midnight, it started. Larry found himself listening intently, knowing what was about to happen. A key turned in the front door lock, followed by the stiff hinges whingeing as they tried to resist the opening of the door.

Pam walked in, slightly drunk, with her blouse untucked from her tight pencil skirt and the zip at the back half undone.

'Where the fuck have you been, Pam?' demanded Frank Fowler. His voice was so loud that lights in neighbouring houses started to illuminate, and front doors opened as the neighbours came out to listen to tonight's episode of The Fowlers.

'Out, just out... getting some last-minute things for

tomorrow,' answered Pam unconvincingly.

'You're lying. You fuckin' cow, you've been with another man again, you fuckin' prostitute, you're such a slut, where's your fuckin' respect?'

Larry could hear the rage turning from red to white in his father's voice. He knew that there would be two more verbal assaults before Frank would move to a physical attack.

'How many times do I have to tell you, Pam. I'll fuckin' kill you and your fuckin' lover boy, I swear I'll break every bone in his body, and you can fuckin' watch while I do it?'

One more shout to go. Larry waited for it, knowing an immediate scream from his mother would follow.

'Fuck you,' shouted Frank, at a volume worthy of a lion's roar.

Frank had reached the point of moving to violence, and he slammed the door behind Pam with such force that the whole house shook. She retreated, cowering and shrinking her size to protect herself against the barrage that would surely follow. Instinctively, she put both arms up to her head to protect herself.

Frank threw his first punch, a boxer-like blow contacting Pam on the top of her head.

Pam screamed.

At the same time, Larry shrieked, stifling his boyish squeal into his pillow while pulling it around his head in an attempt to block the sound from his ears. Then came the second punch and the second scream. Pam cowered, too scared to even try and fight back. Doing so would prolong things, and she would come off worse for sure. Punch three, then punch four, then punch five, they hailed down on Pam, showing no remorse. Frank was swinging his arms frantically at her body now rather than at her head. Despite being in a state of uncontrollable rage, he had an evil, steely cold awareness of what he was doing. He knew that if he pelted her body, other people would not see the bruises and ask difficult questions. Pam wailed and screamed again, fighting to breathe as she was winded over and over again, letting out a whimper or an inaudible word or two when she was able to.

'Please stop…please…' was the most she could utter between gut-wrenching screams and catching her breath.

Larry had heard enough. This time he would do something to help his mum. He had to. Keeping as quiet as he could, Larry crept out of his room and into the upstairs hallway. He held his breath tight, even though nobody would hear him over the shouts and screams if he yelled. 'I'm coming,' at the top of his voice.

Frank kicked Pam's legs from under her with such force that she was lifted off the floor and up into the air. She landed on her back with a loud thud and another scream. As she lay on the floor sobbing and whimpering, praying inside that it had all ended, Frank lifted his heavy boot, ready to bring it down onto her with full force.

Larry launched himself from the fourth stair, landing on his father's back, initially catching him off balance and preventing the stomp from being delivered to his mother.

'You fuckin' bastard, stop. Leave her alone,' screamed Larry, in a tone that wavered between a high-pitched boy's squeal and a slightly deeper young man's voice.

He swung his arms back and forth, punching at Frank's head as his legs gripped his back. Frank rounded on him with ease, dumping Larry on the floor. The boot came up again and was then dropped with full force onto Larry's forearm, with such power that it snapped his radius bone instantly. It let out a resounding crack, like a branch being broken from a sapling. Larry screamed and started to cry. Unable to put up any more of a fight, he scrambled across the floor to join his mum. They lay hugging and sobbing in a huddle on the hallway floor. Frank continued shouting obscenities at them and threw a couple of punches into the wall.

'Don't you ever fuckin' attack me again, you little shit, what the fuck have I ever done to you?' shouted Frank.

He stepped over his wife and son to get to the kitchen and took a beer from the fridge.

'Babe, what's going on?' A younger, drunk half-dressed, blonde woman emerged from the sitting room, where Frank had been before Pam had come home.

'You can fuck off home, get dressed and get out,' shouted Frank, as he pushed past her in the doorway and headed for the sofa.

That night's fight was typical of the violence that Larry had grown up witnessing day after day as a young boy. As he grew older, he witnessed his mother suffering attack after attack. He became numb to it, accepting violence as a part of everyday life.

★ ★ ★

It was no wonder Larry came off the rails in his early teens, turning to crime and violence, always promising himself that he would not be like his father. Nevertheless, he inevitably followed suit. Indiscretions with local girls, his criminal exploits, and repeated run-ins with the police started to shape his future.

It started with petty crime, nicking bicycles or stealing from cars. Larry carried an old spark plug to smash the car windows with before he grabbed the briefcase or handbag that had been left on the back seat, not knowing what treasures waited for him inside. He would simply discard any contents of no value in a ditch or a bin.

From petty theft, he moved on to the burglary of people's homes, carefully choosing the right house to screw-over for the best quality possessions to sell for cash through local pubs, much like his father did. After house burglary, the next step was factories and businesses on the Slough Trading Estate.

Despite his malicious criminal activity, when it came to girlfriends and later his wife, Larry did have a deep sense of morality. He promised himself that he would never lift a finger against his woman, and he kept that promise.

By his early twenties, Larry was a kingpin in the local crime networks. He was an organiser, a manager, and a facilitator. He was feared by most of the other criminals in the area, the young ones and the old guard. He spent most days in the gym working out, mainly to allow himself a fighting chance against his father when things at home turned ugly. His heavy, muscular build allowed him to dominate others, using his presence alone as a threat when they stepped out of line. Larry developed a menacing way of speaking, delivering threats that were taken very seriously. Occasionally he would back them up using a pistol against a forehead for that little bit of added control.

Initially, Larry operated five stolen goods lines, a handler at the head of each, known as a fence. They would move the nicked gear on swiftly and for the best price. Larry reaped the lion's share of the takings, ensuring that his people were paid enough to keep them on the drugs they craved but always in need of more money. In turn, they were happy to do more of his dirty work.

Below his team of fences, he ran groups of younger local kids that specialised in either burglary, robbery, car theft, or theft from cars and vans. The pickings were easy and plentiful; people repeatedly failed to lock up their homes properly or left valuables on display in their cars. Others would walk around without a clue of what was going on nearby, making themselves easy targets for a wallet or car key robbery.

Larry had a strict rule that only men would be robbery victims.

'Blokes can fight back, and they get what's coming; that's fair. Women can't fight back, and they'll just get hurt, so no women.' He would say. That was his directive, and he enforced it.

He grew his empire quickly, building Slough's first organised crime group – or OCG – years before the police even coined the phrase.

By twenty-seven, Larry had complete control of much of Slough and the surrounding area's crime. There were enough layers beneath him that only his closest crime warriors knew of him. Everyone else just referred to him as 'Big-Gun'.

He bought his first home in the neighbouring area of Lynch Hill, allowing him to stay close to his Britwell roots but not be in the thick of it. He moved his mother in with him, leaving his father to fend for himself in the old family home.

At thirty, he was investing his ill-gotten gains into interest-only mortgages, buying cheap houses in Slough, Bracknell and Reading. He rented them to newly qualified nurses, police officers, and council workers. He especially liked the thought of cops living in his properties. It gave him a warped feeling of irony. His endowment policies performed rapidly, as was often the case in the eighties, allowing him to pay back the mortgages extremely quickly and increase the size of his growing criminal empire. He pushed his felonious territory into the financial markets to clean the money that he made through acquisitive crime, drug dealing, and a venture into running brothels in various parts of Slough and Reading.

When he was thirty-one, Larry lost his mother to cancer. He nursed her for three months at home, and then when she was taken to a hospice, he visited her every day without fail for the last month of her life. Her death crushed him. He was alone for the first time in his life. For a while, Larry was off the rails. He fell back into committing burglaries himself, looking for some way to fill the void in his life. The adrenalin rush of doing the crime personally helped, just until he was back in control of himself again.

After his mother died, he never heard from Frank again, only learning of his death second-hand from one of Frank's drinking partners. Frank died three years after Pam from liver failure. His body had finally succumbed to his alcohol addiction.

★ ★ ★

Larry married Sandra at the age of thirty-three. They had only been together for six months, and she was already pregnant with their twin sons, who were born the following year. Until Larry met Sandra, he courted numerous women, often more than one at a time and some were married, a little bit of Pam lived on in him. After he married, Sandra, Larry settled down into something closer to everyday family life, aside from the crime of course.

He moved the family to Kuredo, the house in the well-off end of Ascot, where he managed his empire like a modern-day Caesar. His generals were deployed into the housing estates in most towns in Berkshire, parts of Hampshire, and some new territories in South London.

He grew his reach rapidly as he expanded his territory, muscling in and commanding criminal gangs across the south of England. His financial assets grew exponentially. Larry's organised criminality had gotten so complex and successful that the money he invested in legitimate financial markets meant that his OCG was actually contributing something to the British economy. As a result of the size of his financial enterprise, he was impacting people's lives across the country, if only in some small way. For Larry, crime definitely paid.

Larry still enjoyed keeping his hand in locally. He ran several gangs that operated in the Berkshire towns that he knew so well, convincing himself that by managing these mobs directly, he could make his towns a safer place by keeping other criminals' activities at an acceptable level. He also built a network of informants; criminals that he had managed to get onto the local police's books. This meant that Larry rarely needed to flex his muscles or do any harm himself anymore, only becoming directly involved with what he chose. He simply used his network to get the right information to a grass, who would then hand it on to the police in return for a small legitimate payment. By doing things that way, the filth would do Larry's work for him. They would get a warrant, make an arrest, or look deeper into what they had been told. Whoever Larry wanted out of the way or warned would end up in the cells at the police station and then potentially land in prison.

As far as Larry was concerned, everyone was a winner. He ensured that the police were fed what they needed, keeping them happy and letting them believe they were on top of things and reducing crime. Larry was able to control his network without leaving much of a trace. He would only step in and put a gun to someone's head when the stakes were high, or he felt that direct intervention was required to show everyone that he was still around and very much in charge.

Larry's criminal money-making machine was well oiled, and it ran like clockwork. There was not even much need for cops in his pocket; he kept them for when things got serious, and he needed to buy assistance or information from the police. Larry controlled the crime; he was hidden behind the law itself. Only the trusted few knew who he was and what he did, but those who were in the know referred to it as 'Larry's Law'. Larry liked that. He liked that very much.

PART TWO

DIGGING UP THE PAST
2001

CHAPTER 6

Time Flies

Kathleen stood at the foot of her husband's grave, staring down at the headstone, reminiscing about happy times spent with her husband and family. She thought about Edward as a young man in the Royal Navy, and when they had moved to Burnham, where Leah and then Seth had been born.

Edward Lancelot Hannen

Beloved Husband of Kathleen
Born 26th March 1942
Died 13th September 1978
Age 36 Years

Kathleen visited her husband's grave every year on her birthday, which was also the anniversary of his death. As she stood in peaceful silence, she was transported backwards in a beautiful time warp, her mind filling with sounds of laughter and happy family times. She carried a shard of guilt in her heart about the fact that Edward had died on her birthday, if it had been any other day, he would have been home much later in the evening.

Seth parked his motorbike and took off his helmet. He could see Kathleen stood by the grave. His dad would have been fifty-nine now, and he often wondered how life would have been if the past had played out how it was supposed to. Without the fatal interruption that represented a mammoth turning point for the family's simple life.

Such a colossal change brought about at the hands of a burglar who had chosen the wrong house on the wrong day.

Seth walked quietly up to Kathleen, not speaking until he reached her side.

'Mum,' he said, placing his arm around her shoulder.

'Hello, Seth, here we are again, hey,' she replied.

They stood there with no need to speak to each other, each replaying their own memories, private in thought but with a shared purpose. Providing tranquil support for each other, mother and son, a maternal bond strengthened by a profound mutual loss. Seth thought back to the day that changed his life.

★ ★ ★

Kathleen had finished work at the police station early and gone home for a while before setting off to pick up Seth. She collected him from St. Peter's Church of England School, and they walked the mile or so home to Stomp Road. It was Kathleen's thirty-fourth birthday, and the family had planned to have a special meal at home that evening once Leah was home from secondary school and Edward had returned from work in central London.

As they arrived home and walked onto the driveway, Kathleen saw that the front door was wide open. She knew for sure that it had been closed when she left to get Seth from school.

'Wait outside, Seth,' said Kathleen, as she let go of Seth's hand and kissed him on his forehead. She walked up the driveway to the open door.

'Edward... are you home?' She called from the doorstep, leaning on the doorframe for support, as a mixture of fear and dread began to consume her.

The only reply was silence.

'Edward...' she called again, as she walked tentatively into the hallway.

As she reached the foot of the staircase, she saw the hallway table lying on its side. The vase that had sat on top was on the floor in pieces. The hairs on the back of her neck lifted from her skin, standing straight like soldiers on guard duty. Her heart picked up its pace, and her knees began to tremble.

'Hello... who's there? Please leave.'

Her voice was quivering with terror. Every fibre of her body telling her to turn and run back to Seth. 'Hello, please...' called Kathleen, making one last request for an answer.

Still silence.

'Mum, what's wrong?' called Seth. He was now taking small-boy sized steps towards the front door.

Kathleen edged slowly toward the kitchen. As she approached, she saw the lower half of someone's leg on the floor, the doorframe and wall obscuring the rest of whoever it was. It looked like Edwards' shoe. *It can't be... he's not due home for two or three hours.* She walked up to the doorway and looked further into the kitchen. Edward lay motionless on the floor, a pool of blood surrounding his torso.

As Seth placed his foot on the terracotta step, his ears were filled with a truly gut-wrenching scream. He ran towards his mother; as he reached the kitchen door, he saw Kathleen on her knees in a pool of blood. He could only see his father's legs lying awkwardly on the tiled floor, Edwards's chest and head hidden behind Kathleen's hug.

'Edward, no, Edward, please, no...' Kathleen was hysterical, kneeling over him, trying to pick her husband up while hugging his bloodied chest, his head and arms sagging downward, devoid of any life.

'Dad…' Seth ran toward them, screaming at the top of his voice.

'Seth, please, don't come in here, no, no,' shouted Kathleen, as she stood up dripping in blood and turning toward her son.

Seth ran, but Kathleen's body provided a hard stop as she caught him in a hug. He struggled to get free, now crying uncontrollably, but his mum walked him away, preventing him from seeing Edward's ashen grey face.

★ ★ ★

Stood in the graveyard during those few minutes of thought, Seth was six years old again. Slow-moving tears dripped from his eyes and ran down his cheeks on either side of his face. He wiped them away as he brought himself back to the present.

'Birthday coffee and cake then, Mum?' asked Seth, after they had been standing and reflecting for fifteen minutes or so.

'Yes, that would be lovely, Seth,' she replied, wiping a tear from her eye.

'I'll meet you there then,' said Seth.

He hugged her and headed for his motorcycle.

Every year Kathleen and Seth would celebrate her birthday and Edwards's life over coffee and cake at the Conservatory Café at the nearby Cliveden House.

★ ★ ★

After a challenging end to his probationary period, Seth's career had progressed well. He was good at his job. He had spent a further two years as a response officer, dealing with other peoples fated bastard days. He took his standard police driving course, learning to drive response cars, and got to grips with the basics of investigating crime.

Seth grew to dislike events like Henley Regatta and Royal Ascot more and more. The latter was always hard for him. While most of his colleagues enjoyed horse racing's premier event, it provided Seth with a grim reminder of that dark day back in 1992, when he stumbled across Larry Fowler and then killed a woman. His promise never to be a bent copper returned to his mind again and again, whenever he pushed the rule of law right up to the edge of what was acceptable. Strangely, Larry's voice lived in the back of his head throughout Seth's career, keeping him on the straight and narrow, never allowing Seth to overstep the mark. There was no way Seth would do anything that confirmed his place in anyone's list of bent coppers.

Over the years, Seth's love of investigating crime developed. He joined the CID as a detective and found himself scrutinising all kinds of crime, from simple opportunistic burglaries to complex fraud cases and criminal gangs – or Organised Crime Groups – as they came to be called by law enforcement agencies.

These gangs would prey on vulnerable people to line their own pockets or to feed cash into the complex world of illicit drugs. Seth developed a reputation for being a detective with an attention to detail that was unmatched by his peers, dismantling crime networks and keeping the law on top of the game.

He spent time on the CST, the Criminal Surveillance Team. There he learnt to police covertly, doing short stints working undercover, or staking out criminal activity, watching criminals planning and preparing to commit their crimes, then moving in at the most opportune moment to steal their thunder. Seth learnt that the key to covert work was that it is okay to be seen by your quarry, as long as you were not noticed by them. This exciting work enabled him to take his advanced driving course, learning to drive more powerful cars and motorcycles fast and in dangerous situations. He enjoyed this part of his career immensely, all the action but none of the paperwork.

Later Seth was promoted to detective sergeant, remaining in the role for less than three years before again achieving promotion. Detective Inspector Seth Hannen was a well-respected leader and investigator. He was now in charge of the CID at Slough.

In his private life, Seth was less successful. He married Paula after that fateful meeting at the Royal Ascot Races. Their relationship was repeatedly challenged as Seth fell more and more in love with his job, driven to be everything that a good police officer should be - upstanding and dedicated to the rule of law.

Despite his efforts to move on, and not be haunted by the ghost of the woman he had knocked down, he was constantly trying to balance his personal books and offset the consequences of his poor decision with Larry – he dedicated every ounce of his energy to law enforcement. In his mind, he never managed to get that balance, the heavy darkness always outweighing the light provided by being as good at his job as he could be.

Seth and Paula had a great time in the early days. They began dating the week after they had met, Seth having insisted on taking her number and then calling her to arrange a date in The Nags Head in Sunningdale, where they met for lunch. He often remembered his boyish excitement on that first date, and how they had laughed and exchanged stories of their families and childhood memories.

Seth's modest upbringing in Burnham in Buckinghamshire was a direct contrast to Paula's rather lavish lifestyle in Marlborough in Wiltshire, where her family owned a modest country estate. But they just seemed to fit somehow. It appeared that opposites did attract. A year later, they were married, and the following year Josh was born, Seth's only child.

Seth refused any financial help from Paula's parents, insisting that he and Paula would make their own way in the world. Once married, the police provided them with accommodation. Number One Police House, Stroud Farm Road in Holyport near Maidenhead, had been their home for a short while. They managed to keep things together for just under five years, then his obsession with his career began to unravel his home life. A year later, and they were divorced, Paula moved back to her parents' country estate, and Seth saw nothing of her or Josh for years.

Paula did not ask for anything from Seth, taking only their son and her personal possessions. She left her job as an estate agent in Maidenhead behind, deciding to work for her father's export business instead of being anywhere near Seth.

After they divorced, Seth could not bear the idea of moving back into police single quarters, so he bought a small Victorian house in Maidenhead and set about renovating it. He saw nothing of Paula and Josh until January 2002, when Paula was diagnosed with breast cancer, a mere three months before she passed away. Josh was just seven years old, and despite the loss of Paula, he and Seth failed to rekindle any kind of connection.

It was not long before Seth found himself in another relationship, this time with Charlotte. They had met through one of Seth's colleagues, and they married quickly. Seth moved out of his home in Maidenhead to live with Charlotte, renting his house to another police officer. Despite having deep feelings for each other, Seth and Charlotte soon started to get repeated bouts of buyer's regret after the small registry office wedding. Somehow, the relationship just failed to work. They both had their own unresolved problems. Seth's feelings of responsibility towards his mum took up a large proportion of his spare time, and he was still very much haunted by his father's death. Charlotte had only recently divorced, leaving an abusive relationship behind, and she was not yet ready for a new one.

Their weekly routine would often include an argument, which would typically centre on Seth's working hours, or the amount of time he would spend visiting or calling his mother. He was not mature enough to understand that he needed to invest as much time and energy into his personal life as he did his career. He repeatedly failed to achieve that elusive work-life balance.

Charlotte's ex-husband was a controlling man. When they were married, he had a tight grip on all of the family finances. He dictated what she spent, as well as deciding who she could have as friends. The degree of control was extreme and had caused her to suffer mentally. Despite being divorced, he still attempted to exert his authority on her and their two sons. He would frequently turn up on Charlotte and Seth's doorstep, and a row would ensue, then the police would often be called by a neighbour. That did not help Seth's professional life in any way, and he felt hugely embarrassed by it. His opinion of their relationship was not helped by Charlotte's frequent mental breakdowns. Seth felt that his life was too weighed down with Charlotte's baggage, but it was the continual fights that she had with her ex-husband that played a significant part in Seth's decision to leave.

Seth moved out of Charlotte's house and back to his own on their second wedding anniversary. He often thought that the timing of his leaving was a bit shit, but he was unable to take any more, he had enough on his plate. Seth liked things to be orderly, why wait until they were into year three. He could, and should, have dealt with it all a lot better and been a more supporting husband, if only he had not been so in love with his job. But work came first, and that's where he found his fulfilment and sense of worth.

★ ★ ★

It was a warm September afternoon, so Seth and Kathleen sat outside at Cliveden House. They chatted about everything from happy family memories of Edward, and elderly relatives who had now departed, as well as Seth's career in the police. During this special annual chat, Seth would often consider telling Kathleen about that day nine years ago. About Larry and Scotch, the young woman, and the rottweiler. But every time he thought he had mustered the courage; his nerve would leave him. Sharing his bastard day with his mum would only serve to halve his burden but significantly add to hers. It was better a safely kept secret, in his mind alone.

'Mum, I have some exciting news; I've got a promotion to detective inspector at Slough, on the CID.'

'That's brilliant news, well done. You know your dad would've been so proud of you, that deserves another slice of cake, I reckon,' said Kathleen, as she selected a piece of lemon drizzle from the china cake stand. 'What about you, Seth, outside of work, how is that part of your life?'

'Everything's fine, Mum, you know, I'm chugging along,' he replied.

Seth's only real success in his personal life was the relationship he enjoyed with his mother. She had remained single since Edward's tragic death, and Seth felt a considerable level of responsibility towards her. She meant the world to him, and he saw it as his job to look after her. They remained exceptionally close; he would typically call two or three times a week and visit at least once a month, often taking her flowers and gifts. He would take her out to lunch or to the theatre, doing all that he could to ensure she felt loved.

Seth's sister Leah had moved to Australia with her husband, where they had two children together. Since emigrating, she had not managed to get home once, relying on telephone calls and emails to maintain her relationship with Kathleen. Seth was the local one, and he took the trouble to take care of her as she grew older. He was demonstrably the favourite child. For Seth, his mother was the only woman that was able to truly remain in his heart, nobody else had managed it.

CHAPTER 7

The Praetorian Guard

Larry grew his empire with a shrewd intellect, relative ease, and a degree of business acumen; it all came naturally to him. His decisions were well thought through and informed. He would weigh up the benefits of moving into a particular field of criminal work, then assess the competition before launching a takeover, or perhaps simply dismantling what was usually a crude setup.

Over the years, he established multiple businesses to front-up his money laundering. They ranged from little shops that would spring up in town centres to a small mortgage company. He opened nail bars and hairdressers, always managing to strike deals with landlords for a lower rent to keep the shops occupied in declining town centres. His car wash facilities were generally on disused garage forecourts that allowed space for other criminal activity to carry on unnoticed in the background.

Larry continued to invest in stocks and shares, building an extensive portfolio of financial reserves. He would buy failing endowment policies and personal investment plans from larger businesses if he could see a way of making money or using the venture to hide another form of income.

He would generally staff his small businesses by taking advantage of cheap migrant workers, many of them in the country illegally. He became proficient at human trafficking, exploiting underprivileged workers in Africa and Eastern Europe, bringing them to Britain with a promise of well-paid jobs, only to then trap them in a world of modern slavery.

Larry pushed hundreds of fictitious clients through his books to account for the level of takings that he declared to the taxman. He kept his business manager's work separate from his crime general's work, each type of business having a nominated lead. This approach ensured a sterile corridor between them, saving things from getting too sticky too often, guaranteeing as best he could that an employee would not snitch his activities to the police.

To keep Her Majesty's Revenue and Customs off his back, he played a straight bat with his tax affairs. Pushing his dirty money through his businesses and then declaring every penny. He paid his share of corporation tax, dividend tax, and personal income tax for his and Sandra's paid wage. This tactic kept the taxman away from his door. It allowed him to hide his illicit money behind a sizeable business empire that, without criminal investment, would not function. By appearing as a successful businessman, paying his way in life, he could continue to hide behind the law of the land.

Larry and Sandra's twin boys, Michael and Sean, were privately educated at an independent school on the outskirts of Ascot. Against Sandra's wishes, he had them board at school from an early age so that they would grow up in an environment as far removed from his life as possible. They would mix with other public-school pupils and learn to be businessmen or doctors if they wanted. Larry felt strongly that he could only do what he did because of his roots, the way his parents had lived and treated him helped to make him resilient to the risks of criminal life. His boys would not have the same rhino skin that he had grown to protect himself in the harsh world of crime.

They needed the opportunity to only enter his world by choice, not by default.

Larry had his own personal balancing act going on between the darkness his father bestowed on his mother and the light that he felt his she had deserved. By being the best husband he could be to Sandra, he was, in some way, repaying his father's debt. As a result, Sandra enjoyed a luxurious life, Larry showered her with gifts and extravagance. He treated her like his queen. She knew that Larry carried on dodgy deals and had some shady characters working for him, but she had no idea how far his tentacles reached. He liked to think of himself as a British Al Capone, making tens of millions of pounds from his ill-gotten gains and commanding a small army of foot soldiers.

Larry's world was the other side of the coin to Seth's, but they were both exceptionally good at their chosen careers. Their lives had fatefully crossed paths in 1992 and were about to collide again.

★ ★ ★

Larry sent Sandra off to London with a thick wad of cash and his credit card.

'Go and enjoy yourself, meet the girls, and have a day of luxury; shopping, dinner and a show, go on spoil yourself,' Larry had said, needing Sandra out of the house for the day.

It was the day of Larry's monthly management meeting to discuss how things were going and agree on how to deal with any problems. He would use this meeting to tackle any underperformance by whichever of his teams needed his personal intervention. He liked to hold his meetings in private, so Sandra would always be sent off on a shopping trip or to a spa for the day.

Larry employed several long-standing crooks as his right-hand men, as well as one right-hand woman. His twelve generals were loyal to the last, as much out of fear as out of any respect for Larry. They each ran a designated arm of his criminal setup, taking sole responsibility for ensuring success while also ensuring that everyone else knew that Larry was in charge. He kept their work separate, not allowing anyone to know more than they needed to. Knowledge was power and giving too much of it to one person would risk a coup. This carefully constructed business model helped build Larry Big-Gun Fowler's criminal empire into one of the most substantial in Britain.

Some of Larry's generals had worked with him since being young teenage burglars, thieves, or drug dealers. They ran the street crime scene, which was more localised to London and the home counties. The others looked after IT fraud, counterfeit goods or currency, and exploitation; they worked on a national and sometimes international scale.

Notwithstanding Larry's attempts to keep his sons from his world of crime, they had a large chunk of Frank Fowler's DNA handed down through Larry. As they grew up, they became increasingly interested in Larry's business, and stepped into the world of crime. Michael had become Larry's understudy, learning how it all worked, ready to take over when Larry decided to pack it all up. Sean, however, had specialised in further developing Larry's human trafficking business, frequently spending time abroad to set up the supply chain. Both sons attended Larry's management meetings, often by video link.

Despite their increasing responsibility, his generals got little in the way of financial enhancements or improved terms to match Larry's growing wealth. The local gang generals watched Larry make more and more money while they remained in mortgaged or even council-owned houses. They were not permitted too much of the good life. Larry believed that allowing them to become fat cats would result in showing off flashy cars and watches and then bragging about it, that would increase the risk of loose tongues and prying eyes. Instead, he would offer corporate style rewards, such as tickets to sporting events or gigs played by rock bands.

Only Rebecca Langford, who looked after the money through his investment wing, profited really well from Larry's exploits. She was known in the investment community as a ruthless businesswoman who would take no prisoners. She was as tough as they get, and people rarely crossed her. She had fought off competition from others to climb the career ladder when she worked for Eatmon LLP, a large and successful London investment company. She went it alone at only thirty-two years of age, establishing Langford Investment Management, which had gone from strength to strength. Rebecca was the only person Larry would trust with his finances. Since the early days, Larry had drawn her deeper into his business, trusting her with knowledge of his criminal activities in return for greater financial reward. She was able to work wonders laundering the proceeds of crime, either through offshore accounts or through Larry's small ineffective local business setup, which had plenty of room to apply false profits. Rebecca invested revenue and capital to pay out an income and regular dividends to Larry, which meant all the cash he spent was crisp and clean. She was the only one not paid directly. Her money was paid by way of a commission percentage; the better the funds performed, the greater her take. She also managed the payroll, ensuring that the generals were paid a salary, and they paid their taxes. They disliked the arrangement immensely. They could see that Rebecca had a better financial package than them. She had an expensive car, posh clothes and accessories, and certainly enjoyed the high life. In their view, they took all the risks while Rebecca sat back and creamed off the profit.

* * *

Larry shut his dog away in the kitchen. Buster disliked most house visitors with a vengeance and would bark and snarl at them, making everyone uneasy. That was Larry's job, not Buster's.

The first to arrive was Glen Borland. He was one of Larry's local generals. Glen was a Pit bull of a man, stocky and well built. His criminal persona was an old fashioned one – he would always put his hands up when he got caught – a fair cop was an honest cop in his mind. He had been arrested plenty of times early on in his career, and he took what the law dealt him on the chin. When he started working for Larry, he was afforded Big-Gun's protection which enabled him to become better at his job, and the law left him alone. Borland settled on burglary as his crime of choice and moved up Larry's network as it grew, managing large teams of crooks below him in Larry's structure. Although the early years saw Glen sorting out many of Larry's unfortunate 'sticky' situations, he had managed to leave this aspect of the work behind. Now he controlled the main arm of Larry's local stolen property business. His roots remained in burglary though, and his criminal record supported that, with nineteen convictions and a short prison sentence in his early twenties.

Next through the door was Tony Spiller, only a few steps behind Borland. Spiller ran the kidnap and extortion arm of Larry's empire. He was six foot and ripped, with cropped dark hair, and spoke with the remnants of a Glaswegian accent. He had also worked his way up from dealing with Larry's sticky problems. Spiller had a nasty streak that made him particularly good at the extortion racket, holding the rich to ransom, whether they were upstanding members of the community or the heads of other organised crime groups. His work was much broader than Borland's and was not restricted to Larry's local crime scene, he operated across the south of England. Like Glen, he liked to keep his hand in at the lower level, entertaining himself with torture, which often led to murder.

After Spiller, Rebecca Langford arrived. She was a relatively ordinary looking woman, but when wearing her business suit, which was always a pencil skirt and a matching two button single breasted jacket, her appearance and demeanour were of a woman who would not look at all out of place on Dragons Den or The Apprentice. She was just over five foot seven tall and had a slightly stocky build. Her hair was greying but in a subtle way that nicely flattered her attractively rounded face. She wore her hair down but kept it cut fairly short, as she believed that older women should not wear their hair so that it touched their shoulders.

Tony Spiller and Glen Borland had a fierce rivalry, and neither had any time for Rebecca. Their dislike for each other saw them both wanting to be Larry's high general, his only right-hand man, not one of a group of twelve. Larry, on the other hand, did not want any of the team to think they were more trusted than the others. It kept them sharp and retained a degree of mistrust in the group. The edginess helped to make sure Larry remained in firm control and was able to see risks or threats building.

The rest of the generals arrived individually, each jockeying for the next best seat at the table. They knew who to sit next to or not, anticipating how Larry would run the meeting.

Larry ushered each of them into the large dining room. Larry would always sit at the head of the long table, with six of his generals on each side, appearing like the chair of the board. Glen and Tony always sat opposite each other in the seats directly adjacent to Larry. The table was set up with two jugs of water and a bottle of whisky, each chair having two glasses in front of them, one for each beverage.

'Welcome, Lady and Gentlemen, we all know each other, and we know who's in charge. So, there's no need for fuckin' introductions,' said Larry, opening the meeting with his normal starter.

'I trust you all enjoyed Beckham's injury time equaliser earlier this month. That's us in Japan later this year then, eh boys.'

Larry did not really follow football, but he knew several of his generals did. 'Anyway, down to business, reports please, and don't try and bullshit me, I've spoken to our lovely accountant,' he glanced briefly at Rebecca. 'I know exactly how things are going, so what I want to hear is why they are going the way they are, and if it's bad, what the fuck you are doing about it.'

Larry looked at Tony first. It annoyed Glen that he was going to be last again. For the last three meetings on the trot he had not been chosen to be the first to update.

'Well, Larry, if you've seen the numbers, you'll know everything is fine, no real risks taken this month, and no would-be heroes causing trouble. Everything is just as you like it, tight and tidy.

'On the business front, everyone is paid up on the new business protection service, and nobody is asking any fucking questions. I always say that people handing over money because they are made to feel they want to, is a dead cert – much easier and better than taking it from them by force. I think it could be time to start winding up the more, shall I say… traditional crime. We should focus on extortion, the internet and the people trafficking, and hive off the drug dealing, burglaries and robberies,' said Tony, upbeat and confident in his manner.

He was making sure that Glen could feel the mood, as others around the table nodded in agreement.

'Thanks, Tony, but let's stick to reports, rather than drifting into planning my business for me, shall we...eh?' Larry interjected.

Larry knew the big money was where Tony had outlined, not in local crime, but he felt an affinity with his heritage and enjoyed the feeling of power it gave him. Besides, Glen and his opposite numbers on the local scene lacked the brains for more complex crime, cutting them loose was a risk Larry was unwilling to take.

'Let's move around the table then, Phil, IT scams, what's new?'

Glen sat listening to all the updates about what he saw as la-di-da white-collar crime twaddle, slowly allowing the pressure inside his head to reach a crescendo, only offering support to the reports on the local drug scene and prostitution rackets.

As Rebecca gave her financial update, Glen clocked her new Rolex watch and a designer handbag. He knew they were real; he was proud of the fact he could spot a fake from a couple of metres away. Glen looked down at his old, battered watch, the same one he had worn for years, and felt his bubbling resentment growing.

It was not until after Larry had taken updates from everyone else that he asked for Glen's assessment of the burglary business. Despite sitting to Larry's left and the last in the line, Glen had taken being the final general to update as a sign of his insignificance in Larry's mind.

'No real issues at all, fifteen good quality house burglaries this month, all giving us jewellery and substantial amounts of cash. Two businesses screwed, again good returns, and no problems with the law,' said Glen.

Glen knew that the burglaries provided a steady income, but he was getting weary of the monthly updates that served only for Larry to sit and lord over his apparent power and criminal reach.

'Thanks, Glen, but there's not much detail in there, mate. How many had we planned? Did you get through them all?' Larry pressed Glen.

'You know we bloody didn't, I spoke to you last week about the two big houses we didn't get to. Why the fuck are you asking, just to call me out in front of the others and make me look stupid?' said Glen, allowing his pressure cooker to start releasing steam.

'Glen, pipe down, and watch your fuckin' mouth,' said Larry, less than impressed with Glen's response.

'Larry, if I'm honest, this is just a total waste of fucking time, you speak to us all on the phone every week, you know this stuff. This is just a show, a place to slap us publicly if things are shit, or to put Tony on a fucking pedestal.'

Glen was pushing his luck, and he knew it. But he knew some of the others were feeling the same way, they would often share complaints after one of Larry's highfaluting performance meetings.

Larry saw Glen's rant as a direct criticism and a challenge to his authority and he did not take it well, raising his voice to a bellow.

'If you don't like the way I run things, Glen, you know what you can fuckin' do, you can take me on at a game of fuck-right-off, and you can fuckin' go first, do you get my drift, pal?'

Glen had not expected such a fierce response. But it was the fourth or fifth time, in as many weeks, that he had criticised Larry for something or been interrogated by him over a series of burglaries he had suggested to Larry as a good move. Usually, Glen would back down at this point, but they usually argued in private. With the rest of the generals watching, Glen did not want to lose any more face. The room was silent, the air acrid with a biting atmosphere they could taste. Glen let one more insult leave his mouth in the direction of Larry, raising his voice to match Larry's bellow.

'You're getting fucking greedy, Larry; you and your family do so bloody well out of all this. Look at this place, with your pool, your vintage Aston Martin and a fucking Range Rover, let alone the cleaners and the gardeners. I've given you so many years, made you tons of cash, and I'm still living in a two-bedroom semi on a fucking council estate.

'Your white-collar clean crime crew do well enough. How much of your money are they taking before it gets to you eh, have you ever thought about that?

'As for that cow,' Glen looked at Rebecca. 'She's got all your cash, she seems well enough with her designer clothes and posh car, you need to wake up and smell the coffee, Larry... well, you know what, you're on, I will go first, fuck you,' shouted Glen.

He stood up to leave, purposely knocking his chair over with temper as he did, then he turned and walked towards the door.

'Get out, get the fuck out of my house, go and get some fuckin' air. We will talk about this in a few days, wait for my call, and don't fuckin' think about crossing me, Glen. That would be a big mistake,' said Larry, resolute and bullish in his tone.

They all watched as Glen left the room, then Larry called the meeting to order. 'Anyone else feel like Glen? Does anyone else want to play with me? If you do, it's your move, fuck-right-off if you're on for it.' Larry snarled like his dog.

The room stayed silent as Larry poured himself a whisky and lit a cigarette.

As Glen reached the front door, he paused and glanced back to see if anyone was following him, then he gave a silent two-fingered salute in the direction of the meeting before shouting back at them.

'Fuck you all.'

'Just fuckin' leave, now,' replied Larry, in a forceful tone.

The meeting continued, with eleven generals left around the table.

Glen walked out the door, slamming it shut, and headed for his car. The wheels of the BMW spun on the drive as he sped toward the gates, cutting across the lawn to get around the other cars blocking him in.

★ ★ ★

Glen was an adrenaline junkie, and he had a high temper. He got his kicks from high stakes burglaries, and he preferred to commit them himself when he could. He would generally do the jobs at night, enjoying the possibility of being disturbed by the occupants of expensive houses out in the sticks, although that had only happened a handful of times, early in his career.

Any burglar who wanted to get away scot-free, with the lowest risk possible, would generally choose daylight to screw a house, when the occupants would most likely be out at work. They would knock on the front door and make an excuse if someone answered, or creep round the back if nobody was in. Not Glen, he saw the whole thing as a game, him versus the law. At night the only eyes out there were those of the police and security firms. He liked the adversarial feeling of it being him against the law. He would dodge police cars and watch security patrols from the darkness as they responded to an alarm that he had set off simply to test their response time a few weeks before doing a job.

Glen got home and parked his BMW three series, and quickly went inside. Now was the time to plan his move. Going out on his own and leaving Larry's setup would be a risky business. He needed to do this one big job, then get out of the way for a while and lay low.

Glen saw his trade as highly specialised. A confident bank robber only needed a handwritten note and balls of steel. There was no skill or expertise in robbing banks or old ladies in the park, for that matter. Burglary, however, took planning and skill, and it needed proper consideration of contingency plans. This job had been on his list for a couple of weeks, but the autumn skies were clear, and the moon was bright. He was waiting for there to be no moonlight; Tuesday would be here soon enough. A good night-time burglar would plan the job for the right day and needed specialised equipment and skills to do a decent job.

★ ★ ★

On Tuesday afternoon, Glen pulled a black holdall from his wardrobe and emptied it onto his bed, laying the contents out, putting the tools he needed for the job to one side – a small black anodised shingler's roofing hammer with a replaceable blade on one side and a milled face on the other, a heavy flat-headed screwdriver, a roll of black insulating tape, a rolled-up length of coat hanger wire, a set of locksmith's picks and a bump-key, night vision goggles, a Mini-Maglite torch, as well as a stethoscope, and his woollen balaclava, which was wrapped around a leather ankle holster containing his Glock-42 mini handgun and a small digital camera. Finally, he threw some dog treats onto the pile, along with two pairs of black latex gloves.

Glen pulled on his black jeans with his utility belt to hold some of his tools, then he put on his black t-shirt and threw a black bomber jacket on the bed with his tools. Finally, he put on his black socks and black trainers. He bundled the other bits and pieces back into the bag and then sat down with a couple of bottles of beer to watch some television and get some sleep. Being tired on a job was the worst thing. It allowed silly mistakes to be made far too easily.

At three o'clock in the morning, his alarm buzzed furiously, waking him from his light sleep. Wary of anyone watching his house for movement, he kitted up without turning on any lights. Once ready, he pulled on his black jacket and headed for his car, grabbing his burner-phone as he left the house.

CHAPTER 8

Into the Darkness

On Tuesday the 16^{the} of October 2001, the night was as pitch black as it could possibly be, the new moon reflecting none of the sun's rays. Glen parked his car and walked the last half a mile to the address that he had chosen to be the final burglary he would commit. This was by far the riskiest job he had ever undertaken.

He was now in his early thirties, and burglary was hard work, especially when the houses that he screwed were so well protected. Compared to when he started out, improvements in technology had made security systems much better, making it harder to do a job quickly. Additionally, the police now had much better forensic capabilities and could track you down more easily. Burglary was certainly not what it used to be. This job would enable him to establish his own crime syndicate, without the overbearing and controlling Larry Fowler expecting him to be at his beck and call and holding ridiculous la-di-da meetings. This job was for Glen, not for Larry.

The house was a large property, with several outbuildings, set back from the main road behind thick foliage and a high brick wall. The wall was protected by infrared sensors linked to cameras and an early warning alarm system. The large black gates were firmly shut, held in place by heavy-duty electric motors.

The gates had weight sensors fitted and connected to the alarm to warn of anyone climbing or attempting to force them. The perimeter alone was like Fort Knox. For Glen, this was advantageous because the occupants would take a false sense of security from the boundary protection and the cameras. They would probably be much lazier with the inner security at the house itself.

As Glen walked up to the gates, he saw a notice warning him that the property was protected by security cameras and a monitoring company called Broadlines Security Ltd. He knew this company well. They did not actually monitor camera systems at all. Still, they would respond to an alarm activation pretty quickly, sending a pair of dogs in first, followed by a couple of thugs to search for intruders. If he set the alarm off before he'd implemented his plan, he would have a little over ten minutes to get the hell out and away.

Glen had cased the joint several times and knew it inside out. He had played the plan through in his mind a hundred times, even managing to get inside to check out the basic layout. He was good, very good. The security cameras captured a frame every twelve seconds, the time-lapse footage being recorded to videotape. It would be much easier to deal with than the newer real-time recording systems starting to pop up here and there. Glen just needed to make sure that he left no clues that would enable anyone to identify him later from the footage. Dressed in black from head to toe, he pulled on his balaclava, followed by the night vision goggles, perched for now on the top of his head. Next, he put on the two pairs of black latex gloves. Then he closed his eyes tight for two minutes to get his pupils to dilate and aid his natural night vision while he was not using the goggles. He needed not to emit a green glow or provide a reflective surface that could flare, giving him away to anyone on the road or perhaps being seen from the windows in the house, so the goggles would only be used inside.

As he moved from the road towards the gate, he immediately disappeared into the darkness, his black camouflage doing its job. He would be hard to pick out without a torch being shone directly onto him.

He took the screwdriver out from its place on his belt and the electrical tape from his jacket pocket. First, he tore off a length of black tape and stuck it over the camera lens on the gate's intercom panel, just in case someone inside heard something and connected to the camera to get a close-up view. Then he put a small piece of tape onto each of the large screws that connected the right-hand gate to the electric motor's metal arm. This would minimise any marks made by the screwdriver, preventing any investigation from working out how he had bypassed the gate. The tape would also foil any attempts that police forensics might make to get a mechanical fit between the indentations he would leave and the screwdriver. If they found marks, then the police could potentially link burglaries where Glen had used the same tool. Worse still, they could link the job to him if ever he was caught, and the screwdriver compared to forensic scene reports from historic burglaries.

He made quick progress removing the eight large screws that connected the gate to its motor, carefully placing them aside for later. Once the screws were all out, he pushed the gate. It swung open silently, leaving the motor's arm in its original position. He stepped onto the drive and pushed the gate shut behind him so that it would look normal to a passing police car or security patrol. Then he took out his roofer's hammer and jammed it between the gate and the ground, so the gate would not blow open. The hammer was also a last-ditch escape tool, just in case he was chased by the homeowner or their dog. Either end of the hammer's head would do enough damage to allow him to get away from a fight on the driveway and negate the use of a gun so close to the perimeter.

Stage one complete.

Next, he leant down and unclipped the small leather strap holding the Glock in its holster, making drawing the gun easier. He hoped not to have to use it, but he may have no choice if the occupants disturbed him inside the house.

Glen was careful to walk on the grass, rolling his ankles outward to disguise his natural pronation with any footprints he left behind. The grass was a safer bet over the gravel driveway or the flowerbed. He would neither make noise on the gravel, still one of the best security measures around a house, nor leave detailed impressions of his trainers. He walked to the end of the driveway, disguising his gait and stance in the knowledge that the little red lights pointing onto the drive and surrounding gardens meant that he was being filmed by the infrared cameras. He needed to be confident that he would not be recognised when the footage was played back. He gave one of the cameras a cheeky wave, using his left hand to disguise his right-handedness.

Reaching the house, he took a moment to gather his thoughts, pressing the button on his watch to momentarily illuminate the time while he crouched at the side of the house.

03:34

Early mornings were his favoured time for a burglary. Experience had taught him that the occupants would almost certainly be in a deep sleep and less likely to stir. However, tonight he intended to wake them, he needed their help, but they had to be sleepy enough not to overthink the situation.

He crouched against the wall at the side of the house for a few more minutes, going through the plan in his head one more time. *Right, let's get this done and dusted. It's now or never.*

Glen checked his pocket for the dog treats before taking out his burner-phone and dialling a number that he had saved in the memory. The phone rang inside the house, it took six rings before the answering machine kicked in.

'Hello, you've reached the answerphone of—'

Glen hung up and hit the redial button a second and then a third time. This time the groggy voice of a woman answered the call.

'Hello, Mum, are you okay?' she said. She was clearly half asleep and had no idea who was calling.

'Hello, madam, I'm so sorry to bother you at such a late hour. I work for the electric company. We are dealing with a fallen tree that has damaged overhead cables. I need to turn off the power to get the tree moved and make sure everything is safe before we reconnect you. I'm just calling to let you know that the power will be out for a couple of hours and to apologise for any inconvenience,' he said, disguising his voice. He was taking no chances of leaving any reportable clues.

'Okay, but we'd probably not even have noticed, was there really a need to call at half past three in the morning for God's sake?' came the reply. She was unmistakably upset at being woken up.

'Normally, we wouldn't call, madam, but the houses around here all have security alarms. We'll wake the whole neighbourhood when they all go off due to the power cut, so we need to call and advise you. I'm very sorry to have woken you. If you could just unset your alarm if it sounds in the next fifteen minutes, that would be great. We'll call again when it can be reset if you'd like?' Glen waited for a reply.

'No more calls, please, just fix the power, thank you.'

Then the phone went dead.

Glen sat back against the wall of the house, waiting. Either they would get up and unset the alarm now, or when he set it off getting in, they would assume it was caused by the power being turned off and then reset it. The security company should call the house ahead of responding to the activation.

Within a minute, he saw an upstairs light come on inside the house, then another, this time downstairs. The alarm panel was next to the side door, immediately the other side of the wall to where Glen was crouched. He heard it beeping, counting down to activation, having detected the movement inside. Then he heard six high-pitched beeps followed by a lower-pitched one, the confirmation sound as the keypad had the code punched in to turn off the system. The light went out as the occupant walked back upstairs, but the bedroom light stayed on; now he needed them to go back to bed.

Still in his squat position, Glen moved to a large metal grey box under the kitchen window and pulled out the smallest of his locksmith keys from his pocket. He pushed it into the lock. It slid in perfectly, then with a couple of skilled twists and knocks, the cabinet latch moved, and it was open. Once inside the box, he turned off the mains electricity to the house and watched the reflection of the upstairs light disappear from the lawn as its power source was extinguished. The little red lights on each of the security cameras flickered and died. *That's an unexpected bonus,* he thought. Within a few seconds, he saw that a torch was on in the bedroom. He watched the flickering light move around for a while before it was dark again. Back to his waiting spot for another twenty minutes – plenty of time for them to go back to sleep.

Glen was pretty sure that they would be asleep now. He knew which room they were in and had a good idea of the layout inside the house. He took out his bump-key, a key that he could push into the lock, then give a gentle tap that would throw the levers up and allow him to turn the barrel and unlock the door. *Shit, there's a key on the other side.* The bump-key would not go in.

He took out the coat hanger wire from inside his jacket, unwinding it before poking it through the narrow letterbox while leaning against the glass and looking down at the key sitting in the lock. He bent the wire to the correct angle and worked it towards the key, pushing the end of the wire through the hole where the ring of a key fob would sit. *Thank fuck there's no fob.* Within thirty seconds of wiggling the key with the wire, it came loose from the lock. Glen slowly brought the key out through the letterbox – no point in using the bump-key now. He pushed the key back into the lock, turned it, and then the door was unlocked. It took another two minutes to gather up his tools and ensure nothing was left on the ground.

Stage two complete.

The door opened without a sound, and he stepped inside, closing it behind him before putting the key back in and re-locking it.

The alarm panel emitted an intermittent chirp, indicating power loss, its battery providing power for the keypad and the dim display light. On with the night vision goggles, and everything turned green. Taking slow, purposeful steps, Glen walked past the door to the kitchen, stopping briefly to look inside, just in case anyone was there. As he stood still, he heard the sound of claws tapping the floor as a dog trotted along the hallway in his direction. He pulled the treats out of his pocket and held out his hand as it approached.

'Hello... good boy, here you go.' Glen greeted the dog, keeping his voice down and offering it the meaty treats.

The dog wagged his tail and sniffed Glen's hand, taking the treats before jumping up and putting his paws on his chest. 'Off boy, go on, sod off,' he whispered, as he pushed the Rhodesian Ridgeback away.

The dog trotted off back to its bed. Glen moved along the

hallway, passing several rooms, checking each to ensure no surprises lay in store, before finally arriving at the base of a wide staircase with an ostentatious wooden bannister. His heart was pumping like a turbine at full tilt now, pushing the adrenalin around his veins in a rushing river of blood. He pulled his right trouser leg up, above the gun holster on his ankle. He needed to go upstairs.

Glen put his foot onto the staircase and started to move slowly up the stairs. As he reached the sixth tread, it let out the beginnings of a squeak as he lowered his weight onto it. He immediately froze, then slowly transferred his weight back to the other foot. He stepped over and onto the seventh step. Eventually, he reached the top of the stairs.

The master bedroom was two doors away and at the side of the house above where Glen had been crouched earlier. He moved along the hallway, tight against the wall, the gun now in his right hand and held against his chest, his finger on the trigger. As he reached the door, he stopped and peered through the gap. Two people were asleep in the large four-poster bed, shining bright green in his goggles.

Taking deep quiet breaths, Glen pushed the door open. As he did, the woman rolled over in the bed, turning to face away from him. He walked into the room, and up to the very edge of the bed, he found himself looking down at a middle-aged man. Glen extended his arm, pointing the gun at the man's head, only centimetres from his temple. *I could kill you at point-blank range right now.* A surge of total supremacy overwhelmed him. He had the power of life and death in his hand; he was an emperor, a crime lord. He stood over the bed for three minutes, watching the man breathing deeply, still pointing the gun at his head. He imagined what it would feel like to squeeze the trigger and fire the bullet out of the gun and into the man's brain through his skull. Glen loved the feeling of dominance he got from being in a house while his victims slept, unaware of his presence. When the moment had passed, full of sway, he turned and walked away, leaving the couple to their dreams, not knowing how close they had come to death.

Glen walked back along the hallway and back downstairs, being careful to miss the sixth tread. At the bottom of the stairs, he turned left into a large ostentatious sitting room. He knew exactly what he was looking for. Glen turned off the night vision goggles, lifting them back up onto his forehead and turned on a small torch built into the same unit. He walked over to a large painting that sat above a table. The painting was attached to the wall with hinges, he pulled it back to reveal Larry Fowler's wall safe.

Glen had seen the safe opened tens of times when Larry got his books out during meetings that he and Larry had had in this very room. Larry had no trust in computers, not for his illicit dealings in any case. He was old school, keeping his financial records in one book, his contacts and associate's details in another, and his plans and drug shipment particulars in a page to view diary.

Glen knew that a large shipment of cocaine and heroin was coming into the country sometime in the next week and that Larry had the plans, and importantly which of his criminal generals was running the job, detailed in his diary. He pulled the stethoscope from his jacket and put it in his ears, then he placed the diaphragm against the front wall of the safe near the dial. Next, he moved the dial clockwise, waiting for the first tick, three whole turns, click. Four and a half turns anticlockwise, click. Six turns clockwise, click. *That should be it.* He twisted the dial anticlockwise again, waiting for it to engage the lock.

Nothing.

The door remained clamped shut. Glen repeated the whole routine a second time.

One final turn.

This time the lock let go of its hold, and the safe was open. Glen took Larry's gun out first, placing it on the table beneath the safe, then he pulled out the three hardback books, noticing a wooden box on its side at the back of the safe as he did. After identifying the diary, he opened it up, pulling the long red ribbon to part the pages. Turning a page at a time, he searched for the details of the shipment; after thumbing through six days, he found it, written in Larry's easily understood code.

SHTN – SLG
1000 kg brown dragon – 1000 kg white ghost
plus resin – Grant's crew

That was all that Glen needed to know to be able to get the gear. He had heard of the Southampton to Slough exchange before and knew where it usually took place. He removed the small digital camera from his back pocket and took a photograph of the diary entry. Then he opened the book of contacts and associates and photographed the pages for Slough, Maidenhead and most of South London. He would need them to distribute the drugs later, and for when he made the move from setting himself up to taking over Larry's empire. Just as he was done with the camera, he knocked one of the books from the table to the floor. It took a heavy glass ashtray with it, clattering as it landed on the rug that was sat directly on wooden floorboards.

Glen crouched to pick it up, listening intently for any movement from upstairs. A sound came toward him, along the hallway. As he turned his head, his torch illuminated the figure of Buster trotting over to him, his tail wagging madly.

'For fuck's sake, Buster, piss off back to bed, fuck off,' whispered Glen.

Buster was wide awake though, he often played with Glen,

the only one of Larry's generals he did not bark and snarl at. 'Not now, numb-nuts, fuck off.' Glen tried to whisper forcefully but failed.

He put the ashtray back on the table, then placed the gun into the safe. Then he pulled out the wooden box, curious as to its contents. He put it on the table and opened it up. Inside he found a bundle of newspaper clippings. *They're all about his copper friend Hannen,* he thought, as he looked at a few of the cuttings, he's obviously Larry's inside man in the police. He closed the box and put it back, followed by the three books, being careful to keep them in the correct order. Then he shut the safe, spun the dial to ensure it was locked, and pushed the painting back in place.

Glen walked out of the sitting room into the entrance hall, followed by Buster. Stood at the foot of the staircase, for a moment, he was tempted to go back upstairs and put the gun back to Larry's head, but he decided to leave, not wanting to push his luck. He could not leave the same way that he came in, locking the side door and getting the key back on the inside would take far too long. So, he walked to the front door, carefully slid back the large bolts at the top and bottom, and then opened the hallway drawer and took out a key. He unlocked the centre deadbolt before putting the key back into the drawer. Then he opened the front door slowly, walked out and closed it quietly behind him.

Stage three complete.

Once outside, Glen crept back to the electrical cabinet and turned the power back on, the cabinet door closing with a firm clunk as the lock re-engaged. He left the garden, waving again at the camera as he went, before picking up his hammer and swinging the gate open and then shut again as he walked through. He put the screws back into the gate, shoving the bits of black insulating tape into the pocket of his jeans after each one had been tightened. The gate was reconnected to its electric motor. Finally, he pulled the electrical tape off the camera.

Stage Four Complete.

That wasn't as tough as I'd imagined. All I need now is to get a team together to turn over the drugs run. Glen's thoughts had moved from the job at hand to the next stage of his coup d'état. He jogged back to his car and made good his escape.

CHAPTER 9

Executive Action

'Sandra, you didn't lock the front door up last night,' Larry shouted towards his wife in the kitchen.

'I'm sure I did, Larry, I remember doing it and putting the key back in the drawer,' came the reply.

'Well, it must be your age, that's all I'm saying... at least it's shut, small mercies, eh?'

Larry walked to the side door and picked up the post and his newspaper from the doormat, instinctively twisting the key in the lock, checking that it had been secure overnight. Buster was sat by the door looking at Larry.

'Dog been out for a shit yet?'

'Not yet, I'm only just making the coffee, give me a chance, and please don't swear, Larry,' replied Sandra, feeling that he was having a bit of a dig. *He's in one of those moods.* She thought to herself.

Larry unlocked the door and let Buster out.

'Good job we've got Buster to guard the place if you're going to start leaving the front door unlocked, Sandra,' he quipped, as he walked into the kitchen to pick up the coffee that she had made for him.

'Once, Larry, I've done it once. Who gave me the job of locking up every night anyway? You know what you can do if you want a job done better... do it yourself.' Sandra retorted quickly, she was on form this morning.

Larry chuckled and gave her a wide grin.

'I'm only joking with you, love,' he chirped, as he picked up the mug of coffee and walked towards the sitting room with the newspaper tucked under his arm. 'At least the power's back on, I imagined no bacon and eggs this morning, and that would really be shit. I'm going to have my morning ciggy and read all the doom and gloom in the fuckin' paper,' said Larry as he walked away.

'I'll be with you in a moment,' replied Sandra. 'Pop the television on, will you please, darling.'

Larry walked into the sitting room and pressed the power button on the remote, bringing Eamonn Holmes to life on the large screen. Larry tossed the remote onto the sofa and went directly to collect his ashtray, which was on the table that sat under the safe. Sandra liked Larry's ashtrays out of the way, not in the middle of the room or left on the arm of a sofa. As he picked it up, he noticed it was sitting directly on the table. *Where's the leather mat?* thought Larry, unconsciously looking down to the floor. The small round mat was upside down on the rug, alongside it was a pile of old cigarette ash that had fallen out of the ashtray the previous night when Glen had knocked it off the table. Larry's mind switched up a gear, realising that Sandra had not forgotten to lock the door after all.

'Sandra... Sandra...' called Larry, bellowing towards the kitchen.

'Just a minute, Larry, I can't do everything. I'm still cooking breakfast,' she replied.

'Sandra, call Alison and Sean next door, see if they had a call last night about the power being out, will you.'

'What, why would I do that, are you feeling alright, Larry?'

'No, I'm fuckin' not feelin' alright at all, just make the

fuckin' call, will you, please Sandra.'

Larry knew something was amiss, something serious. After picking up the mat and kicking the ash from the rug to the wooden floor, he pulled back the painting and dialled the code into the safe. Larry opened it to check that everything was still there. As the door to the safe swung open, Sandra called out.

'Alison says they didn't hear the phone ring, Larry, they may have had a call, who knows, what's going on?'

Larry looked into the safe and saw his three books sitting on top of his handgun. *Fuck, some turncoat has been in my bloody safe.* Larry always left the gun on top of the books; it was tidier that way.

Changing through the gears of his mind, he started to eliminate people. *Was this another crime group, or was this something from within? Only I know the combination to the safe...* Larry began running through each of his generals one by one in his mind.

Had they been in, only two or three had the skill to get in and out without being detected...

Or had one of them put someone else up to it...

Phil is a high-level IT scam man, never been near a burglary in his life...

Tony had the skill and probably the contacts to have someone else do it for him, but either way, Buster would have chewed an arm off...

Glen had been with him the longest...

Buster only likes Glen... he'd have let rip if anyone else had been in the house...

Glen, that total fucker, after all I've done for him, all these years...

It did not take long for Larry to be as sure as he could that it was Glen who had been into the safe, but what he was unsure of was why or what the bastard was planning. All he knew was that it would be an assault on his authority, and that he would not allow anything to undermine his position at the top of the food chain.

Larry made a call to Reg Stone. Reg was the general who ran Larry's intelligence wing, ensuring the police were fed information when Larry wanted.

'Reg, it's Larry. Things are getting really fuckin' sticky, I need you to put a call into one of the police informants for me, and it needs to be done fast.'

'Okay, what info needs to be passed, Larry?'

'The three bodies buried up at the old gravel pit on the M4, I need the police to know that they are there, and I need them to be found, sooner rather than later,' said Larry, sounding incredibly pissed off.

'That has all kinds of risks and potential repercussions. Should you not talk to Glen or Tony about this first?' asked Reg.

'Glen is the fuckin' stickiness. Just make sure the police find the bodies, make sure the information is corroborated in some way. They need to take this seriously, and they need to dig 'em up.

'I want it done soon, and I need the investigation watched. If they don't get a suspect from what they find, then I want Glen's name given to them. He needs to be in the frame, is that clear?' said Larry. He was not messing around with his plans, getting straight to the point.

'Consider it done, Larry, I know who to use to do the grassing.'

Reg knew that Glen was one of Larry's best. A trusted man, despite the row that Glen and Larry had at the performance meeting. For Larry to be feeding him to the law, Glen must have stepped badly out of line and was about to pay dearly for it.

'Oh, and, Reg, let this be a warning to you and the others. I will not tolerate disloyalty of any kind or any idea of challenging me. I am your emperor, got that?'

'Yes, Larry, goes without saying,' said Reg trying to pacify his boss.

Larry knew that once the atonement of Glen's wrongdoing had been taken care of, the news would travel fast, and his power and strength would be reaffirmed. Glen would fall out of favour with everyone once they knew Big-Gun had disowned him.

'Reg, it's one of those moments, shit happens... we just have to deal with it now so that it doesn't get any worse. I can't have this hanging around for too long,' Larry delivered his usual view on life and hung up.

As soon as Reg was off the phone with Larry, he made another call.

'Trev, it's Reg, I've got some information that I need feeding to the pigs for Big-Gun, and I need it done now. Is Barry Freeman still on the books?'

'Yeah, mate, he's still one of the best the rozzers have.'

Barry was a drug user and small-time dealer who would often help with manual labour for any of Larry's crime lines in the area. He was less than intelligent but still managed to keep himself out of trouble most of the time. He had passed information to the police regularly for around five years, and enjoyed a decent reputation for giving good intelligence. It was almost always acted upon.

The chain of calls continued.

'Listen in, Barry, it's about the daisy pushers in the gravel pit...'

★ ★ ★

Barry phoned Michelle Gorman. Michelle was a detective constable who worked on a small team whose job was to get information from local criminals that would either help solve a crime, or better still, prevent one. It was usual for Barry to meet Michelle in a coffee shop or in a park once a month, or sometimes by special arrangement if he had some particularly good information. Michelle would always have another officer with her. Working in pairs was safer physically, but it also helped to prevent malicious allegations being made by the informants, who were criminals after all.

Barry sat on a park bench in Salt Hill Park in Slough, waiting for Michelle and her crewmate to show up.

'Barry, what have you got for me that is so urgent, mate?'

Michelle sat down while her colleague remained standing behind the bench.

'Dead bodies, three dead bodies. How much would that kind of information be worth? Any chance of a sub upfront?' asked Barry.

'You know very well that it doesn't work like that, Barry. Once the information has been tested and provided results, then my boss will decide what we pay you.'

Michelle felt like she had to tell Barry the rules every time they met.

'Alright, it was worth a try, though,' said Barry, smirking.

She pulled a small notebook from her pocket.

'Go on then, Barry, tell me more.'

'Three druggies, one tart, two blokes, the blokes were gang members, and she was a bit of a Tom. They're all buried in the old gravel pit up by the motorway,' said Barry, speaking quickly.

'How do you know that Barry, did you have anything to do with their deaths?' enquired Michelle. 'You know if you were involved, we can't absolve you of any wrongdoing you may have done.'

'I know Miche. No, I had nothing to do with it, I helped dig the holes that's it, it was years ago. There's are a few of us that know about the graveyard. I know the man that arranged to put them there and the guy who moved the bodies of the blokes. I can't tell you anything else, or I'll end up in there next, but if you get something from the bodies, you know forensics, and all that, then you might get him that way. I can't tell you any more than that,' replied Barry, somewhat sheepishly.

'Why now, Barry? If the bodies have been there for some time, why are you telling me this now?' asked Michelle.

Barry's information was usually on current criminal activity. He'd never offered information on historic crime before.

'I just need it off my chest, that's all. I've thought about telling you before,' replied Barry, somewhat unconvincingly.

'Okay, Barry, I'll put the information in, but only because everything you've given me before has been sound. It'll be a while before you hear anything back from me, though. This will need further work. I want you to think very carefully about whether you can tell me who was involved. That information could be pivotal in any subsequent investigation. Do you get my drift?' said Michelle.

'A better pay-out?' asked Barry.

'I can't promise, but it's possible, especially if it leads to a conviction, Barry. Just think about it for now. We could always look at providing you with police protection if it came to it,' said Michelle, trying to nudge him towards giving up a name.

'No, I can't. I would die. You or anyone else wouldn't be able to protect me. This is all you're getting, just go and dig 'em up,' said Barry, as he stood up to walk away.

'Thanks, Barry, just think about it, call me if you need to.'

CHAPTER 10

Missing

On an early dismal October evening in 2001, Seth was in his office getting ready to pack-up and go off-duty. Just as he was about to head home, his mobile phone buzzed his leg from inside his trouser pocket. He was tempted not to answer it but pulled the phone out to see who was calling, it was a withheld number, which meant it was probably work-related.

'Hello, DI Seth Hannen speaking,' he knew his day was not quite over yet.

'Seth, can you come to my office? I've got something for you.'

'Yes, boss, I'll be with you in ten,' replied Seth. *Home will have to wait.*

He grabbed his coffee mug, with 'GUVNOR' written around its middle in bold white letters, made himself a coffee and headed off to speak with the chief super.

Seth walked into Sasha Johnson's office.

'Hi Sash, no rest for the wicked, eh.'

Sasha was the personal assistant to Chief Superintendent Dave Martin. Her office adjoined Martin's and had to be walked through to get to the chief super. Part of Sasha's job was to act as a gatekeeper, preventing officers and civilian staff from just walking into his office.

Martin was in charge of the Slough and District Police Command Unit, comprising the towns of Slough, Windsor, Maidenhead, Bracknell and Ascot, and the villages between the East Berkshire conurbations. He had joined the police service only three years before Seth but had flown up the ranks much more quickly.

'Ah, hi, Seth, yes go on in, he's waiting for you,' said Sasha in her usual chirpy and upbeat way, briefly looking up from typing some kind of report.

Seth walked through the second door, knocking loudly on his way in but not stopping or waiting for a response.

'Hello boss,' he said, announcing his arrival.

He put his coffee down on the meeting table before pulling a chair out and sitting down.

Dave Martin looked up from a huge pile of papers, peering over his reading glasses at Seth.

'Seth, have a seat, mate,' said Martin sarcastically, indicating that he had not yet asked Seth to sit down. 'I've got a job that is right up your street.'

He picked up the pile of papers and then joined Seth at the large table.

'What have we got, boss?' asked Seth.

'I need your eye for detail, Seth, and I need the job done at pace. How much work does the CID office have on at the moment?' asked Martin, as he briefly returned to his desk to collect his coffee.

'Pretty busy as usual. The typical Slough level of bulk and serious crime, the guys and girls are working their butts off if I'm honest, Dave.'

'Well, I need you, and a small team if you need them, to break away from the main business and work on a case that the Serious Crime Unit can't take on. It's not something I'd usually agree to, but headquarters are adamant that Serious Crime are chock-a-block with work all over the force, so I've agreed that we'll take the case.' Martin removed his glasses as he looked at Seth.

It was unusual for the SCS not to be able to take on extra work. They would usually pilfer staff from various District Command Units across the force, make up a temporary team, and send them back once the job was done. Seth knew that it would probably be an interesting investigation, but not that juicy if Serious Crime had palmed it off to Dave to allocate to his team.

Dave pushed the bundle of papers across the table towards Seth.

'Don't read them now, Seth. I'll give you a brief synopsis, then you can take that little lot away and digest it in your own time. So, listen in, and I'll go through the basics,' said Dave.

'Okay, I'm all ears, boss.'

Dave Martin continued the briefing.

'We've had several pieces of intelligence that talk of a disused gravel pit near the M4 motorway, between Slough and Maidenhead. Basically, it's been used by an organised crime gang to hide evidence. The bit we are interested in is that apparently, it's been used as a makeshift graveyard for disposing of dead gang members. In short, a long-standing police informant tells us that three people are buried there. The intel looks good, worth following up.'

'Sounds interesting. How do you want me to approach it, Dave?' asked Seth, eager to investigate something more interesting than the burglary and robbery cases he was overseeing in the CID office.

'I want a full review done.'

'Okay...' Seth was waiting for more detail to follow, as was usual with Dave.

'Seth, you know that it would normally take a lot more than

some uncorroborated information to set a full investigation underway, but last week a dog walker's nosey Labrador found an old Nike trainer at the gravel pit. It looked like it had blood on it, so Scenes of Crime had the lab look at it and test it. They got DNA from the blood, and it matches that of a seventeen-year-old gang member from Slough, Joel Waters, who was reported missing back in ninety-five.

'The missing person file was last reviewed twelve months ago. The pile of papers that you now have custody of relate to all our unsolved missing person cases from the last ten years or so. They are all connected to gangs or drug dealing in Slough and the surrounding area. The missing cases seem to match the informant's information, which is why this intelligence needs working on.

'I want you to carry out a full review of each case. Could any of the missing persons possibly be murder victims? If the answer is yes, then I need to be satisfied that they are not buried in that gravel pit. Do I make myself clear?' he asked.

'Yes, perfectly clear, but why don't we just excavate the gravel pit first? That would seem a much simpler way to approach it, especially if we are likely to go that way in the end?' said Seth, questioning Martin's proposed approach.

'Yes, maybe, but the cost of endlessly digging through acres of gravel to potentially find nothing but a huge mountain of stones will be expensive.' Martin's reply was gruff, his annoyance at Seth questioning his plan showing through in his tone. 'This way,' he continued. 'I can make an informed decision as to whether to start a hugely expensive dig or not. At the same time, we will have reviewed all the missing person files and updated the families appropriately.

'If it all comes to nothing, then we'll have still carried out the reviews, which is what we are required to do in any case,' said Martin, looking at Seth.

'I can see the logic, that's why you're the chief super, and I'm the DI,' said Seth laughing.

He picked up the pile of papers, tucking them under his arm, and grabbed his now empty coffee mug.

'Leave it with me, I'll keep you updated.'

Seth walked out of the office, and past Sasha, still sat at her desk; she had finished the report and was now engrossed in arranging Dave's calendar.

'Cheers, Sash.'

'Thanks, bye for now, Seth,' she replied.

Seth walked back towards his office, unaware that the pile of paperwork he had just been given represented what would soon become a very stressful investigation indeed.

★ ★ ★

Seth put on his heavy black leather jacket and slid the files into his rucksack before grabbing his crash helmet from the top of his filing cabinet. As he walked out of the office, he announced his departure to the late-turn CID shift.

'Goodnight, have a good one guys, I hope it stays Q for you.'

It was a long-standing and traditional superstition never to use the whole word *'quiet'*, just in case it brought bad luck in the form of a busy shift.

He walked down the two flights of stairs and along the corridor leading into the back yard of the police station. *It's on days like this that I wish I had a car!* He thought to himself as he lugged his heavy rucksack.

Seth threw a leg over his motorcycle, a gleaming grey Honda Blackbird, an 1100cc beast of a bike. He pushed the key into the ignition and fired her up, and then he was off on the relatively short journey home to his modest house in Cannon Court Road, Maidenhead.

* * *

Seth arrived home twenty minutes after leaving Slough. He rode the Honda over the fine gravel driveway, being careful not to blip the throttle and slide on the stones as he rode up the drive.

He had lived in the house comically named 'Coppers Reach' since 1997. He rented it out for a short time while he and his second wife, Charlotte, lived in her house on the other side of town. He had moved back in just over a year ago and was very happy living on his own. The house was an old two-bedroom Victorian semi-detached property, with a sitting room to the front and a kitchen at the rear. Seth had built an extension to the side to provide a separate entrance hall, which allowed for an ensuite bathroom to be added to the main bedroom.

He unlocked the front door, walked in, and started to punch the code into the security panel, before remembering that the alarm system was broken again. *I really must get this thing replaced sometime,* he thought.

Once inside, Seth poured himself a generous glass of Plymouth Gin, adding a less than generous amount of tonic water, a handful of ice, and a thin slice of lime. He slid a compact disc into the music system, and U2 started singing 'Beautiful Day'. Then he sat down on the sofa and pulled out the pile of papers from his rucksack.

What have we got then? Missing persons are always interesting cases, but this many in one go… He thought, as he opened the first file and read the case overview, which was written up after the last officer's formal assessment of the investigation.

Joel Walters, 17 years of age, missing since April 1995 from an address in Slough. Walters is believed to be an active member of the Slough Massive. A gang involved in selling crack cocaine in the Slough Bracknell and Maidenhead areas. All enquiries have proven negative, with no new lines of enquiry established during this review. I suggest filing the case for a further twelve months.

Well, that doesn't say much, thought Seth. He sat looking through the files, trying to find anything that might link them. The same gang, or perhaps connected associates, but nothing stood out, other than the general drug scene in and around Slough. He opened the fourth file to find a similar update listed for another low-level drug dealer. A gang member who went missing in September 1995, the report was written by the same reviewing officer.

Mickey Stevens, 24 years of age, missing since April 1994 from an address in Slough. Stevens is believed to have been an active member of a Slough gang involved in burglary offences in the Slough and Maidenhead areas. All enquiries have proven negative. I suggest filing the case for a further twelve months.

The fifth, sixth, and seventh files had comparable updates and were similarly vague in detail. Only one file related to a woman. Sharon McCrory, a drug user and petty burglar from Slough.

Sharon McCrory, 23 years of age, missing since August 1992 from an address in Slough. McCrory is believed to have been involved with a drugs gang in Slough. She is predominantly a user and small-time thief. Intelligence suggests that she engages in prostitution from time to time. All enquiries have proved negative - file for a further twelve months.

Seth read McCrory's file, noticing how close the date was to his run-in with Larry Fowler. He thought back to the woman he had mowed down on Coronation Road. The file photograph was of McCrory at the age of eleven; no more recent pictures seemed to exist. She looked healthy at that age, not like a druggy. He was unsure if they were one and the same, but worry had planted and seeded itself into his mind. He sat up most of the night, reading all of the files and filling his mind with the details from the early stages of the uniform investigations – the initial days after they were first reported missing. Then he read through the subsequent CID investigations and the supervisory reviews undertaken each year since the lines of enquiry had dried up.

At three-thirty, Seth pondered the task at hand. *There's really nothing much to go on, without going back to all the witnesses and family members to see if anything has been missed. But that has already been done - twice.*

The file reviews had been more thorough than the closing notes had suggested. We just need to dig up the gravel pit. Seth grabbed a couple of hours of sleep. At six o'clock in the morning, the image of his father's funeral filled his head again, as he woke up grinding his teeth as usual.

After a swift shower and shave, keen to prime his day, Seth got dressed and then made a call before heading back to the office.

'Morning, can you put me through to the Intel Team, please?'

There was a short pause as the line clicked, and he was through.

'Hello, DC Maria Wilkinson, how can I help you?'

'Morning Maria, it's DI Seth Hannen. I'm on my way to work, can I buy you breakfast...?'

Maria knew immediately that Seth wanted a favour. What would it be this time?

* * *

By seven-thirty, Seth was buying Maria coffee and a bacon roll for breakfast in the police canteen. They sat down in the far corner, away from anyone else. Seth outlined the missing-persons cases that he had read overnight and the intelligence that Dave Martin had briefed him about.

'So, Maria, the reviews are all sound, and there's not much more that can be done aside from going on telly and appealing for witnesses. But without any bodies, we won't get anywhere near the real crime TV shows. It's not sexy enough for prime time viewing.'

'Yeah, I get that, but what do you need from me, Seth? You've not bought me breakfast and told me all that, without having something up your sleeve, have you, guv?' said Maria. She knew him too well.

'What I didn't mention was that the reason I'm reviewing the cases is that the information came in through an informant. The details of the informant, as you know, are kept from the file to protect them and keep us from abusing relationships between the police and local grasses.' Seth stated the obvious, expecting a curt reply from Maria.

'Tell me something I don't know, Seth. I work in the intel department,' said Maria, her reply as abrupt as he had expected.

'Really, I hadn't realised, how long have you been there?' Seth winked as he joked with her. 'Maria, I really need you to check the intel system and let me know who the informant is. I need to speak to them personally, not through one of the informant handlers,' said Seth, deciding on the direct approach.

'Shit, Seth, I can't do that, you know I can't,' Maria was

surprised. Seth had never asked for a favour that breached the rules about informants before.

'Maria, I'm a DI. I need this information, it's not like I'm looking to abuse it. I want to potentially solve three missing cases and recover the bodies for the families. It's in the public interest that this is all sorted out. This is not why the rules exist, you know that.'

Maria felt under pressure and not comfortable with Seth's request at all.

'Okay, but this is the last time I help you, guv, this one pushes the favour into rule-breaking, and I really don't want that kind of shit. I can do without being on the end of an internal investigation.'

The pair got up from the table, put their empty plates on the tray rack and walked to the intel office.

Maria logged into the system and started searching through the raw intelligence reports that contained the un-sanitised information, as it was received from the informants.

'Here we are, the informant is Barry Freeman, he's a drug user over in Windsor, been on the books for ages. His handler is Detective Constable Michelle Gorman.' Maria had found the intel entry pretty quickly, as it was the only one talking about buried bodies.

'Can you see if we have a phone number or an address for him, that's the last I'll ask, I promise,' said Seth, pushing his luck now.

'He lives in a block of flats, number three hundred and seventy-four Sawyers Close, there's no phone number, now go, that's enough, guv.'

Although she was a lower-ranking officer, Maria was hard-nosed and confident enough to tell an inspector that the conversation was over. She did not want to be pushed for any more information.

* * *

Seth rapped on the door loudly.

'Barry, it's the police. I need a quick word with you. Open the door, mate.'

'Piss off, I've got nothing to say to you,' the reply came quickly from inside.

Seth crouched down and opened the letterbox, waiting for the initial gust of stale air to pass him by before peering through and into the flat. He could see Barry stood a few metres back from the door, wearing a pair of old boxer shorts and nothing else.

'Barry, grab a hoodie or something and make yourself decent, mate. This is about the gravel pit bodies. We need to have a little talk.'

Seth went straight to the point, hoping that the tactic would work and get him into the flat. Barry obliged and opened the door and then turned and walked towards the sitting room.

'You'd better come in then,' he said, with his back to Seth, as he grabbed a t-shirt off the floor. Shall I put the kettle on?'

'No thanks, you're fine, Barry. Actually, I brought the coffee with me and a bit of breakfast for you.'

Seth never liked accepting tea or coffee from local toe rags. He had been offered too many drinks in filthy mugs and worried that he might end up catching something horrible, or that they would put something in it. He decided long ago not to accept any more offers of food or drink unless it was from a kind old lady coming out of her house with a tray of tea for him and his colleagues at a crime scene-watch.

Today, he wanted to get more information from Barry, so he went via McDonald's and bought two Americano coffees and an Egg McMuffin for Barry. Seth sat and buttered Barry up for a while, letting him sip the hot coffee and telling him how important the information he had given was. That was why a DI had come out of the station, especially to visit him. Seth explained how Barry would allow the missing people's parents to finally be at peace with what had happened to their kids.

'Just remind me how you know about the bodies, Barry? I'm not sure I read that part of the report,' Seth slipped the question into the conversation nonchalantly, hoping that Barry would just give an answer.

'I didn't exactly say how I know about it, don't be sneaky now, copper,' said Barry, who was not as well-buttered as Seth had thought.

'Ah, that's why I didn't read it, that explains it, but how do you know? Just between you and me, it won't go any further. I won't put it into the system. It'll be off the record, so to speak.' Seth expected to be blocked again, not sure that Barry would play ball.

'Let's just say that I helped bury them. I was there all right. I got paid to dig out the gravel and then cover them up again. Then we'd have a short service thing, you know, ashes to ashes, dust to dust and all that shit,' said Barry.

'Who's we, Barry, give me a name,' Seth pushed for more information.

'No, I can't tell you, I want them to be buried properly, I want it off my conscience, but if I give you a name, you'll go after him, and I'll end up buried in the fucking gravel myself. You've got ya lot now, that's all I can tell ya alright.' Barry looked worried. He had already told the police more than he should have.

Seth got the feeling that Barry had probably been deeply involved with the Slough gangs back in the nineties and that he was worried about repercussions. Seth had no idea that his old adversary, Larry Fowler, master of the long game, was behind the information getting to him.

CHAPTER 11

Dig Deep

'Boss, I'm convinced that we have enough to excavate the gravel pit. It won't be a waste of time or money, I promise you,' said Seth, feeling confident.

'That was bloody quick Seth, you've only had the papers a few days, how can you be so sure about it?' replied Martin. He was less than convinced.

'Dave, I went at it from the intel side, not the investigation review angle. The witnesses have all been re-interviewed during the last two reviews. None of the relatives or friends had anything new to add, so it's unlikely that they will be able to add anything now. The intel, though, that checks out, it's good quality information. I obviously can't tell you where it came from, but I've had it verified. I'm sure there are bodies in there. We're good to start a search at the gravel pit, boss.' Seth was careful not to drop Maria in the shit or let Dave Martin know that he had gone directly to the informant.

'Look, I trust you, Seth, get a budget code from Sasha and get the dig sorted. But if you waste my bloody reserve on a negative result, it'll come out of your CID overtime money for the rest of the year, is that clear? Martin continued before Seth could reply. 'This is not a blank cheque Seth.'

Seth knew that money was tight, and that Martin was not

joking. *Barry had better have been straight with me,* he thought.

'Thanks, Dave, you won't regret it, I'll get you a result for sure.'

* * *

The blue and white plastic flapped in the wind as the uniform bobby walked around the gravel pit. He was wrapping the **POLICE LINE - DO NOT CROSS** tape around the occasional tree or anything else that he could find to keep it taut, then walking to the next tree or oil drum until he had encircled the whole gravel pit.

'Top job, mate,' said Seth to the young cop, who must have been no older than twenty-one. He reminded Seth of himself, back in his early days, wet behind the ears and with no idea what challenges lay ahead of him or what trouble he may get into.

'Thanks, sir, I hope it's alright for you,' said the young bobby.

'It's perfect, now get yourself over to the main entrance by the barrier and run the scene log, anyone that comes in must've been approved by me, and they must be logged out again when they leave. Even the guys delivering the excavators when they arrive, no exceptions, got it?' said Seth.

'Yes, sir,' the nervous young officer answered. It was his first crime scene duty.

Seth then turned to the sergeant in charge of the Police Search Team.

'Steve, what's your best guess, mate, how long to search three acres of gravel?'

Seth had mixed emotions about digging up bodies from the early nineties. On the one hand, he was buoyant at the idea of opening up cold cases, and on the other, he was a little concerned at the idea of digging up a female druggy from that time, either way he was keen to get the dig underway.

'This is a barren site, guv, and bodies decompose really quickly in sand or gravel. If we are left with bones mixed with shingle, they won't be easy to find. They could have separated and moved metres over the years. In a field or in moorland, we'd just look for recently excavated relict material. In layman's terms, deposed soil from the grave or changes in vegetation, you know, younger plants among older ones.

'Flying the force chopper over to get some imaging won't help either; this place is like a gravel mini-Sahara. Our only real option is to run a scan with the magnetic gradiometer to start, but I don't hold out much hope. If a body is wrapped in something, it may pick it up, otherwise, we're left with manual probing and mechanical excavation,' explained Steve, who was not as buoyant as Seth.

'Okay, you're the expert, but how long? I don't have a never-ending bag of money here, Steve,' said Seth.

'I don't know guv, four weeks, two months, four months. It all depends on the weather and how detailed you want me to search, how deep you want me to go. As I said, bodies can move in loose ground. Even if there is anything in here, I can't guarantee I'll find it for you,' said Steve, turning to his search team. 'But we'll do our best, eh, guys, we really will, guv.'

'Look, Steve, I need this done inside six weeks, or at least a discovery in that time to justify us extending the dig for longer,' Seth's buoyancy had ebbed. 'If the bodies are here, then they've been buried by criminal gangs. Generally, criminals are lazy creatures, so the graves are likely to be clandestine, so go down a metre or so, I reckon.'

'Let's go for one-point-five metres, guv, that gives us a bit of leeway for any movement that may have occurred over time,' said Steve, who was happy with anything under two metres.

'Fine, over to you, the excavators will be here within the

hour. We have no information about where to start, so carve this place up into a grid and work methodically.'

Seth hoped they would find something sooner rather than later. That way, he would be able to keep Dave Martin on-side.

'It's already gridded, we'll start bottom left and top right and move across in three-metre squares, meeting in the middle. If we uncover something, we'll have to do the whole lot to be sure we don't miss anything. I'll keep you posted, guv,' said Steve.

Two yellow excavators, with sparkling new buckets attached to their hydraulic excavation arms, arrived on the back of a heavy low loader. Once the driver had given her details to the young officer at the barrier, she parked the low loader, drove each excavator off, and signed them over to the police.

'All yours, lads, give me a bell when they need picking up, happy hunting. I hope you find whatever it is you're looking for.'

Steve called his officers together and briefed his team.

'This could be a long one, guys. We'll start excavating in opposite corners of the grid. I want four of you probing, two of you operating the excavators, and two of you at the bucket end, keeping an eye out for what may turn up as we move the gravel. Any sign of something other than stones, then we move to manual excavation. I don't want you digging through and destroying a grave or any other kind of evidence for that matter,' Steve paused, waiting to see if his team had any questions. 'Okay, if anything shows up, we stop, re-brief and decide on how to recover whatever we've got. Are we all clear?'

'Yes, skip.' They replied in chorus.

The search team took it in turns to operate the excavators. Four of them were trained to use plant machinery, so two at a time could dig, changing over every couple of hours. It was late-October. They would be lucky to achieve seven hours of searching in a day once the team had been briefed, set the equipment up, then stopped later for lunch, and ensured the grid was updated. If the search related to a crime in action, then floodlights would be deployed, but financial economy was important on a historic review case. There would be no overtime and no deploying of kit that would take it out of action for any other cases that may need it, not until the team had found something in any case.

* * *

Two weeks passed, and nothing had been discovered at the gravel pit. The search team were not having a great time. They had lost two days to poor weather and were not finding it an exciting search. They were just pushing gravel around.

Jane sat in the cab and moved the two levers again, shifting the gravel forwards to reveal another metre of excavated ground. The officer at the bucket shouted the agreed words to stop the dig.

'Object seen, halt the dig,' he shouted as he raised his right hand, holding up a small red triangular flag.

'Everyone, stay put,' called Steve, as he walked over to constables Jane Whitby and Paul Webber. 'What have we got, guys?'

'Not really sure, skipper, some kind of polythene plastic, could be nothing.'

'Well, it's something for sure, but is it something we are looking for?' asked Steve rhetorically.

Steve was glad the team would have a break from the monotonous gravel shifting.

They set up new barrier tape around the site of the find, carefully pushing steel rods into the gravel at a safe distance from the polythene. As a precaution, the site was now being treated as a crime scene, not a simple search site anymore. They were now all dressed in white hooded paper suits, with polythene shoes and latex gloves.

The team started to work in pairs, carefully removing gravel to reveal more of the polythene from under the stones. Everything was being done with such extreme care that it looked like the site of an archaeological dig. A crime scene officer was now in attendance, so they would periodically stop digging to allow her to take photographs.

Seth walked up to the barrier and signed in on the scene log. He followed a corridor of blue and white tape, pulled tight between the steel poles that had been put up to indicate the common approach route to the now cleared hole in the gravel. He joined Steve, who was waiting for him at the edge of the hollow. It was just over a metre deep, a metre wide and two metres long. Inside lay a roll of blue polythene, apparently wrapped around something, tied at each end and in the middle with blue nylon rope. The team had placed plastic boards all around the item to allow access into the hole without disturbing any more gravel.

'Hi, Seth, we waited for you to be here before we open it up. I thought you'd want to witness it,' said Steve, standing with a sense of pride that his team had found something reasonably quickly and not damaged it with the machinery.

'Thanks, Steve, I appreciate it, a good call to have got SOCO in early too. Right, let's do it,' said Seth, rubbing his hands together.

Annie, the crime scene officer, crouched on the white plastic board, then leant forward and cut through the first piece of rope, purposely leaving the knot tied. She looked up at Seth and Steve, providing a commentary of what she was doing.

'The knot may be important, depending on what we have.'

She cut the second piece of rope and then the third. One of the search team officers filmed her from above. Then moving very slowly, she opened up the outer layer of plastic, which was thick, like builder's polythene. Seth looked on eagerly, expecting to see the remains of one of his missing people, but his eyes were only met with another layer of blue polythene.

Annie looked up at Seth. He gave a nod of his head, indicating that she should pull the second layer back. As she did, the sight of a skeleton came into view. The inside of the polythene was dirty and stained with what would have been bodily fluids leaving the cadaver as it decomposed. The skeleton still had its dark brown hair and was wearing a tracksuit of some kind, both trainers still on its feet.

'No missing footwear. This one doesn't belong to the trainer that was handed in then,' said Steve looking at Seth, who was still staring down into the shallow grave.

'No, looks like there's probably more to be found then.' Seth was feeling a little uneasy.

'I'd say it's probably been here for eight or nine years,' said Annie.

'How can you tell without a pathologist's opinion, SOCO's gut feeling?' asked Seth quizzically.

'No… I bought a pair of those trainers for my brother at Christmas, back in the nineties,' said Annie, looking up and smiling.

Seth's mind wandered back to the 18th of June 1992. *God, please don't let this be her.*

'Sex then?' asked Seth.

'No thanks, I've got a boyfriend,' Annie giggled, hoping her humour was not misplaced.

'Very funny, okay then what gender is it, female?' asked Seth, after sighing at her silly quip.

'Not likely, these trainers are at least a size ten, and by the size of the bones they'd have stood at around six foot tall, I'd hazard a guess at a male, look at the length of those femurs.'

Seth felt the tension leave his mind as he returned to the job at hand, pushing the face of the screaming woman to the back of his head.

'Thanks, get it forensically recovered and taken to the mortuary, I want a forensic pathologist's report as soon as possible. I'll probably have to hand this back to the Serious Crime Unit, now that we actually have some remains, but I want us to have done a bloody good job when the papers go back.

'In the meantime, once this one's moved, crack on with the rest of the dig. There may be more in here,' said Seth.

'We'll sort it, guv, speak soon,' replied Steve.

Seth turned to walk back to the barrier and the CID car waiting to take him back to the police station to brief Dave Martin.

★ ★ ★

Seth checked in at the gravel pit every Thursday, but it took five more weeks of excavation before anything else showed up. It was early December when he returned to witness the removal of two more sets of remains.

The dig had gone well. The second and third discoveries had been found on the same day. As the team removed the gravel from around the second find, they discovered the edge of another piece of polythene. They uncovered what looked like the resting place of a third body, the remains lying at ninety degrees to the second.

Seth followed the same routine, walking up to the scene following the predetermined route laid out by the search team with the usual blue and white tape.

'Guv, good to see you, two birds with one stone today. The one on the right looks like it's been here longer, the polythene is brittle. The one on the left was only inches below the surface at that end,' said Steve, pointing down at the shallow grave.

'Thanks, Steve, let's go again. I think we know what we are about to find. Are there two SOCO's?'

'Yep, Annie will do the first, then we'll remove it, and Bob will do the second. It'll take a little longer, we can't afford to cross-contaminate the two sets of remains, assuming that's what we are looking at here, that is.'

Annie walked down to the same white plastic boarding around the holes. The objects were again wrapped in blue polythene and, as before, tied with blue nylon rope at three points. She followed precisely the same routine, cutting each of the three ropes loose, then folding back the first layer of polythene, then the second. Inside were the skeletal remains of what this time clearly looked to Seth like the bones of a man.

'One trainer missing,' said Seth. 'That'll probably match the one that was handed in. If it does, I reckon that's Joel Waters.

'Based on the remnants of clothing and what he was last seen wearing. The first skeleton is probably Mickey Stevens. But I'm still waiting for a full lab report,' said Seth as he walked away, leaving Steve and his team to await the removal of the remains by the Forensic Recovery Team.

Two hours later, Seth was stood back at the gravesite as preparations were being made to deal with the last set of remains. He outlined the procedure again.

'Bob, you know the drill, the same way as Annie did it, please, cut the rope, don't untie the knot, and then open it up, and we leave the rest to the Forensic Recovery Team.'

Bob crouched down, cut the first, then second and third ropes, and opened the right-hand piece of polythene, then the left. Seth expected to see skeletal remains looking back at him, but instead, all he saw was another layer of polythene.

'Different person doing the wrapping?' his thoughts came out loud.

Bob slowly pulled back the polythene again, first the left then the right, this time revealing another set of skeletal remains. Seth took a deep intake of breath and stepped backwards as he did.

'You okay, Seth?' said Steve, who had noticed Seth's sudden movement.

Seth was unsteady on his feet. Looking up from the grave was a skeleton, but Seth saw something else. He saw a woman screaming back at him. Laying in the open polythene cocoon were the scant remnants of what looked like blue tracksuit bottoms, white trainers, and a well-preserved white shell suit jacket, all hanging off a small set of bones that would have belonged to a woman of slight stature.

Seth's mind travelled back in time, taking him with it. He was again sitting in the black Aston Martin, the woman staring at him in the face, her mouth wide open and her reefer falling to the floor. She was screaming as loud as her lungs would allow. This time Seth heard her wail as clear as day. The shriek of someone about to die.

'Seth, what the hell is wrong, are you okay?' asked Steve, who had seen the colour drain from Seth's face.

'Nothing, really, I'm fine,' Seth snapped out of it. 'It's just the thought of whatever happened to that poor woman, that's Sharon McCrory, I'd bet on it. When women lose their lives to crime, it just freaks me out, sorry, mate, lost it for a moment there.'

Pulling himself together, Seth started to think straight. The woman at Ascot was at least thirty. Sharon McCrory was only twenty-three, and Sharon was reported missing a couple of months after the accident.

'Any obvious signs of injury, Bob?'

'You're impatient today, Seth. It's not like you to second guess the pathologist,' said Steve, who thought something was not quite right with how Seth was behaving.

Seth's eyes were locked to the remains in the pit. He was not looking at his colleagues as he spoke to them or when they replied.

'Nothing obvious, everything looks intact from what I can see. There are possibly old fracture injuries, but they've healed. Pretty badly looking at the angles of the femurs and tibias. I couldn't say anything about the neck or other small bones. So, I won't hang my hat on it, but I'd say no serious skeletal injuries at the time of death,' reported Bob.

Seth listened intently, doing his best to calm his thoughts, forcing his mind to the job at hand, telling himself what he needed to hear. *It's not the woman from that day, it can't be… it's not her.*

* * *

'Good work, Seth. Well done, my budget's still intact, and you can keep your CID overtime money.' Chief Superintendent Martin gave a little chuckle. 'We'll need to hand this all back to Serious Crime now, this is likely to be three linked murders, and God only knows what else. You can get back to the day job now, Seth.'

Martin wanted Seth back in the CID office, dealing with current crime, rather than intelligence about old cases.

'I'd like to stay close to it if that's alright with you. You know, maybe be in on the interviews if they pull someone in?' said Seth.

He was keen to bask in the glory of uncovering the remains for just a little longer and keep an eye on the developments of the investigation.

'I understand, that's fine, but no long periods away from the day job, Seth, got it?' said Martin

'Thanks, Dave, I appreciate it.'

CHAPTER 12

The Van Man

Glen sat alone in a stolen Vauxhall Astra in the car park of Tot Hill Services on the A34, just south of Newbury, munching through a packet of fruit pastels and drinking cheap takeaway coffee. He had decided not to trust anyone else and to do this alone. It was just past three in the morning, and the car park was not that busy. The odd car would arrive, fill up with fuel and then leave. Couples exited the services hotel after an illicit encounter, then went their separate ways, back to husbands and wives after reportedly working late. Glen paid little attention; he was waiting for the black Volkswagen Transporter that would soon arrive and meet the heavy goods vehicle already parked on the bridge over the dual carriageway.

Inside the heavy goods trailer sat a consignment of heroin, cocaine, and cannabis resin that had made its way to Hampshire from Afghanistan. The drugs had travelled through Europe, across the channel and into Britain via Southampton docks. During its journey, the shipment had been divided before being hived off to various markets in Romania, Slovakia, and Germany. What remained was over three thousand kilograms of prohibited drugs hidden among sacks of coffee beans - an amount so huge that it would set new seizure records for the police if they got their hands on it. Glen had thought about just putting his gun to the lorry driver's head, but the consignment was destined for at least eight British crime lords, of which Larry was only one. If he just took the lot, he would be dead within days.

Glen sat quietly in his car, sipping the bitter coffee. A blue light flickered inside the HGV's cab as the driver watched television. The driver was killing time, waiting for his first rendezvous with the men who would take Larry's share of the consignment and move it to an old farm near Slough. Twenty minutes went by before anything interesting happened. Then it arrived, a black Volkswagen Transporter van pulled up behind the lorry. Glen watched intently, trying to see how many of Larry's gang were involved. *Bloody hope there's no more than two,* he thought.

The van drew up alongside the cab, and there was a conversation that lasted around three minutes. The passenger of the van was talking to the lorry driver. *At least two,* thought Glen, as he watched the van draw in front of the lorry and wait a short while. Then they were off, the van leading the way onto Newtown Road, towards Newbury.

Glen was quick to follow, keeping enough distance between himself and the convoy so he would not be noticed. He tucked in behind two other cars to give himself some cover, not wanting to provide a constant set of headlights in their rear-view mirrors. They turned off before getting to Newbury and drove up to Greenham Common, an old Royal Air Force base. The convoy drove through the main gates and onto the industrial estate. Glen dropped back parking up short on the main road to ensure he would not be noticed and set off on foot, running through the industrial estate to see where they were going. The van led the lorry into a vast disused aircraft hangar on the other side of the industrial estate. He was surprised to see the doors stay open after they reversed the goods vehicle in. *Very helpful,* he thought to himself.

Knowing he had time, Glen ran back to the car and drove into the estate behind the line of units and towards the back of the hangar. He turned the lights off then twisted the small screwdriver that was serving as an ignition key, killing the engine but making sure the steering wheel would not lock. The car rolled into the yard, past the industrial units, and stopped directly behind the hangar. *Lady luck is with me tonight.* He pressed the button in on the handbrake and pulled the lever, silently engaging the brake. Then he was out of the car, balaclava on and his handgun out of its holster, held firmly in his right hand with its safety catch off. Glen was sure he would need to fire it tonight, hopefully just as a warning, but who knew what was about to unfold.

He crept around the units and up to the open hangar door and looked inside. *One…two…three… three including the lorry driver, that's okay, I might just be able to handle three thick blokes.* They had to be thick to be running around in the middle of the night doing major drug runs.

The lorry driver was driving a forklift, removing pallets laden with sacks from the back of the lorry, while the other two cartoon characters were just standing watching and laughing. Glen needed to wait until Larry's gear was out of the van and loaded before he made his move.

The sixth pallet had been unloaded, then he heard some broken English as the Polish lorry driver called the two goons over. All three men climbed into the back of the lorry and were out of sight. *They must've reached the separate consignments hidden in the load.* Glen gave them three minutes to be sure that they would be inside for some time. Then he sprinted into the hanger, diving into a roll as he threw himself under the lorry, landing awkwardly on his left shoulder. *Shit, that hurt. I need to stick to burglary. I'm too old for all this shit.*

As he lay on his chest listening to the men moving around inside the trailer directly above his head, he realised that getting out, primed for conflict, was not going to be as easy as getting under the trailer had been. *It's not like the movies,* he thought to himself, wishing he had stayed outside.

There was much shuffling around inside the trailer. Then the driver jumped back out, pushed an empty pallet onto the forklift, and drove it up to the back of the trailer. After lifting the forks up and putting the pallet onto the lorry's wooden floor, he got out of the forklift and back into the trailer. Then, the three men started moving coffee sacks, piling them up onto the forklift's empty pallet.

Glen listened and shuffled forward on his haunches, timing his movements to hide any noise he made behind the sounds coming from above. As his heart rate started to increase, he moved to a position almost level with the back of the trailer. *It'll soon be time.* The driver jumped down, his feet within Glen's reach. He walked around the forklift and got in, initially reversing it, then driving to the rear of the van. Glen watched the forklift's under-inflated tyres as they squidged away on the concrete floor. The two other men got out of the trailer and walked to the van. He lay still, wondering when to make his move, knowing that if he waited too long, he would probably be discovered.

It's either now and deal with three, or let them fill the van first. Glen would rather not involve the lorry driver, he had the rest of the shipment to deliver, which needed to get on its way up the country. Larry's gear would be enough. *Wait it out. I need to wait it out.* As he lay there, he heard movement at the front of the lorry. *Shit, there's a fourth.* Glen lay motionless on the ground, beginning to wish he had decided to just run the van off the road after the exchange. He was out of his burglary comfort zone; relieving other bad guys of three months drug supply was a different ball game altogether. The movement came closer. *A dog, what is it with me and bloody dogs!*

He assumed that the mutt had been hidden in the cab somewhere as the lorry came through customs. The three men seemed to have failed to notice the dog altogether. It was now standing next to the lorry, only a metre or so from Glen. He watched as the four legs became three, then a stream of mustard yellow piss fired its way toward Glen. *Oh, Jesus. Really you bastard. This couldn't get any worse.* But it was about to. The torrent of dog urine hit the floor, narrowly missing him and then flowing away like a river. He sighed a sigh of relief. Then the dog let out a whine, sniffed the floor and got under the trailer with Glen. He tensed up, waiting for the snarling to start. Buster... what the fuck... Larry's here. As Glen's mind moved into panic mode, he heard a voice.

'Buster, over 'ere, now you fuckin' loon.' Larry's voice was unmistakable.

Glen pulled himself up onto the framework of the trailer, trying to make himself harder to see. Larry was now standing in the puddle of Buster's piss. *Well, he can't have looked down,* thought Glen.

'Buster, get the fuck out.' Larry shouted at his dog before walking off in the direction of the Transporter.

'Boys, how goes it, all there as planned?' called Larry, as he walked up to them.

'Yeah, Big-Gun, all is good, fifteen more minutes, and we'll be loaded and away.'

'Good, now listen to me,' Larry looked back towards the lorry. 'I'm anticipating a problem tonight.'

All four men were out of sight at the back of the van now. Glen decided that he needed a plan B. Taking on four blokes would be okay if he was the only one carrying a gun, but Larry would, without doubt, have his gun with him. Larry never got involved in this level of work, not since he was in his twenties. The fact he was here meant that there was more to this than met the eye. Taking Larry on was a considerable risk, but stealing his drugs while he was actually there would be like Glen signing his own death warrant. He silently rolled out from under the lorry, got to his feet quickly, and ran out of the hangar. The black running shoes that he had chosen to be quiet during burglaries serving him well.

Glen ran to the Astra, jumped in and twisted the screwdriver in the ignition to start the engine. He was not so worried about making a sound leaving as he was when he arrived. Nothing, the car didn't start. *Fuck, this can't be happening.* He tried again. This time the wires sparked, and the starter motor turned the engine, firing it into life. He drove out of the main entrance to Greenham Common before parking up in a lay-by that afforded him a good view for when the lorry, the van, and Larry left. *Back to the waiting game.* He thought, making sure that he left the engine running.

While Glen sat in the car, Larry was briefing his two men.

'Boys, it's likely that you will meet trouble before you get the gear to Slough. I'm expecting someone that used to work for me, a fuckin' turncoat, to have a go at relieving me of this stuff,' said Larry grimacing.

'Who boss, who would have the balls to do that?'

'I think you mean, who would be fuckin' stupid enough to do that,' retorted Larry.

'Ah, Yeah... sorry, boss.'

'Anyhow, who is not important,' continued Larry. 'What's important is your fuckin' response.'

'Boss, they won't get away with it, we'll leave him wishing he'd never been born.'

'No, I want you to let him have the gear. You need to put up a fight, but you need to lose. Understand me? I want him to get the stuff.' Larry's tone was one of total seriousness.

'Right… If that's what you want, boss, but this gear is worth millions, why would you—'

'It is what I fuckin' want,' interrupted Larry. 'Don't ask questions, just do as you're fuckin' told. It's bad enough that I'm even awake at this time of night, let alone talking to you pair of fuckin' idiots in a freezin' cold aircraft hangar.'

'Okay, Big-Gun, consider it done.'

'Buster, with me,' he shouted, calling his dog to heel and smiling to himself.

Larry patted his hand on the pile of hessian sacks and turned to walk out of the hanger with Buster. The three men watched as he left. The dog jumped into the back of the Range Rover, then Larry closed both halves of the tailgate, got in and drove away.

Glen watched Larry's car leave Greenham Common and drive off into the distance. *How the fuck did I miss him arriving…? Not long now.*

The two men slammed the rear doors of the Transporter shut, said their goodbyes to the Lorry driver, and left.

Glen saw lights approaching from the airfield, faster than when Larry had left. *The height and size must mean that they belong to the van, not the lorry,* thought Glen. As the van exited the junction, it turned right towards Newbury. Glen set off, keeping a good distance behind. As he followed the Transporter, a white Ford Transit van drove into the airfield and towards the hangar.

Glen followed the Transporter along the A339 into Newbury, where it re-joined the A34 heading North. He knew that they would head for Slough and a drug kitchen on an old farm, where Larry centred his drug operation. That was where the drugs would be cut, then mixed with anything from ground glass to dried faeces, before being repackaged ready for sale on the street. If Larry had not turned up, then he would have taken the van before it left Greenham, but his plan had been scuppered. Glen had never been to Larry's farm, but he knew that Larry would have other people there, waiting to receive and check the delivery, and they would be armed for sure. Glen needed to intercept the drugs haul before it got to Slough, which allowed him about forty-five miles to make his move, to find the right spot to run the van off the road. The motorway would not be an ideal place, but he had no option. He had no idea how far the farm was from the Slough junction at the other end. Turning the van over near residential streets and houses would cause too much interest. If it got too noisy, the residents would call the police for sure.

The van joined the motorway at junction thirteen. *I need to do this before we get to Reading, before the busier section.* Glen's heart was thrusting his blood around his body at an alarming rate. This really was not his game; he had planned everything to be easier than this.

He followed the van for three miles. The motorway was quiet, with very little traffic. *Right, fuck it, it's all or nothing.* The van was hogging the centre lane. Glen accelerated to get closer, pulling into lane one and alongside it. They were doing seventy-five miles an hour as he steadied his speed to match that of the van. The passenger looked out of his window, and their eyes locked before the passenger mouthed 'Fuck off,' and gave Glen the finger.

Glen lowered his window and sounded his horn to get the passengers attention again. As he looked over from the van, Glen brought his gun into view and then pointed it out of the car window. A look of surprise and panic washed over the man's face. There were expletives as the passenger turned to the driver, then the van started to accelerate.

Glen let the van move away before dropping in behind it,

then he moved out to the third lane and pulled alongside again. He accelerated past and then moved sharply left, shoving the car directly in front of the van. He hit the brakes – hard. The anti-locking system kicked in immediately.

The van driver followed suit, instinctively braking to avoid a collision. He tried to steer the van around the Astra, lurching quickly to the left, the offside of the van clipping the back of Glen's car as the van slid onto the hard shoulder.

Glen felt his car jolt forward with the impact and released the brakes to prevent being thrown off course. He pulled onto the hard shoulder ten metres ahead of the now stationary van.

In his panic, the driver had stalled the van's engine and was desperately trying to turn it over, but it was still in gear. Each turn of the starter motor resulted in the van hopping forward, taking it closer to the Astra.

Glen was out of the car in a flash and running toward the van, his right arm outstretched, pointing his gun at the driver. He moved his arm to the right, squeezing the trigger as he did. The small handgun let out a loud crack as it sent its bullet searing through the air, past the van and into the woodland to the side of the road. *Point made,* thought Glen.

'Out, out of the van now, get out now and do it slowly, leave the keys.' Glen shouted as loud as his lungs would allow, dispensing a threatening tone to try and hide the stress he was feeling. The two men sat still, not reacting. *If they drive off, I'll have to put one in the tyre, or the driver, thought Glen, as he weighed up which would be the best option.*

He shouted again. 'Don't fuck me about, the next one has your name on it,' Glen was now standing in front of the van and aiming the gun through the windscreen at the driver's head. *Come on, lads, play ball.* 'Last time, out, out now,' he shouted, upping his volume.

The passenger door opened first.

'Out, and close the door, stay there, by the side of the van, don't come any closer,' demanded Glen.

The man did as he was asked. Then the driver opened his door and stepped from the van.

'Alright mate, you win,' he called to Glen.

'Round the other side, with your mate, don't shut the door.' Glen gesticulated with his handgun.

The driver started to walk in front of the van towards his companion. Glen could see that his right hand was empty. As he walked, he suddenly rounded and lifted his left arm, turning towards Glen, letting off a shot from a handgun.

Glen flinched. *A fucking cuddy wifter,* he thought, referring to him being left-handed.

The two men stood frozen still on the hard shoulder, pointing their guns at each other. Glen looked into the other man's eyes, trying to weigh up his opponent. *Was the shooters blood really cold enough to kill another man?*

'We can't stand here forever, pal. What's the plan then?' asked Glen.

'The plan is that you walk back to your car and fuck off.'

'After all the trouble I've taken to get here. Not a chance in hell, matey,' said Glen.

As the two men glared at each other, Glen missed the passenger walking to the rear of the van.

'What are you doing?' shouted Glen as he heard the doors open. There was no reply. Glen saw movement through the front window, the passenger was doing something just behind the seats.

'Get him the fuck out of there,' shouted Glen.

'Or you'll do what?' replied the driver, laughing at Glen.

Then the passenger reappeared at the side of the van. Pointing a gun in Glen's direction.

This really isn't going well. Glen was as far as he had ever been from his comfort zone now.

'Put your gun down, tiger,' shouted the driver. 'The odds aren't in your favour, mate.'

Glen started to slowly lower his weapon, squeezing the trigger as he did. The bullet left the muzzle with another resounding crack, met almost instantly with a shriek of pain from the driver as he dropped his gun and grabbed his knee with both hands.

The passenger let a shot off in Glen's direction. Glen felt the pain at the same time that his ears registered the sound. The bullet had shot between his arm and his body, grazing his ribs as it went, then embedding itself in the rear of the Astra.

Glen let another bullet out of the gun in the passenger's direction, who was now moving quickly towards the van's driver. The shot missed by a mile.

'Look after your mate, leave this, now,' shouted Glen.

'Okay, just take the gear and piss off,' came the reply.

Glen had expected more fighting talk, not a surrender, but he would take a step-down in preference to an extended gunfight at the side of the motorway. The incident had lasted no more than five minutes, but more than a dozen cars had driven past in that time. Depending on what they had seen or heard, the police could be along soon.

'Take the Astra and fuck off. Leave the guns,' said Glen.

Glen watched as the passenger pulled the wounded driver, who was still wailing, towards the Astra. He pushed him into the passenger seat before getting in himself and driving away. Glen ran to the back of the van and slammed the rear doors shut, before climbing in and driving off, making sure to let the Astra get away from him.

Glen left the motorway at the Bracknell exit and drove to a small dead-end lane that led to a wastewater pumping station, where he had left his own van parked earlier that night. He reversed the Transporter, parking parallel with his van. After opening the rear doors of both vans, Glen set to transferring the hessian sacks from one to the other, enjoying the smell of coffee beans as he did. Then he doused the Volkswagen in petrol and set it alight before he drove home, feeling smug with his achievement.

He parked his van next to his BMW, went indoors and set to patching up the graze from the bullet, which was still oozing blood. *Lucky old fucker, that could have been a lot worse.*

★ ★ ★

At ten o'clock the following morning, Glen went to his van, opened the doors and pulled two of the sacks toward him. He took out his pocketknife and sliced the first sack open, coffee beans poured out onto the floor of the van. He thrust his hand in, feeling for what was hidden among the beans. Nothing, just beans. *Shit.* He cut another and repeated his search, finding nothing but more coffee beans – a third, then a fourth, then a fifth, only coffee beans in all of them.

'Fuck it, I've been bloody had. Larry, fucking Larry.'

Glen was speaking out loud, his mind darting around, playing with anger, fear, and trepidation all at the same time. *This is bad, very bad. Larry must know about me getting into his safe.*

★ ★ ★

'Big-Gun, it all went to plan, other than a bloody bullet in my shitting knee.'

'Don't go near a hospital. We don't need that kind of attention; they'll call the pigs for sure. Go home, I'll get someone to come and see to it.'

Larry was extremely pleased with the outcome. He knew for sure now that Glen had crossed the line; he was now on the outside and would get what was coming to him. Larry would see to that. By ensuring that Glen had failed to take his drug haul, he had reaffirmed his authority. The news was sure to travel fast; Larry was still Caesar, still the Big–Gun.

★ ★ ★

After Glen had set off tailing the Transporter, the white transit van loaded Larry's drugs and left, taking a different, cross country route to Slough. By the time Glen realised that he had got nothing but coffee beans, the drugs were already being cut, weighed, and bagged at Larry's farm.

CHAPTER 13

Operation Shingle

'Seth, it's Philippa Parker from the Serious Crime Unit. Long story short, we're about to make an arrest in relation to the three sets of remains that you dug up.'

'That's great news, Philippa, anyone I know?' asked Seth, feeling the warmth of glory returning.

He was glad that his work at the gravel pit was progressing but still felt a degree of trepidation after the shock of seeing the remains in the hole and initially believing that they belonged to the woman he had mowed down.

'You might do, he's an organised crime man from Slough, worked his way up from being a low-level minion, a bloke called Glen Borland. Anyway, I thought you'd like to know. It's not cut and dried by any means. His fingerprints showed up on the blue polythene sheeting from the two sets of male remains - every single sheet. Partial prints, but good enough to make a comparison for an arrest. Not enough on their own to prosecute, but his DNA is present on the remnants of their clothing as well, so we are off to a good start. Time will tell.'

Philippa was always straight to the point and did not exaggerate, preferring to err on the side of caution.

'No, I haven't heard of him before. So, can I help out? I'd like to stay involved,' asked Seth. He hoped Philippa would be receptive to some additional detective experience on the team.

'Well, you can sit in on the interviews if you like. I could do with a good second officer in there, watch for any blunders in Borland's story or apparent weaknesses in whatever he says. You up for that?' said Philippa. She knew that Seth would be.

'For sure, Philippa, when are you bringing him in?'

'We're doing a warrant on his house, early doors tomorrow to guarantee as best we can that he's home when we go in. Meet me at Slough Police Station at five for the briefing. I'll call you if anything changes, otherwise I'll see you in the morning, bright and early.'

'Thanks, Philippa, I appreciate being involved, see you tomorrow morning,' said Seth.

Detective Chief Inspector Philippa Parker worked for the Thames Valley Police Serious Crime Unit. She was a career detective and had been involved in many grim investigations at ranks from Constable to Chief Inspector. She had been with the unit in her current role for three years. In essence, her job at the SCU was to deal with the juicier investigations involving murder and serious organised crime. The less severe crime would be investigated by the smaller local CID units that covered the local police areas in the three counties that made up the police force area, the counties of Berkshire, Buckinghamshire and Oxfordshire. Philippa being on a case meant that no stone would be left unturned; every lead would be followed up.

Philippa was a woman who did not mince her words, to the point of being brash but not arrogant. That was her style, and anyone that did not like it had to just deal with it.

★ ★ ★

Seth walked into the briefing room as Philippa stood up,

shuffling a small pile of papers before speaking.

'Now listen in everyone,' she said, then waiting for the room to fall silent.

'Thanks for coming in early today. This is Operation Shingle, a search warrant at seventy-five Woodford Way on the Britwell estate in Slough. We're doing the house, the garden, and the garage at the back. As well as the search, we are looking to arrest Glen Borland, who lives at the address, for three murders that happened in the nineties.

'The basics are that following information received from a covert human intelligence source, which was investigated by Detective Inspector Hannen from CID at Slough,' she nodded towards Seth, and he raised his hand to the room. 'The skeletal remains of one woman and two men were discovered buried in an old gravel pit by the M4 Motorway. DI Hannen will be assisting us with the interview of Borland.

'Anyway, the remains were each wrapped in blue builder's polythene and tied with blue nylon rope, all three wrapped in essentially the same way. After the remains were recovered, Scenes of Crime managed to harvest partial fingerprints from the polythene. When overlaid, the prints match those of Borland. Further to that, the lab has managed to get DNA matches for him, so we know he had at least some contact with the two male gang members before they were buried.

'I'll be making the arrest, but if anything goes wrong, and one of you ends up with hands-on Borland, then the arrest is on suspicion of the murders of Sharon McCrory in 1992, Mickey Stevens in ninety-four, and Joel Waters in ninety-five, and also for failing to allow the proper burial of those three people. All I want to disclose for now is that marks found on, or with, the remains indicate that he may be responsible for the murders. We're not disclosing the fingerprints and DNA until we speak to his solicitor.

'Now, I want a regular house containment. There is a possibility that his girlfriend will be with him, but we are not expecting anyone else. Once we have him, I want the house searched really well, guys, very detailed, fingertip stuff. We are looking for anything that links him to the bodies, notes, diary entries, anything at all. If in doubt, contact me, and I'll decide if we seize what you have as evidence or not.

'If you seize anything, take it to Lee. He's on exhibit officer duty for the day.

'I'll wait outside until you're in and secure. No cockups, please, people. If he does a runner, we'll not catch up with him for ages. Everyone clear?' Philippa stopped for breath.

'What radio channel boss,' asked one of the uniform officers.

'Sorry, I missed that, channel forty-eight, it's just for this job, and the control room is running it. Right, let's get to it.'

Philippa indicated towards the door with a wave of her arm. The chairs clattered and scraped the floor as the detectives and uniformed officers filed out of the briefing room, heading towards the two marked police vans waiting for them in the back yard of the nick.

'Seth, I'll see you at Maidenhead; we'll take him there for the interview. I'll introduce you to DS Linda Graham; she's the lead interviewer. She'll appreciate your input,' Philippa said as she left the room.

The vans set off in convoy, followed by Philippa and the exhibits officer, Detective Constable Lee Quinn, in an unmarked car.

* * *

Within minutes of leaving the yard at Slough Police Station, Larry's phone chirped on his bedside table. Larry had programmed his mobile, so his watchmen's messages had their own alert. He pulled himself up in bed and read the text message.

WARNING
old bill is out in sluff
2 vans plus CID

Larry generally had little interest in the day-to-day street-level goings-on in his empire. That was the concern of his generals, but the police interfering with his business was another matter. He needed to feel in control. Larry had established several business continuity plans to ensure that he minimised any losses at the hands of the police. His early warning network was just one of them.

Larry's Slough watchman lived in a block of flats that overlooked the police station's rear gates. His job was to ensure Big-Gun was warned of any police activity that looked like it was lining up to be a raid. He had no idea who Big-Gun was, but he was paid well for his night-time surveillance and early warnings.

When Larry received the text warnings from any of his watchmen, he would decide whether there was enough concern to activate his business continuity plan and warn the appropriate parts of his network or to just let the police run with whatever they were doing. Sending an alert to his gangs would undoubtedly result in kilograms of drugs being flushed down toilets. Anyone who knew they were wanted by police would flee from their houses and go and hide somewhere safe. His drugs factory on the farm would lockdown, load up the vans, and get any drugs out and away.

Larry scrolled through the entries in his phone. When he found the one he was looking for, he pushed the green button and waited for an answer.

'Morning, Larry, I can't really talk right now,' came the quiet, almost whispered voice.

'I just need to know what you boys in blue are up to in Slough this morning,' asked Larry.

'Alright, all I can say is that it's an arrest for three bodies dug up at a gravel pit. Does that help?' The voice on the end of Larry's phone remained quietly spoken.

'Thanks, that'll do.'

Larry hung up before sending a text back to his watchman.

NO ALERT NEEDED

As Larry had instigated the dig with the intelligence fed to the police, he knew that they would be after Glen Borland. He smiled to himself, put his phone back on the bedside table and went back to sleep.

★　★　★

The convoy pulled up just short of the entrance to Woodford Way. The officers lined up at the side of the vans, waiting for the order to approach the address.

'Okay, go get him,' said Philippa. 'Call me in when you have the house secured.'

The sergeant in charge led the way, followed by a pair of officers in protective gear and carrying the big red key, a heavy steel battering ram used to open doors quickly. The other ten officers followed behind in single file, approaching quietly.

The sergeant issued his instructions.

'Two of you to the back door, two more on the back corners and two at the front, one on each corner. Ensure you keep a line of sight with each other, don't leave your points until I confirm that we are in and secure.'

The officers moved quickly to their positions and signalled their readiness to the sergeant. The remaining four uniformed officers prepared themselves at the front door. The pair of detectives stood to the side, waiting for the door to be breached. The radio crackled in their earpieces.

'Rear door is locked sarge, over,' came the message.

'Many thanks, all received, trying the front door, wait-one,' replied the sergeant.

The officers checked the front door. If it was unlocked, it would buy them more time to get to Borland while he was asleep.

'Front door is locked, sarge. We'll be using the big red key, standby.'

'On the count of three…one…two…three, go, go, go.'

The sergeant marked the off.

The lead entry officer was wearing long black leather gauntlets and a riot helmet. He swung the heavy steel ram back and then thrust it forward at the wooden door with all the might he could muster. It impacted the door just below the lock with a loud crack. As the door frame immediately gave way, the door swung open and slammed into the wall inside the house; wooden splinters flew everywhere. The entry officers quickly moved to one side while four officers ran into the house, shouting as loudly as they could.

'Police, stay where you are, nobody move, stay still.'

Two of the officers checked the dark unlit downstairs rooms, while two went upstairs, their torches showing the way, still shouting at the top of their voices.

Glen Borland was up and out of bed like a shot, taking the duvet with him, leaving his naked girlfriend sprawled across the bed. He had no idea what was happening, he headed for the wardrobe to grab his kit bag, going for his gun. As he opened the wardrobe door and put his hand on the handle of the bag, he felt the weight of someone on his back.

'Police, on the floor now, get on the floor,' shouted the officer as he pushed Borland down.

As he was pushed to the carpet, and before he knew it, he had the knee of a police officer on his back between his shoulder blades.

'Keep still, don't resist,' shouted the officer, bellowing at the top of his voice and calling for support from other officers to assist with handcuffing him.

Two more officers entered the room, stopping for a moment as they saw the sleepy forty-something naked blonde woman scurrying around, not really trying to cover her modesty. One of the officers threw the duvet in her direction before taking out his handcuffs and helping to cuff Borland's arms behind his back. The woman sat back on the bed, wrapping the duvet around her as tightly as she could.

'Get the fuck off him. What the fuck are you doing, you bastards? He's done nothing wrong, leave him alone,' she yelled.

'Keep quiet and stay there,' shouted one of the officers.

At the same time, Glen started to shout.

'Shut the fuck up, Tracy, this has nothing to do with you. Get dressed and go home. I'll call you when I'm back from the cop shop.'

'He's talking sense,' added one of the officers, throwing a pile of women's clothes in her direction.

Tracy dropped the duvet and started to get dressed.

'Use the bathroom,' said one of the officers.

'Fuck off, copper, I'll get dressed where I like. You take an eyeful and have a wank thinking about me later,' said Tracy, smiling as she picked up her clothes.

Tracy had been brought up to have a low opinion of the police. She was not going to risk being accused of flushing anything down the toilet if she went to the bathroom.

Glen was pulled to his feet and pushed onto the end of the bed. As he sat pulling on his boxer shorts, Philippa Parker walked into the room.

'Glen Borland, I am arresting you on suspicion of the murder of Sharon McCrory in 1992, Mickey Stevens in 1994 and Joel Waters in 1995, and for preventing their lawful burial. You do not have to say anything, but it may harm your defence if you do not mention when questioned something which you later rely on in Court. Anything you do say may be given in evidence. Do you understand?'

Philippa glanced at Tracy, who had stopped dressing. She stood in just her knickers and bra, staring at the scene before her.

'You can get dressed. Nobody is interested in you prancing around half-naked, get dressed and get out of the way, but we'll need all your details before you go anywhere,' said Philippa.

Tracy finished getting dressed and walked downstairs.

'Get some clothes on him and get him to the van and away, while the others finish up with the search,' said Philippa. 'Oh, and well done,' she added.

Philippa walked downstairs, taking a moment to speak to the sergeant in charge.

'Good job, sarge, get the place searched and take your time. I don't want to risk missing anything.'

Then she turned to Lee Quinn, who was sat ready to receive any seized property. 'Lee, call me when you're done and let me know what we've got, please, so I can decide how to approach the initial interview.'

Once dressed, Glen was marched to one of the vans and bundled into the prisoner transport cage at the back before being taken to the custody suite at Maidenhead Police Station.

★ ★ ★

The search took just over four hours. The officers seized Glen's grab bag, which contained all the tools of the trade for his life as a burglar, and the Glock-42 mini handgun that he always took on his jobs. They also recovered an old roll of blue polythene from the garage and a partially used reel of blue nylon rope.

After Glen had been processed, he was locked in a cell at Maidenhead Police Station. It was not unfamiliar to him. In fact, he had been in this very cell before, when he was once arrested for burglary, early in his offending career. On that occasion, the evidence against him had been damning, he had been well and truly bang to rights. Yet, he avoided being charged, something he was sure Larry had arranged.

As he tucked into his microwaved all-day-breakfast, Glen considered his predicament. There was no Larry to get him out of trouble this time. In fact, he suspected it was Larry who had gotten him here, and if that was the case, then it would be part of a bigger plan for Glen's future. Larry would be pulling strings, considering the long game.

CHAPTER 14

Full and Frank

Seth parked up his motorcycle in the back yard of Maidenhead Police Station, then made his way up to the third floor to meet Philippa. The old single quarters had been converted to offices. Seth tried to work out where his old room was in relation to Philippa Parker's office.

As he walked along the corridor, he saw Philippa walking quickly in the opposite direction.

'Seth, team up with Linda; she is the interview lead. She's down in the custody block now,' said Philippa as she hurried past Seth.

'The briefing Philippa, I've not had a full briefing, only the ops briefing earlier,' he replied.

Seth was shocked at Philippa's hurried approach. It was most unlike her.

'Sorry Seth, it's Gordon. He's just been taken to hospital, a heart attack. I've got to go… Linda will fill you in,' and she was gone.

Philippa was married to Gordon Parker, an old school detective inspector, who had retired from the job a couple years ago.

When Seth had been a detective constable, he once worked for Gordon. He was a nice guy and an outstanding detective.

But always ended up in the police bar or down the pub after work, with two or three pints of beer accompanied by pork scratchings and a packet of cigarettes. Seth had fond memories of working with Gordon and he was sad to hear about the heart attack but not that surprised.

Seth made his way down to the custody suite and buzzed his way in. There he found Detective Sergeant Linda Graham setting up the interview room ahead of the first interview with Glen Borland.

'Hello boss, you must be DI Hannen?' she asked, as he walked through the door.

'Yeah, you're Linda then, please call me Seth.'

'Thanks for coming over to help. We're short of experienced interviewers on this case. The plan is that I lead, and you do the second officer role, that alright with you?' said Linda, looking up from her pile of neatly organised papers.

'Yes, but you'd better brief me, Linda.'

'Well, as far as the recovery of the remains goes, you know that part as well as we do. Stevens' skull has a blunt trauma fracture to the back of the head, the same with Waters. As for McCrory, no obvious cause of death, we're waiting for skeletal toxicology reports, but with the remains being nearly ten years old... we're not holding out much hope.'

'Right, and the forensics that gave you the suspicion to bring him in... partial prints, wasn't it?' Seth enquired.

'Yes, we got nine separate partial prints from the polythene wrapping. None on McCrory's, five on Waters' and four on Stevens'. They were all partial due to time-related degradation, but the lab has put them together, and when overlaid with each other, we almost have a whole thumbprint. Add that to Borland's DNA harvested from Stevens's clothing, and there was enough to bring Borland in.

'He's predominantly a burglar, but he did a bit of drug-running years back. The intel suggests that he's a general foot soldier for the organised crime scene in Slough. There's lots of intel about his escapades, but not much has stuck to him in recent years. Any questions?' said Linda, hoping that would be enough to get going, but Seth wanted more information.

'The warrant, what did that bring up?' asked Seth.

'Blue polythene and rope, similar to what the remains were wrapped in. We still need tests done to see if there is a mechanical fit between the cuts in the polythene, but it's old and dirty. It was under a load of crap in his garage. Oh, and a burglar's tool kit and a handgun, but I plan to save that for the second or third interview. I don't want to muddy the water early on. Can we start now... please?' said Linda, impatient to get going.

'That'll do for now. I can read the papers later before the second interview. If I'm only working as the second officer, listening for gaps in his story or continuity issues, my knowing less will probably help, if I'm honest,' he replied.

Linda smiled at Seth, giving him a thumbs up.

'Grab a seat then, and I'll fetch him from his cell. His solicitor's here, and they've had their chat. I'm starting the interview in order of reported disappearance, so this interview is for Sharon McCrory,' said Linda, as she left the interview room.

Seth chose the chair furthest from the door, on the police side of the table, so he would not have to get up when Linda returned with Borland.

The door opened, and in walked a detention officer, who showed Borland and his solicitor into the room.

'Take a seat, Mr Murphy.'

The slightly weedy and untidy looking solicitor sat down opposite Seth. He extended a hand and introduced himself as Linda sat down beside Seth. Borland sat next to his solicitor, opposite Linda.

Seth looked towards Borland. He immediately went cold and felt like the ground was opening up beneath him, sucking him downward. Borland looked like the same was happening to him. They stared at each other as if they had been transported back in time, each recognising the other immediately. *Glen Borland is Scotch... Fuck, this could be the end of my career,* thought Seth.

Glen's mind was racing too, *Fuck... Larry's copper friend, this is some kind of fit-up. I am so screwed now.*

Seth broke his transfixed gaze and unwrapped two audio cassettes, taking them out of the plastic cases and sliding the cassettes into the tape machine before closing the flaps. There was a clunk, then a long beep, as the tape machine started recording on its double deck.

Linda started the interview while Seth tried to compose himself.

'Okay, this interview is being tape-recorded on an authorised recording device. At the end of the interview, the tapes will be sealed, and you and your representative will be invited to sign the seal. You will be advised how to obtain a copy of the recording. We are in interview room number one at Maidenhead Police Station. The time is twelve thirty-two hours on Friday the 21st of December 2001.

'I am Detective Sergeant Linda Graham. For the purposes of the tape, I'll ask those in the room with me to identify themselves.' She looked at Seth, who took a fraction longer to reply than would be usual, still shocked that he was in a room with Scotch all these years later.

'Detective Inspector Seth Hannen, from Slough CID.'

Seth nodded at the solicitor, indicating that he was next.

'Mr Paul Murphy, solicitor and legal representative for Mr Glen Borland.'

'Thank you,' continued Linda, looking up from her papers. 'Glen, you do not have to say anything, but it may harm your defence if you do not mention when questioned something which you later rely on in court. Anything you do say may be given in evidence. Do you understand?'

'Yeah, I've been cautioned before.'

'What is your full name and date of birth?'

'Glen Angus Borland, the 24th of June 1966. You can call me Scotch if you like detective sergeant. I'm known as Glen Scotch Borland; it's a whisky thing. You probably remember me as Scotch, don't you, Inspector Hannen.'

A short but acutely uncomfortable silence followed Borland's introduction.

'Do you two know each other?' asked Linda.

'No, not at all, not unless we've met in the distant past, and I don't remember?' said Seth, trying to remain as calm as possible and shrugging off Borland's comment.

Glen shrugged his shoulders.

'Must have muddled you up with another pig, sorry it was years ago.'

Linda continued with the formal start to the interview.

'Thank you, Scotch... Glen, do you understand why you are here?'

'Yeah, you dug up three dead people.'

'And you were arrested this morning on suspicion of the murder of Sharon McCrory, Mickey Stevens and Joel Waters, is that correct?'

'Yeah, I'd have thought you'd know that really, being the police and all that.'

'I just want to talk about Sharon McCrory initially, so did you know her?'

'Nah, not that I'm aware of unless we've met in the distant past, and I don't remember, eh Detective Inspector.'

Glen appeared calm as he answered the initial questions put to him by Linda, but inside, his head was racing. He was more concerned that Seth was sat in the interview than by the questions he was being asked. He knew for sure now that Larry had wanted him arrested. Larry would have made sure that the police had been given the information that would later lead to his arrest and conviction. *That must be Hannen's part in this*, he thought.

When any of Big-Gun's boys got nicked, and it was clear it had been orchestrated by Larry, they knew to play ball and fess up, or they would face a far worse fate back on the streets. If they grassed Larry up to the police, then they would face death for sure. They would either get taken out while on bail, or if remanded, they might get a shank in the gut while in prison.

The only option was to put your hands up. Play it Larry's way and take the punishment dealt by the law. Once in prison, Larry would have someone on the inside make contact and give you a brief as to what you needed to do to reprieve yourself while you were banged up. It would either be an order to take out another prisoner or run something criminal from the inside. Larry's reach knew no boundaries.

The thing that was worrying Glen the most was precisely why, or how, Larry's cop friend from all those years ago was involved, but he had no way of finding out.

Linda was into her interview stride now.

'Sharon was reported missing on Saturday the 28th of August 1992. Do you remember what you may have been doing back then around that time of the year?'

'That was nearly ten bloody years ago; how would I remember that?' answered Glen laughing.

'Well, that's reasonable, but can you tell me what you remember from that year, anything at all?'

'Yeah, I saw Nirvana in concert at Reading Festival, and my

dog Zeus died. I lost him that year; he was a rotty. Didn't Freddie Mercury die that year as well, or was that the year before? I can't remember.'

Borland looked directly at Seth and saw him squirm; he recognised the same anxiousness in his face that he had seen back in 1992.

'Go on, maybe thinking about Zeus will help you remember something else?'

'He was my best friend. The whole thing was tragic really, such a sad incident.'

'Tell me about it?' prompted Linda.

'Nothing to tell you, he was run over, head stoved in, I almost reported it to a copper I saw in Ascot the same day, but he had his own problems by the looks of things.'

Seth found himself sweating profusely. *How could one day, and one stupid decision, come back again to haunt me like this.*

'We might be able to look that up on the system,' said Linda, deciding to move things on.

'So, tell me—' she was interrupted by Borland.

'Can I be straight with you…? I'll tell you everything, start to finish, I'll come clean.'

Seth squirmed in his seat, McCrory's face screaming at him in his mind.

'My client may need to take further legal advice,' Murphy interjected, putting his hand on Borland's shoulder.

'No, I don't need to take advice, I just want to tell the truth, get it done and sorted, I didn't murder anyone, but I did help to get rid of the bodies. I'll tell you everything I know.'

Seth's mind was running wild now, his world teetering on the brink of collapse. He had to interrupt the interview.

'I think in fairness, you ought to speak to your solicitor before you say any more. This is a serious allegation, and I'm not about to lose an interview on a technicality. I'm pausing the interview to allow Mr Borland to consult with Mr Murphy. The time is now o-seven-forty-eight hours.'

Seth pushed the stop button on the cassette recorder, then he stood up and looked at Linda, indicating that they should leave the room while Borland and Murphy spoke in private.

Linda was raging.

'What the fuck happened in there, Seth? He was about to squawk without even being pushed. You screwed that up. I don't care if you're a hotshot DI. You were bang out of order, guv.'

'Trust me, it'll be fine. We can't risk a breach of the codes of practice for a quick confession. We'd lose it in court once a clever barrister gets hold of it,' said Seth, who was doing his best to sound purely professional, hoping his stress was not showing through and giving him away.

'Breach, what breach, there was no breach, I'm going to Philippa, I don't want you in this interview; you're a bloody liability.'

Linda moved to walk off, but Seth took hold of her arm.

'Linda, I've been asked to do this interview with you, I'm the DI, and I'm telling you that I am working it with you. Philippa has gone to the hospital; her husband has had a heart attack. It's you and me on this interview, and if you don't like it, then it'll be me and someone else.'

The custody officer called Seth over to his desk.

'Boss, there's a call for you. Apparently, it's about Borland.'

Seth took the phone.

'Hello, DI Hannen speaking.'

'Ah, Seth, my friend... long time no speak,' said the voice at the other end of the line.

'Who's speaking, please?' asked Seth.

'Seth, you don't recognise me. I'm fuckin' disappointed,' replied Larry Fowler.

Seth could hardly believe his ears; could this get any worse than it already was? He had been relieved to have an excuse to walk away from Linda, hoping the take the opportunity to calm himself down. But the sound of Larry's voice put the brakes on him regaining any of the control he needed.

'How can I help you, sir?' asked Seth, trying to sound official.

'What's wrong Seth, don't want to say my name in front of your colleagues?'

'How can I help you? I'm pretty busy, so you need to be snappy.'

'I'm just checking in, Seth. I believe you are dealing with my old pal Scotch Glen,' enquired Larry.

'Yes sir, that's correct,' replied Seth, wondering what was coming next and looking around to see who might overhear him.

'Well, I just wanted to say, Seth, that if he says anything that could in any way incriminate me, I expect you to make it fuckin' go away. I don't think I need to say anymore, do I?'

'I'm sorry, sir, but I can't guarantee that; your friend is subject to a criminal investigation and that is governed by the Police and Criminal Evidence Act.'

'Don't be silly, Seth, you know very well what I fuckin' mean. I like you, if ever you decide that you want to earn some decent money, you know where I am. You'd be very welcome to join me in business.' Then, without a further word, Larry cut the call.

Seth turned to the custody sergeant.

'Did that bloke ask for me in person or just the officer in the case for Borland?'

'He asked for you specifically, Sir,' the sergeant replied.

The realisation that Larry must have at least one contact in the station sent a shiver down Seth's spine. He must either have someone that fed him information or was ready and waiting on the end of a phone. Who was it, and what else did they know? Seth felt fear joining his anxiousness; the emotions gripped his mind as he and the still annoyed Linda headed back to the interview room.

★ ★ ★

The tape machine beeped again. This time Seth ran through the introductions, then he moved onto the questioning before Linda could manage to get a word in, glancing at her as he started.

'Glen, you've had time with your solicitor. Are you happy that you have been appropriately advised?'

'Yeah, I've been advised to make no comment to your questions,' replied Borland.

Seth breathed a sigh of relief as he and Borland locked eyes again.

Linda's antenna was on high alert, and she noticed Seth's reaction immediately. Interviewing is as much about reading people as asking the right questions; Linda was one of the best there was.

'But I've decided not to take the advice. I want to talk,' Glen added.

The atmosphere tightened again.

Murphy looked at his client, knowing he could do nothing more to intervene.

'Tell us what happened, take your time, no pressure.' Linda got in quickly this time.

'I did know of Sharon. She was a smackhead, used all the time, couldn't get enough of the stuff. That's why she was called Shmack. She'd nick anything and sell it to buy more heroin, and she'd shag anyone for a few quid. Back in ninety-two, she couldn't function without the stuff; she was a fucking mess. Her dealer was a bloke called Matt, had a green Ford Capri, total spanner he was, nearly died a few years back of an overdose.

'Anyway, I heard back then that she was dead. I heard that she overdosed on some bad shit. I never met her, and I have no idea how she ended up in the gravel. The other two, yeah, I buried them. Me and some local drug-runner took them there after they were done in.'

'Who asked you to do that, Glen?' asked Linda.

'No, I can't tell you I've been as straight as I can be with you, I didn't kill those blokes, but I did put them in the ground,' replied Glen. 'If you've got my DNA or something, it'll be on those two, not on Shmack.'

'Glen, I want to keep this interview to Sharon. I'll cover the other two in our later interviews. So, in short, you deny anything to do with the death or burial of Sharon McCrory, is that correct?' asked Linda.

'Yeah, nothing to do with me. I know nothing at all about what happened to her.'

Seth's mouth dropped open as he listened, and his mind filled with questions. *Was Glen telling the truth, or was something else going on here? Has Glen just saved my bacon for some reason? Was McCrory the woman from the crash or not?*

Seth's reaction was not lost on Linda. She decided not to challenge him again but to just keep watch, trying to work out Seth and Borland's connection.

★ ★ ★

Glen Borland was interviewed a further two times and gave what is known as a 'full and frank' interview on both occasions, admitting to his part in disposing of Mickey Stevens and Joel Waters, but he vehemently denied any part in their disappearance or death. He refused to say anything about anyone else's involvement, fearful of repercussions from Larry Fowler.

Linda Graham, for her part, remained suspicious of Seth and the link he may have had to Borland in the past.

★ ★ ★

DCI Parker took the case to the Crown Prosecution Service for a charging decision. She telephoned Geoff Atkins, one of the senior crown prosecutors, and outlined the partial fingerprints on the polythene and the DNA results. The forensics and his confessions would surely bring about a charge for preventing the lawful burial of two people, but anything more would be a bonus; their disappearances and subsequent deaths would probably remain unsolved for now.

Geoff had worked on and discussed many cases with Philippa in the past. He was an experienced and trusted crown prosecutor.

'Philippa, I've read the papers and listened to your case. I'm sorry, but for once, I disagree with you,' he said.

'You disagree, Geoff? Surely, we must have enough for the disposal offence. He's admitted it for God's sake, and we can place him with the wrapping material and the clothing they were wearing.'

Philippa was surprised; they usually saw eye-to-eye when discussing charging decisions.

'Philippa, you've taken me the wrong way, yes you do have enough for that, but I want you to charge manslaughter on the two men and add on the disposal offence. The injuries to the heads of each of them indicate a violent death. I can't approve a manslaughter offence for the woman without an apparent cause of death, and there's no contact proven between Glen Borland and the remains, so no disposal charge either, I'm afraid.

There's plenty of work to be done on the case between now and court; we can discuss the details later,' he said confidently.

Philippa was flabbergasted. In her view, it would be impossible to prove Borland committed manslaughter. If there was enough evidence, the injuries indicated a common method, pointing toward an execution, which would be murder, not manslaughter. Geoff had lost his mind.

After Geoff had finished speaking with Philippa, he picked up the phone to make another call. The phone hardly rang the other end before it was picked up.

'Hello.'

'Hi, it's Geoff Atkins. It's done. Borland will be charged and remanded. I've approved manslaughter as the primary charge.'

'Thanks, Geoff, that's good news. I'll let Mr Fowler know, bye now.'

Geoff put the phone down and went back to reviewing another police file needing a charging decision.

Borland was charged with two counts of manslaughter and two counts of preventing the lawful burial of a body. He was remanded in custody at HMP Reading, pending his initial appearance at court.

★ ★ ★

Philippa Parker was convinced that there was more to know about the disappearance and the death of the three people that ended up in the gravel pit. She wanted more than just Glen to be dealt justice for his part in the burials; she still wanted to identify the killers and all those involved.

She filed the case with an action for it to be reviewed every twelve months, just in case anything new cropped up. All she needed was one lead, and Philippa would get her teeth back into it.

★ ★ ★

Glen pleaded guilty to preventing the lawful burial of both men but not guilty of their manslaughter. The jury concurred and found him not guilty. Nevertheless, the judge took a dim view of Borland's involvement and handed down a harsh sentence, citing their violent deaths as increasing the likelihood of murder, which made preventing their proper burial a more serious matter. Glen received six years in prison for his part in disposing of their bodies. With luck, he could be out after somewhere between three and four years.

★ ★ ★

Two and a half years into Glen's sentence, Larry received a telephone call from the governor of the Isle of Wight prison.

'Good afternoon Larry, it's Howard Jenkins. I thought that you'd appreciate a call. It's about Glen Borland.'

'Hello Howard, I thought Glen Borland was in fuckin' Belmarsh, not your gaff,' replied Larry.

'He was found hanged in his cell yesterday. I don't know anything else. Any deaths in custody are shared with us all, just in case there is some kind of pattern developing. Anyway, I thought you'd want to know Larry.'

'That's a shame, he was one of my best once, been with me a long time, shit happens eh Howard.'

Larry hung up the phone.

Borland had been moved to a cell on his own, following a fight with his cellmate. That night Glen had tied a torn-up bedsheet to the sprinkler attachment in the ceiling of his cell and hanged himself. He was not discovered until the following morning.

PART THREE

LONDON CALLING

CHAPTER 15

Moving On

'Professional Standards Department, Superintendent Clive Landon speaking.' The phone was answered promptly.

The day after working with Seth, Linda Graham called the Professional Standards Department.

'Hello sir, I'm after some advice. My name's Detective Sergeant Linda Graham. I wanted to talk to you about some concerns I have regarding an officer on the Slough CID. I work on the Serious Crime Unit, and he joined me on a manslaughter interview. The things the prisoner said and then the officer's reaction just made me really uncomfortable; I think something really odd is going on,' explained Linda.

'Go on, I'll need more than that to be able to advise you,' replied Landon.

'Well, the prisoner made comments about knowing the officer from the past. They were made in a way that sounded like the two of them were familiar and that the prisoner knew of something that the officer had done, something that was bad. It may be just me, but it felt wrong, guvnor. Then, just as the prisoner said he would tell us everything, the officer stopped the interview and prompted legal advice.'

'Who is this officer you're talking about?' asked Landon.

'Detective Inspector Seth Hannen from Slough CID,'

replied Linda.

'Okay, I appreciate the call. You are right to have raised concerns, even if they turn out to be unfounded. Can you make a duplicate of the working copy of the tape and drop it at my office in Langley? I'll have a listen, and if I share your concerns, I'll get it investigated to see if we have anything to worry about. How does that sound?' asked Landon.

'That sounds good guv, I'll get a copy over to you later today if that's okay, thank you.'

Linda ran off a copy of the tape and drove to Langley Police Station just the other side of Slough. It was a small building that housed a team of local beat officers on the ground floor. Upstairs was home to the Langley office of the Professional Standards Department. They oversaw any complaints and discipline issues for the southern part of the Thames Valley Police force. The small team was headed up by Superintendent Clive Landon, who was known to investigate anything that breathed. He was a man of principles, the slightest hint of anyone not having the integrity and ethics expected of a police officer, and he would be down on them like a ton of bricks. He had one objective in life, and that was to hunt out wrongdoing and rid the police force of the cause.

Linda parked her car and went into the station, walking upstairs and tapping on the locked door to the PSD offices. The door opened quickly, and she was met by Landon.

'Hello Sir, I'm Sergeant Linda Graham. We spoke earlier.'

'That was bloody quick. This must be really bothering you. Please come in.' Landon beckoned her into the office.

'I've got the tape for you, guv,' said Linda as she walked in.

'Okay, let me sign for it, then you can play it to me and explain your concerns,' he said.

Landon was not about to take possession of the tape without completing the audit trail first. Once the paperwork was correct, he pulled out a cassette player from his desk drawer, and they sat down to listen. Linda played the tape from the start, talking over it as the introduction played.

'This is the normal formal intro; this part is all fine, no real issues at this point, although I could certainly feel an atmosphere in there,' said Linda.

'Police regulations don't talk about atmospheres Linda, I'll need more than an atmospheric change to look into anything,' replied Landon.

'I know, guv, I was just trying to paint a picture. It just felt off from when Borland and DI Hannen first saw each other, that's all.'

Linda tried to hide the flush that had crept up to her face from her chest and neck, visually displaying her awkwardness.

'Sorry, I didn't mean to embarrass you, Linda. You know I deal with facts and reasonable assumptions, not hunches, alright?' said Landon, not really managing to put her back at ease.

'Listen to this part,' continued Linda, as she pushed the play button again.

'What is your full name and date of birth?'

'Glen Angus Borland, 24th of June 1966. You can call me Scotch if you like detective sergeant, I'm known as Glen Scotch Borland, it's a whisky thing! You probably remember me as Scotch, don't you, Inspector Hannen.'

'This is when things first looked dodgy to me. If you could only see their faces at this point, guv. DI Hannen was ashen white and clearly uneasy,' said Linda. She set the tape machine to fast-forward. 'I asked if they knew each other, as I wanted to check out any familiarity before we continued. The answer from DI Hannen was really strange, and he was really acting odd and fidgety,' said Linda, as she pushed play again.

'No, not at all, unless we've met in the distant past, and I don't remember?'

'At this point, Borland shrugged his shoulders and smirked at DI Hannen and me. They definitely know each other, I'm absolutely sure of it, and there's more to it than that, guv, there's something wrong here.'

'Must have muddled you up with another pig, sorry it was years ago.'

'There were more instances like this. Borland mentioned his dog. It was hit by a car or something. Again, DI Hannen looked really uncomfortable,' said Linda as she pushed the fast forward button, watching the counter numbers move higher.

'I'm getting your point; it does sound strange,' said Landon.

'Now this is when the interview was stopped by DI Hannen. Borland said that he wanted to come clean and tell us everything, his solicitor suggested legal advice, but Borland refused. DI Hannen interjected and pushed for a break. We were about to be given an unprompted confession of some kind. Still, DI Hannen decided it would breach the code of practice under the Police and Criminal Evidence Act. She pushed the play button again.

'I think in fairness, you ought to speak to your solicitor before you make any confessions… I'm pausing the interview to allow Mr Borland to consult with Mr Murphy…'

'DI Hannen claimed that he didn't want to lose the investigation on a technicality, and we left Borland and his brief chatting for twenty minutes or so. When I challenged him, he threatened to interview Borland without me or to continue questioning with another officer,' said Linda, looking at Landon and hoping that he did not think that she was bonkers. She hoped he would agree that her concerns were worth looking into.

'Look, Linda, I agree, things do sound odd, but just him and Glen Borland knowing each other does not give me an investigation into Seth Hannen. I also agree that it's odd that he would deny knowing Borland unless perhaps he'd dealt with him years ago and lost a case or something. Then perhaps he'd not want Borland thinking he had one up on him,' said Landon, who was playing devil's advocate.

'I know, sir, but the look on his face and that of Borland's said so much more than that, you needed to be there,' replied Linda, resolute in her tone.

'Well, I wasn't, was I, but you were, so I'll get Seth Hannen looked into, just to be safe. If we end up going any further, I'll need a statement from you about the mannerisms of them both to put some context around the recording. I would write that statement now if I were you, while it's all fresh in your mind, then seal it in an envelope and tuck it away. We'll only need it if we take things to the next step. Leave it with me,' said Landon, bringing the discussion to a close.

After Linda had left, Landon listened to the tape from start to finish before sealing it in an evidence bag and locking it in his desk drawer. He picked up his phone and called Liz Davenport, one of his top discipline case investigators.

'Liz, it's Clive Landon. I want you to do some digging into a detective inspector. Seth Hannen, he works on CID at Slough. Get the detail behind his last vetting assessment and his financials, and then check all intelligence ever recorded for a man called Glen Angus Borland. He's also known as Scotch. He was born on the 24th of June 1966. If there are any links at all, I want a thorough, in-depth assessment of the connection. Got it?'

Landon waited for a response, while davenport wrote the details in her notebook.

'Okay, boss, I'll get it sorted and update you as soon as I have anything,' replied Davenport.

★ ★ ★

It was three months before Clive Landon decided that Seth needed to be spoken to. Seth was at home eating breakfast when the doorbell rang at just after six on an unremarkable morning in March 2002. He walked from the kitchen to open the front door and saw Clive Landon and Liz Davenport stood on his doorstep.

'I assume you've not popped by for a coffee Clive,' said Seth, knowing that a visit at home from PSD meant that there was a problem.

'No, Seth, we need to speak to you about an allegation that has been made,' replied Landon.

Seth felt his chest tighten and his heart rate increase.

'Alright, am I being arrested, or is this an informal chat?' asked Seth.

'Neither actually,' replied Davenport. 'You're not being arrested, but it is a formal chat. We'd like to do it at Langley, less obtrusive than popping into your office at Slough.'

'Shall I meet you there then?' asked Seth.

'It would probably be better if you came with us in our car, if I'm honest. I've let Dave Martin know that you'll be late in Seth, you'll be back at your desk by midday, I'm sure. It's just routine,' said Landon, smiling.

Seth grabbed his jacket and walked to the car with Landon

and Davenport. Half an hour later they drew up into the back yard at Langley Police Station. Landon and Davenport led Seth into the meeting room on the first floor.

'Have a seat Seth, can I get you a coffee?' asked Landon.

'Yeah, that would be great, black, no sugar thanks,' replied Seth, as he sat down.

Landon looked at Davenport. 'Mine's white, no sugar Liz,' he said, smiling at her.

Liz Davenport tutted under her breath and went to make the coffees, returning five minutes later with a tray of mugs.

Seth had been nervous when interviewing Glen Borland, but he was less worried today. The stress that he had felt earlier had subsided. The car journey had given him time to think. If Landon had anything concrete, then he would have probably arrested him. Seth decided this was either a rubber stamp to close an investigation or a fishing expedition on Landon's part.

'Seth, I'll be straight with you. I had a report from another officer who had concerns about an investigation that you were involved in, specifically the interview of Glen Borland,' said Landon.

'Yes, I remember the interview. I guess there are no points for guessing who had concerns, Clive,' replied Seth.

'No, it's not hard to fathom, but that's why we are here, Seth, any allegation or concern of misconduct, and we'll take a look. It keeps us all legitimate and authentic.'

Landon opened up a couple of cassette tapes and set up the machine. He pressed the record button and then ran through the introductions in much the same way as Linda had done during the interview with Borland.

'Right Seth, before Liz runs through things, I need to ask you. Do you know Glen Borland in a personal capacity, or in any capacity at all that would undermine your position as a police officer?'

Seth thought for a moment, unsure if Landon was setting him up to fail. *Did Landon know something that was going to come out later in the discussion?*

'No… I don't have, and never have had any kind of relationship with him whatsoever,' replied Seth, feeling distinctly uneasy at delivering a half-truth to Landon.

'Thank you, Seth, that's very useful,' said Davenport picking up the conversation. 'I've been looking into Borland in some detail, as well as digging deeper into your latest security vetting assessment. I'm happy to say that everything I found on your file and in your financials for the last five years checked out fine. I have no concerns on that front.

'As far as Borland goes, he has a chequered history. There is lots of intelligence about him running a group of criminals committing burglaries to high end houses and having links to the Fowler family, formerly of the Britwell estate in Slough. He appears very close to Larry Fowler, who is a businessman suspected of high-level organised criminal activity.

'Our concern, Seth, mirrors that of Sergeant Linda Graham. Why would he claim to know you or have had dealings with you in the past?

'I have no idea, have you asked him?' replied Seth, knowing that they probably would not have.

Davenport ignored his churlish question and continued.

'Anyway, my digging into Fowler and Borland drew some attention from people in high places. I must have set off some kind of tagging alert. I got a concerned call from the Home Office, asking why I was looking so deeply into a relationship between Fowler and Borland. I was basically warned off—'

'Thanks Liz,' Landon interrupted. 'The point is Seth, we are concerned that if you have any connection with them, that it could put you or your colleagues in danger. So, I wanted to hear from you as to whether you two were connected?'

'No, I told you I have no relationship with Borland, and certainly not with Fowler,' said Seth, looking at Landon and Davenport in turn.

'Thanks again, Seth, but I need to make it clear that we will be monitoring you for a while, just to be sure everything is as it should be.' Landon was straight to the point.

'Right… okay, what are you saying, Clive,' asked Seth gingerly.

'I'm saying that I am concerned. Being warned off by the suits in the Home Office is unusual, so I am saying that if I see a connection between you and Borland, or you and Fowler, I'll be getting you suspended for a full investigation. This is a warning shot, Seth; one you need to take heed of.'

'Thanks Clive, but there's nothing for you to be concerned about, really there's not,' he replied.

'Well, that may be the case, but I wouldn't be doing my job if I didn't put you on the officers of interest list,' said Landon.

Seth understood very well what Landon was saying. Basically, Clive Landon thought there was something to the concerns held by Linda Graham, but he had been unable to confirm them. Seth was now on the PSD radar. If he put a foot out of line, he would move quickly from the radar to the microscope. Being told about the Home Office call had resulted in Seth slowly beginning to comprehend the extent of Larry Fowler's reach.

★ ★ ★

Outwardly, Seth had managed to leave the events of that day in 1992 behind him. He had escaped their return to his life during the investigation into the three gravel pit bodies and the subsequent PSD interest in him, Glen Borland and Larry Fowler. Inwardly, the missing person investigation and his second brush with Glen and Larry had really affected him. He had trouble sleeping for a year or so after the investigation, and he was constantly worried that it would resurface again. He had tried his hardest to commit the incident to the annals of his personal history, but that was hard to do when there were reminders all around him.

So, in the Summer of 2003, Seth decided it was time to leave Thames Valley Police behind him and head off to the capital, where he could do his job with little or no chance of Larry and his cronies encroaching on either his professional or personal life. The Metropolitan Police were advertising for chief inspectors, Seth took it as a sign and applied for promotion in the Met.

★ ★ ★

Dave Martin took the letter from Seth and placed it on his desk, reaching for his reading glasses.

> **Dear Mr Seth Hannen,**
>
> **It is with great pleasure that the Metropolitan Police Service wishes to offer you the position of Detective Chief Inspector, on promotion and transfer from Thames Valley Police…**

'You're deserting us then, Seth?' said Martin, peering over the top of his glasses.

'Boss, I've tried for promotion here twice with no luck. The Met is a bigger beast, there'll be more opportunity there for me to do some serious fraud investigations and maybe even counter-terrorism work.

'If I'm honest, working the patch where I grew up is really hard on the personal front. Especially when you end up dealing with witnesses you know from school, or worse still, offenders.

I need to do this, it's the right thing for me right now,' said Seth.

He felt a little guilty at the thought of leaving some good friends and colleagues behind, but by the following February, Seth had started his new policing chapter.

Seth's decision to transfer to the Met served him well. His career progressed just as he had hoped; he was happy and fulfilled, the only downside was the commute to London from his home in Maidenhead.

Seth worked initially as a detective chief inspector on a borough CID team, overseeing criminal investigations in much the way he had done at Slough. Then he qualified as a tactical firearms commander and spent a short time back in uniform working with a cadre of officers commanding spontaneous firearms incidents across London.

Seth's penultimate role was working in the Counter-Terrorism Command Unit. He worked mainly on developing intelligence and providing investigational support following the July 2005 London terror attacks. Once that work was complete, he moved to the Met's Serious Fraud Investigation Unit for the last few years of his service.

He managed to push the screaming woman, Scotch, and Larry Fowler to the back of his mind, preventing the incident from unconsciously popping up in his head without an invite. He had convinced himself that the younger Seth had made one bad decision. He was not, and never had been, a bent copper. Larry Fowler was wrong.

In 2016, thirteen years after joining the Met, Seth began a routine fraud investigation, which would bring Larry Fowler back into his life. Fate conspired against Seth once again.

CHAPTER 16

Clever Woman

Emelia DiSalvo worked for a small investment company in London, owned by Rebecca Langford. She had worked there since leaving university and was well-liked and good at her job, but then she was good at everything she did.

Emelia had done well at school and then at university too; she studied at Imperial College London and obtained a first-class honours degree in engineering and computing. She loved the complexity of designing computer systems and writing software that was robust and hard to break into. Her degree had served to formalise the skills that she already had, rather than adding that much to them. She naturally understood the theoretical and practical aspects of programming and always seemed to push computing boundaries further than others could.

Emelia was always viewed as a bit of a geek at school; not many of the girls had the same level of interest in computing as she did. When studying her A-levels, she was in a class of fifteen students, thirteen of which were male. Being slim and attractive, and knowing it, she was as much the centre of attention as the computing itself. During the two-year course, most of the class had asked her out on a date at one stage or other, but none of them got a look in.

Alan Fitzgerald was the computing teacher at Norwich's

Loxbury School. He had not long qualified and had just moved from his first school to teach A-Level mathematics and computing at the private school. He was tall and dark, in his mid-twenties and obviously kept himself fit.

Emelia's teacher was why she had turned down all the offers of romance from the boys in her class. She had a massive crush on Mr Fitzgerald, but he wore a bright shiny gold ring on his wedding finger. Although he did secretly enjoy the attention his pupil gave him, he was in no way interested in teenage infatuations. He valued his job far too much and was very happily married, and he made sure that Emelia knew it.

Emelia had to be content with her fantasies. She realised from that point onward that it was older men that held her gaze; she enjoyed an older man's confidence.

From the age of eleven, Emelia had been a full-time boarder at Loxbury. She worked hard at school but was certainly no angel, loving to find out things that she was not supposed to know. She would often be caught snooping around the staffroom or other parts of the school that only staff were meant to be in. She was naturally curious to the point of being nosey, and she enjoyed it.

Her nosiness first paid dividends when she found the questions and answers to the upcoming mock GCSE exams on the deputy head's desk. The usefulness was not that she would be able to cheat and enhance her grades; she was already well able to excel at the exams. The benefit was selling the information to some of her classmates and making money from the enterprise. Not so brazen to simply sell the exam paper; that would be far too dangerous, and she would get caught if someone snitched on her. Instead, she used the information she had obtained, offering paid study advice to fellow students, helping them revise precisely the right subject areas to do better in the exam than they otherwise would have. Emelia recognised that people clamoured for valuable information, and they would often pay to get it.

When the time came for Emelia to take her A-levels, she took things a stage further. She wrote a computer programme, hacking into the examination board's mainframe server to steal the exam questions, the real ones this time, not the mocks. Far too intelligent to need the answers herself, she went back to her original audience and again sold study advice for a premium. This time she was able to charge a higher fee, based on the success of her previous coaching exploits before the mocks. Emelia felt no guilt of any kind; she was simply helping others achieve their greatest potential and making herself some extra money along the way.

At university, Emelia knuckled down and learned as much as she could about how mainframe computer systems and servers operated, as well as how large industry and corporations protected their data.

As part of her applied computing study, she designed a system to protect the university's computers servers. Emilia identified flaws in the system that her lecturers and the university IT team had been blind to. When they assessed her design, they became extremely uncomfortable, so much so that they upgraded the system.

During her final year at university, Emelia toured the career fairs. She was uncertain about where to take a career, alternating between a profession in computing or something more exciting like policing or the Army Intelligence Corps.

Her father had always wanted her to follow him into the military, but she had never really been drawn to a uniformed career. Despite that, she knew that her father would be incredibly proud if she decided to join the armed forces or served her country in some way.

★ ★ ★

Emelia's father had served as a pilot, flying jets in the Royal Air Force. He always told Emelia that the military had given him the best years of his life. He retired as a squadron leader and set up his own business, running a small chain of Italian restaurants and several continental food shops, and a few rental properties.

He would buy old, dilapidated houses or flats, do them up himself, sell them quickly to realise a profit, or rent them out. His property flipping worked well. Over time, he built a highly successful business, which enabled him to buy a modest country home on the outskirts of East Dereham in rural Norfolk and pay private school fees for Emelia. The country property provided stables and ample room for Emelia to play and explore during her early childhood and school holidays.

Her father's business exploits enabled Emelia to live in London during her time at university. She lived in one of her father's properties, rent-free, with four other students paying rent to live in the house.

He was an honourable man, and he pushed Emelia to be the best that she could be in everything that she did. His encouragement and total faith in her ability to achieve anything she desired helped mould her into a highly confident woman who generally got what she wanted.

★ ★ ★

At the last careers fair of the year, just ahead of her finals, Emelia came across Marc Pashley looking after a stall on behalf of Langford Investment Management Ltd. Marc was in his early thirties, smartly dressed in a well-cut three-piece suit from Huntsman & Son on Saville Row. He wore his tie tight, in a perfectly symmetrical Oxford knot, and sported black brogue shoes made by Church's. He oozed new money, but in a very traditional, almost old-fashioned way. He was dashing indeed and immediately caught Emelia's wandering eye. She made a beeline across the hall, grabbing his attention as she sashayed towards him.

She had no real interest in financial investment. Still, she knew that she liked the look of the well-dressed, slightly older guy, sitting patiently waiting for would-be employees to come and speak with him.

'Emelia, Emelia DiSalvo,' she forcefully held out her right hand, which was met quickly by Pashley's in return.

Her father had always told her to get the handshake in first. *'It demonstrates that you are a strong woman Emelia, not a woman to mess with,'* he would say.

They shook hands, Emelia sustaining her grip a little longer than would be usual, making Pashley blush a little and giving her the upper hand.

'So, what are you offering us today,' asked Emelia, the ends of her lips curling upwards with a hint of a smile.

Pashley was quick with his reply.

'That depends on whether you're looking for business or pleasure?' he said.

He was well-spoken, clearly public school educated, with a slight air of arrogance about him. As their hands parted, he offered Emelia a rather corny wink of his eye. Emelia was equally fast with her retort, the word investment catching her eye from the stalls small sign in front of Pashley.

'I take pleasure in any business, or indeed any ventures that I devote my time to. But it always needs to be a worthy investment!' said Emelia, flirting with him.

Pashley nervously explained what the company did and that they were looking for whizzy computer geeks to design some cutting-edge software. The new system would help the company make fast, time-critical financial decisions, fractions of a second ahead of the competition, getting in on the money early.

The work now started to sound attractive to Emelia, something right up her street, and a good-looking chap to work with to boot!

'Why not come in for an interview?' asked Pashley, hopefully.

'What, just like that, what about a formal application form or something?' said Emelia.

'My boss, Rebecca Langford, she likes to recruit people for their attitude, if you have the skill for the work, and she likes your approach, she'll take you on. If you don't perform, she'll let you go. She's pretty ruthless really, but she's good to work for, and she pays well. Go on, you know you want to.'

Pashley winked again, continuing to flirt with Emelia as he held out his business card.

'What's your number then, Emmy?' asked Pashley.

'Wow, steady tiger, my name's Emelia. I get to choose who shortens it and to what,' she said, cutting him down with a steely stare.

'I'm sorry, way too familiar of me, pop your number on here, Emelia, and I'll get the office to invite you in to see Rebecca.' Pashley handed her a pen and a small pad.

'Okay then, why the hell not? After all, what have I got to lose?'

Emelia wrote down her name and mobile number on the pad and handed it back to Pashley before turning to leave.

As she walked away, she turned her head and blew him a kiss, following it up with a wry smile.

★ ★ ★

'Take a seat, Miss DiSalvo. Rebecca will be with you shortly'.

Emelia could see Rebecca Langford sat in a designer chair at a large modern desk in her glass-walled office. She was on the telephone talking loudly and looking stern. The door was open, and Emelia could just about hear some of Rebecca's conversation.

'If you expect me to invest your money to the best of my ability, I need your trust; you can't question every decision I make. If you continue in this vein, I'll have to ask you to take your business elsewhere. I am good at what I do, so let me get on and do it.' Rebecca sounded like she was very much in charge. Emelia liked that.

Rebecca put the phone down and walked to the doorway.

'Sorry about that, you're Emelia right? Please come in, let's have a chat.' Rebecca's tone had changed to being much more friendly.

Emelia held her hand out, Rebecca accepted it, and they shook hands. Emelia gave her usual firm handshake that ended with that slightly longer hold.

Rebecca was not fazed at all by Emelia's tactic. She looked at her and ever so slightly tilted her head to the left, with a quizzical expression that said, *'Don't try and take the upper hand with me, young lady.'*

Emelia found herself blushing. It was the first time that her handshake trick had failed to achieve the desired effect. She sat on the black leather two-seater sofa while Rebecca returned to her desk.

The pair chatted for two hours, Rebecca curious to know about every aspect of Emelia's life, from her childhood and her parents through to her choice of degree at Imperial College.

Emelia also asked plenty of questions of Rebecca. Where had she worked before? How had she built up her business in very much a man's world?

'So, do you have any big-cheese kind of clients, Rebecca?' asked Emelia. This was the question that ended the interview.

'Emelia, asking me about my clients before you even work here, that's pushing too far. My clients trust my discretion. Many are top businessmen and women, some are in the public eye, and many try to stay out of it. If, and that is a big if, you work for me, it's only then you learn more about the clients we serve, is that clear?' Rebecca glared at Emelia.

'Yes, I'm sorry if I was inappropriate,' replied Emelia.

She felt embarrassed by Rebeca's response. This was her first discussion of any kind with a successful and powerful businesswoman. It was clear that she had much to learn in the art of effective corporate conversation.

Rebecca was clearly riled; her face had turned to stone. The interview came to an abrupt end, and Emelia was politely escorted out of the office.

She thought she had blown it; Rebecca had seemed pretty stern about her asking a few questions about her clients. But two weeks later, Emelia had a call from Rebecca.

'I like you a lot, Emelia. You remind me of me when I was younger. I'd like you to work for me, not on the client side of the business. I need your computer skills, what do you say, will you come?'

'Yes, I'd like that very much indeed. My course is nearly over, so I can start as soon as I finish university if that works for you?' asked Emelia.

'Slow down Emelia. First, you need to know my requirements of you. I expect total and absolute commitment and loyalty to me and my business. I work hard, and I expect you to do the same. If you cross me or do anything that harms my business in the slightest, then you are out.' Rebecca's voice was soft and calm, despite delivering a stark warning.

'Okay… of course, I can be loyal, and I won't let you down,' said Emelia, not really sure what to say in reply to a warning that sounded more like a roasting for something she had already done wrong.

'Great, my personal assistant will keep in touch and deal with the details.'

So, in 2003 Emelia started working for Langford Investment Management Ltd as a computer systems designer, working on a new cutting-edge piece of software. Her work would give her access to the very core of the company's business. There would be nothing that Emelia would not be able to see.

CHAPTER 17

Back to the Valley

'Seth, it's Philippa Parker from the Serious Crime Unit at Thames Valley. How long's it been? Twelve or thirteen years, maybe?'

'Philippa, wow, this is a surprise, to what do I owe the pleasure?' Seth had not spoken with Philippa Parker since he had transferred to the Metropolitan Police.

'Well, it's about the investigation we worked on; remember the bodies in the gravel pit?'

'How could I forget that Philippa, yes it was back in 2001, which makes it fourteen years,' said Seth. He thought that investigation was far behind him.

'I've had the case reviewed again, Seth. I've always been concerned that it would have taken more than just Glen Borland's involvement to dispose of those bodies. We never got to the bottom of what had happened to them before they died, and that sits uncomfortably in my mind. It's too easy to just put it down to gangland fallouts and organised crime. Those people still deserve justice,' said Philippa, speaking fast and excitedly.

'But that's not what you called to tell me, is it Philippa?' asked Seth, who was feeling a little uneasy.

'Well, it is partly, the review turned up some compelling new evidence, forensics have moved on a lot, Seth. As you know, the harvesting of DNA has improved in leaps and bounds; it's so precise now. Anyway, we've identified some new DNA on the clothing of Sharon McCrory, and what's more, we have a match,' said Philippa, now ecstatic in her tone.

Seth's heart raced, picking up its pace from its regular rate to an uncomfortable one in an instant. Then his mind took over. If he had been linked to Glen 'Scotch' Borland in any way, then he would have had a visit, not a phone call, especially after the warning he had been given from Clive Landon.

'Congratulations Philippa, thanks for letting me know, I appreciate it—'

Seth was not expecting to get much detail now that he was not with Thames Valley Police. He was about to say his goodbyes when Philippa interrupted him.

'You played such a major part back then, developing that intel and recovering the remains, and then sitting in on the interviews. I wanted to ask if you fancy an away-day. Come and help me question the suspect? I'll keep you up to speed and let you know when we plan to make the arrest, and then you can come down here for the interview. You were so keen to remain involved, and I'd be pleased to have you back in on this, Seth. What do you say?' Philippa pushed him for an answer.

Seth thought for a moment. The last time he had involved himself in this case, he ended up on the end of an internal investigation and a warning. It had all gotten too close to exposing his past for all to see. He really did not want to open that can of worms again. Yet, something was telling him he ought to join forces with Philippa again if only to keep an eye out for any involvement from Larry Fowler.

'Well, I still live locally, so if I can spare a day from the office here, I'll happily come along. But I can't promise you anything; I'll need to have it approved this end,' replied Seth, tentatively agreeing to Philippa's offer.

Knowing that the investigation had been reopened, Seth decided that it would be better to stay close rather than wake up one morning to another surprise knock on his door. If, for any reason, this new suspect knew of Seth's connection to Larry Fowler or Glen Borland, or worse still, they knew of the accident itself, things could get very ugly indeed for Seth Hannen.

★ ★ ★

In April 2015, Seth found himself back in the custody suite at Maidenhead Police Station, being briefed by Philippa Parker about the arrest of Matt Hopkins. His DNA had been found on the clothing that was worn by Sharon McCrory's skeleton.

'This is a cold case review Seth, so the team is small on this one. I'm doing the interview myself this time, and I want you in there with me.

'Hopkins has been arrested on suspicion of murder, but as before, all we have is a connection to the clothing, so on its own, it represents nothing more than contact.

'He's a long-time drug user and small-time dealer, with proven associations with Glen Borland, so it all fits together quite well.' Philippa paused to take a breath.

'Certainly sounds like it,' said Seth, feeling slightly nervous but remaining in control of his thoughts and heart rate.

He listened intently as Philippa briefed in her usual style, offloading all the information in one big hit.

'The interesting part is that despite being arrested on suspicion of murder, he has flat refused to take any legal advice of any kind. He doesn't want to speak with a solicitor or have one present in the interview. He says he has nothing to hide, so he doesn't need legal representation. It looks like he may actually want to talk to us about what happened,' said Philippa.

Seth's mind let some of its control go, and his heart rate started to pick up.

Philippa had not changed much since Seth had last seen her. She was still the same dogged investigator, always keen to get to the very bottom of an investigation. No tin can could have too many worms for her, and she would just keep tugging them out one by one until she had the whole story. Her determined scrutiny worried Seth. If any of this investigation led back to Fowler, he was sure that Larry would be thrilled to burn a cop to save his own bacon. He began to feel like history was repeating itself. *I wish I'd not come back to help*, thought Seth, as they headed to interview room number one.

The room was the same as he remembered it, aside from now looking rather tired and run-down. The interview started in the usual way; However, the questioning was being audio-visually recorded this time. Technology had moved on since Glen Borland's interview.

After the introductions, Philippa started with a wide-open question, hoping that Hopkins would talk freely and tell them more than they knew. She would be hugely disappointed if they ended up with only another body disposal charge. She wanted to know about the killings and who was responsible for them.

'Matt, to put things very simply, I'd like you to tell me everything you know about how Sharon McCrory ended up dead and buried in a disused gravel pit. Start at the beginning.'

Matt told Philippa and Seth how he had dropped Sharon off in Ascot one morning during one of the royal race days.

'She was going to do over a few houses, or cars, whatever looked worthwhile. There was lots of opportunity with the rich toffs in town,' said Matt.

He described taking her there in his car, dropping her off, and then driving away to deal cocaine and cannabis to wealthy drug users.

'Within an hour, I got a call from Scotch Glen; he wanted my help moving her body, she had been knocked down by a car, and he needed her gone.'

Seth took a deep breath as panic began to take over. Despite everything he knew, he had managed to convince himself that the woman in the gravel pit was not the woman that he killed on that day. Now things looked to be very different. He knew for sure that his initial investigation into the gravel burials had resulted in him digging up his own victim. *I should be the one being interviewed, and before the day is out, I probably will be.* His face had drained of colour and taken on an expression that shouted guilt and fear.

Matt continued to describe the part he played on that fateful day.

'Anyway, I drove back and helped Glen put her into the boot of my car, then he sent me on my way to get rid of her body.'

'And you took her to the gravel pit on your own?' asked Philippa.

There were a few seconds of silence. Seth sat waiting for some kind of revelation that would implicate him and unravel his life. His mind instilling a frantic anxiety that just kept on rising. He was now sweating and struggling to maintain his facade. Matt told his story.

★ ★ ★

Matt drove the Capri back towards Windsor, trying his best not to let panic take over his mind and control his actions. As he wondered what the hell he was going to do with Sharon's body, then the answer came to him from the boot of the car.

'Aagghhh,' a short series of whimpers and coughs, followed by a second, and then a third, each time growing in volume.

Sharon felt the agony from the impact; her legs, back, and

head were screaming with pain. She was unable to think or comprehend much of what had happened. All she remembered was a shiny black car and that copper's face. After that, her memory was blank.

'Alright, babe, it's me, Matt, hold on. I'll get you to your flat. I have no fucking idea what's going on. I thought you were dead, babe, thank God. You'll be alright, I promise,' shouted Matt.

He felt relief that getting rid of Sharon's body was no longer an issue, but a new panic started to seize his mind. He thought of the state that Shmack was in. *I'm no doctor, what the hell do I do...* his thoughts rambled as he drove.

He pulled up in the exact spot where he had picked Sharon up from earlier, then quickly got out of the car and rushed to the boot. After opening the tailgate, he pulled Sharon onto her bum. She looked like death itself, much paler than usual with an expression of sheer agony on her face. The gash on the back of her head was still bleeding, and her tracksuit bottoms were ripped open, her mangled legs peeping through the holes in the fabric.

'Aagghhh,' she groaned again as he moved her.

'Can you talk? Can you see me? Do you need a hit?' asked Matt. He had no idea how to check if she had any serious head injuries or even how to take her pulse. He did know her legs were terrible, horribly twisted and out of alignment.

'Aagghhh, what the fuck happened? That cop ran me down, fucking wanker,' Sharon spoke for the first time.

'A cop... what are you on about? There was no cop there,' said Matt, even more confused now. 'I got a call from Big-Gun's man to come and get you. When Scotch Glen calls, you just get on with it. If Big-Gun's involved, it's heavy shit. He thinks you're dead, babe.'

The sense of panic started to return as Matt wondered what

he was going to do. Putting an arm around Sharon's middle to support her slight frame, he dragged her from the car. She could not put any weight through her broken legs; they just dangled, sending searing shafts of pain through her body as her feet were dragged along the pavement. Matt heaved her towards the flats, just as one of the neighbours sauntered out of the opposite block. The elderly woman stopped dead in her tracks as she saw Matt dragging Sharon, groaning and screaming, towards the entrance to the flats.

'Stoned again, love, had some bad shit earlier, I need to get her indoors, fancy giving me a hand darling?' called Matt.

The woman looked down and hurried away, wanting nothing to do with whatever was going on.

Once inside the flat, Matt put Sharon on the mattress and arranged her works. He made up a syringe of heroin, prepping her arm and injecting it into the vein.

'Wow… that feels a lot fucking better, thanks,' said Sharon, her groans turning to a deep sigh of relief.

'Bite the spoon handle,' said Matt, holding out the wooden spoon he had just used to tighten the tourniquet.

'What the fuck… why?' came the weary reply; she was tripping now.

'I've seen it in films; It makes it hurt less or something. I need to straighten your legs, babe,' replied Matt.

Sharon bit hard on the spoon as Matt pulled her right leg straight.

'Aagghhh,' she screamed a blood-curdling yell. Then he took hold and pulled her left the leg. 'Aagghhh, for fuck's sake, stop.'

Then he grabbed the broom from the kitchen, pulling the head off before snapping the handle in two. He used a pair of Sharon's stockings to tie the broken broom handle to her lower legs, one half handle to each leg.

'You can't go to a hospital, there's no gear there, and Scotch Glen and Big-Gun will soon know you're not bloody dead. Or if they don't, if there was a fucking copper in that car, he'll work it out for sure. If he's involved with Scotch, he's a bent copper. We can't risk it.

'I'll do my best to look after you. I can keep you in heroin to help keep the pain down while your legs heal.'

Matt liked Sharon, but more to the point, he did not want to be in any kind of trouble with Big-Gun, *time to stay low.*

Matt explained to Seth and Philippa that about two months went by with Sharon being bedridden in her flat. He took her food and kept Sharon topped up with heroin to control the pain in her legs. She had only been able to move from the mattress when Matt was with her. He would pull her up and drag her to the bathroom so that she could use the loo. If he was not around, she just emptied her bladder where she sat, resulting in the room becoming pungent. She smelt awful and had become even thinner than she was before. Her legs had healed badly. The bones were misaligned, making her legs look strangely angled below the knee.

* * *

Seth had hardly asked any questions during the interview; he just sat listening intently to what Matt was saying.

His revelations about Sharon seeing a cop driving the car almost made Seth jump up and run from the interview room. He wanted to travel back in time and just arrest Larry for being drunk in charge of his Aston, or just take the tunnel back to the station and push history through a different sliding door.

Learning the truth for the first time about what had happened to Sharon McCrory, that she had not been dead at all, felt strange. His mind was reformatting and uploading new files and information.

'One day, I went round to give her some more brown, a McDonalds and help her have a shit, but she was fucking dead. I called Scotch Glen, and he sent Barry Freeman round to take Shmack away.'

'Thank you for that, Matt,' said Philippa, before looking at Seth. 'Can you tell us anything about the accident, how Sharon became injured in the first place, why you had to go and get her from Ascot?'

'No, honestly, Scotch Glen never told me anything about it. I just knew that Big-Gun had wanted her body moved quickly, and Scotch had been asked to sort it out. I don't know anything else at all,' replied Matt.

'Who's Big-Gun Matt, can you tell us that?' she asked.

'Sorry no, he's a big-time crook, only his closest blokes know who he is, but the rest of us know what will happen if we cross him. He's in charge, and he calls the shots around here,' said Matt.

'The police officer, do you know anything about the cop she mentioned?' asked Seth, then holding his breath.

'No, that must have been bollocks. She was always high. She'd had a hit before I dropped her off,' replied Barry.

Seth calmed his nerves. He knew the accident had not been reported and that only four people knew that it happened. Borland and Sharon McCrory were dead that only left Larry and him.

Matt was charged with preventing the lawful burial of Sharon McCrory. Given that it had happened so long ago and that he had been entirely upfront with his involvement, he was released and bailed to attend court.

★ ★ ★

Sharon McCrory had died alone in her flat.

'Aagghhh, I'm getting up', Sharon spoke out loud to herself. 'Matt will be round to see me in an hour or so.'

She pushed herself up, sitting against the wall, then bent her legs, using her arms to help them move. As she tried to stand, the pain burnt through her legs and up into her back.

'Aagghhh fucking hell,' she screamed out at the top of her voice.

In a hospital, her legs would have been realigned, placed in plaster. Then physiotherapy would have started a week or so ago, none of that here, just the liquid fire to ease the pain.

She sat back on the bed, her legs throbbing so hard, the extreme discomfort not subsiding in the slightest.

Sharon made up a syringe, then another two. She grabbed the stocking, wound it tight around her arm, and then sent more bronze liquid into her veins. *I need this bastard pain to stop, just for a bit,* she thought as she picked up the second hypodermic and plunged it into her arm. Then she picked up the third, injecting the last of the brown liquid into her veins to chase the previous dose. The hit was huge, the pain subsided, and then it was gone, replaced with the hedonistic freedom she craved.

Sharon lay motionless on the mattress, drifting in and out of consciousness. The heroin began to suppress her heart rate, slower and slower. She felt her extremities feeling the heavyweight that she knew. But it became heavier than ever before; she could not move a finger, let alone an arm. She opened her eyes for one last time just as her heart managed its final beat, and then her breathing stopped, the room faded to black. Her hearing was the last of her senses to leave her.

The door opened.

'Shmack, I've got you Mackey Dee's, how are—' death interrupted Matt's voice. Life stopped clinging to Sharon's body; the pain had gone for good now.

Matt shook Sharon, trying to wake her up, convinced that she had just passed out from a heroin hit. After fifteen minutes, he realised that was not the case and gave up his efforts. He sat down on the mattress next to her and called Glen Borland.

'Scotch, she's dead, Shmack's dead this time,' Matt spoke into his phone, Glen not yet having even spoken.

'What the hell are you talking about, you stoned again or something?' came Glen's reply.

'Shmack was still alive when I picked her up a couple of months back, but she's dead now,' said Matt, crying as a mixture of nervousness and grief took over his emotions.

'Why the fuck didn't you tell me she wasn't dead, you were supposed to deal with it, you cock,' said Glen, shouting into the phone.

Glen was angry but also worried about the knock-on with Larry. 'Right, I'll get Barry to come and help you. Help him bag her up, and then she can go to the old gravel pit by the M4. This might just work out alright. He'll be there after dark.'

Barry Freeman arrived at the flat just after midnight. He wrapped Sharon's body in two sheets of the blue polythene sheeting, that he had collected from Glen's garage and then tied nylon rope at each end and in the middle of her body. He carried her to the boot of his car, tossed her in and slammed it shut.

'Glen says to give it a week or two, then report her missing, no detail, you just haven't seen her since today.'

'Alright, got it,' replied Matt, as he watched Barry drive away with his mate Shmack in the boot.

CHAPTER 18

I Smell a Rat

'Mum, it's me, Emelia, what's wrong? I've told you not to call me on a workday, you know how busy I am here in London,' said Emelia. She was returning a missed call from her mother, Carol DiSalvo.

Carol was taken aback by Emelia's brashness. Her daughter had toughened up since moving to London to study, and now even more so working at L.I.M. Emelia had worked for Rebecca for thirteen years, and she seemed to be getting all the busier. It appeared that Emelia was ever more distant and would only really entertain a call from family at the weekend. Even then, sometimes weeks would pass with Carol and her husband Errico not hearing from their daughter at all.

It did not help matters that Carol and Errico disliked Emelia's boyfriend Marc Pashley intensely. Pashley had shortened Errico's name to Eric the first time they had met, even after her father was introduced as Errico. This overfamiliarity irritated Emelia's parents.

Although Errico was known to all his close friends as Eric and his former RAF colleagues as 'Rocket Ric', he felt strongly that it was his call to decide when to allow anyone to shorten his name. It was his name, after all.

Actually, Errico hated his name. He was born in England and

was fourth-generation English Italian. His father had insisted on a tradition of giving the boys in the family an Italian name that could be shortened to an English one if they wanted later in life.

'It's your father. He's gotten us into trouble, serious trouble,' said Carol, trying hard to stay calm and hold back her tears, doing her best to disguise her anguish.

Errico was a self-made man, having worked hard to build his business from scratch. Two years ago, he sold his restaurants and his small property portfolio, to invest his capital back into the Italian family business with his cousin Luca. Luca lived in Brindisi in Italy and ran a large family business that had substantial assets. He had handed the capital over to Luca, who managed the finances well and ensured an income for Errico and Carol, enabling them to continue living very well.

'Mum, you'll need to tell me more than that. I don't understand what you're talking about. What trouble can Dad have possibly gotten into?'

Carol offloaded the story that only she and Errico had known until now.

Luca had been involved in the family business for years, taking over from his father when he had passed away. His relationship with Errico had pretty much always been long distance and conducted mainly over email and telephone calls. They were a similar age, and as children, they had visited each other; well, Errico and his parents had visited the family back home in southern Italy, rather than Luca coming to England that often. Luca had only visited the UK once. Nevertheless, the two of them had a family bond, and they had helped each other in business over the years.

After Errico left the RAF, Luca invested a significant amount of money into Errico's property business, allowing him to get things off the ground and make sure the venture worked. In return, Errico had agreed that when the time came, he would wind up his restaurants and property portfolio and invest the capital back into the family business, only keeping his continental food shops. Errico kept his word, and he sold off most of his portfolio, releasing over three million pounds in capital. He used some of the money to invest in an income bond to eventually leave for Emelia. That was Errico's way of ensuring that he could leave some kind of legacy to his only daughter if everything went wrong.

Carol explained that Errico had put almost all of their capital into the Italian family business, not really knowing how or what it would be used for. The family firm had been in existence for years. He was confident that the money would be safe. Family meant family; he could trust Luca to ensure a long-term income.

A month ago, Carol and Errico heard of Luca's tragic death. After a business trip to the north of the country, he was driving home from Brindisi airport when his car had left the road and struck a tree head-on. Luca was killed instantly. The Polizia di Stato had found that no other vehicles were involved. Luca had been drinking heavily on the flight, and the police found the alcohol in his body. They concluded that the crash was an accident and needed no further investigation.

Having received the news, Errico made the obvious inquiries about the family business's funds, only to find a gaping hole. Nothing was left. In fact, the business was nearly two million euros in debt.

Two weeks later, Errico received the first death threat, and he took it seriously. It was clear that Luca had been tangled up in something very dark indeed, and the people involved wanted the money they were owed. Errico was now on the debtors' list, to the tune of just over two hundred thousand euros, and he had no means to raise the money within the four weeks he had been given. He had considered going to the police, but the family back in Italy had made it clear that they did not want to involve the authorities. They told him that going to the police would cause more problems than it would solve. Errico was trapped, with no option but to try and raise the cash.

Emelia was floored. She had always viewed her father as an honest and upstanding man who had grown up staunchly supportive of both the British and Italian establishments, only switching national loyalty depending on who was winning the rugby. The thought of him being involved in dodgy business, or even organised crime, made her feel sick. Even if he had not really known what was going on, he was savvy enough to have asked about his investments. *He must have known something,* thought Emelia.

'Mum, I think I can help, but I need a little time. I'm not sure that I can raise all of the money you need. Give me three or four weeks to see what I can do with my investments. Get Dad to call me please. I need him to buy some time, and I will let you know how things go.'

She put the phone down abruptly, not really knowing what else to say. The truth was that she was not sure what to do or how she could raise that kind of money quickly. Emelia knew that things must be really serious for her mother to call. Her parents never discussed money with her, they kept their finances very private indeed. She knew she needed to do something before lives were at risk, the lives of her parents.

* * *

Emelia was up early the next day. She dressed in a grey business suit that was well cut and hugged her figure and a pair of black trainers that she wore for her commute. She grabbed her black leather Mulberry tote bag that contained her workbooks and a pair of patent leather heels that would add almost two inches to her height when she arrived at work. Then she dashed out of her front door and headed for the train.

Emelia took up her usual place in the first-class carriage, in one of the single seats next to the door. She preferred sitting there as she did not have to put up with any of the annoying businessmen that would sit with their legs wide open – man spread – as she would often refer to it.

Emelia sat with her notebook open, drawing a mind map and working out what avenues she had available to start raising some liquid cash to help her parents. This was going to be more complicated than selling exam paper advice at school.

Having designed and written the L.I.M software, she knew it inside out and was already working on the next software update. Her mind wandered between work and her parents as she mapped out possible solutions. *Intervening and slowing the automated decision making at the right point and then skimming off some of the profit before it hit the clients' accounts wasn't beyond the bounds of possibility.* The problem would be Marc, her boyfriend, he was now working as head of audit and governance, and he knew his business very well. If the yields started to look drastically different, he would spot it quickly.

As usual, the tube was totally packed, so she stood just inside the door, pushed tightly against the other commuters. She hated it, but at least nobody had tried to squeeze her bum, or worse still, lewdly push themselves up against her.

She exited St. James' Park tube station, ran up the steps and out of the station and headed to the serviced offices of L.I.M in nearby Broadway.

When she arrived at the office building's main door, she saw Marc Pashley stood outside finishing off a cigarette. He gave her a friendly pat on the bum as she walked past him.

'Wow, no good morning kiss today,' chirped Pashley as she rushed by.

Emelia stopped, turned around and walked back to him.

'Sorry Marc, I've got lots on my mind today,' she said, leaning forward and kissing him tenderly on the lips and smiling as the kiss ended. Then she squeezed his cheeks between her thumb and forefinger and gave his face a friendly shake.

'Lunch... let's do lunch today, Marc, but it may be a late one; my diary is rammed,' she said. She needed him to believe she was just busy with work, not fixing her parents' financial problems.

'Okay, deal,' he replied.

Emelia switched her trainers for her heels, and they walked into the office together.

Emelia had done very well at L.I.M; her software made considerable differences to the company's investment strategies. She had deployed algorithms that accurately predicted the direction of individual stocks and shares, enabling the system to make automated buying and selling decisions across the full range of L.I.M's portfolios.

Most of the clients were private individuals, investing capital to make sure it grew faster than the rate of inflation.

Emelia sat and started writing code that she would insert into her original program as a patch. She planned to slow things enough to enable a millisecond of extra time. Her patch would only affect the accounts belonging to clients who had chosen the higher risk investment portfolios. They were used to seeing more significant fluctuations in the value of their investment. As long as the year-end figures had grown well enough, the greedy bastards were always happy.

* * *

It took Emelia two days of writing and rewriting code to have the patch ready to install. She had verified it on the original test platform that she had designed and built and was confident that she could hide it.

Everything was set up and timed to be uploaded onto the company system overnight Saturday into Sunday.

'It's Friday, poets' day,' called out Pashley as he stood up from his desk. 'Let's go out and get pissed, girlfriend.'

Emelia looked up from her desk.

'Do you mind if I meet you at the Adam & Eve? I've got just a little more to do to make sure the system is running well for next week,' she answered.

Emelia hoped he would be keen to get a pint down his neck and leave her alone in the office, so she could finish up preparing for the installation of the patch.

'Sure, what's your poison tonight, bubbles or a gin and tonic?' he asked as he pulled on his suit jacket.

'I'll take a double Bombay Sapphire and slimline tonic, I'll be with you before they've finished adding the lime, I promise,' she blew him a kiss and watched as he walked out of the door.

Emelia was the only employee left in the office now. She needed to link her laptop to the server before she went, and a wired connection was the safest way to deploy the update.

She swivelled her chair around and stood up, picking up her laptop as she did. Then she walked to the server cabinet, glancing towards the office door to ensure the coast was still clear. Despite being the only person in the office, her heart was racing. She felt so nervous. This was not a silly schoolgirl venture to cook the examination books – this was serious – she was about to trigger a significant chain of actions.

She opened the glass cabinet and plugged the long yellow network cable into the server, connecting her computer to the system. Then she plugged the mains adapter into a spare socket to ensure that the laptop would not die over the weekend. Just as she flicked the mains power switch, she heard the office door open. *Shit, who the fuck is that?* Her mind started to race, trying to think of reasons why she should be tampering with the server last thing on a Friday night.

Emelia swung her head around, still kneeling at the base of the server cabinet, but she could not see who it was. Her view was obscured by the line of desks and screens between her and the door.

As she stood up, the blue cable pinged out of the server. *Shit!*

'I left my wallet on the desk. Are you ready yet?'

Marc had returned to the office, having gotten to the pub and not been able to pay for his order.

She managed to pop the cable back into its slot as she stood up, closing the glass door as she walked towards him.

'I'm ready!' she said, deciding not to make any excuses for why she had been at the cabinet. After all, she did run the IT system. Emelia glanced back at the server tower as they left the office together, the magnetic security lock on the main door clunking shut behind them as they left the building.

★ ★ ★

'Mum, I've managed to free up some of my cash. Everything will be fine, I promise,' said Emelia.

Carol knew Emelia had done well with her financial investments due to what she had learnt at L.I.M, but she had not thought in a million years that she would be able to get all the money they needed to see off the Italian debt. She was so relieved and full of gratitude that she did not ask any probing questions.

★ ★ ★

To Rebecca Langford, trust was everything. She had worked extremely hard since leaving Eatmon LLP to establish her own successful investment company. Her clients trusted her implicitly, and that was important when you were responsible for investing vast sums of their money. Some of her clients were high profile figures, some less so, and they wanted it kept that way, clients like Larry Fowler.

Rebecca valued loyalty highly, and she expected everyone she employed to be loyal to her. The only thing she placed a higher value on was money. She paid and treated her staff well for their allegiance, running a flexible office that allowed people to work hours that suited their home lives. As long as the work was done and done well, Rebecca was happy.

Now at the age of sixty-six, Rebecca was still a single woman. She relished the good things in life, enjoying a small but close circle of friends. Her father was an old-fashioned stockbroker, and he taught her that money could buy anything you needed in life. You just had to invest it wisely and spend it cautiously, and then take the joy it provided at face value.

It was two weeks after Emelia had inserted the patch that Rebecca realised things were not quite right. She was not quite able to put her finger on it, but she smelt a rat. She asked her long-time friend and confidant, Peter Grimes, to look over the accounts. He would often come in and carry out an in-depth independent audit and assessment to help Rebecca understand any anomalies that cropped up from time to time.

'Come in, what news do you have for me?' Rebecca invited Grimes into her office.

'There is bad news, Rebecca, someone in your business has set up a skimming racket,' said Grimes, his voice full of seriousness.

'Well, we knew that was probably the case. But how much is missing?' said Rebecca, getting straight to the point.

'It's not that easy to tell, it's all well buried behind deals and transactions, lots of small amounts here and there. I think it's all over the accounts, but mainly the higher risk portfolios,' said Grimes, frowning as he spoke.

'Rebecca, can I have a word, please?' came the voice of Marc Pashley, poking his head into her office.

'No, Marc, you bloody can't. You can clearly see that Peter is with me today, so go and find something useful to do with your time will you please?' snapped Rebecca.

'Sorry...' he said as he scurried off.

'My apologies, Peter, please continue.'

'So, Rebecca, my best assessment is that something in the region of three million pounds is missing. Pretty big in the scheme of things, but three clients seem to have been hit harder than the rest.'

'Who, which three clients?' said Rebecca, her face had turned to concrete. Her expression did not change at all as she listened intently.

'Mr Phillip Owens, Mrs Cynthia Clark in the United States, and Mr Lawrence Fowler. Mr Fowler's portfolio is the largest of the three and so has suffered the biggest hit, relieved of something like two million pounds.'

'Thank you, Peter, do you have any idea which of my staff may be responsible?' asked Rebecca, keeping her view to herself and waiting to hear Peter's first.

'I do, but I'm an audit consultant, not a criminal investigator. It's been cleverly done, Rebecca, making the losses almost look like an error. It's probably best that we invite the police in to assess the records that I've pulled together. Then you can decide whether to take the culprit to task yourself or have the police arrest and prosecute them. The key will be acting fast if you want to recover the money,' said Grimes, looking intently at Rebecca's now frozen face.

'I understand your point, but I will need to advise my clients about any investigation. Mr Fowler, in particular, will not be happy. He is a dangerous man, one that may well take matters into his own hands,' said Rebecca, unusually letting details slip about her client.

'That, Rebecca, is none of my business, I'm only suggesting that this should be looked at by the police. Any issues that you have with your clients is your problem.'

Grimes stood up and handed a file to Rebecca. 'That has all the numbers in it. I have detailed all the impacted accounts, with approximations of amounts missing. With this paperwork, the police should have an easy time with any criminal investigation. Let me know if you need anything more from me. I'm only too happy to come back and assist,' said Grimes, as he left Rebecca's office.

Once he had left, Rebecca picked up the telephone and called the Metropolitan Police.

'I'd like to report a significant fraud. I need to speak to someone in the fraud squad, please.'

CHAPTER 19

Rebecca's Law

Rebecca sat at her enormous desk in her high-backed leather swivel chair, sipping peppermint tea from a bone china cup.

One Friday in July 2017, Rebecca had arrived at her office particularly early, before any of her fourteen strong team had made it into work. She needed to be ready for what was going to be a stressful day, a day that she had looked forward to with glee but also dreaded in equal measure for the last three months.

Since reporting the skimming fraud to the police in April, she had become increasingly frustrated at how long it took them to investigate her report. Especially considering that she had supplied all of the files and numbers that Peter Grimes had given her. At last, they had pulled their finger out and were taking the action she had wanted.

'We need to be completely sure of what we are looking at, Ms Langford,' they had told her.

She sat contemplating the potential fallout of what lay ahead in the day. She just hoped that she would be able to keep anything from appearing in the press or on social media. Still, she doubted she would be able to prevent people from gossiping. Today could start one of the most challenging times for her company, one she needed to mitigate as best she could.

She had decided not to tell Larry anything yet. She was still unsure about what he might do when he discovered the shortfall in his funds.

By 8.45am, Marc Pashley was sitting at his desk, Emelia at hers. The row of desks that separated them were laid out in pairs, full of portfolio managers, investment associates, and Marc Pashley's small audit team.

The office had been full for around half an hour. Typically, everyone was at work by 8.15am, and today was no different. Rebecca Langford sat quietly at her desk, her mobile telephone in her hand as she waited for an expected call. She was looking through the glass at her staff at work. She knew what was about to happen, and she watched as the scene before her unfolded.

The main office door opened, and a well-dressed man and woman walked in. He was tall, with short dark hair, in his late forties and wearing a good quality suit and carrying a slim leather document folder. His partner was a younger woman, quite a bit shorter than he was, emphasised by her wide hips and stocky frame. She had blonde collar-length hair and round gold-framed spectacles and was also wearing a business suit. They both oozed an air of confidence. The woman walked slightly behind the man and seemed to be watching him as if following his lead.

Emelia immediately identified them as police officers, and she felt her skin flush as her mind started to frenzy. She looked down at her computer screen, trying to look as if she had not noticed them walk in. She moved her hand from her keyboard and removed the anti-glare screen from her monitor before adjusting its angle to allow her to see the officers on her screen, mirrored from the reflection on Rebecca's glass office wall. Not a great view, but better than nothing, and better than actually looking up at them.

The tall man reached into his pocket and pulled out his telephone. As he put the phone to his ear, Rebecca answered hers. Emelia could see that they appeared to be talking to each other. *This has been set up. Rebecca knew they were coming this morning.* Emelia's mind was now racing ahead of her thoughts. *My time's up. How did they manage to unpick the software patch?* Emelia had buried her work deep in the system.

The cops walked across the office floor. Emelia sat tight. Running would do no good as the police were between her and the door. Where would she go anyway? They would catch up with her in no time. Running would make her appear as guilty as sin itself, *stay put, sit it out, and hope they are here for some other reason.*

She kept her head down, avoiding looking up. *This is stressful, so stressful,* she thought. Not looking up probably made her look guilty. Everyone else had looked up and wondered what was going on, but the stress was taking over her senses. Her hearing was only listening to the panic inside her head. All the other sounds were now blocked out. Her eyes joined her ears, slowly shutting down, her peripheral vision starting to turn black.

Rebecca pointed her finger and directed the officers to the correct desk while she spoke into her phone.

The suited woman walked over to the desk and leant forward, placing both hands on its edge and then moving the keyboard out of reach. She looked around at the male officer, who gave her the nod.

'We need to speak to you, and we can't do it here,' she said gruffly.

The male officer lifted his hand and firmly placed it on Marc Pashley's shoulder, then nodded again, indicating that it was his colleague's arrest.

'Marc Pashley, my name is Detective Sergeant Williams, and this is Detective Chief Inspector Hannen. I am arresting you on suspicion of fraud, as I believe you defrauded Langford

Investment Management by way of defalcation between May 2004 and today's date,' she cautioned him before asking for a reply.

Pashley looked up at her, he was ashen white, and his hands were trembling. He had broken into a cold sweat, and he felt sick, very sick.

'Defalcation, what do you mean?' was Pashley's reply to the caution.

William's let out a little chuckle before she spoke.

'Skimming the books Mr Pashley, lining your own pockets with money belonging to the clients of Langford Investment Management.'

Seth looked over at Rebecca Langford and nodded his head as he pulled Pashley to his feet.

'Hands behind your back, please,' said Seth, as he turned Pashley around forcefully.

Seth slapped the handcuffs around Pashley's wrists, taking time to push the locking pins in to keep them from over-tightening when Pashley sat in the unmarked police car. He then frog-marched him towards the door and out of the office, holding onto the thick black plastic bar between the cuffs. At the same time, DS Williams followed, carrying Seth's leather folder.

Emelia had almost blacked out; she was shocked and relieved at the same time, the sense of relief inducing an immediate feeling of shame. Her boyfriend had just been arrested. Her head filled her mind with questions. *What the hell had just happened? Why had they taken Marc? Were they even actually police? Who did she say she was? How had they identified Marc as a skimmer? He can't have had any involvement in stealing from Rebecca. I know Marc wouldn't do that.* Her thoughts echoed around her mind as she tried to make sense of it all. She felt so cold, shivering as if she was stood at the North Pole. She was desperately trying not to let anyone else in the office notice her unease. *I look more like a guilty woman than I do a shocked girlfriend.*

She was about to run out of the office and follow the police to confirm what she had witnessed had actually happened when Rebecca Langford's office door opened behind her.

Rebecca was holding an empty glass in one hand and a teaspoon in the other. The office was a babble. Everyone had started gossiping as soon as Marc was out of the office door.

'I told you it was him, bloody greedy druggy.'

'That slippery thieving bastard.'

'Emelia must have known, don't you think?'

'When did the police interview you?'

They all seemed to have some kind of knowledge of what had just happened.

Ting, ting, ting, Rebecca tapped the glass with the teaspoon, the sound brought the room to a hush, and everyone looked in her direction.

'I'll thank you all for stopping your gossiping. Get back to your work, please,' said Rebecca. She spoke quietly to ensure that everyone listened intently.

The office behaved like a single organism. Everyone started work again within an instant, but the air had changed. It was now charged with an atmosphere ready to electrify anyone who walked in.

'And one more thing,' Rebecca spoke again. 'If a word of this hits any social media sites or the press, then those responsible will be dismissed, is that clear?'

Rebecca did not wait for a reply; she knew that they all recognised that she was not joking. She ran a tight ship and demanded obedience from her staff at work as well as at home. She turned to walk back into her office, looking at Emelia as she did, who was still shaking and had turned a ghostly shade of pale.

'Please step into my office Emelia if you'd be so kind.'

Emelia stood up, almost losing her footing as her head began to spin and everything started to turn black. She stole support from her desk to steady herself as her vision returned.

'Sorry, I must have stood up too fast,' she declared, in Rebecca's general direction.

Rebecca glared at her.

'For God's sake, pull yourself together. Get a cup of tea with extra sugar, then into my office. We need to speak.'

Emelia sat on the black leather two-seater sofa in the corner of Rebecca's office. To her surprise, Rebecca's demeanour had made a complete U-turn. She sat down and placed her hand on Emelia's knee, offering comfort as she started to speak.

'Emelia, I'm so sorry, I could not tell you about Marc. The police were concerned that if they interviewed you, you might tell him what was going on, giving him a chance to cover his tracks. They've been investigating him for over two months, looking back at his files. He started to steal from the company shortly after he moved to audit and compliance. The police have been watching his bank account. They'll be at his flat soon to look for any more evidence. I know you two have been together for a while, but he is a bad man, greedy and deceptive. I'd suggest that you—'

'Wait...' Emelia butted in, her head still spinning. 'Marc can't have been skimming money, he—'

Rebecca placed her finger gently on Emelia's lips.

'Emelia, I know it's hard for you to take in, but it's true. The police have all the files from his computer. They can show where some of the money has gone and how it was skimmed. There is still a large hole in some of the higher risk accounts, but the margins are much smaller, and it's harder to establish how and where the money has gone. They will question him about that. Go home, take the rest of the day off, we'll speak again tomorrow.'

Emelia was stunned at Rebecca's supportive approach; it was not what she was used to.

'Thanks, Rebecca,' she said.

'Oh, one more thing,' said Rebecca, as Emelia stood up.

Her voice had returned to its usual harsh and uncompromising tone.

'Yes,' replied Emelia.

'Every employee's computer records, and associated transactions have been downloaded and passed to the police. If anyone was in this with him, rest assured they will get what is coming to them.'

Emelia took the words as a blatant warning rather than a statement; it was reminiscent of the unwritten contract Rebecca once described to her. She picked up her coat and bag on the way out of the office, her mind still putting together what had just happened.

* * *

Seth unlocked the handcuffs while Kath Williams explained the circumstances of the arrest to the burly custody sergeant.

'Thank you, DS Williams. Marc Pashley, I'm authorising your detention at this police station to enable officers to interview you about the alleged offences. You have the right to consult a solicitor, to have someone informed of your arrest, and to consult a copy of the codes of practice relating to your treatment while in police detention. Do you want to exercise any of those rights?' asked the sergeant.

Pashley made no reply. He just stood there staring into space.

'Empty your pockets onto the desk, please,' demanded the woman behind the high custody desk.

She took Pashley's full name, date of birth, and address,

before moving on, asking if he had ever self-harmed, had any medical conditions or used drugs.

'No to all of that stuff, I'm not sure why I'm here. I'm just an investment banker,' he said, declaring his innocence.

Seth searched Pashley.

'What have we got here then, Marc?' asked Seth, holding up a small polythene bag of white powder and nodding at Kath Williams.

'You're also under arrest on suspicion of possession of a controlled drug,' she said, then cautioned him again.

Pashley shrugged his shoulders nonchalantly as he replied.

'I'm fucked already. What difference is a bit of coke really going to make.'

He was taken to a cell, where he sat and waited, before being interviewed.

During his interview, Pashley confessed to skimming money from L.I.M's clients for his personal benefit. He claimed to have used the money to sustain a rampant cocaine habit, spending hundreds of pounds a week, as well as treating his girlfriend to meals out. He had been living beyond his means for years.

Seth and Kath managed to track down and account for just over ninety-six thousand pounds of stolen money. That left a significant financial hole in Rebecca's company funds which remained unaccounted for.

Despite the gap, Seth secured a decision from the Crown Prosecution Service to charge Pashley with the total amount. The forensic accounting report that Rebecca had supplied provided strong evidence to support the fact that he had taken all of the money.

★ ★ ★

Rebecca informed Larry of the missing funds. She explained

how she had robustly involved the police, how they had failed to trace all of the money but had charged Pashley with the crime.

Larry sat in the back of the courtroom and watched as Marc Pashley pleaded guilty to fraud. His barrister tried to mitigate the circumstances, blaming his heavy drug addiction on repeated child abuse that he had suffered at the hands of his stepfather. But the Judge was having none of it. She was very clear that Pashley had abused a position of trust and authority over other people's finances. She sentenced him to serve five years at Her Majesty's pleasure.

Larry Fowler had been in the public gallery throughout the trial. As Pashley was walking away from the dock, Larry caught his attention.

'We'll fuckin' speak later, you can count on that,' Larry mouthed the words silently as he raised his hand and waved.

Pashley was initially sent to Belmarsh Prison, where he was supposed to only serve two months, while he waited for a space to be found for him in a lower category prison. Larry Fowler had other plans, and within a few weeks, Pashley learned that he would serve out his sentence at Belmarsh, where things would be much grimmer.

★   ★   ★

Marc Pashley suffered a merciless existence in Belmarsh. Being a well-spoken white-collar criminal, he was easy pickings for the hardened thugs he was doing time with. Not a day passed without him being punched or spat at. Pashley had been inside for two months when a message was delivered to him from Larry Fowler.

'Hello, pretty boy,' said a gruff voice.

Fifteen inmates were in the tiled shower block, showering

off after exercise.

'Hello…' replied Pashley, unable to hide his nervousness.

He knew something was about to happen.

'The soap jokes… you know it's all bollocks don't you, mate,' another man was now speaking with his mouth only an inch or so from Pashley's ear.

'Well, that's very good to hear,' replied Pashley.

He let out a laugh, trying, but failing to hide the uneasiness in his voice.

Without warning, Pashley felt his arms grabbed and pulled outward from either side of his body, one man holding each wrist tightly. They pulled his arms out and then spun him around to face the white tiles. He could not move, his arms being pulled so hard, he thought they would come off as easily as a spider's legs.

'It's not the soap. It's the fucking shower gel you need to be worried about, pal. There's no fanny in here for me to have any fun with, you bitch,' the voice was behind his head.

His feet were kicked apart as the gruff man pushed up against Pashley. He pushed his erect penis firmly between Pashley's buttocks.

'You are my bitch now, Marc,' whispered the man. 'Big-Gun said that I could help myself. I'm in here for life, and I need to fuck something to keep me sane.'

Then the man slapped a handful of shower gel between Pashley's buttocks and rubbed his hand vigorously up and down in the crack of Pashley's arse. The next thing Pashley felt was a powerful knock to the side of his abdomen, followed by searing pain. He gasped for breath, letting out a stifled groan as he tried to hide the pain, winded by the blow.

'You sound like you're ready. I love a woman that groans,' said the man's voice, before laughing with his mates.

The next thing Pashley felt was the agonising pain of the man entering his anus. Pashley tried to shout out, but the man's hand covered his mouth and stifled his attempts. The other men laughed as the gruff prisoner violently thrust himself back and forth, the pain intensifying with each thrust.

Finally, it stopped. The man let out a sigh of satisfaction and then pulled himself out. Pashley immediately felt what he thought was a second powerful punch to his side and more searing pain. He looked down to see a river of red washing away into the drain of the shower and a white shank laying on the floor, covered in his blood. He had been stabbed twice. As the shock set in, his legs started to fail.

'Guards… help, quickly. Pashley's fucking stabbed himself, stupid little fucker,' one of the men shouted out for help as they let go of Pashley's arms. His legs were unable to take his weight, and he hit the tiled floor with a slap.

Pashley's assailant crouched down to speak to him.

'Big-Gun says that he'll wait for you. He wants his money back, the money the police didn't find, until then, you can be my wife,' he said. Then he slapped Pashley's buttock, stood up and walked away.

Pashley was raped and beaten by the same man every week until he was released from prison, having served three years of his sentence.

CHAPTER 20

US Relations

It was nine months after Seth had managed to get a conviction against Marc Pashley that he would meet Emelia DiSalvo for the first time. He arrived at the very plush residence that is the formal home to the Minister of the Embassy of the United States of America. A large white house in Kensington with security cameras outside and the door attended by two men in suits, who were not just there for show.

'Good evening, and welcome. May I take your name? My colleague will take your coat?'

Seth gave the man his name, which was ticked off the guest list, and then walked into the entrance hall, handing his coat to the second smartly dressed man standing at the door.

Seth had been asked to accompany his boss Superintendent Pete Marsh, to represent their department at the drinks reception. The event was being hosted by the Minister to recognise Anglo-American efforts to tackle organised crime. There were over two hundred people in attendance, all dressed in lounge suits. Most of them from various law enforcement agencies from either side of the Atlantic but based in the United Kingdom.

Seth quickly found his boss in the main reception room.

'This is very nice Pete, thanks for getting me the invite.'

'No problem, Seth, you deserve it, and it's a nice bash. These kinds of things are one of the last perks left in the job, few and far between these days,' said Pete, as he lifted a full glass of white wine. 'Now, it's a social, you're not working, so get yourself a drink and do some networking. You never know, you may find someone who can help you with a job after you retire in a few years, that time is fast approaching Seth.'

Pete smiled and turned, leaving Seth to seek out a drink and some hors d'oeuvres. Seth scanned the room. He recognised a few faces from the Metropolitan Police and some from the National Crime Agency, generally Inspectors and higher-ranking officers. A smartly dressed man holding a silver tray approached Seth.

'Can I get you a drink, sir?'

'Perfect timing, can I have a gin and tonic please, ice and a slice of lime,' replied Seth.

The man walked away, quickly returning with a generously filled gin glass.

'Here you are, sir, enjoy,' he said, handing Seth the drink.

As Seth took hold of his glass and turned to walk into the soirée, he came face to face with an attractive woman standing immediately in front of him. She was a tall olive-skinned woman with long dark hair and a striking bone structure to her face. She wore her trouser suit very well. Seth was struck by her presence, feeling an immediate and magnetic attraction to her. As he stood there, she thrust her hand out to greet him.

'Hi, nice to meet you,' said Seth, as he engaged her in a handshake.

'Hello, Emelia, Emelia DiSalvo,' she said as she shook his hand with her signature firm grip, holding onto Seth's hand a little longer than he had expected.

'Seth Hannen,' he replied, as their hands parted.

'So, what do you do for Anglo-American crime fighting?'

she asked, the corners of her lips turning up as a smile started to make an appearance on her face.

Seth smiled back.

'I work for the Metropolitan Police,' he said.

'Well, I guessed you probably were a policeman or something, but that doesn't really give me much more to go on, does it?' She said, teasing him.

'Oh, nothing that exciting. I've worked on a few things over the years, but recently I oversaw an investigation into a fraud that impacted some high-profile American businessmen and women. Hence my being here today, it really wasn't that special,' said Seth. He purposely played down his capabilities as a detective, not mentioning any of his counter terrorism work.

'And what about you, Mrs... Miss... DiSalvo, what do you do in that regard?' Seth asked, hoping to establish Emelia's marital status more than find out what she had done to deserve an invite to a cocktail party.

Emelia did not disappoint, picking up on Seth's flirtatious manner of questioning.

'Oh, it's Miss DiSalvo, very much a Miss. But really, please call me Emelia, you're not at work now.' She smiled at him again.

'Well, hi Emelia,' said Seth, smiling as he took a sip of gin.

'So, tell me about this fraud investigation. Was it anything juicy?' said Emelia, dodging the second part of his question.

'Oh no, not juicy at all. You may have read about it in the papers though. A few million quid skimmed off the books of a small local investment company in St. James,' said Seth.

Emelia's face brought about the slightest glimmer of recognition in his mind. 'Have we met before? You do look a little familiar,' he asked.

'No, I'm certain I'd remember a handsome police officer if I'd met him before,' replied Emelia, continuing her flirtatious approach.

Emelia felt her face flush a little. She had instantly recognised Seth as one of the police officers that had come into the L.I.M offices and arrested Marc Pashley. 'Juicy enough for the papers...' she said smiling.

'Well, yes, anyway, you didn't tell me what you do for a living and how you got an invite to be here tonight. A conspiracy theorist would think you'd dodged my question,' said Seth playfully.

'Oh, to be honest, I'm a plus one. I've done absolutely nothing to help Anglo-American crime fighting, aside from making up numbers and helping to fill this place. Nothing as exciting as you. Mr... Mrs...?' said Emelia, her smile breaking into laughter.

Seth joined in, and they laughed in concert.

'Well, it's Mr, Mr Seth Hannen, very much a Mr, without a Miss or indeed a Mrs, just me. But really, please call me Seth, you're not at work now...' he said, making sure he flirted back, and that it was noticed.

'Well, Seth, it's very nice to meet you too,' said Emelia, smiling at him again.

'Excuse me, I'm sorry to butt in, but I wonder if I may have a word DCI Hannen?' said a man's voice, joining them from Seth's left.

The man took a step closer, making it clear that he was not going away. A look of annoyance washed over Seth's face. He ignored the interruption and finished talking to Emelia.

'Emelia...' he said, pausing as he passed her his business card. 'Call me... soon I hope?'

'I'd rather you call me really,' said Emelia, avoiding having to share her business card.

She smiled and scribbled something on the back of Seth's card before passing it back to him. Then she held out her hand,

Seth engaged her in the farewell handshake, again caught off guard by that fractionally prolonged grip.

'Bye then, perhaps another time,' he said.

Seth turned his body toward the man that had spoken to him but maintained his gaze with Emelia as she walked away towards the adjacent room.

'DCI Hannen,' said the voice.

'Sorry, yes, nice to meet you,' replied Seth, redirecting his attention to the man that had spoken to him. 'How can I help you?'

'Very smooth Detective Chief Inspector, very smooth indeed.' Seth had been called out for his flirting.

'My name is Xavier Addington. Your charming colleague Pete Marsh pointed me in your direction.'

Xavier was a man in his late fifties. He was well over six foot tall and very slightly overweight, wearing a shimmering blue suit and white shirt, with a flamboyant pink and green tie. He did not have the appearance of a typical civil servant. Despite having a rather extravert appearance, he carried himself very well indeed, and his clothes had a look of quality about them.

'Okay…?' Seth said quizzically.

He was unsure why Pete had sent Xavier over to him. He started to scan the room, hoping to see Pete and summon him to join the conversation, but he could not see him.

'I'm sorry, but I'm not sure why. I'm feeling a bit caught off guard,' said Seth. He thought openness was probably the best approach.

'Ah yes, that was my poor introduction, but I was caught a little by surprise with your previous encounter. It was fascinating to watch though,' quipped Xavier, smiling at Seth.

Seth was now feeling extremely uncomfortable. He was reminded of when he met with his first wife at Ascot races, quickly followed by his fateful encounter with Larry Fowler.

Please don't let this be one of those moments, thought Seth, as he waited for Xavier's next move.

'So… shall we start again,' said Xavier, offering Seth his hand.

'Seth Hannen, DCI Seth Hannen,' replied Seth, as he accepted Xavier's offer of a handshake.

'Xavier Addington, I work for the Home Office. Your boss Pete tells me that you will be retiring from her majesty's constabulary in around two years from now?'

'Yes, that's right, I'll have done my thirty years. I plan to hang up my cuffs,' replied Seth, still unsure where the whole conversation was leading.

'Well, I run a small department in the Home Office, it's closely linked to law enforcement, and we are always looking for chaps like you. Perhaps you'd give me a call when you finish the policing thing?'

'I was planning on taking a few years to decompress, if I'm honest. I want to take some time out and just see where life takes me. But I appreciate the offer, thank you,' answered Seth.

'Well, just in case you change your mind, let's exchange business cards, pop your personal mobile number on there as well, Seth. You never know. You may be tempted back to work,' said Xavier.

Seth took a moment to think, *what the hell, there can be no harm in keeping my options open.*

'Okay, but I'm sure I'll probably just sail off and live somewhere by the sea. There's really nothing to keep me in London after I leave the job.'

Seth pulled out another business card and scribbled his private mobile number on the back before swapping it with Xavier. *Now to find Emelia and resume our chat before we got so rudely interrupted.* He wandered off into the room that he had seen her heading toward. There was no sign of her. So, he spent the next couple of hours chatting and exchanging business cards with various American and British law enforcement officials from countless parts of the establishment. All the while keeping his eyes peeled, just in case he managed to see Emelia DiSalvo.

As Seth walked out of the front door, he reached into his pocket and pulled out the business card that Emelia had written on to see what she had penned. He expected to see a mobile phone number or something. Instead, he found his next appointment.

> Meet me at the Churchill Arms
> at 9.30
>
> See you there E x

Seth looked at his submariner, just past nine. *Perfect timing!* He set off striding confidently towards the Kensington pub.

★ ★ ★

Seth walked into the pub and directly up to the bar.
'Double Plymouth Gin and tonic please, ice and lime.'

Seth ordered his drink and scanned the pub for Emelia, but he could not see her. After his gin had been prepared, he turned and walked towards a small empty table next to a window, just inside the door to the pub. The table had a leather-covered captain's chair on either side. He selected the one that gave him the best view of the door and the bar so that he could see her arrive.

Emelia walked in promptly, just seconds before half past the hour. Seth watched her for a moment as she walked towards the bar, not scanning for Seth at all until she reached it. She still looked as attractive as his first gooey-eyed impressions had led him to believe a couple of hours earlier. She wore a figure-hugging business trouser suit, modest high heels, and a white blouse. She appeared very business-like and ordinary, but she carried herself in anything but an ordinary way. Her long wavy auburn hair was untied and reaching past her shoulders, framing her face beautifully. Seth moved to get up and join her.

'No, stay there. I'll be over in a moment,' she said.

Seth sat back down and lifted a hand to acknowledge her.

'I'll have one of whatever he's drinking,' said Emelia to the barman while looking in Seth's direction.

Seth was quick to offer his hand for a handshake before Emelia had the chance to offer hers. His timing was almost uncomfortable, as Emelia had not quite gotten to the table as he stood with his arm awkwardly outstretched.

Their hands met and engaged in the handshake. It felt different than before, more intimate, still firm, but less formal on both their parts. Emelia still held her grasp a little longer, in fact, quite a lot longer, but so did Seth this time. They smiled at each other before leaning in and delivering a mutually polite kiss to each other's cheek, then finally parting hands and lowering themselves into the leather chairs.

'I really didn't think you'd come,' said Emelia, opening their conversation.

'There was no way I was going to miss a chance of another chat with you,' replied Seth smiling. 'I'm sorry we were so rudely interrupted by that chap.'

'Oh Xavier, I think he managed to work his way around the whole party, butting in to ensure he got a word in with everybody. Those things are all about exchanging business cards and building your network. You never know when someone you meet could be useful to you. If you've lost a card or not linked up with them online somehow, then you'll rue the day you didn't network properly. I'm glad that we networked…'

'Do you network a lot? You sound very well-practised. I thought you were just making up the numbers. Who did you go with?' asked Seth, remembering that she had said that she was a plus one.

'That's two questions, Seth. I thought police officers only asked one question at a time. Otherwise, the answer could be ambiguous.'

Emelia chuckled as she teased Seth.

'Good point. You clearly know how to network, so tell me, what were you doing at an Anglo-American drinks party celebrating international law enforcement?' enquired Seth.

'I don't want to talk about work, it's really not important, and it's so boring really. Let's talk about you Seth, what makes you tick?' said Emelia, again dodging Seth's enquiries. 'Give me two truths and a lie. That's a good way to learn about someone,' she swiftly moved the conversation on.

Seth was hooked and was getting drawn in. He was attracted to Emelia and was easily driven in the direction that she wanted.

'Okay…' Seth thought for a moment, pondering the delivery of his three statements.

'Come on then, out with them,' said Emelia pushing him to speak.

'Number one, the most important woman in my life is my mother. Number two, I'm older than I look and will be a pensioner in a few years. And thirdly, I'm really not interested in taking you for dinner sometime soon,' he smiled and then laughed.

The evening continued with them chatting and getting to know each other while drinking more gin and sharing lots of laughter. Before they knew it, the pub was calling last orders, and it was time to hit the road.

'As much as I'd like to suggest a club, I'm not sure I'd be fit for work in the morning,' said Seth, hoping a nightclub was not actually the next destination.

'Absolutely not my scene at all,' replied Emelia. 'Where's home for you?'

'I'm on the train to Maidenhead, then a short motorcycle ride home, well normally. It'll be a taxi tonight after all that gin. You...?' replied Seth.

'Me, I'm on the Northern line to Highgate. I have a little house there. I'd ask you back for a coffee, but I'm not sure that would be proper, would it?' said Emelia, smiling.

'No, probably not, not on a first date anyway. I like you a lot, but I don't want to fuck it up on the first night. I've had a great time, you're very easy to talk to. Perhaps we can do it again sometime?' said Seth.

He had a good feeling about Emelia. She had ignited a flame in him, one he certainly had no plans to extinguish too quickly. He was wiser now compared to his younger years.

'Thank you, I appreciate your candidness... You're a good man Seth... I think! If you're catching a train from Paddington, I can get the Circle Line from there. We can tube it to Paddington or walk and talk if you like?'

'Let's walk, there's plenty of time, it's dry and only about two and a half miles if we cut through Hyde Park, plus, a little longer in your company sounds perfect to me,' replied Seth.

The pair strolled chatting all the way to Paddington. By the time they reached the station, their hands had joined, walking hand in hand. They politely kissed and said their goodbyes, arranging to see each other again early the following week.

★ ★ ★

The chance meeting with Emelia had set Seth on a path to his third serious relationship. Seth and Emelia dated regularly, visited each other's homes and soon became a couple.

Seth and Emelia's romance blossomed as they found that they had much in common. They both enjoyed keeping fit and would run and cycle together. They even joined a gym and worked out together on the weekends. In the October after they met, they flew to New York for a long weekend, where they enjoyed soaking up art galleries', culture, and the little hidden gems of the city. Of course, Seth had to visit the NYPD and swap some kit he had brought along – badges and a wall plaque.

As time went on, they were living in each other's houses on alternate weekends. Seth introduced Emelia to his mum, and Emelia took Seth to Norfolk for a weekend at her parents' house. She told him all about her childhood, the boarding school and the summer holidays out in the fields with her pony.

Seth had matured. He knew now that relationships needed investment and that you only got back what you put in, so he reigned in his working hours, making sure that Emelia appreciated that she was important to him. They would meet for lunch when he was at work, and despite his protestations, Emelia would often pick up the tab.

'You can get the next one,' she would often say, but then pay for the next lunch anyway.

Seth could not fathom it, he was on reasonably good money as a Detective Chief Inspector, but he almost had trouble keeping up with Emelia when it came to available cash for their socialising.

She continued to dodge questions about her work, putting her expensive lifestyle down to a lucky break on the stock market and a private income from her investment portfolio. Seth did not want to push it, hoping that she might open up about her work life when she was ready to.

PART FOUR

LONG SERVICE
2020

CHAPTER 21

A Night at the Yard

'Mark Pashley gets released today, Larry. I've just had a call from the police witness care unit.'

'Rebecca, that's fuckin' good news, thanks for letting me know,' replied Larry Fowler.

Larry put the phone down before calling Tony Spiller to pass on the news and set the wheels in motion to get his money back from Pashley, or at least make him pay for the theft in some way, shape, or form.

★ ★ ★

The prison gates slid back, and Marc Pashley walked out onto the street outside Belmarsh Prison. He was a free man again, but without a job or anywhere to live.

Having been repeatedly beaten, raped and generally abused while he was inside, he was now a man intent on revenge. Pashley stopped and looked back at the prison gates. They were now closed behind him, like a finished chapter of a book. His life had been wrecked by his cocaine addiction, but he blamed other people, not himself. He was now at the bottom of the social ladder; no more tailored suits or business lunches lay in store. At least he had been allowed to set up his unemployment benefits before he had been released from prison. Still, money would be tight, very tight indeed.

Pashley had a rail warrant in his pocket that would get him back into central London, where he planned a mix of sofa surfing and sleeping rough on the streets. He headed straight for the Docklands Light Railway at Woolwich, where he exchanged his travel warrant for a travelcard, allowing him to move around central London all day.

It took just over an hour for Pashley to get into the city. He walked up the steps of Oxford Circus Underground Station and disappeared into the crowded streets. London was full of smiling shoppers and tourists, all having fun and spending insane amounts of money on designer clothing, new mobile phones, and Swiss watches. Just like he used to do when he was earning – and stealing – good money.

Marc Pashley was still wearing his three-piece suit and brogues from before his time in prison – they had been returned to him upon release. The first thing to sort out was some more appropriate clothing for his new lifestyle. A suit really was not going to be all that useful. Then he would need a decent sleeping bag, a rucksack, and some toiletries for his nights on the streets.

It took him three hours to steal what he needed. The first few attempts at thieving clothes went wrong. He found himself being watched intently by store detectives; he was not used to shoplifting and looked far too furtive and suspicious.

By the time he ditched the more upmarket stores, things got much easier. Although rather messy, he still looked reasonably well dressed in his suit, so he drew less suspicion in the lower end of the market. He chose a large discount clothing store, where he managed to get into the dressing rooms without being checked. Once he had tried the clothes on, he removed the security tags from the clothing with brute force, leaving tiny holes and tears in the garments. Dressed in his new outfit, he put his own clothes onto the hangers, and left them hanging in the dressing room. Pashley walked back out into the street wearing a pair of blue jeans, a black sweatshirt with a t-shirt underneath and a green military-style jacket. The trainers would be easier for street living than the brogues he had left behind.

By six in the evening, he was sitting in a McDonald's restaurant, munching his way through a Big Mac meal. He now had a decent rucksack, which contained a well-insulated sleeping bag, a pay-as-you-go mobile phone, a survival knife, some toiletries, as well as some cash in his pocket. He finished up his food before leaving the restaurant and wandering the streets while the shoppers and tourists disappeared, then he set off for his first night as a rough sleeper.

Pashley spent three weeks sleeping on the streets, trying to work out how to exact his revenge. His days were monotonous and boring. He used the little money he had to buy his main meal each day, which would usually be breakfast. He ate in cafés or fast-food restaurants and collected loyalty tokens and stamps to save up for a free meal. Lunch would usually be a mix of food given to him while he sat on the street begging, or sometimes remnants from discarded fast-food packets in dustbins.

After he ate in the evenings, he would sit and wait for darkness to arrive and the crowds to dissipate so that he could roll out his sleeping bag and get some sleep in a bus shelter or a shop doorway. He used old, flattened cardboard boxes as a makeshift bed. Each night was worse than the last, they grew colder, and he became more and more hungry, craving simple food to fill his belly.

With the loneliness of street living came the early stages of mental illness for Pashley. It started with long and detailed conversations with himself, spoken out loud as he walked the streets. When he was not talking to himself, his mind would replay the assaults he suffered in prison. He would alter the facts to allow himself to be victorious and fight off the prison bullies. However, they would still overpower him and win. The only way he could quiet his mind was to cause himself physical harm. He would either use his knife or pieces of broken glass, usually pushing them into his thighs and twisting them into his flesh. The resultant pain would distract his mind. As his desperation grew, so did the feeling of having been wronged. Pashley needed someone to pay for his pain.

★ ★ ★

It was now six weeks since his release from Belmarsh. At just after six o'clock one Friday evening, Pashley sat on the steps to a building in Trafalgar Square eating a packet of sandwiches that a passing woman had been kind enough to buy him. He was dishevelled and unshaven, with an untidy beard and in desperate need of a haircut.

He sat watching passers-by hurrying home from work or travelling towards their Friday night drinking scene. He sat wondering how to get himself out of his situation, wishing that he was back in prison, where the meals were hot and free, and the beds were warm. As afternoon turned into evening, Pashley sat blind to the passers-by that would stare at him. Some would toss fifty pence, or even a pound coin, into his upturned cap that sat on the pavement in front of him. He would soon have enough for breakfast the following day.

As he sat there, he drifted into his routine moment of self-pity, thinking about who was responsible for his situation, looking to blame anyone other than himself.

It was seven o'clock when fate would interrupt Pashley's self-absorption, a two-pound coin clattered into his hat as a man and woman walked by.

'Get yourself a coffee, mate.'

He had heard that line so many times.

'I get free coffee every day, pal. There are cafés that allow people to put one in the pot for the homeless, but thanks anyway,' said Pashley, mumbling to himself.

For no apparent reason, he looked up and saw the man walking away, hand in hand with a woman.

Marc started talking, mumbling out loud to himself.

'Surely not, is that Emelia?'

'Certainly looks like her, Marc,' he replied back to himself.

'It does indeed! What are the chances?'

'It is her. It is Emelia.'

He quickly rolled up his sleeping bag and stuffed it into his rucksack before running down the street after the couple, quickly catching them up.

'It has to be her.'

'Well, she walks the same, it might be.'

'Marc, it is her. Look at her hair; it's the same.'

'You're right. It's Emelia for sure.'

'The bitch, you need to do something Marc, she needs to pay.'

'She will, I'll make her pay, she took way more money than me, and I did time in prison,'

'Sod the time, Marc, it's her fault you were fucked up the arse every week.'

'You're right, Emelia caused that. She needs to pay.'

After his arrest, she had never contacted or visited him in prison. Emelia had not attempted any communication with him in any way whatsoever. He hated her for that.

Pashley followed the couple from Trafalgar Square and along Whitehall towards Westminster. As they rounded Parliament Square and joined Victoria Street, he ran up behind them before slowing to a brisk walk and overtaking them. He walked ahead and dived out of sight into a shop doorway. Then he immediately exited, stopping briefly as if to get his bearings.

As he stood there, he saw Emelia walk past, hand in hand with Seth Hannen.

'Jesus H. Christ Marc, did you see that?'

'Yeah, talk about rubbing salt into the wound mate, the cow is only seeing that fucking cop.'

'That's it then payment time, don't you think?'

'Yeah, Yeah, let's go and sort this out.'

Pashley felt a rage bubbling inside, taking control of him. His hand dived into his pocket, reaching for the survival knife he had stolen. It was not until he had already pulled it out and moved his other hand to open the blade that he realised what he was doing. He quickly folded it back away and put the knife back into his pocket before resuming his surveillance.

'Not yet, Marc, pick the right moment.'

'You're right. I don't want to end up back in prison.'

'No way, better wait, just bide your time.'

Pashley now had a sense of purpose again. A feeling that had not touched his senses since before he was arrested. It felt good. He felt alive again. Alive but angry.

★ ★ ★

Seth and Emelia walked into the Feathers Pub in Westminster. As they entered, the whole place erupted with cheers and clapping.

'Yay, here he is.'

'The top man is here.'

'For he's a jolly good fellow.'

As they joined the party, Seth turned to Emelia.

'You knew about this, didn't you?' he asked, already knowing the answer.

Emelia just smiled and gave him a huge hug. Seth had thought they were having a private drink to celebrate the end of his policing career, but Emelia had been in on the planning with Pete Marsh. Her job was to get Seth there without raising his suspicions.

The pub was busy, full of serving and retired police officers, all keen to buy Seth a drink.

'What'll it be, Seth, old boy?' was the question asked throughout the evening.

'Plymouth Gin and tonic,' was Seth's repeated reply.

There must have been over two hundred colleagues from throughout Seth's career that had come to say farewell. Even Jonesy and his old single quarter's buddy Mark Rivett had turned up. Jonesy had retired and then gone back into the police as a well-respected civilian, making sure new officers understood how to gather and present evidence, mentoring and advising them on file preparation. Mark had retired after making Inspector. He ended up running the Operations Team as he had hoped, cutting the numbers of officers deployed to events and replacing them with private security firms, just like he and Seth had talked about years ago.

Of course, Superintendent Pete Marsh was the compere for most of the evening. Seth felt genuinely humbled and slightly embarrassed by the turnout.

Nobody noticed the dishevelled homeless man sat keeping warm in the corner of the bar, mine sweeping the odd drink or plate of food that had been left unattended. Pashley took the opportunity to remove a couple of wallets from unattended coats and pocket a few quid in cash.

'That's tomorrow's lunch sorted.'

'Good going, Marc, now get back to the job at hand.'

He sat back down and watched the proceedings, keeping his watchful eye on Emelia and Seth, trying to control his dark cocktail of jealousy, resentment, and anger.

The evening rushed by, farewell speeches, the giving of gifts and finally the hugs and goodbyes.

'Keep in touch, Seth and enjoy doing what you've not had time to do, and look after that woman of yours; she's a keeper,' said Pete Marsh, who was the last of the group to leave.

The pub was now almost empty.

'Thanks, Pete, I really appreciate tonight, it was very humbling. Take care mate,' said Seth, as he shook Pete's hand firmly, then he turned to Emelia. 'Thanks, gorgeous, that was a great night.'

After gathering up his leaving gifts, they kissed and headed out of the door not far behind Pete.

'I hope you'll remember it in the morning, let's get back to the hotel and get you tucked up in bed,' said Emelia.

She took Seth by the hand and led him back towards their hotel.

Pashley, now with a full stomach for the first time in weeks and slightly drunk for the first time in years, followed them out of the pub. He was careful not to be noticed, staying close enough to see where they were going but far enough back to be out of immediate sight if they turned around.

Seth and Emelia walked into the lobby of the Great Scotland Yard Hotel. Emelia collected their electronic key from reception and took Seth to their room.

As soon as they left the lobby, Pashley walked into the hotel.

'Hi, I have a room booked for tonight,' said Pashley to the receptionist.

'Okay, Sir, what name is the booking under?'

'Mmm…Marc…' said Pashley, his words stalled. He had failed to think ahead.

'Mr Marc, what?' asked the receptionist, not sounding convinced.

'Langford, Marc Langford,' replied Pashley.

There was a pause while the receptionist checked the computer system.

'I'm sorry, Mr Langford, but there doesn't seem to be a booking in your name.'

'Oh, that's strange, I'm with the Hannen Party. We've just been at his police retirement bash in Westminster. I had specifically booked the room next to Emelia DiSalvo and Seth Hannen. This really is not what I'd expected from an establishment like this.'

Pashley had kicked into gear.

'Ah, okay, you're with Miss DiSalvo. I can call her, they've just returned. I'm sure she'll confirm,' said the receptionist, warming to Pashley.

'I'm not with Emelia, well not anymore! Anyway, I'd rather you didn't disturb them. Me and the chaps from the station have a surprise for Seth in the morning. Is the room available or not?' asked Pashley.

'It is, sir. I can book you in if you like. Do you want to settle now or in the morning?' asked the receptionist.

'The morning, I think, I need to speak to Emelia about who's covering the bill, but either way, the morning will be splendid,' answered Pashley, hoping that he would not be asked for a credit card.

'Okay, Mr Langford, I'll pop a note against the room. Here is your key, the Wi-Fi code is on the back. Oh, and please feel free to use the minibar. I just need an address for the system, please.'

Pashley gave an address that he was not sure even existed, then took the key and walked towards the stairs.

'Oh, what time is breakfast served, my man?' he called out as he walked away, feeling very chuffed with himself.

'Breakfast is served from seven, Mr Langford, sleep well.'

Pashley let himself into his room, undressed, showered and then set to making himself a drink from the minibar. His room was at the end of the corridor. He had only one neighbour, the room that housed Seth and Emelia.

Pashley heard movement in the room next door. He moved as close as he could, pushing his ear against the wall. As he spoke quietly to himself.

'They're having rampant sex.'

'She's shagging with you right here, Marc.'

'I know how fucking rude is that?'

'You used to fuck her, she was yours once, Marc.'

'Do you think I was better than the cop?'

'Probably not, by the sound of it anyway!'

His mind was unrelenting, firing images into his head, goading him, slowly boiling his anger like a kettle. He imagined them naked on the bed, Emelia's body writhing under Hannen the cop.

'No, she'd be on top.'

'Yeah, she likes being on top, well she did with you, Marc.'

'She looks good on top too.'

'Yeah, but you used to cum too fast Marc, he's lasting longer than you ever did.'

'Fuck off, that's not true. I gave her what she wanted.'

Pashley painted a picture in his head, thinking back to when he had been Emelia's lover – when she had been his. He pushed himself up against the wall, listening intently and imagining himself next door in place of Seth, caressing her beautiful body and kissing her lips. Pashley began to feel aroused and started to rub himself through his jeans, unable to take his thoughts away from the scene that his mind had created. He could just make out their voices and their pleasure laden moans. He pushed himself harder against the wall and heard Seth groaning and then Emelia's voice.

'I love you, Seth.'

That was it. He could not listen anymore; Pashley broke away from his daydream and his emotions turned instantly from desire to rage. Uninvited thoughts ravaged his mind, taking him back up against the wall in the shower in prison, only this time his mind had put Seth in the role of the burly prisoner pushed up behind him. He pulled himself away from the wall, throwing his glass across the room and then upturning the coffee table, sending a lamp crashing to the floor.

'No, you bastards, stop tormenting me,' shouted Pashley through his disturbed rage.

'What was that?' said Seth.

'No idea, a drunken argument next door I'd imagine, ignore it and keep your mind on me,' replied Emelia.

Pashley picked up the pieces of glass. He pushed one of the fragments into his thigh and slowly twisted it into his flesh, watching the blood appear, oozing through and soaking the blue denim of his jeans. Once he had gouged two more holes in his leg, he put the pieces of glass into the bin and tidied the room.

He took another shower, washed and dried his wounds, and then shaved off his beard before climbing into bed. He lay still trying his hardest to banish the image of Emelia and Seth engaged in their passionate naked lovemaking. Once his mind cleared, he began thinking about how he would exact his revenge. *Tomorrow, tomorrow will be my day, a day for me.*

★ ★ ★

The morning came quickly. Marc Pashley had been awake since five o'clock, lying in bed still fixated on Emelia and Seth in the room next door. He imagined them curled up asleep together, naked and smelling of sex. He laid back on the bed and masturbated, imagining it was him in bed with Emelia.

By ten to seven, he was shaved and showered again, his hair brushed and looking comparatively tidy. Then he made his way downstairs, checking briefly to see if the receptionist had changed since the previous evening.

Where the male receptionist had sat, a young brunette woman was now in his place. *That's a relief.* Pashley took advantage of a hearty full breakfast before moving to the lobby with a fresh cup of coffee. He sat down, choosing a seat in the corner so that he could see the reception and the doors out to the street. Reading the free newspaper and enjoying the temporary comfort of the hotel, Pashley settled in to wait for Emelia and Seth to come downstairs.

As the lobby started to get busy, Pashley noticed two men sat on the other side of the atrium. Both were well built, one with a particularly bent nose, the other with not much hair. Both were dressed in dark clothing and looked like nightclub doormen. They were drinking coffee in silence, the larger man reading a newspaper, while the other seemingly stared into space. Their interest piqued whenever anyone walked up to the reception desk.

Pashley spoke to himself.

'*They must be some of Hannen's mates from last night.*'

'*Police officers?*'

'*Yeah, don't look at them, Marc. You'll get clocked for sure.*'

He did not need to get arrested for failing to pay his hotel bill and then end up having his parole breached. He shuffled his chair, so he was obscured from the men's view, then he picked up his cup and sipped his coffee while he waited.

CHAPTER 22

30 Years Done

'Wakey, Wakey sleepy head, coffee's here,' Seth felt his face being gently stroked. It was just past 10.30am, and he had not expected to sleep in quite so late, paying the late checkout fee was definitely the right idea. *Well done, Emelia.*

'How does it feel then, no longer being a cop?' asked Emelia, placing the cup of hot black coffee that she had just made onto his bedside table. Seth's brain slowly started to stir, pushing his usual waking image to the back of his mind.

No, he was no longer a cop. Just over thirty years of loyal service to Her Majesty had passed by so quickly. He had enjoyed a successful career in the police force, challenging at times, but it had turned out alright in the end.

His career had been tinged with the sadness of a private life that seemed to lurch back and forth at the behest of the stresses of his job. Those stresses had destroyed not one but two marriages, both of which Seth regretted losing, especially the first because he had completely missed his son growing up. He had not been there for him when his teenage years had taken him down the wrong path, putting them on opposite sides of the law for a while.

For the past couple of years or so, things had felt right for the first time in so long. Emelia had been the key. Before they met,

Seth had imagined that he would end up retiring from the job still single. He had assumed that he would end up surfing the illustrious dating websites, swiping left or right, trying to work out which of the women had the least baggage. Or which of them would not eat into his soon to mature police pension. Seth liked that Emelia was almost ten years his junior; it made him feel younger. She was a perfect fit. She had no children, was financially and personally independent, and had never until now found the right man. There was no annoying ex-husband in the background, constantly popping up in discussion or haunting the relationship. Everything was well in Seth's world.

Seth pulled himself up in bed, still groggy from a night of old stories and gin – lots of gin. *Why did I not just drink beer?* he thought to himself, sticking to double Plymouth Gin and tonics all night was now taking its toll on his ability to think straight.

'I'm not actually sure how it feels to not be a cop yet Emmy, I think I may still be a bit pissed,' declared Seth, answering her question.

Seth was the only person Emelia had ever allowed to call her Emmy. No one else had ever managed to get away with it or indeed get emotionally close enough for her to be comfortable with it. She was Emelia to everyone, but it felt right being Emmy for Seth.

Seth glanced over to the other side of the bed to see Emelia wearing his pyjama top, an NYPD t-shirt that he bought when they had visited New York. He could see the shape of her breasts pushing against the grey fabric.

'I'm sure I was wearing that when we went to bed!' he looked at her with a wry smile on his face.

'Are you telling me you remember nothing of last night?' she quipped back at him, playfully prodding him in the ribs with her fingers, then she spider walked her hand lower and pulled the cord undone on his cotton pyjama bottoms.

'It started out on you but ended up on me!' said Emelia, laughing playfully as she leant in close and whispered into his right ear. 'Need a reminder, old man?' She bit his ear lobe, then moved back away to pick up her coffee.

Seth loved that they still flirted with each other in this way. It kept things light.

He had not planned on having a leaving do at all. But having so many people together at The Feathers had been fantastic. He felt that he had said goodbye to policing properly. It was now time to start a new chapter. As he sipped his coffee, Emelia snuggled into his side, placing her hand on his chest.

'I am so very proud of you, Seth,' she said, looking up at his face and catching his eye. 'Last night, I learnt so much more of who you are and what you've done at work over the years. All those people coming along is a real testament to the great policeman and friend you are to them, Pete's speech was just perfect.'

Seth reached down to the pile of clothes beside the bed and pulled out two sheets of stapled and folded paper from the back pocket of his jeans. He read the handwritten note, scripted in black fountain pen ink in Pete's unmistakably flamboyant handwriting.

In case you get too pissed and wake up unable to remember old boy, and don't spend all of that lump sum too quickly! All the best, Pete.

That was typical of Pete Martin, he was a great boss, as well as a very good friend and confidant, but he would have hated the idea of Seth not remembering what he had said in his speech. He was a bit vain like that. Seth needed a reminder in any case. *How well he knows me,* thought Seth as he unfolded the slightly crumpled sheets of paper. He started to read through the speech that Pete had delivered at the end of the evening.

Seth Joined Chad Valley Police in 1990 at the age of 18...

Chad Valley Police is what some Met officers call Thames Valley Police, in a friendly yet slightly provocative way. Referring to the counties-based force as a toy town compared to the hustle and bustle of the capital's police service.

Having worked in both forces, Seth knew that this was not true at all. He had an equally challenging time in Slough and Reading as he did in London. With the main difference being fewer available resources in the counties, his Thames Valley colleagues often had a tougher time. He gave up this argument long ago, realising that it did him no favours with his Met colleagues.

Seth read the rest of the speech, slowly taking in what Pete had said about his distinguished career. Pete had briefly outlined some of Seth's roles in Thames Valley, including his short spell on the surveillance team, before moving to investigations on CID. Then he went into a little more detail about the Met part of his career. He spoke about the serious crime investigations and his work on SO15 working on intelligence-led operations to combat terrorism in London and the wider United Kingdom. Pete commented on Seth's work following the 7/7 terror attacks in London, being careful not to disclose anything too detailed about what Seth and his team had been assigned to.

As Seth read lines like *beyond the call of duty* and *intrepid determination to see justice done,* a tear welled up in his eye. It was really over. The job he had sold his soul to had come to an end. All those years, long shifts, late nights, and giving up friends and opportunities to put the job first had led to one last piss up with the great people he had worked with, a speech, and some gifts.

Seth had a small box of stuff that now represented the sum of his career, including a set of six gin glasses, a framed set of badges and epaulettes from his hardly worn Chief Inspectors' uniform, and a battered and engraved stainless-steel Zippo lighter. The lighter was engraved with 'DCI Seth Hannen, 30 Years' Service' on one side and the Met Police coat of arms on the other. Despite feeling strangely familiar, the lighter puzzled Seth as he had not smoked for many years now.

As he sat quietly contemplating the ride he had been on, he realised that Emelia had fallen asleep. Her head was resting on his chest and her hand on his stomach, the tips of her fingers pushed just under the corded band of his pyjama bottoms.

His mind wandered as he held back the tears. Had the job been worth destroying his personal life twice? He thought back to Paula, his first wife. She was in some ways very similar to Emelia, extremely affectionate, with a down to earth approach to life. She had dark hair and dark eyes as well.

Seth looked down at Emelia again, her breath caressing the hairs on his chest as she breathed deeply. He really hoped that he had got it right this time. With no police career taking up all of his attention, he was sure that he could make this relationship work. If he could just keep the ten-year age gap from feeling bigger as he got older.

Seth's mind then briefly took his thoughts to his second marriage and to Charlotte. That one had been a total fuck-up on his part. The fights, the arguments, and his reaction to the constant appearances of her ex-husband on the scene.

His mind shifted quickly back to the present and how lucky he was to come out of two failed marriages with his pension intact and a beautiful woman by his side – a woman who he loved so much. He hoped that in time he could develop some kind of relationship with his son Josh, even if it was only through Facebook or text messages to begin with.

Seth slowly pulled the duvet back and slid from the bed, trying not to wake Emelia. It was now nearly eleven o'clock, and they had to check out by midday. He and Emelia had not discussed plans for his first day as a police pensioner. He imagined it would include a classy lunch in town, a leisurely walk around some of the London sights, as well as visiting a few places that were significant to his career.

He walked over to the ensuite bathroom, looking back at Emelia as she turned over in bed. He could see the creases of her bottom as the NYPD T-shirt rode up on her body. *God, she's beautiful*, he thought to himself as he dropped his pyjama bottoms on the floor.

The shower was hot, steaming up the ensuite bathroom with a thick fog-like mist, making it hard to see anything. Seth could just make out the shape of Emelia standing outside the shower door, she was now naked, and he hoped that she would join him in the shower.

Emelia took hold of the shower door handle and slid the glass door to one side before stepping in and putting her arms around Seth's body. She pushed her fingernails into his buttocks, making him wince with the agreeable pain. They kissed and hugged, both in a happy place, enjoying the moment for a while. His hands on her hips and hers on his, neither of them moving, just allowing the hot water to caress their bodies as they stood still, feeling the love that they had for each other.

Neither of them could have known that the day was about to turn sour.

★ ★ ★

Seth and Emelia walked out of the lift and across the lobby to the reception desk. Seth wore a clean pair of blue denim jeans with a red and blue embroidered leather polo belt and shoes without socks, as summer boat shoes should be worn. His blue and red check shirt was neatly tucked in with his top two buttons unfastened at the collar. His sleeves were rolled up to reveal his father's old military Rolex Submariner. The watch was a valuable collector's piece, but Seth had no interest in its value.

Emelia was also dressed well. She wore tight white jeans that hugged her figure perfectly, turned up at the bottom to show her ankles, and a loose-fitting pale blue thin cotton jumper. Her designer tortoiseshell sunglasses were perched atop her head, ready to drop into place as soon as the sun came out. She wore flat brown leather shoes, not her usual heels, in preparedness for the day she had planned, wandering around London with Seth.

Marc Pashley put his coffee cup down and watched them intently. He felt the resurgence of rage he had experienced the previous night welling up inside him. He was flooded with emotion, unable to regulate his feelings in any way at all. As Pashley watched, so did the two men on the other side of the lobby. They were devoid of expression, keeping their beady eyes on Seth and Emelia, as well as on Pashley, all three watching and preparing to pick up the follow.

As the receptionist leaned forward to hand the hotel bill to Seth, Emelia quickly snatched it away. The startled receptionist almost lunged to grab it back.

'This one's on me... The next one can be on your pension,' said Emelia, looking at Seth out of the corner of her eyes and smiling at him.

'Do you have any plans for the day?' asked the receptionist politely

'Well, as a matter of fact, we do. We're off for lunch at a

lovely restaurant in Old Street, then we'll just potter around the city, letting our mood take us. Today is a special day,' replied Emelia, smiling at Seth again.

'That sounds lovely,' said the receptionist, as she handed Emelia's Coutts' banking card back to her.

These moments always amused Seth. He still wondered how she managed to live a life of relative luxury yet not have to go to work every day.

'Do you mind if we leave our bags here and pick them up later?' asked Seth.

'Not at all, I'll call the porter,' replied the receptionist.

They left their overnight bags and walked towards the door hand in hand, briefly glancing at each other and smiling. Seth smiled inwardly too as he thought to himself, *retirement is going to be good, very good indeed.*

As they left the lobby, Pashley was quick to his feet, grabbing his rucksack and running over to the reception desk.

'I'm so sorry, I've just missed my friends. I'm supposed to be meeting them for lunch,' he said to the receptionist.

'Who are your friends? Perhaps I can help,' she replied.

'Mr Hannen and Miss DiSalvo, I don't suppose they mentioned where they were going... did they?' he asked.

The receptionist hesitated for a second and then decided that since Pashley knew their names, he must be a friend. It would be alright to say where they were going.

'They're off to Old Street for lunch, sir,' she replied, still feeling a little uneasy about telling him.

Pashley hurried out onto the street, confident in the knowledge that if he lost Emelia and Seth, he would be able to look for them in Old Street. As he left, he failed to notice the other two men get up and follow him through the door and out onto the street.

CHAPTER 23

Waiting

Seth and Emelia walked out into the busy London Street; it was already fast approaching lunchtime. They walked directly towards Shoreditch, where Emelia had booked a table for two at The Clove Club on Old Street, one of London's highly rated modern European restaurants. They occasionally broke hands as they dodged tourists with heads down on their phones or local workers making lunchtime dashes, their hands quickly came back together again. Seth gave Emelia's hand an extra squeeze each time their palms met.

Pashley followed, keeping between twenty and thirty paces behind Seth and Emelia, closing the gap as they approached junctions so as not to lose sight of them. Behind Pashley, the two other men followed on, another twenty paces further back.

'So, I've talked lots about getting to this moment, Emmy, but not much about what's next for us. It's kind of crept up quickly over the last six months, and I've not really mentioned what I'd like to do... us to do,' said Seth, looking at Emelia.

Emelia looked back at him quizzically.

'I'm getting the idea you are about to suggest something big,' she lifted her eyebrows as she finished her sentence. *Please don't spoil what we have by proposing now Seth, I'm not ready for that, not yet.* Emelia was willing him to say something other than anything to do with marriage or even moving in together. She liked what they had now.

'Well, I was thinking that things are pretty hectic, what with me still living down in Maidenhead and you up in Highgate. We spend as much time travelling between our homes as we do with each other,' said Seth, not picking up on Emelia's mood.

He felt ready to take their relationship to the next stage, and for him, that meant moving in together. He would be happy using either of their homes to do that.

'Let's talk about it after lunch, it could be quite complicated, and I don't want our relationship to change too quickly,' said Emelia, evading the subject.

Seth's mood dropped a little, he had hoped that she would immediately agree, and the love he felt would be reciprocated with an agreement to live together.

As the couple walked, chatting and holding hands, they failed to notice that they were being watched. Followed by the quick-stepped Marc Pashley, who was so interested in his quarry that he did not see the two men behind him. Pashley walked with obsessive purpose, occasionally talking out loud to himself.

'That was me once. Bitch,' he muttered to himself as he watched them laughing and holding hands, apparently without a care in the world.

Seth and Emelia walked into The Clove Club.

'Table for two, in the name of Emelia, Emelia DiSalvo,' she squeezed Seth's hand as she spoke to the maître d' looking after the front of house.

'If you'd like to follow Louise, she'll show you to your table,' came the reply.

As Seth and Emelia walked into the restaurant, the young maître d' turned and watched them. To be more accurate, he watched Emelia. His eyes were fixed on Emelia's behind. He had no interest in Seth, *those white jeans, and that arse!* Seth had noticed the young man's wandering eye, and felt a fierce alpha male jealousy as well as feeling slightly smug.

'Excuse me mate, any chance of a table?' The maître d's gaze was interrupted by the two men that had sat in the hotel lobby opposite Pashley.

'Have you booked gentlemen?' he asked.

'No, should we have,' the larger man with the bent nose replied.

'Not at all. Lunchtime is usually fine. I can probably fit you in. Give me a couple of minutes.'

Seth and Emelia took their seats at their table, choosing to sit side by side rather than opposite each other. They both liked to people-watch, and The Clove Club provided a great view of the kitchen staff working away behind a peacock blue tiled servery. They would be able to chat and watch with interest as their food was prepared.

The two burly men sat behind Emelia and Seth, one with a view of them and the other with a view of the door.

While Seth and Emelia were sitting down, Marc Pashley took his seat at the Bike Shed Motorcycle Club, a restaurant hidden under the railway arches immediately next to the Clove Club. He sat outside at one of the street-side tables so that he could see if they left and joined the street again. With a pint of beer in his hand and food on the way, he was prepared to wait as long as it took for them to come back out. He would sit and bide his time, enjoying as many beers as he could afford to buy with last night's stolen cash while he waited until the opportunity to make his move presented itself.

* * *

A couple of hours passed before Seth and Emelia walked out of The Clove Club. They turned left and walked directly away from the Bike Shed Motorcycle Club towards Old Street underground station. Pashley was lucky to see them leave. He had consumed one beer too many and had literally just returned from the toilet and stuck his head out onto the street to check on Seth and Emelia.

He ran after them to get close enough to maintain his follow, his stride slightly affected by the alcohol. As he ran past the Clove Club, he ran straight into the two men from the hotel lobby.

'Sorry mate,' he said, as he regained his balance and continued his jog. The two men looked at each other before then joining the foot convoy.

'How was that then? Did you have a good lunch?' asked Emelia as she took Seth's hand in hers.

'Perfect Emmy, just perfect, thank you.'

'Good, what do you want to do now?'

'Well, I'd really like to get across town and visit the National Police Memorial if I'm completely honest. I don't want to be in any way glum or anything, but after thirty years' service, it feels kind of right to pay a little respect to those that did not make it all the way through their career,' said Seth, hoping that Emelia would be okay with the idea.

'It's your day Seth, if that's what you want to do, then let's do it. I'm just happy to be able to do it with you.'

Inside, Emelia thought it was a little odd of Seth to want to see the memorial. His office was not far from it, so he could have gone to see it any day of the week.

'Old Street to Moorgate, then to St. James Park is probably the best route,' said Seth.

He knew the underground network pretty well.

'No, it's more changes, but if we get it right, Old Street, to London Bridge, to Westminster, then St. James Park will be slightly quicker,' replied Emelia. She never liked to be outdone.

Pashley stayed far enough behind them so that if he needed to, he could dive into a doorway or dart down another street to avoid being seen. He had waited some time for this moment, and he was not going to let it get away from him. As Pashley walked, he allowed his thoughts to drift back to his time in Belmarsh. The memories of the degradation and the bullying he had been through started to bring the red rage back into his head. *Today I repay you for my suffering.*

Pashley reached into his coat pocket and felt the handle of the survival knife. The opportunity to use it at the leaving do had not presented itself, there were too many cops around, albeit off duty, but all the same, it was way too risky. If he had made his move there, he would have ended up back inside in a flash. Now he hoped that he would find the moment to pull the knife in a busy street and sink it in, in one blow, and then just walk on by before anyone knew what had happened. He had been stabbed in prison with a shank, and he knew that initially, it would feel like a heavy punch. By the time the pain had been realised as a knife wound, he would be away, disappearing into the crowd. He fiddled with the knife in his pocket, pulling the locking blade part of the way out, then letting it flick back into the handle under its own pressure.

Pashley walked behind Seth and Emelia, speeding up enough to slowly gain on them, getting closer and closer with each step that he took. He was now about eight paces behind them. He just needed to time it right.

Seth and Emelia turned into the tube station, quickly followed by Pashley. Seth pulled out his wallet, ready to swipe his Oyster Card on his way into the underground. He and Emelia joined separate queues for the turnstiles, still stood side by side.

'I'll race you,' said Emelia, smiling at him.

'You're on, but you'll lose.' Seth smiled back.

Pashley moved in closer, pushing the blade of his knife through the inside of his coat pocket and out into the open, his hand still concealed in his pocket. His heart rate upped its pace as he thought about what it would feel like to push the knife through the fabric and then into skin. He lunged as he took a huge step forward, moving the exposed blade furiously onward towards its target. As his arm extended, his coat opened. The knife was inches from its target. He raised his left hand to grab Seth's collar, intent on pulling him back onto the blade. Then just as he was about to make contact, he felt a huge pressure on his neck, followed by an enormous downward weight. At the same time, his legs left the ground. As he fell, his left hand groped for support, he took hold of Seth, and they both tumbled backwards. The pair landed on the ground in a heap, Seth's wallet falling from his hand. As Emelia turned to see what had happened, she felt herself being pulled forcefully from the side and away.

'Seth,' she called.

'I'm okay,' answered Seth

Pashley rolled away, grabbing the wallet as he got back up and onto his feet. He ran out of the station and back onto the street, not stopping to look back. He just ran as fast as his legs would take him, sprinting with all of his might.

'What the hell happened there,' said Seth, as he got back to his feet.

'You alright, mate?' asked another man in the queue.

'Emmy, where are you?' shouted Seth.

He looked to either side, the queues of people staring at him, unsure of what had just happened. There was no sign of Emelia. She had simply vanished. Then he jumped the turnstile, frantically searching to locate her, but to no avail.

'Emmy...' he called out again, but there was no reply. Emelia was nowhere to be seen. She was gone.

Seth was quickly grabbed by the two underground attendants.

'Oi, you either swipe in and pay, or you don't ride the train,' one of them shouted at Seth.

'It's okay, I'm a police officer.'

Seth reached for his police warrant card in his jacket pocket. It took a nanosecond for him to remember that he was not a police officer anymore. There would be no warrant card and badge waiting to be pulled out to prove his identity.

'Sorry, I was a police officer yesterday, but I've just retired,' he said, knowing that he sounded pretty lame.

'Alright, mate, of course you were. Off you go then… get out unless you swipe and pay.'

Not only was his warrant card not in his pocket, but his wallet was missing. *I must have dropped it in the tumble,* he thought.

'My wallet did you see my wallet?' asked Seth of the two men now looking at him in disbelief.

'Here we go… no, I've not seen your bloody wallet. Out, now mate,' said one of the attendants.

The other man flashed the barrier with his staff card and pushed Seth through as it opened. Seth stood on the street side of the barriers looking between the feet of the travellers, frantically looking for his wallet. He put his hand inside his pocket one more time, just in case. No wallet, just a small piece of paper. He pulled it out and unfolded it to find a message scrawled in block capitals.

CALL THE POLICE AND

EMELIA DISALVO DIES

BEST REGARDS BIG-GUN

Seth must have tried searching the underground station at

least five times. He asked the staff if he could view the CCTV and then tried to do the same at one of the buildings opposite the entrance, each time getting short shrift. Seth walked the length of the road and spoke to the shop and restaurant owners all the way along one side, retracing his steps as far as The Clove Club, asking at each shop and hotel if he could look at footage from their security camera's. Every time he was met with the same negative response or a request for his police identification, which of course, he could not provide. Then he repeated the exercise on the other side, all the way back to the entrance to the underground.

Eventually, he walked into a small bookshop immediately opposite the station. It was called the Murder Club, and it specialised in crime-related books. *Well, that's ironic,* thought Seth as he pushed the door open and the old brass bell above his head rang.

An older man was sitting in a leather chair reading a copy of The Mallorcan Bookseller by Pete Davies. He was behind an old dining room table being used as a makeshift counter, and the till itself was an antique.

'I don't suppose by any chance you have any CCTV in here, do you?' asked Seth, almost second-guessing the reply that would come.

'What's it to you, my friend?' the man answered.

Seth introduced himself. He explained that he was a recently retired cop and described what had happened at the underground station and that Emelia was now missing – then he waited to be told where to go.

'This is terribly exciting,' the bookshop owner said. 'I've had nothing like this since I left the job in ninety-six.'

'You were a police officer?' asked Seth.

'Yes, young man, I was a detective inspector in Hackney. I may now just sell crime books, but I'll be buggered if the security in this place isn't the best you've ever seen. Let's fire up the hard drive, follow me,' he said.

The old man locked the front door, turned the cardboard sign to display 'closed', and then led Seth into the back of the shop. As they walked through the peeling interior door, the light became brighter. In the back room was a large safe, some plush filing cabinets and a smart desk with a modern computer sat on it.

'The older books sell better from what looks like a run-down shop, people think they're getting a bargain,' said the shop owner, laughing as he spoke. 'Right, you'll want the entrance to the railway station then, last hour or so?' he asked.

'Yeah, that'll be perfect, thank you,' replied Seth.

'I'll run the footage. If you want to capture and save a still image, hit the control and tab key together, okay Seth.'

As the computer played back real-time footage from the shop window, Seth had a clear view of the front of the station. He saw himself and Emelia walking in, closely followed by what looked like a drunk vagrant. There was a commotion when he had fallen, and it looked like two men had run for Emelia. They pushed the vagrant out of the way as they grabbed her, then they pulled her out of the station and bundled her into a black cab. He saw the vagrant pick something up and run. *That explains my wallet, thieving bastard,* he thought.

Seth saved a dozen images to file, and the old man dragged the footage and the still images to a memory stick. Then they walked back into the front of the shop.

The till pinged as the drawer opened, and the old man took something out and wrapped the memory stick in it.

'Good luck, youngster, this has all your stills on and the full moving frame mp4 file. I hope you find her,' he said, as he held his hand out to Seth. 'This should get you back home.'

He handed Seth the memory stick, which was wrapped in a

fifty-pound note.

As Seth left the shop, the old man called after him.

'Life after the job is fine. It takes a while to adapt, but the water's warm, I promise you.'

He offered a smile and a wink as Seth left the shop and headed for the railway station, wondering what to do next. He expected to receive contact from Larry Fowler at some point, but why had he taken Emelia?

Once at Maidenhead Railway Station, Seth unlocked his panniers and pulled out his rucksack, pushing the memory stick into one of its zipped pockets and fastening it shut. Then he pulled out his helmet from the top box and kitted up before setting off for home.

★ ★ ★

Marc Pashley kept running until he was sure that neither Seth nor the other two men had followed him. He ran from the street into a café, arriving at the counter out of breath and sweating profusely.

'I'll have a skinny latte and a chunk of carrot cake, please, darling.'

The woman behind the counter looked at him, doubting his ability to pay for his order.

'That'll be nine pounds and twenty pence, and I'm not your darling,' she said, not moving to prepare anything until it had been paid for.

Pashley pulled out Seth's wallet and offered one of the cards to the contactless payment machine. It responded with a reassuring ping, and he looked at the woman smiling smugly.

'Extra-hot milk, please… darling' he said.

As he sat drinking his latte, Pashley rifled through Seth's wallet.

'Thanks for the coffee mate, very kind of you.'

He pulled out a few banknotes from the main compartment and stuffed them into the pocket of his jeans, then he emptied the small change pouch, the coins followed the notes to his pocket. Two credit cards and a debit card. Pashley began discussing the contents of the wallet with himself.

'They'll be cancelled within an hour or so, Marc.'

'You're right. I can only use them a few times, then I'd better chuck them.'

'Good plan.'

He tugged out a pile of receipts before stuffing them back in where the cash had been. Then he took out a photograph of Seth and Emelia. It looked like they were in New York somewhere, high up over the city. She looked stunning. Pashley gazed at her picture for the best part of five minutes, then he folded the photograph down the middle and tore it in half. He put Seth back into the wallet and Emelia into his pocket. Finally, he took out Seth's driving licence.

Pashley used Seth's Oyster Card to travel across London, arriving at Paddington station just after four in the afternoon. He bought a single ticket to Maidenhead using Seth's credit card. The ticket for anytime return was over the contactless payment limit. He would have to work out the return trip later. He walked towards platform twelve to catch the four twenty-eight train that would have him in Maidenhead by about ten past five. As he got onto the first carriage, he chucked Seth's wallet down between the step and the platform, sending it on its way to the ballast below. He stepped up, turned left and walked through the almost full compartment, finding an empty seat next to an attractive young woman.

'Mind if I sit here?' he asked

'Be my guest,' she replied, looking at him and instantly wishing she had said that she was waiting for her boyfriend or something.

Pashley sat down and moved so that his thigh contacted the woman's leg. He felt her warmth briefly before she squirmed and moved in close to the window to avoid his touch. He felt aroused, imagining more than being sat in a railway carriage with her. She was the first woman Pashley had been this close to since being locked up. He smiled to himself and pushed his legs wider, making contact again. This time she had no room to move. He sat with a grin on his face, and began talking to himself.

'Feels nice, Marc.'

'She's very fuckable.'

As he laughed, the woman moved to stand up.

'Excuse me, I'm off at the next stop,' she said, making an excuse to get away from him.

As he moved off the seat, she pushed past him, dropping her handbag onto the floor of the carriage. The contents went everywhere. Pashley bent down and started to pick everything up.

'Just leave it. I really don't want your help,' she said, the tension evident in her voice.

'I'm sorry, it wasn't my fucking fault,' he said.

She scooped her belongings into her bag and walked hurriedly away into the next carriage.

Pashley stood up, then turned and sat back down, sliding the box of matches he had picked from the woman's possessions into his pocket.

★ ★ ★

Emelia had been pulled so quickly from the underground station, she was out and into the road before Seth and Pashley had gotten up off the floor.

'Scream or shout again, and it'll be the last breath you take, do you understand me,' the taller man, with the crooked nose, whispered into her ear threateningly while holding her right arm tightly in his grip.

'He's not joking, princess,' said the second man.

They walked her quickly out onto the street and into a black cab waiting immediately outside the station with its door open. It pulled away as Pashley sprinted past and away from the station.

'Drive, go,' shouted one of the men at the driver.

'Please, where are you taking me? There must be a mistake,' said Emelia.

'Shut the fuck up. There's no mistake,' shouted the driver.

'On the floor, get on the floor now,' the larger man in the back shouted at Emelia.

'What?'

'Get on the fucking floor now,' he pushed his face up close to hers, the spit from his mouth landing on her face as he shouted. Emelia got down onto her knees. No sooner had she done so, and a black cloth bag was put over her head. Then what felt like a cable tie was pulled around her neck, holding the bag tightly in place.

'Where are you taking me, what are you—' she was interrupted by her head being violently pulled toward one of the men.

'Shut up, I'm done with all your fucking questions. Open your mouth again, and you'll get a mouth full of cock,' all three men laughed.

Then she felt the grip of one of the men's thighs pushed tightly on each of her ears, holding her head still. *Oh my God, I'm between his legs, she thought,* feeling sick.

After another twenty minutes, the cab drove into a workshop under a set of railway arches. The door of the cab opened, and Emelia was pulled out violently. Her hands were zip-tied behind her back, and her ankles tied tightly together. She was thrown into the back of a van with bench seats in it. All she saw was darkness. She could smell the same man that had held her head between his legs. He sat next to her, holding her head down hard against the seat while she lay on her side, not daring to move.

The door slid shut, then Emelia heard the driver's door close, then the van started and pulled away.

CHAPTER 24

Ignition

The gravel crunched under the tyres of Seth's motorcycle as he pulled up on the driveway. He was exhausted. His efforts to locate Emelia had not proven fruitful, and he was beginning to wonder if he would ever see her again, alive at least. Investigating on his own was more demanding than having an entire CID office working for him. Still, he had the video footage that may help.

Seth got off the bike as it started to rain. As he removed his helmet, drops of water ran down his neck on the inside of his jacket. He popped the pannier open and took out his rucksack, suffering a heavy feeling of déjà vu, as his mind snuck back to when he had taken the missing-person files home to study them before Sharon McCrory and the two young men had been found at the makeshift graveyard. It was clear to him what Larry would do to Emelia if he did not get what he wanted. He knew that if he did not track Emelia down soon, then she would probably end up dead.

Seth unlocked the front door and went indoors to meet his study partner, a double Plymouth Gin and tonic with ice and a slice of lime. He sat down on the sofa and turned on the television to provide some white noise while he mapped out everything he knew about Larry and what he thought he knew about Emelia. *How were they connected? What was going on here?*

Three hours passed, and Seth had not really worked out a plan of action. Nothing had screamed out as a clue that would help him locate Emelia or understand why she had been taken, unless Seth himself was the connection. He sat pondering his next move as his brain felt like it would implode.

★　★　★

Marc Pashley walked past again, watching for the downstairs lights to extinguish, waiting for Seth to go to bed. Each time he walked around the block, he got wetter and wetter in the unrelenting rain. As Pashley walked along Cannon Court Road for the fifth time, the downstairs light went out. He walked up the driveway, trying not to crunch the gravel as he approached. As he entered the back garden from the side of the house, he saw that only an upstairs light was on, shining onto the lawn and the field behind the house. He stepped into the shadows to shelter among the laurel bushes at the bottom of the garden, watching and waiting.

When the bedroom light went out, he pushed his rucksack into the bushes and walked away, leaving Cannon Court Road via the field at the back of the houses, then along Furze Platt Road and into the Esso garage no more than half a mile away. He walked into the garage and to the till.

'Hi, I've run out of petrol. Do you have any of those plastic cans that I can buy and fill up, please?' asked Pashley.

'On the forecourt, between the kindling and the stack of screen wash.'

Pashley walked outside, grabbed two of the green five-litre plastic cans and filled them up with unleaded petrol before returning to the cashier.

'Twenty-eight-fifty-two please,' said the cashier.

Marc started a monologue with himself.

'Should have kept Hannen's cards, mate.'

'Shut the fuck up, Marc.'

'What? you okay chap?' asked the cashier.

'Yeah, that's a bit fucking steep,' said Pashley, as he rifled around in his pocket for Seth's money.

'The cans are seven-ninety-nine each and the petrol's twelve pounds fifty-four, mate,' said the cashier.

Pashley pulled out some crinkled notes and a handful of change.

'That'll wipe me out. Can I just take one then, please?' he said to the cashier.

'Sorry chap, you've pumped it now, it's pay for both, or I call the police.'

Pashley pushed the pile of money across the counter, not bothering with the amount. It took a minute or so for the cashier to sort and count it.

'You're two-pence short, chap,' he said smiling.

Pashley sank his hands deep into his jean pockets, desperately searching for more change. As he fumbled, he noticed a small tray of coins on the counter.

Need a Penny? Please Help Yourself

He took two pence from the tray and thrust the coins at the cashier.

'That's for when you're only one-pence short, chap... you're two pence adrift,' the cashier smiled again, enjoying watching Pashley's annoyance.

'For fuck's sake, just put the payment through. I need to get back to my car,' said Pashley, half shouting as he turned to leave the garage.

SIMON BOWDEN

'Do you want a receipt?'

'No, fuck you, jobsworth,' he shouted as he left.

Pashley walked back towards Cannon Court Road, a can of fuel in each hand. He strode across the open field at the back of the houses and stopped outside Seth's house. It was now almost one in the morning, and all the lights were still off. He pushed the cans of fuel under the laurel bushes and walked off. *One more hour to be sure,* Pashley thought to himself as he walked away, the rain still lashing down, causing his trainers to pick up clumps of mud from the ploughed field.

At two o'clock, Pashley returned and pulled the cans of petrol from under the bushes and walked slowly through the back gate and into the garden. He placed the cans of fuel under the kitchen window, took out a mini torch from his jacket and turned it on. Then he made his way across the garden to a small wooden shed to find something to force the kitchen window. The door was locked in two places and was solidly built, so despite his best efforts, Pashley was unable to get enough purchase to force it open. The frustration started to bubble inside him. He was drenched to the skin, covered in mud, and cold. He took a couple of minutes to compose himself and think. He needed to get something to force the wooden sash window to Seth's kitchen. As he looked over the low fence into next-doors shrubbery, he noticed what looked like a large garden spade pushed into a freshly dug vegetable patch. Pashley jumped the fence, grabbed the spade and jumped back into Seth's garden.

He put his torch back away, then pushed the blade of the spade between the bottom of the sash window and its frame, wiggling it in as far as he could get it to go. Once there was no more room for movement, he leant onto the handle and pushed it down to force the window upward. The spade lost its grip and slipped out of its crevice, sending the handle quickly downward

282

under the full weight of Pashley's body. As he fell, he struck his head on the stone windowsill, splitting open the skin of his forehead.

'Fuck,' he cursed under his breath, trying his utmost to remain calm, his temper telling him to just throw the fucking spade through the window. He resisted the urge, managing to hold it together.

Pashley pushed the spade back into its slot, the other way up this time. He pushed harder and changed his angle of attack. As he pushed down and inward, he heard the wood starting to creak a little.

'One more go should do it.'

He tried again, pushing harder this time. Crack. The window flew up, and it was open, and he had a way in.

Shining his torch into the kitchen, he looked for an intruder alarm sensor. There it was, in the corner of the room, up high. He turned the torch off, expecting to see a little light flashing on the passive infrared sensor, but it remained dark.

'The alarm's not on, Marc,' he said to himself, as he picked up the petrol cans and pushed them through the window one at a time. Then he climbed into the kitchen and stood still, listening for any movement from upstairs. The house remained silent. He took the cap off one of the cans and made his way to the base of the stairs, stopping again to listen for movement. Pashley was shivering now, partly from being wet and cold but also due to his nervous energy. He climbed the stairs leaving muddy footprints behind him.

Once he had reached the landing, he started to empty petrol onto the carpet, dropping fuel outside both bedroom doors, before slurping some onto the tiled floor of the bathroom. He could just make out the sound of someone snoring in the back bedroom. Not wanting to wake them, he went into the other bedroom, emptying more petrol onto the bed and then the ensuite bathroom. Then he descended the stairs, slopping glugs of petrol as he went. By the time he reached the downstairs hallway, the first can had been emptied. He discarded it and went back to the kitchen for the second, removing the cap and repeating the process downstairs, emptying glugs of petrol around the sitting room, then finally going back to the kitchen. Pashley climbed back out of the window and stood on the wooden decking, looking into the dark interior of Seth's house. The smell of petrol was so strong, *no time to hang about now.* He took a box of matches from his pocket, slid it open and took one out. With a flick of his fingers, he struck the match across the side of the box. Nothing happened, no spark, no flame. He tried a second and then a third, but none of them would light. The box had become damp in the rain and would not provide a spark for the match to ignite. Pashley clicked the torch back on and shone it into the house, lighting up the area by the cooker. *Yes, matches.* He climbed back in and grabbed the box, giving it a shake to check its contents, then he turned and climbed back out.

Back in position on the decking, he slid the box open to find four matches, taking the first one out and striking it. The flame took hold immediately. He threw the lit match through the window, but almost as soon as it left his hand, the flame extinguished itself.

'For fuck's sake,' he cursed to himself in a quiet whisper.

This time Pashley held two matches together and struck them simultaneously, leaving one unspent in the box. The flame took hold immediately again. Leaning into the window, he threw the lit matches into the kitchen, slower this time, watching as the matches separated, the two small burning sticks falling toward the floor. As the first one landed, it just sat on the tiles burning. The second one landed thirty centimetres further in, creating a flash as it hit a small puddle of petrol. Flames shot upward in a ball of fire before retreating, the pool of fuel burning furiously but in isolation from the rest of the petrol.

As Pashley stood watching, he slid the matchbox open and took out the last match. Just as he was about to strike it, there was a terrific whoomph as the rest of the petrol further into the kitchen accepted the flame. A rush of fire was sent racing through the ground floor and up the stairs.

Pashley felt a stifling wall of heat hit him through the window. The darkness was now replaced with bright orange flames producing thick black acrid smoke. He turned and ran, back towards the safety of the field, where he stood in the shadows, watching the house as it succumbed to the raging fire.

* * *

It was twenty minutes before he saw the pulsating blue lights of a fire engine joining the orange haze. The sound of sirens merged with the crackle of the fire. Pashley could see the neighbour's lights were on. *They must have called the fire brigade.* Soon another fire engine arrived, closely followed by a police car. He could hear the shouts of firefighters and police officers as the initial chaos turned into an ordered attempt to extinguish the furiously burning house.

Pashley basked in the satisfying glow as his thoughts turned again to his time in prison. The attacks, the rapes and the change his life had suffered upon release.

'That's payback. We're even now Detective Chief Inspector Hannen, see you in hell one day,' he said to himself, as he pulled his rucksack onto his back. Satisfied with his evening's work, he turned and ran through the field, flicking up chunks of mud as he headed back towards the safety of the road.

Emerging from the field, he slowed to a walk, heading back on himself towards the entrance to Cannon Court Road as another set of blue lights screamed past him. Pashley walked along the pavement in the direction of Maidenhead town centre, planning to wait for the train to take him back to London and then disappear back into the city streets.

As he walked, passing parked cars along the road, the side door of a van slid open.

'Oi, Pashley, Marc Pashley,' a voice called to him.

He turned just as two men jumped from the back of the van, heading straight for him. Their faces were lit by the streetlights, and Pashley briefly recognised the heavily bent nose. It was the two men who had sat in the lobby of the Old Scotland Yard Hotel the previous morning. Before he could break into a run, he felt a blow on his head, and the lights went out. All was dark. The men dragged him into the back of the van and slid the door shut.

As the van sped off, it passed another police car with blue lights flashing as it headed for the blazing house. Pashley's assailants set off towards Slough. As they drove over the bridge that crossed the River Thames the passenger threw Pashley's rucksack into the river.

★ ★ ★

The firefighters doused the house to ensure that the flames did not reignite while their colleagues checked the inside. The watch commander's radio crackled into life as he was updated by his team.

'One person reported – deceased,' he shouted, to the police officer, who gave him a nod and fired up his radio.

'Oscar Charlie Two-One to control, fire service reports a single person found appears deceased. For information, the property is Coppers Reach, Detective Chief Inspector Hannen's house. He's now a Met officer. Request you make contact with the Met and advise them accordingly, over.'

The radio remained silent for a couple of seconds.

'Roger that, any indication as to the deceased's identity? Over,' came the reply.

'Negative, I'm advised that the body is badly charred, unable to confirm at this time, over.'

The Control Room Inspector called her opposite number in London to be advised that DCI Hannen had retired and was no longer a police officer.

'We do still have a contact number for him, though, if you'd like his personal mobile number. If that would help you?'

The Met officer passed the details back to his Thames Valley colleague, who dialled the number, expecting the line to not register or to go directly to an answerphone.

'Hello, Seth Hannen speaking,' a sleepy voice answered the phone.

'Hello, sir, is that former DCI Seth Hannen?' asked the control room inspector.

'Yes, that's right, how can I help you? Who is this?'

'I'm sorry, Mr Hannen, forgive me, I didn't expect you to answer. This is Inspector Sidhu at Thames Valley Police control room. Can I ask if you still own Coppers Reach in Cannon Court Road in Maidenhead?'

Seth was quiet for a moment, taking a few seconds before he answered.

'Yes, that's my house... why are you calling me?'

'Mr Hannen, there's been a fire at your house. Do you know anybody that may have been inside, anyone at all?' asked Inspector Sidhu.

Seth's heart skipped a beat as panic began to fill his head.

'Yes, my mother's been there for a couple of days, while she has a new kitchen and bathroom fitted at her house. Have you found her? Is she alright? asked Seth, almost knowing what the answer was going to be.

'I'm so sorry, Mr Hannen, the fire service has found the body of a person at the property, upstairs in the back bedroom, we can't confirm their identity at this stage, but it would appear that—'

'I'm on my way. I'm leaving now,' Seth butted in before hanging up the phone.

He sat on the edge of the bed in silence, his head in his hands, as he started to cry. Why had he decided to stay at Emelia's house tonight? Why hadn't he gone back to Maidenhead?

★ ★ ★

First, his father, then his mother, both taken too soon, both having suffered at the hands of criminals. Again, Seth listened to the vicar reading the prayers, his eyes clamped tightly shut as he struggled to understand why his life had suffered so many tragedies, so many sad events had been thrown his way.

Leah, Seth's sister, flew to England immediately, for the first time since she had emigrated. Within days of arriving, she found herself with Seth, back in the church that held their haunting childhood memories. They held a small private memorial service for Kathleen, as it would be a few weeks before they could lay her to rest. The post-mortem and criminal investigation needed to get underway.

Leah had called Seth's son and persuaded him to come to the church, and after some arm-twisting, Josh had agreed.

'I'm really sorry, Dad,' said Josh.

'Thanks, Josh. This kind of thing shows you how none of us know what's around the corner. Life is just too short,' replied Seth.

'Maybe it's time that you two let the past go. Your dad is the only immediate family you have now,' Leah interjected, looking at Josh.

'What do you think Josh, shall we give it a go?' asked Seth.

There was a short pause before Josh replied.

'Yeah, why not, Dad, I'll unblock you on Facebook so that you can add me. Call me sometime. Maybe we'll have a beer and go from there?'

'That sounds good, Josh,' replied Seth.

It was a very rare occasion for Seth and his son to be in the same place, even rarer that they spoke more than two words to each other. The death of Seth's mother had made him think about family; he needed to keep those that he had left close. Leah and Josh were his only living relatives now.

As Seth stood in the church, his father spoke to him in his mind, *Men don't cry, they are tough, come on be a man like me.* This time he answered his father. *Sorry Dad, but you're wrong, it's real men that cry.* Then he thought about Emelia, *I am not losing anyone else. I'll get you back, Emelia, if it's the last thing I do.*

CHAPTER 25

The Tunnel

Emelia had been taken out of London by two men. She had no idea where she was or how long she had been in the second vehicle. Her pupils were as wide as they could be, but she was still unable to see anything from inside the darkness of the hood. Her other senses tried their hardest to fill in the gaps for her. She worked out that she was in a van by the shape of the seats and how it moved along the road. The same two men from the taxi were still with her; their voices and body odours were distinct. The more confident bolshy man had been on the phone several times, clearly taking instructions from whoever was in charge.

The van came to a standstill. Emelia listened as the driver got out and slammed the door behind him. Then the side door of the van slid open. She could just about make out the light from a torch breaking through the fabric of the thick black sack still over her head. *It must be dark outside.* Her senses were her key to survival now, so she switched them to high alert.

'I'm pleased to say that we are finally here Emelia, I hope you had a pleasant fucking journey,' said the same voice that had whispered into her ear earlier.

Still unable to see anything, she listened to every sound. She needed to either work out where she was or at least listen for clues that could help her get an idea. Emelia heard the sound of the two men getting in and out of the van. She felt the cold blade of a knife on her skin as it slid between the cable tie and her ankles. Then there was a rough wrenching as they cut the cable ties free from her legs. A vice-like grip took hold of each of her upper arms, and she was pulled out of the van, one man on each side, her arms still tied behind her back. Emelia's legs dropped from the doorsill then hit the ground with a thud. The pain shocked up through her shin bones, and she took a sharp intake of breath and bit hard on her lower lip, not wanting to offer any confirmation that she was in pain. Then she was dragged along what felt like smooth tarmac until they came to a stop. A wooden gate slowly scraped the ground, and she was pulled quickly through the opening. Her legs struggled to keep up on what felt like uneven broken concrete underfoot.

Then without warning, she felt like she was falling. Her feet scrabbled to find the steps, missing most of them as she was pulled down for what seemed like an age. The air got colder, and she smelt an old dampness. The men's footsteps and voices started to echo off nearby walls. *I'm underground. Where the hell am I?* Emelia tried her utmost to remain calm, but her body started to fill with panic. She felt herself being rammed into something cold and hard at chest height, then the hands moved from her arms to the shoulders, pushing her toward the ground.

'Sit the fuck down,' said the confident man's voice.

They tipped her off balance as she dropped to the floor, landing heavily on the base of her spine. Emelia bit her lip again as her body absorbed the pain. A knife cut through the thick cable ties that were holding her wrists together. Her arms were wrenched quickly upward as she felt new cable ties drawing in tight, clicking as they tightened, holding her arms up above her head against what felt like cold metal. A fat hand pushed her head to one side, the man's fingers pushed between the plastic tie and the fabric of the bag. For a moment, she was unable to breathe. Then the cable tie lost its grip as it was cut loose, and the bag was taken off. She was in a poorly lit tunnel. Although the light was dim, her eyes were already accustomed to the dark from being inside the bag for so long. Her brain started to take in her surroundings. Two high arches covered a walkway divided by a white metal fence, and metal pillars supported the tunnel roof.

'Don't you go anywhere now gorgeous,' said the confident one.

Then the two men turned and walked away in the direction they had come from, leaving Emelia tied to the railing. The men reached the end of the tunnel, flicked a switch, and then left along with the light, locking the door as they went. Emelia sat still, in pitch darkness again, wondering what they had in store for her. *Who are they? Why am I here? Come on, Emelia, focus.*

She sat in the cold for what felt like days, but in reality, she was only alone for just over three hours.

Tony Spiller unlocked the door and pulled it open before flicking a switch, sending power to the ineffective low voltage lighting. Emelia listened as the footsteps got closer. They sounded heavy on the concrete floor as the silhouetted figure of a tall man came into view.

'Who are you, what do you want,' she called.

'Ah, hello Emmy, my name's Tony. I've got you something to eat.'

Spiller threw a brown takeaway bag in her direction.

'How am I supposed to eat anything with my hands tied up,' she shouted angrily.

'That's your problem, not mine,' laughed Spiller. He bent down in front of her, pushing her legs wide open so he could crouch between her legs and get close to her. 'I do love to be between the legs of a beautiful woman,' he said, laughing as he picked up the bag.

Then he pulled out a burger. 'Open wide darling, I've got some meat for you,' he said, as he stuffed the burger into her mouth, pushing it all in. Emelia coughed as she tried not to choke, her mouth and throat full. 'There you go. I'll be back in a while, I'm just off to get your boyfriend.'

Spiller stood up and walked back out of the tunnel, stealing the light from Emelia as he cut the power.

Emelia spat the burger from her mouth. She sat on the concrete floor, hopelessly trying to work out a way to escape. She was exhausted. The more she tried to figure a way out, the harder it became to think. Her thoughts drifted into a dream, and then she was asleep.

Emelia was woken by the sound of a struggle. The tunnel was dark; no lights had been switched on this time. She could hardly see a thing, only her ears giving up any clues about what was happening. She heard writhed footsteps and a man protesting, struggling against the efforts of at least two other men. Then came the sound of cable ties being zipped up and a man's grunts as she heard boots being laid into him. Then the footsteps sauntered away, and all was quiet.

Her arms cramped, and she wriggled to get relief from the cramp that attacked her shoulder muscles.

'Who's there?' a man's voice came from the darkness. Emelia stayed still and quiet. 'Who's there? Please help me, I need help,' the man called out again.

'Marc is that you?' asked Emelia, in disbelief.

'What, how do you know my name, who's that?'

'Marc, it's Emelia, Emelia DiSalvo.'

'Fuck, Emelia, they got you too. They want the money back. They think you and I have the money stolen from Rebecca Langford. It belongs to a man called Fowler, you need to admit taking all that money Emelia, give it back to them, for fuck's sake.'

Right, so Langford Investment Management is the link here, thought Emelia.

'I don't have any of Rebecca's money, Marc. You did the skimming, not me. Anyway, that was ages ago, why now, why wait so long?'

'I was warned in prison that he was waiting for me. He had me targeted in there, long slow torture until I was released. Where are we Emelia, do you know where we are?' said Marc.

'No, I think it's probably some kind of old access tunnel or something.'

Emelia and Marc had been taken to the long-forgotten Slough underground station that would have been the last stop on the District Line before the idea was shelved in the 1950s. They were in the abandoned access tunnel under the main A4 road that passed through the centre of Slough. It had remained locked up since the plans had been shelved, only being accessed for an inspection every five years or so.

Emelia and Pashley sat in the darkness, occasionally talking to each other, but mostly sitting in silence. They sat contemplating their own fate and wondering what lay in store for them.

Marc stopped talking to himself out loud, leaving his mind to argue with itself in the background. At the same time, Emelia sat thinking through different scenarios, each time looking to work out an escape plan.

★ ★ ★

Over the next five days, they were visited once a day, always late at night. They were given food and water by a man and a woman, not the two men that had initially brought them there. Eventually, late on the sixth day, the dim light seeped back into the tunnel, followed by the sound of footsteps. Four men and a woman walked up to where Pashley was tied. Only one of them spoke. It was Tony Spiller.

'So, Marc… what to do with you,' he said, looking at Pashley in the torchlight.

'I don't have your fucking money; you have to let me go, please,' said Pashley.

Spiller and his pals laughed at him.

'My boss wants me to speak to you about some financial issues. Now that you've stewed for a while, I'm going to have some fun getting you ready to talk,' said Spiller.

'What do you mean? I can talk to you now. I'll talk to anybody, just let me go,' said Pashley, sounding desperate.

He was about to ask another question when he was kicked, the black boot of one of the men hitting his abdomen like a train.

'Are you really ready to talk?' asked Spiller.

Pashley gasped for air, unable to speak. 'I didn't think so,' said Spiller.

Another boot launched at Pashley, this time contacting his head, opening up the cut he had sustained when he fell onto the windowsill a few nights earlier. The force of the impact ricocheted his head off the white metal fence behind him, splitting the skin on the back of his head wide open. His neck and back started to warm up as the blood from the wound soaked into his shirt. Then Spiller and his crew turned and walked towards Emelia.

'Are you ready to talk yet, pretty lady?' asked Spiller.

'Why, are you going to lay the boot into me too?' she asked back.

'No, why would I do something to damage a pretty thing like you?' said Spiller, crouching as he spoke, leaning forward and stroking Emelia's hair.

'No, there are much nicer ways to make women talk,' he said, as he leant in closer and stroked Emelia's cheek with the back of his hand. He moved his head in close to hers and sucked air in through his nose, sniffing her neck.

'Leave me alone,' she said, glaring at him.

'You smell lovely, turns me on,' he whispered in her ear.

'Piss off,' said Emelia, then she spat in his face.

Spiller grabbed hold of her hair and pulled it hard, forcing her head back and to one side. He wiped the spit off his face with his fingers and then pushed them into her mouth.

'You can have that back slag,' he said in a calm, cold voice, enjoying his fingers being inside her mouth.

Emelia bit down hard, and Spiller grimaced but did not make a sound. He let go of her hair and moved his left hand to her crotch, grabbing hold with a firm grip.

'Let the fuck go of my fingers,' he said, as his grip tightened between her legs.

Emelia let go of her bite, and Spiller pulled his fingers away, leaving the metallic taste of his blood in her mouth. 'Try anything like that again, sweetheart, and you'll get more than my hand down there. It hurts if you're dry,' he said, smirking.

'Fuck you,' said Emelia.

He leant forward, kissed her and then stood up, looking towards his four henchmen.

'You two grab him and take him to the farm, I'll come with you. You two follow with her, keep her in the van once you're there, and watch her mouth – it's fucking dangerous – Big-Gun wants Pashley first.

Spiller's top two henchmen set about untying Pashley and taking him to the farm. Both Carl and Grant had been recruited from working on the doors of local night clubs. They were old school bouncer types – hit first and ask questions later. They spent most of their spare time in the gym working out to ensure the steroids they would take had the desired effects on their muscular physiques. Spiller had nicknamed them Mugger and Thug. Mugger was the bigger man, the leader. He had ambitions of moving up in Larry Fowler's empire. Thug followed him around like a puppy, never far away, always in his shadow.

★ ★ ★

Tony Spiller and his two muscle men parked the van in an old barn and then led Pashley to a stubbly field, the old mown barley stems stabbed at his legs. The cuts on Pashley's head were still seeping blood. His shirt was now soaked in sticky congealed blood, sticking the fabric to his skin. They walked to a dark unlit corner, farthest from the barn, near to a small copse of birch trees, coming to a stop next to a large oblong pit. The hole had been recently dug and was still muddy from the rain earlier in the week. It looked like it was ready for a funeral.

'Marc, this my friend is for you. A lot of effort has gone into digging this hole. My two boys, Mugger and Thug to you, would love some appreciation for their hard work,' said Spiller.

Pashley did not say a word; he just stood there between the two men, feeling his knees starting to lose their torque and preparing to give way. He stood, desperately trying not to show his inner fear.

'Now then Marc, my boss, Mr Fowler, has some questions that he wants to ask you. He'll be arriving in a moment, whilst we wait, why don't you try it for size?' said Spiller, nodding towards the hole.

'What, I'm not fucking getting in there,' screamed Pashley, as he tensed his body, trying to pull away from the grip of Thug and Mugger. His two chaperones increased their vice-like grip on his upper arms.

'In you get now, Marc,' said Spiller, raising his voice.

'No, fuck off, I'm not climbing into my own fucking grave, I'm not going to be buried alive,' shouted Pashley. His voice started to crack as tears began to roll down his face; they were joined by a meek sob that developed into hysterical crying.

'Stop your fucking blubbing. We would never bury anyone alive, would we lads…' said Spiller, his two cronies laughing as he spoke.

'No, I bet you wouldn't,' came Pashley's answer.

He struggled with all his might, trying his best to break away, twisting and contorting his body, desperately attempting to free himself like a fish caught on a hook. The grip on his arms was unrelenting, his struggles were in vain, and he found himself falling to the bottom of the pit.

'Lay down, stop pissing me around and lay on your fuckin' back,' shouted Spiller before spitting into the pit.

Pashley gave in and did as he was told and laid down on his back, looking up out of the abyss, his eyes met with the bright white light of a powerful torch. All he could see was white, everything else blinded from his sight.

Spiller unzipped his fly, freeing himself from his trousers. He aimed at Pashley's chest and then released the hold on his bladder. As he lay there, Pashley felt the warm liquid hit him on the chest, then it moved up to his face catching him unaware. He coughed and spluttered, not managing to prevent a swallow.

'Fuck, stop, please,' begged Pashley as he wiped his face.

Spiller shook the last few drips off, tucked himself away and pulled his zip back up, just as Larry Fowler walked up and joined the three men.

'Don't have too much fun now, Tony, eh,' He said as he arrived.

The four men stood at the edge of the pit, two on either side, all looking down at the urine-soaked Marc Pashley.

'Hello Marc, I hope you've been keeping well, mate,' said Fowler.

'Who are you,' replied Pashley.

'Well, shall we say that you owe me a lot of money, Marc. You, my friend, are here to pay a debt, and a debt you shall pay indeed, one way or another.'

'You're Larry Fowler! You've got the wrong man,' said Pashley.

'Oh no, Marc, we have the right man. You see that money that you stole from Rebecca Langford, well that was my money. You skimmed the wrong account, my friend, I want it all back, every last penny, do you—'

Pashley interrupted Larry.

'I don't have your fucking money. Ask Emelia about it,' he screamed, still blubbing.

'Shut up and don't interrupt me. If you don't pay me back, you can be sure that you have found your final resting place. The pit that you're in represents the hole that you managed to fuckin' dig yourself by stealing from me,' said Larry, becoming increasingly annoyed.

'I spent everything I took. I can't pay it back. It's all gone. Why would I be living rough if I had any money? Please, you have to believe me.'

Pashley was now talking through deep gasps as he lost control, crying uncontrollably like a child.

'I know about that money, Marc, but what about the rest, eh? There is nearly two million fuckin' quid of mine missing. That's a lot of money, Marc, and it's not yours or your little ex-girlfriend's either. I want it back,' said Larry, his voice becoming louder with each word. 'I'm done with pissing around Marc, where's the fuckin' money. Just tell me, and you can go on your merry way.'

'I don't have it... honestly... I don't know what you're

talking about, I beg you... you have to believe me... I only took money for drugs. I didn't take that much,' screamed Pashley, as he became increasingly stressed, his words now coming out in short bursts.

'Calm him down for fuck's sake,' said Larry looking at Mugger. 'Get in there and calm him down now. I can't bear this pathetic crying lark.'

'Me boss?' exclaimed Mugger, looking back at Larry.

'Yes, fuckin' you, who else was I looking at, Jack fuckin' Frost?'

Mugger jumped into the pit, landing with one foot on the soil and one on Pashley's groin.

Pashley let out a squeal of pain.

'I said to calm him down, don't make the noise worse,' said Larry.

'Stand up, stand up now,' shouted Mugger, as he grabbed Pashley by the lapels of his jacket and pulled him to his feet.

The two men stood in the pit facing each other, the top of their heads just below the surface level of the field. Mugger looked up at Larry, who responded with a nod. The next thing Pashley felt was a tremendous blow to his gut, almost lifting him off his feet as he was pushed to the back wall of the pit. The second blow came shortly afterwards but felt twice as powerful. His body was now resting on the wall of the pit with nowhere to go. Then came the knee to his groin, which sent Pashley falling to the ground, the agony shooting up to his abdomen as his balls seared with pain. He found himself kneeling in front of Mugger.

'There's no point in prayin', Marc, God's not fuckin' listening today. It's his day off,' said Larry, laughing.

Pashley's ears did not hear Larry's dark humour. His body had shut everything down except the pain receptors in his brain, and they were working overtime.

Still kneeling, Mugger's knee came back for another agonising visit. The man's knee contacted Pashley's face with a crack, his nose moved sideways, taking up a new position, just left of centre.

'That's much better, Marc, you've stopped fuckin' blubbing at last,' said Larry, smirking as he spoke.

Pashley had indeed stopped crying. All he could do now was murmur and groan as the pain from his injuries raced through his body directly to his brain.

'Now, Marc, you sit down and make yourself comfortable while we give you a rest. This will only make you stronger Marc, pain is just the body letting go of weakness, you know,' said Larry, pulling a cigarette from a fresh packet and lighting it before taking a long draw of nicotine filled smoke.

'Marc, you have until I finish this ciggy to tell me where you and little miss pretty have hidden the money. If you don't… well, let's just say that she'll be next for a little intimate interview with Larry. What says you, Marc, ready to tell me yet?' said Larry, speaking quietly again, calmed by the nicotine in his veins.

'Larry, mate, I honestly don't know, I only took the money I used on drugs, I'm telling you the truth,' said Pashley, speaking in a splutter, through a mouth full of phlegm and blood.

Larry took another long draw of his cigarette, which burned down quickly as he sucked in.

'It's Mr Fowler to you, Marc. I am not in any way your mate. We both know that what you say is not true. You see, Rebecca looks after my money, she does an outstanding job at it too. She has a good handle on what goes on, and I am assured that you have that money. I waited for your release so that I could speak to you personally, Marc, don't fuckin' disappoint me. Please don't do that,' said Larry, as he drew in another huge lung full of smoke.

'I don't have it,' replied Pashley.

'Would you like to finish my ciggy Marc?' he asked, as he bent down and passed what was left of it to Mugger, who was still in the pit with Pashley.

'No… no, I don't smoke anymore,' replied Pashley.

Mugger sucked on Larry's cigarette; the end glowed bright orange in the darkness of the pit. He bent down to a squat, up close to Pashley. Then he took hold of Pashley's face with his gloved hand and pushed his head hard against the dirt wall of the pit, his hand half covering Pashley's mouth. Mugger took the cigarette from between his lips.

'Here you go, mate, you finish it,' he grunted.

Then without any warning, he pushed the hot cigarette up Pashley's left nostril as hard as he could, twisting it as it went in. Pashley screamed with pain as the inside of his already battered nose blistered with the heat of the burning tobacco. Then he just sobbed quietly as the cigarette smouldered inside his nose.

'Marc, lay down, take a load off,' demanded Larry, as Mugger heaved himself out of the pit.

Pashley lay on his back, coughing as the blood and phlegm ran down the back of his throat. The pain in his groin and nose throbbing rhythmically, in time with his heartbeat.

Larry lit a second cigarette and started to suck on it as he spoke.

'Well, Marc, I'm really done with asking any more questions. It's clear that you've chosen your destiny and that of your little tart. I am, of course disappointed, I really don't enjoy hurting women, but I need to put all my faith in Emelia now. I hope that she will see sense and tell me where you two thieving bastards hid my money,' said Larry, as he nodded at his henchmen.

Marc was expecting to feel the thud of heavy soil hitting him as he was buried alive. The pain he felt would soon fade as he ran out of air and went to sleep for the last time. He heard a metallic click, followed by a second. *Shit, they're going to shoot me. If I'm going to die, that would be better than sucking in soil and suffocating.* He felt a massive wave of regret that he had ever snorted that first line of cocaine, his addiction had brought him here. He had done this to himself.

'Open your mouth, Marc,' shouted Larry.

Pashley was totally broken and did as he was told, shutting his eyes tight and preparing for a bullet or a sod of soil. He was waiting to die.

The taste of petrol was pungent. He coughed and sputtered as the blue liquid from the jerry can moved from his mouth down his body to his legs, then on to his feet. Two whole cans of premium unleaded were emptied onto his body, soaking his clothes and pooling on the floor of the pit.

'Shit, for the love of God, please no,' screamed Pashley.

'It's too late. You should have told me when I asked, Marc,' said Larry as he turned to walk away.

'Please, please don't do this,' cried Pashley.

'What goes around comes around. I'll pass my condolences to your husband in Belmarsh.'

Larry laughed as he started to walk away from the edge of the pit. He was followed by Mugger and Thug, their silhouettes disappearing from Pashley's view. Pashley lay on his back, listening for movement, silently praying to God. He heard nothing. Dare he get up and scramble out of the pit? *Five minutes I'll give it five minutes.* He lay on his back, not knowing what to do, his heart pumping adrenaline filled blood around his body.

Larry and his men stood only three metres from the pit, watching to see if Pashley would dare climb out. As Larry took the last draw of his cigarette, he called out to Pashley.

'Here you go, Marc, you can finish this one off too.'

Then he flicked the cigarette stub. It twisted as it cartwheeled through the air towards the pit, letting small pieces of bright orange ash loose as it went. The stub landed just short, teetering on the edge of the pit.

'Are you there pl—' called Pashley.

He was interrupted as the stub toppled downward, igniting his petrol-soaked body with a flash and a whoomph, the flames launching high into the air. After the sound of the ignition, Pashley's screams started loud, then faded to nothing. He had yielded quickly.

'What the fuck have you done,' shouted Emelia as she was dragged into the field by two more of Larry's thugs.

'Hello sweet lips, your old boyfriend is in there, and that is where you will fuckin' end up if you don't tell me what the pair of you did with my fuckin' money. You'll be next, I promise you that. I'm sure you appreciate that I'm not pissin' around,' said Larry, glaring at Emelia through the dark.

Emelia felt the heat from the fire as the smell of burning flesh started to fill the air. The hot, pungent smoke brought Pashley's terror with it as it infiltrated Emelia's lungs and then the rest of her body.

'Take her back to the tunnel, while the boys sort out what's left of Pashers here,' said Larry, then he walked away, followed by Mugger and Thug.

PART FIVE

UNSEEN LAW KEEPING

CHAPTER 26

Now Recruiting

'Hello Seth, it's Xavier Addington from the Home Office. I think it's time we had that chat about you coming and working for me.'

Xavier's telephone manner was as abrupt as he was in person.

'Mr Addington, it's really not a good time right now,' replied Seth.

'But you've finished with the boys and girls in blue. You must be ready for that new challenge?'

'To be honest, no, not quite. I have some problems to sort out before I can even think about any kind of work,' said Seth, not wanting to get sucked into providing lots of detail.

'Seth, listen… if one of those problems is Emelia, I mean finding her… Or anything to do with Lawrence Fowler. I'd say that they are one and the same as my own problems.'

Seth paused for a moment.

'What, how do you know about Emelia and—' he was interrupted by Xavier.

'Seth, come to the Home Office. I'll meet you and explain what I know. See you this afternoon?' said Xavier. He already knew Seth would agree to come and meet him.

'Look, Emelia's been gone for nearly a week now, my mother is dead, and I've been warned off going to the police by

Larry Fowler. This is really heavy shit Xavier, I don't know how much time I have to sort it all out,' said Seth.

'Just come to the Home Office; you've got nothing to lose. I can help you, I promise,' replied Xavier calmly.

Seth paused to think again before answering.

'Okay then, the main building in Marsham Street? I'll see you as soon as I can get to you,' said Seth.

'You won't regret it. I'll see you soon,' replied Xavier before hanging up the phone.

★ ★ ★

Seth walked into the large lobby to be greeted almost immediately by Xavier Addington, who was instantly recognisable in his well-cut suit, which was just a shade brighter than you would expect of a business suit, complemented with a pink and white check shirt and cobalt blue tie.

'Hello Seth, welcome to the Home Office. It's been quite a journey you've had getting here,' said Xavier, holding out his hand to welcome Seth.

The men shook hands, and then Xavier led Seth towards the security desk.

'Not really, I got the tube from Highgate, forty-five minutes door to door at worst,' replied Seth, puzzled by Xavier's comments.

'I don't mean today, Seth. I mean, the thirty-year journey you've had getting here, that's been quite something. I've been briefed on all of it. You're a man of resilience, Seth, a man of moral fibre, one that I feel we can trust,' said Xavier.

'I'm not too sure what it is you're referring to,' said Seth, feeling slightly uncomfortable.

'I know all about you, your two failed marriages, and Emelia, of course, I witnessed that meeting in Kensington. The Thames

Valley years and the Met ones too. Anyway, let's get you through security, and then we can talk. We have much to discuss.'

Seth joined a queue of people waiting to visit various parts of the building. His briefcase, wallet, coins, and watch all went into a tray and were x-rayed. He walked through a metal detecting arch before being patted down by one of the security team. Once issued a temporary pass with 'must be escorted' printed in bold red letters, he was led by Xavier through an airlock security door entry system.

'Can I get you a tea or coffee?'

'I'll take an earl grey tea, no milk thanks,' replied Seth.

The pair walked downstairs to a large café, not speaking as they walked. Seth waited as Xavier bought two cups of tea. As he stood at the back of the café, he saw a man in his fifties walking away and up the stairs. Seth could not quite catch a view of his face, but his gait seemed strangely familiar. He brushed the thought aside, unable to pinpoint what it was that he recognised.

He had been in the building before but was unsure of exactly why he was here now. The uncertainty made him feel anxious, especially as Xavier seemed to know an awful lot about him. Just mentioning Emelia and Larry was enough to confirm that.

'Right, let's go upstairs to my office, don't look so worried, Seth,' said Xavier, as he led Seth toward the main set of lifts in the large atrium area.

The lift was almost full. Seth stood with Xavier at the back behind another eight people.

'Fifth floor, please,' Xavier spoke to the woman nearest the buttons.

The lift jolted and moved upward, stopping at each floor, people getting in and out as it went. By the time it reached the fifth floor, Seth and Xavier were the only ones left. The doors opened, and they walked out, met immediately by a heavy metal door with a security lock. Xavier placed his finger onto a glass screen. A green light moved up and down the glass, and the lock gave a reassuring clunk as it unlocked.

'One second, Seth, I need to add you as a visitor,' said Xavier.

He typed Seth's details into the touch screen computer, scanned his thumbprint again, and asked Seth to place his thumb on the screen. A red light moved up and down under his thumb twice before turning green as the display let out a high-pitched beep.

'That's it, come in Seth, welcome to the Civil Intelligence Service, Section Three.'

In all his years working with the police, dealing with a myriad of government agencies and departments, including MI5 and MI6, Seth had never heard of the Civil Intelligence Service.

'So, what do you do here, and why are you interested in me?' asked Seth.

'All in good time, Seth, come into my office, and I'll fill you in,' replied Xavier.

They walked through a large open plan office. All the desks were extremely tidy, with no papers or folders anywhere. Everything was digital, and each desk was devoid of anything personal. The workstations were laid out so that nobody could see anyone else's computer monitor. All the monitors had privacy screens on them, obscuring anything from view as Seth walked past. Xavier led Seth into one of only three enclosed offices.

'Have a seat, Seth. I'll just see if Patricia is free; she knows that you're coming in.'

Seth was still trying to figure out what exactly was going on. He sat down, placing his tea on a small meeting table surrounded by four chairs.

'Ah, hello Seth, I'm so pleased that you agreed to come in,' said a smartly dressed woman as she walked into the room, offering her hand to Seth, who stood up and obliged.

They shook hands and sat down as Xavier walked in behind her and closed the door.

'Seth, this is Patricia Daniels. She runs the department,' said Xavier.

'Nice to meet you, Patricia... I think?' replied Seth. 'Is there any chance that you can turn a light on for me? I'm feeling like I'm being kept in the dark?'

'That would probably be fair, Seth, I'll start with a bit of background. That will help shed some light, I'm sure,' said Xavier, as he started to put the light on for Seth.

'Shortly after the First World War, MI5 – Military Intelligence Department Five – was created to protect this country. It was one of several military intelligence departments that now make up the Secret Service. In 1964 the Government moved all of the MI departments out of the Home Office, but the ministers at the time were uneasy, not comfortable letting everything go.

'The Home Office kept a few staff back, and the Civil Intelligence Service was born. We have three sections. Section One looks after the raw intelligence, basically putting together everything each police force gets and building a bigger picture. We pass some up to the Secret Service and some on to the National Crime Agency. About five per cent of it stays with us. We deal with the layer between what the blue lights look after and what MI5 deals with.

'Section Two develops intelligence on an international basis, working with foreign counterparts and MI6, joining the dots.

'Section Three consists of a couple of small operational units; one looks after covert activity and the other out in the field leading our investigations.

'Patricia runs the service, and I look after Section Three. That's what we call it. It's easier to refer to it that way. I get the fun bit and oversee the operational work and recruit new operatives for the field. We recruit mainly from the police and the NCA, and occasionally we'll take on some ex-cons. However, they are a little more complicated. It's my job to recruit our operatives, oversee our operations, and keep the service under the radar,' said Xavier, pausing for breath.

'That all sounds great, but what does it have to do with me? Are you telling me that I'm being recruited?' asked Seth.

'I've been waiting for you to finish your time with the boys in blue. We have a system that tracks every police officer's career, training, and expertise. It flags up to my team those who may be useful to us, then it's a human's job to keep an eye on them in the last few years of their service and make recommendations to me. You are one of those recommendations. I'd like you to be one of our field operatives,' said Xavier, finally getting to the point.

'What, be some kind of secret agent or something?' asked Seth, laughing as he spoke.

'The only thing secret about us is our existence,' said Patricia. 'Xavier has outlined what we do in simple terms. You'll know that things are obviously more complicated than that. We are enacted through old legislation, almost hidden in the statutes. Our field officers are certainly not real-life James Bonds, no gadgets, no luxury cars. You get a telephone that works as a radio. It's a prototype from the new Emergency Services Network; we are testing the system for the programme rolling it out. You'll also get a gun if you've passed the police firearms suitability assessment and training course or one of our equivalents.

'We police what the police can't get to. The high-level organised crime lords are our target; we infiltrate and gather intelligence. We decide whether to let them carry on, feeding what we have to the police to allow them to dismantle the criminal organisations. Or, if that is not likely to work, we take executive action ourselves, taking the organisations apart in a more aggressive and less conventional way.'

Seth was intrigued as much as impressed. The work sounded interesting, but he still wanted to know about their connection to Emelia.

'And Emelia, how does she fit into this?' he asked.

Xavier picked up the question.

'We'll talk about Emelia in a moment. Let's finish with you first, Seth, then we can move onto her,' he said, looking towards Patricia.

'Before I can approve Xavier contacting a prospective recruit, the team carries out an extremely intrusive assessment. You completed the Developed Vetting assessment and were interviewed as part of the screening you needed for your job in the police,' said Patricia.

'Yes, that's right,' replied Seth, wondering what was coming next.

'Well, that information came to us, and we took it to another, much deeper level. I have to be honest, yours was concerning at one point,' continued Patricia.

'Go on,' said Seth. His interest was at a peak now.

'You received a payment into your bank account in 1992 for eighty thousand pounds. That money came from Eatmon LLP, a London investment firm. Rebecca Langford worked for them at the time, and she is closely connected to one of our targets, Lawrence Fowler. He has moved up the crime food chain, from local gang lord to one of the national players.'

Seth felt his stomach churn as the events of twenty-eight years ago flooded back to his head yet again. *I suppose it all had to come out at some point.*

'Do you need me to explain?' he asked.

Xavier took up the lead again.

'Let us explain first Seth, I think we may know more than you realise we do…'

'Okay, go on,' said Seth.

'You believe that payment was made by Lawrence Fowler to pay for your silence after a regrettable accident that you were involved in. Now, you know you didn't kill Sharon McCrory, but nevertheless, if you'd just come clean at the time, you could probably have saved yourself an awful lot of stress over the years.'

Seth turned pale as he began to realise the extent of Xavier and Patricia's knowledge of his life.

Patricia took over the talking from Xavier again.

'Our extensive investigations showed that your father's trust fund had matured and paid out on your twenty-first birthday. It was all checked out, and we found that there was no need to be concerned.'

'What… my father's trust fund? I don't understand.'

'That money was always yours, Seth. It had nothing to do with Lawrence Fowler, well, not much anyway. Your father, Edward, set up a modest investment with Eatmon when you were born. The fund matured on your twenty-first birthday in 1992 and was paid in accordance with the fund's conditions. Rebecca Langford was supposed to send you a letter detailing the payment, but it appears that she didn't send it, allowing you to believe that the money came from Fowler. We imagine that she took the same amount from Fowler's funds and lined her own pockets, letting him believe that he'd paid you off. To a degree, you and Larry were both puppets in Rebecca Langford's quest to make more and more money for herself.'

'Fuck… sorry, I didn't mean to swear, it's just…'

Seth was floored by what he was hearing. 'How do you

know where the money came from, and Rebecca Langford's involvement with Larry,' asked Seth, looking for the missing parts in the puzzle he was trying to piece together.

'Good question Seth,' said Xavier, picking up the lead again. 'We've been watching Fowler for several years now, we get a lot of information that we feed into the police, so it's not been the right time to take him out of the equation yet. He has contacts in the Crown Prosecution Service, the police and a few business and financial institutions. Once we map it completely, we can remove the kingpin.

'Anyway, we picked apart his financial dealings with Eatmon, and that alerted us to his portfolio manager, Rebecca Langford, so we started watching her business deals and her private account. She took Larry to her own company when she set that up in 1993. Some years later, we needed a closer look at her operation; we needed to be in the room, digitally speaking.'

'Does this link to Marc Pashley? Is he one of your people?' asked Seth.

'No, Pashley is just a greedy man. His little operation was a surprise to us; we weren't looking for small internal criminal activity. Your involvement in investigating Marc Pashley had the potential to derail the work that we'd been doing for some time. Rebecca Langford has some very dubious clients, and we have been able to learn an awful lot about how the country's crime lords fit into the financial system,' said Xavier.

The dots still were not joining up for Seth.

'Can we talk about Emelia? Do you know where she is? How is Larry involved in her disappearance?' asked Seth, wanting to move things on.

'Yes, to the first question, and no to the second, I'm afraid,' said Xavier, as blunt as ever. 'Emelia works for me,' Xavier delivered Seth's next surprise.

'What...?' exclaimed Seth.

'I recruited Emelia from university, then we worked to get her into Rebeca Langford's company. We needed to use her exceptional computer skills to deliver what Rebecca needed and harvest information to map the financial dealings of the country's biggest crime lords. Rebecca looks after a lot of criminally obtained cash, cleaning it up for the organised crime groups behind it.

'Emelia designed the systems to plug us in. After Pashley's arrest and conviction, we needed to get her out. Her relationship with him had the potential to cause suspicion in Rebecca's mind,' said Xavier.

'I didn't know that she worked for Rebecca Langford. Why did I not know that?' asked Seth.

'Why would you?' answered Patricia.

'And my second question? Do you know where Emelia is now?' asked Seth.

'No, not yet. Emelia's been working on something else. She's been working on recruitment – her job was to help me vet you. The personal vetting side, that's why you met her at the reception in Kensington…' Xavier paused to let Seth process what he was hearing.

Seth was shocked. All this time, Emelia had been playing him, just tagging him along to pass information back to Xavier. This was one blow too many. His mind started recalling events, times that he thought were special. *No wonder she's always dodged the work and the moving in together questions.*

Patricia broke the silence.

'Before your mind starts to torment you, Seth, you need to know that I hadn't planned for you two to become close. The relationship that you have now is a real one. It may have started out on false pretences, seeds sown by us, but I hadn't foreseen Emelia developing feelings for you. That was certainly not the plan. You know that undercover officers of any kind can't go forging sexual relationships with their targets. It's no different with us. We may work behind what the public sees of the law, but we are still bound by it.

'Emelia properly declared to us that she had feelings for you. By that time, I was satisfied that you were suitable, and I cancelled her assignment. I immediately placed her on desk duties until we could recruit you and bring you into the fold,' said Patricia.

Seth was trying his hardest to work everything out. He was in overdrive. The last few weeks had been among the most stressful periods of his life. His mind was doing its best to keep up. He was trying to determine which parts of his past were still true and which were now turning to lies and misunderstandings. What he was hearing was flooding him with tsunami of emotion.

'Can we take a break? I need to take this all in,' replied Seth.

Xavier took Seth back down to the cafeteria and bought him another cup of earl grey tea.

'You can sit here, but don't leave without one of my staff or me. You'll be challenged without the appropriate tag around your neck Seth.'

'I understand. Can you just give me thirty minutes?' replied Seth.

'Okay, I'll come back and get you,' said Xavier, leaving Seth to find a seat.

Seth sat sipping his tea, slowly trying to work out who the people in his life really were. *What other surprises do they have?*

★ ★ ★

Seth sat down, back in the same chair in Xavier's office, opposite Patricia and Xavier, readying himself for the second half of the strangest meeting he had ever attended.

'Seth, before we go any further, I need to know if you're willing to work with us. We've already invested quite heavily in you. But I can't make you join the team, despite hoping that you will,' said Patricia kicking off part two.

Seth sat quietly for a moment, considering his feelings, trying to divorce those about Emelia from everything else in his mind before answering.

There was a minute or so of silence.

'Yes, I am, I'll need more information about the remit and everything, but in principle, yes, I'll work for you.'

'Good, I'm pleased to hear that. We need to get some signatures from you, get your bank details for salary payment, and issue you with an identification card. Then we can get down to business,' said Xavier.

'What about Emelia? What are you doing to find her?' asked Seth.

'Don't worry about her; Emelia can handle herself. We monitor the police intelligence feeds, and once we get a lead, we'll intervene and extract her,' said Xavier confidently.

'You must have some idea where Fowler would have taken her. You've been watching him after all,' said Seth.

'No, we only know that Fowler has her and Pashley somewhere. He has no idea who Emelia really is. He thinks she worked with Pashley to steal money from his portfolio. Emelia worked on inserting patches into the L.I.M systems to extract information for us. Any missing money over and above that taken by Pashley is likely to have been hived off by Rebecca Langford herself,' said Xavier, as he picked up the telephone in the office and punched in four numbers. 'Amy, can you bring in Seth's folder, please.'

The office door opened, and a young woman walked in and handed a large, sealed buff envelope to Xavier.

'Thank you, Amy.'

Xavier took the envelope, opened it and tipped the contents onto the table.

'Seth, I need you to read and sign the contract. It's just employment stuff. This unit is governed wholly by employment law regarding its employees, no police regulations here. Then the bank details form, with a signature please, and the third document is the Official Secrets Act declaration, you'll have signed one before.'

Seth read through the bland contract documentation and signed all the documents, adding his bank details to the salary form. Patricia then passed him a pre-printed identification card complete with a photograph borrowed from his police personal file.

'That was a bit presumptuous,' said Seth, not sure whether to laugh or cry.

They had well and truly reeled him in. They were very good at their job.

'Welcome to the team Seth, it's good to have you on aboard. Xavier will brief you on your first assignment, and don't worry, we'll get Emelia away from Lawrence Fowler's grasp,' said Patricia.

Seth put his hand into his pocket and pulled out the memory stick containing the footage and stills of Emelia's abduction.

'There may be something on here that can help us. It shows the point that Emelia was snatched at the underground station,' he said as he handed it to Xavier.

Xavier took the memory stick from him.

'Thank you, I'll get it looked at and let you know of anything useful. There is one more thing… come with me will you,' he said, walking towards the office door.

Seth followed Xavier out of the office.

CHAPTER 27

First Assignment

Xavier led Seth through the open plan office and through a set of double doors and into what looked like a police briefing room.

'Have a seat, Seth, and please open the file; it contains details of your assignment. The pin code is set as the numbers from your postcode and then your mothers date of birth. You'll be asked for a new code once you put that one in.'

In the middle of the table was a plastic folder marked in red with the word confidential in capitals and sealed with what looked like a security seal. Seth sat staring at it, wondering what his new career was going to look like. He was sure that it would be quite a bit different to his previous one. He picked up the file marked for his eyes only and opened it. Inside was a computer tablet; he pushed the power button and tapped in his passcode. The tablet prompted him for a new security pin. Once he had reset it, the details of his first assignment popped up on the screen. He knew before he started reading that his assignment related to Emelia DiSalvo's extraction from the grips of Larry Fowler's organisation.

'I'll be back in a moment Seth, there's someone I'd like you to meet,' said Xavier, somewhat mysteriously.

Xavier walked back in, followed by another man. The man

with the familiar gait.

'Seth, I think you've met Glen before?' said Xavier, turning to Glen Borland as he spoke.

'What... what's he doing here? I don't understand,' said Seth, clearly baffled by Borland's presence.

'Hello Seth,' said Glen.

'This is probably a bit of a shock, Seth, but Glen works for us now and has done for a while. We contacted him while he was in prison and fabricated his death to get him out. You see, we've been looking for a way into Lawrence Fowler's world for some time. Emelia's work at Rebecca Langford's office has helped build a good picture of Fowler's finances. We also now have a good part of the country's broader criminal network mapped financially, as well as how their money is cleaned up. But we needed to understand the operational world that Fowler runs. Glen has given us that insight.'

Seth was dumbfounded. He had already had his fair share of surprises from Xavier, first the fact that Emelia worked for Section Three and now that he and Glen Borland were on the same team. He was at the point of expecting his mother and father to be rolled in next; nothing seemed to be impossible in this place.

'Right, what's the deal, how does all this fit together, how does he help us get Emelia out of trouble?' asked Seth.

'Well, I'm putting the two of you together on this. What better than a career detective and one of Larry's former generals working as a team? Glen is your new partner, and this will be his first field operation,' said Xavier, smiling through his words.

Seth and Glen looked at each other, inhaling an extra-large lungful of breath at the same time.

'Let's get you two briefed, shall we,' said Xavier turning on a large screen. 'Lawrence Fowler, you both know him. He still lives at a house called Kuredo in South Ascot. Glen, you know the size and extent of his criminal empire. We believe that he has police officers, crown prosecutors, customs staff, lawyers and possibly judges on his payroll. Emelia's work tells us that they are paid by way of dividend payments from Langford's investment company, all of which is declared and dealt with, totally above board to maintain a low profile.

'He generally only deals with his management team - his generals - but he does occasionally get hands-on with some of the criminal activity himself. He works with a few thugs that he can trust and his watchmen keeping an eye on the police. Would you agree, Glen?'

'Yeah, that's pretty much how he works,' replied Glen.

'So, from what Glen has given us, we don't think he will want to harm Emelia. He has a soft spot for women on account of how his father treated his mother. That doesn't put her out of danger because we believe that Tony Spiller is likely to be in charge of holding her and Pashley. If that's the case, we may have trouble ahead. He's not so compassionate.'

'So, what's the plan, how do we approach this?' asked Glen.

'I was just getting to that, Glen,' said Xavier. 'the key is that we cannot afford this organisation to become a known entity that is entirely out of the question, a tactical parameter. By the same token, if we alert the police to the circumstances of Emelia's disappearance, we risk undermining the work we've done so far to monitor Fowler and the other crime lords in this country. If Emelia's parents report her missing, or the police believe they are dealing with an abduction, then they'll swing into full kidnap investigation mode. We don't need that at all; Emelia knows that, so she won't fold under interrogation. We need to get to her before the police receive any information or intelligence about her disappearance.

'You two need to go to Larry, in your own capacities, Glen as a former member of Larry's team and Seth as an ex-cop, now considering that offer he made you… you want to work for him now.

'Between you, you need to find out where Larry is holding Emelia, then sort out extracting her. We only have one chance of success. Once you've burned your natural cover with Fowler, you'll be permanently outside his circle, and we won't get back in.

'The files on your tablet contain everything we know about Fowler and his organisation, including Tony Spiller. Take it away, study everything and come up with a plan, a plan that will work. But whatever you decide, you're working together on this, understand?' said Xavier, looking at Seth and Glen in turn.

He hoped that he had not pushed things too far by putting Seth and Glen together so early, but it was as much a test of their fit with the organisation as anything else.

★ ★ ★

Seth and Glen left the Home Office and headed for the train station, choosing to walk along the Embankment rather than taking the tube. Seth was the first to break the silence.

'Glen, I need to understand something.'

'Fire away, what's on your mind, mate?' replied Glen.

'I just need to know why you didn't mention me in the interview about Sharon McCrory,' asked Seth.

'That's simple. I thought you were working for Larry, grass you up, and I'd be in deeper shit. It was safer to say what I did,' said Glen.

'Simple as that then?' replied Seth.

'Pretty much, yep, you don't cross Larry without an insurance policy.'

'Okay, I have no idea how our lives have ended up in the same place again, but given we seem to be working for the same outfit now, it would seem a good idea to just get on with it, don't you think?'

'Seth mate, I have no trouble working with you at all. I was recruited months ago; it bought me an early release from prison. As unlikely as it may seem, I'm very happy to be putting my skills to a better purpose than just burglary and drug shit. Life didn't give me many breaks as a kid. I went to the wrong school, hung out with the wrong crowd and then got involved with Larry as a teenager. I was doomed from the start,' said Glen.

Seth listened as Glen told him about his early days with Larry Fowler and his offending. He held nothing back, telling the whole story, right up to Xavier's approach when he was in prison and how he ended up working with Section Three.

'Wow, your life has been very different to mine. I appreciate you telling me. You obviously know that Emelia and I are... well, we're together. I need to do this my way, properly. I've run many kidnap and missing person enquiries over the years, I know what I'm doing,' said Seth, as they crossed the Thames.

'No offence Seth, but if this needed investigating in the traditional way, the police would have the case already. This is not a missing person enquiry. This is a locate and extract operation. One that needs to protect the identity of Section Three,' said Glen.

He had become Mr Corporate surprisingly quickly.

'I'm not talking about a slow burn step by step missing person investigation, Glen, I'm talking about a fast-paced kidnap enquiry, we need to make contact with Larry and negotiate, and we need to do it fast,' said Seth, who was feeling a little put down by Glen.

'We're on the same page, well, at least in terms of making contact anyway, but there won't be much in the way of negotiation. We don't have anything to bargain with. It'll be more likely to be threats and demands Seth, that's Larry's language. I am on this with you because I know him so well. At the moment, matey, I'm your best friend, and the only way we can get this done is through me and my connection with Larry,' said Glen, feeling puffed up and important.

They arrived at Waterloo station twenty-five minutes after leaving the Home Office. Glen handed the left-luggage ticket to the attendant, who walked away, returning with a black holdall which he passed over the counter. Glen unzipped it, checked the contents, and then stuffed his still sealed file inside.

'What's in there?' enquired Seth.

'Just kit, don't worry, it's all issued and approved. It's just not the kind of stuff we are allowed to carry into the Home Office. It would set off the alarms and look pretty bad on the x-ray machine if you get my drift. Where are we off to Seth? We need to plan for tonight,' said Glen.

'My place is a burnt-out shell; it's back to Emmy's house in Highgate. There's a spare room you can use. We'll run through the documents and work out our plan. It's about forty minutes from here; we can take the Northern Line.'

'We'd better get a move on. Let's go and get this thing planned,' replied Glen, as they set off.

* * *

Seth unlocked the door to Emelia's house.

'Come in, can I get you a coffee?' he asked Glen.

'Cheers, yeah white with two sugars'

'So, what is in the bag,' said Seth, pushing Glen to disclose its contents.

Glen put the holdall on the kitchen island, unzipped it, and pulled out the plastic file, setting it to one side.

'Electronic case papers, and other shit,' he said smiling.

'Yeah, it's the other shit I am concerned about,' replied Seth.

Glen started taking out the rest of the bag's contents, providing Seth with a commentary as he went.

'Cable ties, gaffer tape, gloves, night vision kit, two burner phones complete with push to talk capability, credit cards – billed back to the department – and the last few bits are my own tools of choice for getting into houses, should I need to,' said Glen smiling, as he handed Seth a phone and one of the credit cards.

'And that, you didn't mention that?' Seth pointed at what looked like a shoulder holster.

'Ah yes, that's a fucking gun Seth, I thought that was bloody obvious. It's Home Office issue, pretty much like my old one from the burglary days. To be honest, I've only ever shot someone once, but it always made sense to have a gun in my old world. Xavier seems to think it's sensible now too.'

'Great, I'm working with an ex-con, who up until now has been well and truly on the opposite side of my table, and he is armed, you couldn't bloody make it up,' quipped Seth.

'Okay, enough of your kit envy, I need to brief you,' said Glen, slurping down a mouthful of coffee.

Seth sat opposite him and listened as Glen unloaded what had clearly already been discussed and planned with Xavier.

'Alright, we know that Larry's behind Emelia's disappearance. He'll most likely be using Tony Spiller and his cronies to do his dirty work. That poses a problem. Tony is a vicious bastard and is far more likely to hurt or kill someone.

'Larry believes that Emelia was working with Marc Pashley to skim money away from Rebecca Langford's investment business. You know all about Pashley's skimming enterprise, Seth,' said Glen.

'Yes, I put him away for the fraud, but we never tracked down or accounted for the missing millions,' replied Seth.

'That's because he didn't have it. Rebecca had been taking

large slices of cash from Larry's investments for years. Once Pashley's activity was found out, she tried to pin the whole fucking lot on him. Larry has no idea it was down to his trusted investor. He thinks that Emelia or Pashley have the money hidden somewhere. Anyway, our first step must be to speak with Larry. I think I can use you to get to him at his house. The only hurdle to overcome is that he thinks I'm dead.

'Then we need to get to Spiller and take him and his cronies out before they harm Emelia,' Glen smiled as he finished speaking.

* * *

Seth and Glen headed off at one o'clock in the morning, Seth driving Emelia's Mercedes convertible. They made good progress, crossing London to Wembley, then taking the A30 out of London to pick up the M25 before dropping into Ascot through Bagshot. They arrived fifty minutes later and pulled into Coronation Road.

'You ready for this, Seth?' asked Glen.

Seth took a deep breath and closed his eyes for a second.

'Yeah, as ready as I'll ever be, let's get this done.'

CHAPTER 28

Return to Kuredo

The Mercedes drew up at the gates to Kuredo in Coronation Road. The last time both men had been at the address, their worlds had been very different. Seth lowered the car window and pushed the intercom button. There was no reply. After pressing it twice more, a light came on in the house, and the intercom crackled to life.

'Who the fuck's there,' asked Larry Fowler.

Glen leant over from the passenger seat to speak.

'Larry, it's me, Glen... I need to talk to you.'

There was a long silence before Larry answered.

'I thought you were fuckin' dead, Scotch. What the fuck do you want? We didn't part on good terms. You've got a nerve coming back here at all, let alone at this time of night. Fuck off,' said Larry. He had no interest in entertaining Glen in the middle of the night.

'Wait, Larry, I've brought Seth Hannen with me. He's out of the pigs now, wants to work with you... with us,' said Glen.

They sat and waited, but there was no reply. Seth buzzed the intercom again.

'Larry...come on mate, why would I even bother coming to see you after the way we fell out? This is legit,' said Glen.

'I don't fuckin' believe you,' you'll excuse me if I don't

fuckin' trust you either,' said Larry.

'He's being upfront, Larry, it's me, Seth Hannen, I'm working with Glen,' said Seth, speaking into the intercom.

'Wait there,' came Larry's reply.

Seth and Glen turning up together was enough to pique Larry's interest; he had to find out what was going on.

Seth and Glen watched as more lights came on in the house. After a couple of minutes, a figure exited the side door. The security lights lit up the driveway illuminating Larry's silhouette as he walked slowly but purposely up to the gate. He was dressed in a heavy dressing gown and wearing slip-on shoes. When he reached the gate, he took hold of the bars and peered through. He was standing exactly where Seth had seen him last, in 1992. Larry was older and slower, but he still had an intimidating air about him.

Larry looked at the men and nodded before stepping back. He took a small remote-control keypad from his dressing gown pocket and held it up for them to see. He pushed the button and then turned and walked back towards the house while the gates opened behind him.

Seth slipped the Mercedes back into gear and drove in, driving slowly behind Larry. He parked the car in the same spot that he had parked the Aston years before. He noticed that the flashy Aston had been replaced by an all-electric Tesla saloon. Larry was clearly looking to portray the persona of an environmentally conscious businessman.

Seth and Glen looked at each other briefly and nodded, then Seth popped the boot open and got out of the car. *Back into the lion's den,* he thought, as he grabbed Glen's holdall from the boot and handed it to him. Larry had already gone back into the house, leaving the side door open for them to follow.

'If he goes to open the safe, we need to stop him. That's where he keeps his gun,' said Glen keeping his voice low.

They walked into the house to find Larry stood in the hallway waiting for them. Larry was now in his early seventies, but aside from the white hair in place of the blonde, and some wrinkles, he still looked like the Larry that Seth remembered. The last time he was here, Seth had felt sick. Back then, he believed that he had taken an irreversible step to be a bent copper and that he had accepted a payoff from Larry. Although he still felt a significant degree of responsibility for the outcome, he found himself stood there now, knowing that the money was not Larry's and the woman had died from a drug overdose. Seth still felt anxious. The very survival of one of the most important people in his life rested with Larry.

'Come in, lads, this is most unexpected,' said Larry as he led Seth and Glen through towards the sitting room.

Glen dropped his holdall at the kitchen door as they walked. As they passed the bottom of the staircase, Larry shouted out. 'Sandra, we have two very special guests; we're going to need a pot of coffee.'

'You're joking… really, now?' replied Sandra from the bedroom.

'Come, let's go sit, said Larry, as he led them into the sitting room. 'Have a seat, Seth. I need a quick word with your man Glen here.'

Seth sat in the same spot he had occupied on his first visit to the house. The room looked familiar; it had the same antique wooden furniture, but with a new flat-screen television, and the sofas had been replaced. Larry led Glen back out of the room and closed the door behind him.

'What the fuck is this Glen, what's your game?' he said.

'I had a bad time inside Larry, so they gave me a new identity and moved me to another clink. I've been out a while now. I regret trying to do you over; it was wrong of me. I knew the only way I'd get you to consider having me back on the team would be to bring you something valuable. That's why he's with me. Seth Hannen retired from the pigs, and I approached him a few weeks back. I put a little pressure on him to work with me, to come over to the dark side. His contacts inside the police could be useful to us. Come on, Larry, you always said you could use him, and you've still got some dirt on him, enough to keep him loyal. You can't lose,' said Glen, hoping that Larry would buy the story.

As Larry was about to speak, Sandra came down the stairs, having hurriedly dressed.

'Sandra, you remember Glen here. He's done his time and has come back to work for me, the thoughtful soul... Glen, would you give Sandra a hand in the kitchen? I want to have a private word with Seth before we all have a joint pow-wow.'

'Hello Sandra,' said Glen, as he followed her toward the kitchen picking up the holdall on the way. 'Where's the dog?'

'Oh, Buster died a couple of years back Glen, broke Larry's heart,' replied Sandra.

Larry opened the sitting room door, went inside and closed it again.

'Seth, Seth Hannen, well I never.'

'Hello Larry, long time no speak,' replied Seth.

'Yes, it's odd that the man you helped put away should come out of prison and befriend you don't you think? I'm not buying this newfound alliance, not yet anyhow.'

Seth felt his nerves prickle as his senses became more alert. He was truly in uncharted waters now, with no back up other than an ex-con, who he did not really know or yet trust.

'Larry, I spent my whole career fighting with what happened here before. You, the car, the woman, the money. I was lucky to get through unscathed, lucky to keep my job and my sanity. I lost my mother recently and—'

Larry butted in before Seth could finish speaking.

'Yeah, I heard about that. My deepest condolences, Seth. You know that had nothing to do with me, don't you?'

'I had my suspicions to be honest, I still don't know what to think,' answered Seth.

'Well, it was not me Seth, Marc Pashley was responsible for the fire at your house and the death of your poor mother. But what goes around comes around. Let's just say he now knows what it feels like to be burned alive,' Larry smiled. 'Anyway, I'm still not convinced about you and Glen-boy, what's the fuckin' deal, it smells iffy, but I'm not sure which of you is hooky here,' said Larry

Seth was not sure what else to say. *Where is Glen? Hurry up!*

'Coffee's ready…' called Glen, as the door swung open, and he walked in with Sandra.

Seth turned to see Glen marching Sandra into the room. She had black gaffer tape over her mouth, and her arms were tied behind her back. Glen had his left arm linked through the crook of her elbow and his gun in his right hand. The muzzle was pushed upward under her jaw. He pushed her onto the second sofa. Sandra's eyes were wide open; she looked terrified, tears streaming from her eyes.

'Tie him up,' called Glen to Seth, pulling a couple of heavy-duty plastic cable ties from his back pocket and throwing them toward Seth while keeping the gun still trained on Sandra.

Seth looked shocked. He had not discussed this with Glen. He picked up the ties and pulled Larry to his feet, and bound his arms behind his back before pushing him across the room and sitting him next to Sandra.

Glen pulled out another handful of cable ties that protruded from his back pocket and held them out to Seth.

'Tie their feet,' he said.

Seth tied their ankles together before then adding an extra tie to hold their legs together.

'Now I understand, you are working together, you pair of turds, are you bastards going to tell me what's fuckin' going on. I assume neither of you actually want to work with me?' said Larry, who looked like he was about to overflow with rage.

'We are here about Emelia DiSalvo,' said Seth.

Sandra looked confused, staring at Larry but unable to speak through the tape.

'Oh, that bitch, she's… how would you say it, Seth, helping with enquiries,' replied Larry. 'What Tony does to her is his business, but she owes me a lot of money, and I want it back.'

'You're looking at the wrong woman Larry, your thief is much closer to home. Try looking at Rebecca. I did warn you years back,' said Glen.

'That's fuckin' bollocks. Rebecca wouldn't have the guts to cross me,' replied Larry.

'You see, Larry, Emelia is very close to Seth here. Seth has lost a lot and does not want to lose this woman. We need you to tell us where she is, and we need to know now.'

'Fuck off, nobody tells me what to do,' said Larry, smirking.

'You two cowboys don't have a chance; what the hell are you going to do, beat an old man? I'm seventy-two now, for fuck's sake.'

Glen sauntered over to Larry and stopped.

'Larry, I don't give a shit how old you are. It was you that put me inside, not Seth, you. I owe you for that,' he said as he drew his arm back, then swinging it downward at Larry. The handle of the gun contacting Larry's cheekbone with a whack, sending Larry's head pivoting.

Sandra screamed through the tape on her mouth as Larry's skin opened and let out a stream of blood. Seth watched, not sure how he felt. This was a new kind of law enforcement to him, one which he was certainly not entirely comfortable with.

'Fuck you,' said Larry, glaring at Glen.

Seth walked over and sat to Larry's right.

'Larry, Glen here is clearly willing to hurt you, and maybe Sandra as well, if you don't help us find Emelia. I know that you don't want to help but believe me, this will go very badly for you if you don't.'

'Why are you working together? I still don't understand that bit,' asked Larry.

'That's not your concern Larry, let's just say it's a mutually agreeable arrangement,' said Seth.

As Seth stood up, Glen whipped his hand again, hitting Larry in the same part of his chin, before swinging his arm back again in the opposite direction. Larry shook his head as he regained his senses.

'That is quite enough,' a voice came from the door behind Seth and Glen.

They turned at the same time to see a man standing in the doorway. He held a gun with a silencer in his outstretched hand, pointing it directly at Glen.

'Michael, sorry to have woken you,' said Larry, smiling at his son.

Michael was now in his late thirties and had been back at Kuredu

for a couple of days, working on Larry's new business opportunities.

'You disgust me, beating an old-age pensioner... what's this all about, Dad?'

'Michael meet, Glen and Seth, you might remember Glen, he used to work for me, and Seth's a bent ex-copper, now fully embracing crime it would appear. It seems that they have a fuckin' grievance with me of some sort,' said Larry.

'Drop the gun,' shouted Michael.

'You drop yours, pal,' replied Glen, turning his gun towards Sandra's head.

Michael smiled as he pulled a mobile phone out of his back pocket, pressed the home button and spoke to the phone while still pointing the gun at Glen.

'Call Tony,' he said before holding the phone to his ear.

'Hi Tony, it's Mike... yeah, I know it's late, I'm with my Dad. Things are a bit sticky this end, if you get my drift. How's the DiSalvo woman?'

There was a pause before Michael Fowler continued speaking.

'That is good Tony, Dad wants to make it clear that if she continues not to talk, that she needs to pay the ultimate price. Are you with her now?'

Another period of silence.

'Excellent, I have someone here that needs to know that she is okay. Call me back in two minutes on video,' said Michael, as he looked towards Glen.

They both lowered their guns but kept eye contact. Michael picked up a remote control and turned on the large screen television, then he connected his phone, mirroring it to the screen. The phone buzzed, and Michael answered it. Spiller smiled at the camera, his face appearing on the television screen.

'You remember Glen, don't you, Tony?' said Michael.

'I do, mate. Yeah, of course, I thought that shit bag was fucking dead. Is everything okay over there? What's going on, Mick?' asked Spiller.

Michael swung the phone round to show Tony the room, stopping briefly so that he could see Sandra and Larry tied up on the sofa, with Glen and Seth standing in front of them.

'As you can see, things are not as they should be, but Glen and Seth here are interested in the fate of the DiSalvo woman.'

Spiller passed his phone to one of his men. They walked along the poorly lit tunnel with white painted walls. The image from the phone became a little blocky as it started to lose its signal just as Emelia came into view. She was sitting on the floor, her hands above her head tied to the railings.

'Emelia, say hello to my friends,' said Spiller.

She looked up at the camera, her face was dirty, and she looked exhausted. 'She's a pretty one. I might need to have her before the night's out,' chirped Spiller, grinning back at the camera. He laughed as he knelt in front of Emelia. The phone's camera zoomed in as Spiller grasped hold of Emelia's breast and squeezed. He leant forward, stuck his tongue out and licked her cheek as he laughed.

'Thank you, Tony, for that important update, now back to me in the studio. We'll bring you more news as and when we get it. Oh, and Tony, if you don't hear from me by morning, kill the bitch,' said Michael before he hung up the call. 'Now drop the gun,' he aimed his pistol back at Glen, who threw his gun across the room. It landed at Michael's feet.

'Alright, you've made your point,' said Glen.

'Now you two be good chaps and sit the fuck down,' said Michael, as he picked up the gun and walked over to Larry and Sandra.

He pulled open a drawer in a small cabinet, took out a pair of scissors, and then cut his mother and father free and handed Glen's gun to Larry.

'How the tables turn, eh,' said Larry, as he wiped the blood from his chin. 'Tie 'em up.'

'Michael picked up some of the cable ties that Glen had left on the floor and bound Seth and Glen up. Larry walked over and took a full swing at Glen, replaying the scene from earlier.

'Wait here, Michael,' said Larry, as he walked toward the door, leading Sandra out of the room.

Larry went upstairs and got dressed before returning to the kitchen. He led Sandra out to the Tesla and drove away while calling Michael.

'I'm getting your mother out of here, I'll take her to a hotel, get her settled and then come home, and we'll sort this out. Just keep that pair of fuckin' turds with you, okay.'

'Yes, Dad, I'm on it. They're not going anywhere,' replied Michael, as he put the gun down on the coffee table and sauntered up to Seth.

'You, bastard pig,' he said, as he swung hard and low at Seth.

His clenched fist contacted the side of Seth's head, sending him sideways across the sofa. Then he threw a punch at Glen before lifting his foot and planting his heel hard into Glen's crotch. Glen buckled over on the sofa, the pain shooting through his groin.

Michael moved and lifted his foot again to do the same to Seth, who raised his tied ankles upwards as quickly and with as much force as he could muster. His aim was spot on, his feet contacting Michael Fowler hard between the legs, causing his knees to fail. As Michael fell towards the floor, Seth leaned into him, managing to administer a head butt, the main force of which came from the speed of Michael's fall. Michael groaned as he fell sideways, his head landing at Glen's feet. Glen lifted his feet up, and then he drove them downward onto his head. The second blow had taken away Michael's consciousness. Seth and Glen looked at each other and smiled.

'Not bad for an ex-copper,' said Glen.

'Thanks, and all from the comfort of the sofa, now what?' replied Seth.

Between them, and in a somewhat uncoordinated manner, they managed to get to the scissors and free themselves before tying up and gagging Michael Fowler.

Seth held the phone up to Michael's face and unlocked it, scrolling through the contacts until he found Tony Spiller's phone number. Then he pressed the speed dial for the Section Three night-office from the phone that Glen had given him earlier.

'Hello, this is Seth Hannen. I'm assuming you guys can access what the police can? If I give you a mobile number, can you get a trace on it? I need to know where it is, and fast.'

'Sure, we'll get onto it straight away,' came the reply.

'Thanks, let me know as soon as you get something.'

Seth took Michael's gun, leaving Glen with Michael at Kuredo. As he drove the Mercedes back towards Ascot High Street, his phone rang.

'Seth, it's Glen, head for Slough, they'll get more to you soon… and Seth take care mate, Spiller is a nasty piece of work.'

★ ★ ★

When Larry returned to Kuredo, he found Michael tied to a bar stool in the kitchen, trussed up like a kipper and gagging on a sock thrust deep into his mouth, held in place with a plastic cable tie tight around his head.

'What the fuck happened to you, you fuckin' little twat? Where have they gone?'

Michael's eyes were like saucers as Glen walked in behind and thrust his gun into the small of Larry's back.

'No more fucking about now, Fowler,' shouted Glen.

He tied and gagged Larry, being careful to keep the pair apart. Then he poured himself a glass of Larry's whisky, pulled up a stool on the opposite side of the kitchen island, and sat down.

'If it's okay with you guys, I'll just sit here and mind my own business while I wait for Seth to get back,' he said.

He sipped on the whisky awaiting Seth's update.

CHAPTER 29

The Follow

Ten minutes after leaving Kuredo, Seth's phone rang on the car's Bluetooth system. He answered quickly, hoping it was news on the phone trace.

'Hi Seth, this is Judy at Section Three. I have some good news and some not so good news for you.'

'Right, what do you have?' he asked.

'Well, we've run Tony Spiller's number with the mobile phone supplier, which has given us an international mobile equipment identity – an IMEI number – there's something really odd with his phone. I can't get a trace, not even historical position data. It's just not pinging anything back,' said Judy.

'I hope that wasn't the good news.'

'No, the good news is that I've been able to get data for telephone numbers called from his phone. I've run a check on the most frequently called numbers, and I've run traces on their locations against the time you and Emelia were at Old Street. I've managed to identify a number that I believe was at the scene of her abduction. That phone's IMEI relates to a smartphone with a global positioning chip. So, when it is back on and picks up a GPS signal, I'll be able to pinpoint it for you and down to a couple of metres,' said Judy, sounding pleased with herself.

'Great, but that doesn't tell me where to go now, does it.

Where do I start, any ideas?' Seth was less pleased.

'Yes, well, I can help there a bit,' said Judy.

'And?' replied Seth, he was used to a more succinct update on cell-site work from his old police authority's bureau, with less chatter.

'I ran a historical check on the IMEI, starting from the time stamp on the CCTV you supplied. The trace showed that the phone first went to a small works unit under a railway line, then it moved again to a warehouse outside London. A twenty-two-mile journey from Old Street to a place called Horton Industrial Park in Poyle near Slough. There are a few industrial units there. That's where I'd start looking, Seth. I'll call you if I get a trace from the phone,' said Judy.

'Thanks, Judy, that's really useful. Bye for now,' said Seth before he hung up the call.

Seth knew the Horton and Wraysbury patch from his days with Thames Valley Police. It was about a ten-mile drive, but he needed to turn around and go cross country through Virginia Water and Stanmore. He turned the car around and floored the accelerator, the gears kicking down on the automatic transmission as he sped on his way.

Seth arrived in Poyle at just after three-twenty in the morning and quickly located the industrial estate. There were six cars and a van parked in the spaces at the front, next to the entrance gates. He parked alongside them, got out of the Mercedes, and walked up to each vehicle to check for heat on the bonnet, then he slid a finger through the wheels and onto the front brake disks. He had learnt years ago that with insulation under the bonnet, you may not always be able to feel the heat from the engine. But checking the brake disk for heat would often give away a recently driven car. All were completely cold.

Next, he walked around the industrial estate; there were ten units, all of which were in darkness. He took out his phone and took a photo of the name board for the estate detailing the ten businesses and their units. Then he walked back to the car and got in to check the companies on the internet.

The car park was too well lit. He would be seen too easily if he stayed parked there, so he moved the car across the road and into a driveway to Horton Park. It looked like a mobile home site, *could be a traveller site, not ideal,* thought Seth. He was parked up for no more than five minutes before the lights in one of the homes came on. *Time to move on already.* He started the car, drove back onto the main road and parked up in the car park of a pub, giving him a good view down the road. He would easily see anyone arriving at the industrial estate.

Two hefty men walked towards Seth along the pavement, from the direction of the mobile home site. *They're out late,* he thought to himself. His mind was back in cop mode, almost getting out of the car to have a chat and ask what they were up to, but he remembered he had left the police; he worked for a different outfit now. The men walked past the Mercedes, glancing at Seth as they did. He paid no attention to them as they walked on along Poyle Road, redirecting his gaze back to the entrance of the industrial estate. *Come on, Judy, I need more than a historic hit on a location. This could be a complete waste of time.* His mind wandered to Emelia. *Was she just playing me for Xavier, or is there really something more to our relationship? What if—*

The passenger door of the Mercedes opened, interrupting Seth's thoughts.

'Oi, mukka, what was you doin' down by Horton Park?' It was the heavier of the hefty men he had walked past.

Seth was caught off guard, jumping with surprise.

'Just lost mate, nothing more.'

'Then fuck off, mukka,' snapped the man.

'Look, I just need to rest up a bit. I've been travelling ages,

I'm lost, and I just need some kip,' Seth was bluffing big time.

The driver's door opened, the other of the two men was standing by the door.

'What you up to mate?' he said.

'I just told your friend, I'm just resting,' said Seth. He had a feeling that things were not looking good. Previous run-ins with travellers had not gone well. The ones he had previously met generally did not like the police. Despite Seth not being a cop anymore, he oozed the persona of a police officer. Thirty years of policing had indelibly marked him, making him easy to spot as a cop.

'I think you need to get out and have a chat,' said the man at the driver's door.

'No, I don't think that would be a good idea,' replied Seth.

As Seth went to pull the driver's door shut, his phone rang. *Shit, that'll be Judy.* 'Look, guys, I really need to take this; it's an important call. Can we just go our separate ways?' said Seth, despite thinking that his request was unlikely to be agreed to.

'Out, or I'll punch your lights out where you're sat, posh boy.'

The phone stopped ringing. Seth stepped out of the car and was immediately pushed by the man standing at the driver's door.

'Mind your step mate, you'll hurt yourself,' he said.

If ever there was a time when he needed a police radio to call for urgent assistance, now was it. The place would be flooded with cops from miles around if a call was put out from an officer in distress. But he neither had a radio nor was he a police officer anymore. As he steadied himself, the other man pushed him back again, he was in a game of tennis, and he was the ball. The third shove came with a punch to the gut from the larger of the two men. The other man took Seth's legs out from under him with a striker's penalty kick to the calf muscles. Seth hit the deck. In a fight, the last place you wanted to be was on the floor. Seth instinctively took up the defensive position taught to him year on year in his officer safety training. He backed up against the car, holding his body up with his arms, and flailed his legs, kicking out to try and prevent the two men from getting close enough to get a strike in. It did not stop them trying though, as the boots came flying toward Seth, he remembered the gun Glen had made him take with him.

'Take the car, you can have the car, if you just let me be, I just need to get my phone, and you can keep the car,' shouted Seth, at the top of his voice.

The kicks slowed, and the men stood laughing.

'Alright mate, you are giving us the car yeah, no reporting it nicked or anything, we can have your car, yeah?'

'Yes, just let me get my phone. I need my phone for a taxi,' said Seth, as he got to his feet.

'The passenger side, go to the passenger side,' said one of the men.

Seth did as he was asked. As he walked around the car, the larger of the two men got in and sat waiting to start it. Seth leant in and opened the glove box, pulled the gun out and pointed it at the man in the driver seat.

'Get out of my car, slowly, do it now,' he said, slipping back into his firearms commander set of orders.

'Behave, posh boy, that's not real, you wouldn't know what to do with it, fuck off out of my new car, posh boy.'

He chuckled at Seth as he started the car's engine.

Seth moved his aim and squeezed the trigger. The silenced muzzle let its charge go with a muffled thwack, the bullet whizzing past the man's face and hitting the wall of the pub.

'The next one won't miss, I promise you,' said Seth. He felt a strange sense of power that he had never experienced before. This was very different to being on a police firearms operation.

Despite the edgy adrenalin rush it gave him, he was unsure whether he liked the feeling.

The man outside the car spoke next.

'Fuck me, Jon, let's just piss off, mate.'

The bigger man got out of the car, and they backed away, walking back toward where they had come from.

If they were travellers, they could be tooled up and back within twenty minutes, thought Seth, as he got into the car and locked the doors. He unscrewed the silencer and slid it into the glove box before pushing the gun into the waistband of his jeans and then getting his phone out and calling Section Three.

'Judy, so sorry I missed your call, had a spot of bother this end,' he said calmly.

'Hi Seth, I thought you'd fallen asleep or something. The second phone is back on, and I've got an IMEI trace running. It's heading your way from Slough, no more than half a mile away now, if that,' said Judy.

As she finished speaking, a black multi-van drove past Seth and headed towards the industrial estate, turning left into the entrance.

'Where is it now?' asked Seth.

'Hold on, it's just stopped… it's in the Poyle Industrial Estate. You should probably be able to see it.'

'Judy, you are a star indeed, thanks so much. I'll speak later if I need anything else.'

'Thanks, Seth, bye.'

Seth reversed the car further back in the pub car park and into the shadows from the bushes at the back and out of sight from the road. If the travellers returned, he wanted them to give up and turn back, thinking he had gone.

He got out, locked the car and set off at a slow jog towards the industrial estate. His money was on the unit listed as Value Meats Pet Food, as it was the only one of the companies listed that did not show up on a Google search. As he entered the estate, he could see that one of the units was now lit up. Sure enough, it was Value Meats.

He got to a position where he could see what was going on. As he watched the van being unloaded, his heart stopped. A woman seemed to be giving directions, while a man pulled what could only be a body bag from the rear of the van, letting it thud to the floor under its own weight. *Shit, I'm too late.* As he stood transfixed, his phone buzzed. Seth ducked around a corner and pulled it out to read the text.

E's phone was last live
At your current location - Judy

So, she was definitely here at some point; this must have been where they first brought her. The man and woman pulled the body bag into the unit and then locked the doors shut, then they climbed back into the van. Seth sprinted back to the pub car and stood behind the bushes, watching and waiting to see which way the lights would turn. As he watched, he saw a group of nine or ten men walking in his direction. *Shit, the travellers are back.* At the head of the group were the two men that had caused trouble earlier. Seth stood watching as they got closer. Still no van. *Come on, hurry up*—Fifty metres to go. The larger man from earlier was carrying what looked like a sawn-off shotgun. Still no van. Then Seth saw the road light up with the glow of vehicle lights. The van was on its way out of the industrial estate. *Yes, let's get out of here,* thought Seth. The van reached the junction with the main road. Seth watched, ready to run to the Mercedes and take up his follow. The van sat at the mouth of the junction, stationary.

Meanwhile, the posse of men was closer still, talking and bolstering each other's ego as they walked along the pavement.

Forty metres, thirty metres. The van turned right toward Seth. He ran to the Mercedes and jumped in, started the engine and kept the lights off. Just as the group of men passed the hedge that Seth had been hiding behind, the van passed him. The larger man raised the shotgun and pointed it at the Mercedes as Seth put his foot to the floor. The wheels spun as the car lurched forward, reaching the road quickly, the group of men running toward him. *That was bloody close, thank fu—* His thought was interrupted by the sound of the twelve-bore releasing its lead shot, followed immediately by the sound of the rear window shattering as the pellets hit the car. Seth instinctively shrugged his shoulders, pulling his head downward, waiting to feel the pain of the lead hitting him. Nothing, no pain, he had managed to avoid injury, but only just. Then another bang as the shooter let the second barrel loose. This time there was no breaking of glass, but also no pain. The shot had missed its target, and Seth was now moving at speed around a bend, taking him to safety.

In the commotion, he had lost the van. He dialled Judy's number on the car's Bluetooth speed dial. She answered quickly.

'Hi Seth, are you tailing the van now?'

'Long story short, I've lost it, not sure if it's ahead of me or if it's turned off.'

'I thought you were trained in surveillance stuff, hold on.'

The line went quiet aside from the sound of Judy frantically typing on her keyboard. 'Looks to be heading for Windsor or Slough Seth,' said Judy.

'Thanks, I'm heading that way; they must be bloody motoring. Keep monitoring Judy. I'll call if I don't get back in contact with the van.'

Seth pressed the accelerator, hoping to catch sight of the van's rear lights soon. As he entered Datchet, he saw the taillights of the van three hundred metres ahead of him. They travelled through Datchet, then Windsor, and into Slough, turning right onto Windsor Road. As he headed towards the A4 and passed Slough Police Station, Seth glanced at the illuminated sign above the main entrance. *Life was simpler when I was in the job,* he thought to himself, almost wishing he could just park the car and go up to his old desk in the CID office. The van drove on for a short distance before turning onto Stoke Road and then immediately left into the Old Market Yard car park. Seth drove into Brunel Way, parking the Mercedes at the railway station, doing his best to hide the car's damage by reversing into the parking space in the back corner.

Seth checked that the handgun was still securely in the waistband of his jeans and then ran back to where he had seen the van. As he got to Stoke Road, a police patrol car cruised by, causing him to instantly slow to a walk, not wanting to draw attention to himself. He walked along Stoke Road, past the car park and towards the town centre, glancing back to keep an eye on the van.

Two people got out of the van in the car park. They looked around before walking up to a panel of white hoarding that surrounded a cleared demolition site, then they disappeared behind a small tree. Seth watched as they pushed the panel aside and squeezed through the gap before moving the panel back into place.

Seth turned around and ran back along Stoke Road and then into the car park and up to the point that they had used to get into the fenced-off site. He felt unusually nervous; the thought of having no immediate backup, no real communications options, and just the gun in his belt made him feel uneasy. Then he remembered the phone that Glen had given him had a push to talk function, effectively allowing it to use the mobile network as the carrier for walkie-talkie type communications.

'Seth to Glen, are you receiving, over.' There was no reply from Glen. 'Seth to Glen, over.'

There was a short hiss, then Glen's voice came out of the phone. 'Yes, mate, I'm here; what's with all the over stuff?'

'Sorry Glen, hard to drop police radio protocol,' said Seth.

'Fair enough, what do you need? I'm just keeping Larry company. Any news on Emelia?' asked Glen

'No, not really. I'm at the Old Market Yard car park in Slough. I think Spiller and a woman have just gone into a cleared demolition site behind the car park. Any idea what they may have in there?'

'No, none at all… mate, Spiller will be tooled up, watch yourself,' warned Glen.

'Cheers, Glen, I'll update you later.'

Seth took a deep breath and then pulled himself up to get a view over the hoarding. About halfway across the site was an entrance to a set of steps that went down into the ground. The man and woman were just disappearing down the steps and out of sight.

CHAPTER 30

The Descent

Emelia had been tied to an old wooden chair. Her ankles were tied to the front legs and her wrists to each side of the upright backrest.

'Now then, Emelia, you saw what happened to your friend Marc Pashley. He paid the ultimate fucking price for stealing from Mr Fowler and then not telling us where the money is hidden. Please don't let me have to take a similar course of action with you,' Tony Spiller spoke quietly into Emelia's ear.

Emelia said nothing. She just glared at Spiller defiantly.

'You can play the quiet game if you like, but you'll just end up in a hole, getting the same treatment as Pashley. Want to be burned alive, do you?' Spiller said chillingly.

It was not just a threat, he would execute Emelia if he needed to, and he would enjoy doing it. 'What do you think, Mugger…Thug… how should we make her talk?' said Spiller, turning to his wingmen, grinning and rubbing his hand on his groin.

'Do you want her to talk or groan, Tony?' said Mugger, laughing as he sat down on another chair, over near the wall.

Emelia found herself thinking that she was probably going to be raped and then murdered. How had her life come to this? Why had she been so receptive to Xavier when he approached her at University? Where the fuck was Section Three now, and where was Seth, surely at least Seth would come and find her.

Spiller walked up, straddled the chair, and sat on Emelia's lap so that he was facing her.

'Now, are you going to tell me what I need to know, little Miss Pretty? Mr Fowler wants his money back. Marc Pashley has paid his debt; it's just you now. How are you going to pay yours?'

Spiller leant in and licked Emelia's cheek, running his tongue up to her forehead and then ending his slimy assault with a kiss.

Thug pulled a sack trolley with a large lorry battery on it towards Emelia. The battery was wired up to a rheostat, a control unit for changing the output voltage. Hooked on the trolley handle was a long brown pole connected to the rheostat by a length of electrical cable – the device looked homemade. Thug parked it next to Emelia's chair.

'This is a very rare thing, Emelia… You see, these are hard to get hold of, probably because they're banned in most countries. This is a picana Emelia. I was taught how to use it in Argentina. It really is a lot of fun,' said Spiller.

He pulled a pair of paramedic's scissors from his back pocket and handed them to Mugger, who had walked back over to them.

'Sit still darlin', this won't hurt a bit,' said Mugger, as he started to cut away her clothing.

He cut all the way up both sleeves of her cotton jumper, then through the shoulders and collar, before ripping it from her, pulling her bra away with it. Thug stood watching and laughing.

'What the fuck are you doing, you bloody pervert, leave me alone,' shouted Emelia.

Mugger said nothing but continued to cut her jeans from her legs, leaving the rags hanging down from the chair, Emelia now sitting just in her knickers.

'Stop, leave me alone, for fuck's sake stop,' protested Emelia.

Tony started talking again.

'Shut up, slag, now let me finish what I was explaining. The picana is a bit like a cattle prod. It delivers a high voltage electric shock to a torture victim; that's you by the way, this little dial here lets me raise or lower the voltage. Trust me, sweetheart, it fucking hurts,' said Spiller.

He nodded to Thug, who picked up a full bucket of ice-cold water and threw it over Emelia. She took a sharp inhale of breath as her body reacted to the cold. Before she could breathe out, Spiller pushed the picana against the middle of her chest. The pain was immense and instantaneous as the electricity travelled through her body. Each of the four thousand volts felt like a nail being hammered into her.

'Hurts, doesn't it? It's not even turned up full whack yet,' laughed Spiller, before telling Thug to turn up the voltage.

'All set, boss, that's six thousand,' said Thug.

Spiller moved the bronze tip of the picana toward Emelia, holding it ten centimetres from her skin. He moved the tip up to her mouth.

'Shall I put in here?' he said, before moving it down to her crotch. 'Or maybe you'd like it in here. I reckon you're probably a bit kinky like that, aren't you?'

Mugger and Thug laughed like a pair of naughty schoolboys.

Emelia held her breath, not knowing what he was about to do, which part of her body was about to be violated.

Spiller moved the picana to her chest, holding it a couple of centimetres from her skin. Emelia flinched in anticipation of the pain. She took her bottom lip in-between her teeth and bit.

'The money, where is the fucking money hidden,' asked Spiller.

She was so tempted to explain that she worked for a secret

government department and that it was actually Rebecca that had syphoned a big chunk of Fowler's money away from his investments. That Marc Pashley had been Rebecca's coincidental and useful scapegoat. But that would blow her cover, and potentially out Section Three to the wider public, she had to hold her nerve, for now anyway.

'I have no idea. I was not involved with Marc Pashley's scam. I don't have your money,' she said, starting to sob.

Spiller moved the tip of the picana slowly forward until the two bronze tips contacted her left nipple, then he pushed hard. Emelia screamed as every muscle in her body tensed up, pulling tight against the pain. Spiller pulled the wand back. Emelia took a deep breath, taking a brief opportunity to breathe without any pain. Spiller prodded again, to her right side this time. The electricity repeated its agonising effect on her body. At the same time, Spiller took great pleasure watching her almost naked body writhe in the chair.

★ ★ ★

The hoarding scraped against the concrete as Seth pulled it back. The small gap allowed him just enough space to squeeze through. Once an office building or something, the site was now completely wiped of any sign of its existence, awaiting redevelopment. Chunks of concrete lay randomly, interspaced with weeds and small bushes that had seeded and taken root over the years since the area had been cleared. Seth crept towards the staircase, using only the moonlight to assist his vision. He looked down from the top of the square hole in the ground. The stairs led down to a landing then a second set of steps went further into the darkness. At the base of the steps was the outline of a door, a splinter of light indicating that it was very slightly open.

He switched his phone off, just in case Glen fired up the

push-to-talk and inadvertently alerted anyone to Seth's presence. He checked the gun in his waistband and started slowly down the steps, ready to turn and run back up if anyone came out of the doorway. Each step let out a scratchy crunch as his shoes disturbed the bits of debris. In all his time working in Slough, he had never known about this underground place. As he reached the first landing, he knelt on one knee, straining to listen, to check if anyone was nearby on the other side of the door. He heard nothing, so he took the tentative steps to the bottom of the stairwell.

Seth slowly opened the door and stepped into the dimly lit passageway. The white walled tunnel was about one hundred metres long. At the end, it branched left and right. *What is this place?* thought Seth.

As Seth was entering the tunnel, Spiller and his henchman were still having fun torturing Emelia with the picana.

The junction in the tunnel split two ways. One side led right and down more stairs. The other went left, a long, dimly lit continuation of the walkway, encased by white painted brick walls, with a white railing along its centre. Seth went right, descending two more flights of stairs into pitch blackness. There was so little light that having his eyes open or shut made no difference to his vision. He pulled his phone from his pocket, switched it back on and hit the torch function. Pointing the light into the darkness, he could make out the shape of what looked like an underground train platform. A sign on the wall said Slough in large letters, District Line written beneath. There were no rails, just an empty track bed. The station had never been finished. Seth turned the light back to the stairs and ran back up. He turned the phone back off before moving slowly along the long tunnel with the railing. A sound came from far ahead.

★ ★ ★

Spiller was enjoying watching Emelia squirm each time he touched his rod to her body. Emelia sat in the chair, hoping to pass out and get some relief. She was way past answering any questions now, just sitting waiting for the tip of the picana to make contact with her skin. Taking deep breaths, Emelia tried to think of Seth, their night out, and the morning after, how they were planning the rest of their lives. She wondered if Xavier would have spoken to Seth yet. How would Seth react when he found out she was deployed to recruit him.

Mugger threw another bucket of water, immediately waking Emelia and banishing any chance of unconsciousness. Almost immediately, Spiller pushed the end of the picana into Emelia's abdomen and ran the tip up and across her sternum to her neck. As she opened her mouth to scream, she passed out.

★ ★ ★

Seth walked along the tunnel staying close to the wall as he got closer and closer to the sound of a man and a woman speaking. His hand touched the gun in his waistband, as much out of self-assurance as of readiness. With each step, he felt his heart rate increasing as the adrenalin rocketed through his blood, providing him with the nervous energy he needed. He could just make out the figures of the man and woman that he had followed into the tunnel from the van. They were moving in and out of an alcove in the tunnel. *That must be where Emelia is,* he thought. They disappeared back out of sight. Seth took more cautious steps towards them. As he reached the point where the wall veered off to the left into the alcove, he found himself glued to the spot. The white painted bricks were cold against his cheek. Not sure what to expect, he slid his head toward the edge of the wall and peered around the corner into the gloominess. The talking had stopped, and he could see the man and woman, their backs toward him. The floor was wet with fresh water. Where was Emelia? He could only see the two of them.

'Who's there?' said the woman, as they both turned around.

Seth pulled his head back, *stay put or move to the fight.* Despite being unsure of what course of action to take, he knew he really only had one option available to him. Whether he stayed put, walked into the open, or tried to leave, he would be discovered for sure.

The feeling of being alone overwhelmed him again. He would need to get used to it if he was to remain with Section Three.

Seth stepped out into the opening and looked into the darkness. He could just make out the shape of two people.

'I'm here,' he declared.

'Who the fuck are you?' asked the man.

'I'm Seth Hannen, Tony,' replied Seth.

'Tony? Oh, you mean Spiller, he's not here mate, so you can just sod off you wanker,' came the reply.

'Yeah, right, pull the other one. Where's Emelia?'

'Seriously, fuck off, mate, Tony's not here. I don't give a toss who you are. We work for Tony. If you want to speak to him, then I'll pass on your regards.'

Seth had got the wrong man. Where was Tony? Where was Emelia? Something was amiss, and Seth felt out of sorts. He had anticipated more resistance, a more aggressive or violent response. He had also expected to find Emelia; his spirit started to wane as he realised that he was not yet any closer to finding her.

In his previous life, he would just make an arrest on suspicion of conspiracy to kidnap and go from there. But stood here now, he was unsure how to deal with the situation. *The gun will change things.* Seth needed to be the aggressor to get a response and the information he needed.

★ ★ ★

'Wake her up. This is no fun if she can't feel it,' Spiller shouted at Mugger.

Mugger threw another bucket of water over Emelia. The cold, sharp shock stimulated her senses again. She opened her eyes to see Spiller advancing, pushing the picana toward her chest.

'No more, please no more. I don't have your money.'

Spiller placed the picana on the ground and then pulled out a folding knife from his pocket. He opened the blade and held it against Emelia's cheek. 'Would losing parts of your body make a difference to your appetite to talk to me perhaps?'

He drew the flat of the blade down her cheek with just enough pressure for Emelia to feel the metal but so as not to draw blood. Then he brought the blade around to her chin and down the contours of her neck, past the dip between her clavicles and onto her chest, bringing it to rest at her left nipple.

'Shall we start with this one?' he whispered.

'You sadistic bastard, do you hate women that much?'

Spiller pushed the blade to draw the slightest amount of blood.

★ ★ ★

Seth pulled the gun from his belt and pointed it at the man in front of him, hoping that would be enough to change gear and get them to offer up more information.

'Let me make this clear, I need to know where Emelia DiSalvo is, and I need to know now.'

They looked unperturbed, just looking at Seth and smiling.

'Or what, you'll shoot us and still not know where she is?'

Seth lowered the gun, squeezing his hand as he did. The gun fired, sending the bullet between the man's legs.

'Yes, if I need to,' he said.

'Firing a shot at the floor is a little different than shooting someone. You're not a seasoned shooter, mate, just fuck off.'

Seth squeezed again. This time the bullet contacted flesh, tearing a hole in the man's calf, just missing the bone. The man's body crumbled; he fell to his knees, letting out a scream as his hands grabbed at the hole torn in his leg, blood flowing onto the floor.

'Okay, okay, we get the point,' the woman spoke for the first time.

Seth moved closer, holding the gun at arm's length.

'Where is Emelia? Is she alive? Tell me where she is. That's all I need to know, then I'll sod off?'

'She's with Tony at the farm,' the woman spoke nervously, while the man lay on his side clutching his leg and groaning on the floor.

'Who was in the body bag?' asked Seth.

The woman looked surprised.

'Pashley, Marc Pashley, how do you know about that?' she said.

'I'm asking the questions, where is the farm?' Seth retorted, prodding the air with the gun.

'Birch Wood Farm. It's on Village Lane between Slough and Beaconsfield,' the woman's reply was unforced.

'I need your phones and your van keys,' demanded Seth.

The woman put her hand into her jacket pocket.

'Stop,' shouted Seth. 'If I see anything other than a phone or keys, your leg gets the next dose of lead, take your hand out slowly, very slowly.'

She pulled out her phone, holding it between her forefinger

and her thumb.

'Chuck it over here,' said Seth, keeping his distance.

The phone landed at his feet. 'Now your mate's phone, who has the van keys?'

'Ryan has them both,' said the woman. She leant down and slowly put her hand into the man's jacket pocket.

Seth was sweating in the cool tunnel. His adrenalin-fuelled bravado had taken its toll on his nerves. He had his finger poised, ready to respond at the sight of a gun emerging from the jacket pocket. The woman's hand came into view, holding a phone and a fobbed key.

'Throw them here,' demanded Seth.

She did as she was told, not questioning anything.

Seth leant down, keeping his eyes on the two of them as he picked up the mobile phones and the van keys, pushing them all into his jacket pocket, he paused as his heartbeat slowed a little.

'Now that wasn't so bad, guys, was it?' said Seth as he stood up. 'I'm going to leave you here for a while, Ryan. I just need to borrow your mate and your van for a bit. What's your name?' he said as he looked at the woman.

'Karen, my name's Karen,' she replied.

'Right, come with me then, Karen,' said Seth, indicating that she should walk in front of him along the tunnel.

Karen walked ahead. Ryan had stopped groaning but still lay with his hands clamped tightly around the wound in his leg.

'Keep holding that tight. The blood will clot soon enough, mate,' said Seth as he started to follow Karen along the tunnel back towards the entrance.

They reached the door to the tunnel. Seth exited first, with the gun still pointed at Karen.

'Shut the door and lock the padlocks,' he said.

'Okay, mate,' said Karen, doing as she was asked.

'Now face the door, hands up high against it and legs apart.'

Seth tucked the gun back into his belt and started to pat Karen down. He placed his left foot up against the inside of Karen's; he would feel movement from her foot early if she decided to turn and run or fight. First, Seth used both hands to feel Karen's arms from her wrists down to her armpits, one arm at a time, then he moved his hands around to her chest and searched her torso.

'Is there anything in your pockets that could cause harm to either you or me,' he found himself slipping into routine police search terminology.

'No, are you Old Bill?' asked Karen, suspecting that he was.

'Old, Old Bill,' answered Seth, I'm on the other side now. Lift your right foot.'

Seth searched one leg, then the other. Once he had finished, he stepped back and took the gun back out. 'We are going to Birch Wood Farm, Karen, and if you put a foot wrong, you will have a new hole somewhere in your body, stay here for two minutes. I need to make a call.'

'Okay, mate, I'm not going anywhere,' she replied.

Seth climbed the first flight of steps and then pushed the push to talk button on his phone.

'Glen... are you there, mate? ov—' He stopped himself from finishing his last word.

'Seth, yeah, all good here mate, you found Emelia yet, hurry the fuck up?'

Glen moved out of the kitchen so that he could speak out of earshot of Larry and Michael.

'Not yet, but soon, I hope. Have you heard of Birch Wood Farm?' Seth asked.

'Yeah, well kind of... I know that Larry has his drugs factory and other shit set up at a farm. I've never been there myself - I was his burglary man. Only the drugs and exploitation bods were allowed anywhere near it.'

'I think that's where she is. I'm with one of Tony Spiller's cronies, a woman called Karen. We're going over to the farm now,' said Seth.

'Karen's a wuss, just keep the pressure on her, and she'll do what you want. Her priority is survival, so she'll run before she fights.'

'Cheers,' Seth found himself beginning to trust his unconventional new partner.

He ushered Karen to the van, putting her in the driver's seat, before getting in himself and passing her the keys.

'Birch Wood Farm, and don't piss me around, Karen,' said Seth. The van set off, heading north out of Slough.

CHAPTER 31

Farmyard Animals

Emelia was exhausted, still tied to the chair and alone in the barn. Her wrists and ankles were red, raw from her contortion and struggles in response to the picana. She sat shivering from the cold, covered in mud, her knickers wet from the buckets of water repeatedly thrown over her, and her feet buried in the resulting muddy pool under the chair.

'I can't get hold of Big-Gun; his phone just rings out,' said Mugger.

'He's probably gone to bed; it's late. We should pick this back up in the morning,' replied Spiller.

'Let's have one more go at the slut. She'll talk this time, she has to,' said Mugger. He wanted to be the one that forced Emelia into talking and get recognition and kudos from Larry.

'Okay, let's have one more go then, we'll use the rope this time,' said Spiller.

He picked up an old coffee bean sack that contained a long rope and walked back into the barn with Mugger, Thug following behind as usual.

Emelia's head was slumped to one side, her eyes shut.

'Shall I wake her up, Tony?' asked Thug, laughing slightly.

'No, I'll wake her a different way.'

Spiller tied a loop in the rope. A Jack Ketch knot - the

hangman's noose. Then he threw the rope over the barn's central beam, catching it as it fell back down. He pulled the hessian coffee sack onto her head, then gently pushed the noose over Emelia's head before taking hold of the other end of the rope and taking up the slack. Emelia remained asleep, blissfully unaware of what was about to happen. Spiller steadied himself readying to heave her upward. Then he leant back and pulled with all his might. Emelia was hoisted upward, her neck bearing the weight of her whole body and the chair. Her lungs screamed for oxygen, waking her instantly as terror filled her brain. Unable to breathe or see, she thought she was about to die; either her neck would snap, or she would suffocate.

'Ready to talk to us yet, honey?' shouted Spiller.

Emelia was silent, unable to utter a sound, her neck crushed by the rope. Her were eyes wide open and bulging inside the sack, the brown hessian began to turn black as her blood rushed to her vital organs. Her mind was unable to form a single thought. Her hands frantically trying to move from their fastened points on the chair, desperate to grasp the rope and try to release the pressure. Spiller let go of the rope, and the chair hit the ground with a wet thud, sending a shock through the base of Emelia's spine and up to her neck.

★ ★ ★

Seth sat in the passenger seat, with the gun trained on Karen. The van sped along the lanes, north out of Slough; Karen clearly knew where she was going. Seth's mind was desperately trying to formulate a plan. Sitting in the van was the easy bit, but he headed closer to uncertainty with every metre he travelled. He was trapped in a collapsing time frame, one that he could not yet see a way out of.

'Tell me about the farm,' said Seth.

'It's a fucking farm, barns and fields and shit,' answered Karen.

Karen kept her eyes on the road, focused on the job at hand. She would rather be driving Seth to the farm than laying in the tunnel with a bullet wound in her leg. Karen was given all the 'just do' jobs. Taking orders was easy and required nothing much in the way of thought. She was less than intelligent and failed to realise that Ryan would milk the fact that he took a bullet to protect Big-Gun's organisation, while she had just succumbed to Seth's demands and given away the location of Big-Gun's farm. Ryan would end up being the lucky one.

'You know what I mean, how many buildings, who is there, where's Emelia being kept?'

'Look, I just do stuff for Tony, I know jack shit. I know where the farm is, been there a few times, I've dropped stuff off and picked stuff up, but that's it. Me and Ryan just help him sort stuff out,' replied Karen.

Seth got the feeling that she was being straight with him. He sat quietly for a while, trying to build his plan of action.

'Slow down a bit. I need some time to think.'

As the words came out of his mouth, the flashing blue light in the mirror hit his eyes.

'Let them go past, don't drive like a twat.'

Karen slowed the van, but the blue lights did not overtake. Instead, the police vehicle's headlights flashed and were quickly accompanied by a short whoop-whoop of its siren.

'Shit, we're being pulled over. Will they know you?' asked Seth.

'Probably, most of them do.'

Karen pulled the van over to the side of the road. For the first time in his life, Seth was not pleased to see a copper. Sat in a van with a locally known shit-bag and carrying a gun was not on his bucket list. He wound down the window and moved the door mirror so that he could watch what was going on. One of them walked towards the passenger door, the other to the driver's side, speaking into his radio.

'Morning, what's the rush then? Can you get out of the vehicle, please?'

Karen got out and walked around to the passenger side of the van, followed by the police officer. Seth stayed put, hoping not to become engaged in discussion with the police, watching as the officer spoke to Karen. The second officer stood a little way back, keeping an eye on both Karen and the van's passenger door. He was in the backup role, there in case Karen kicked off or Seth made a move to get out of the van.

'There's no rush, officer,' said Karen.

'Well, you were certainly going faster than thirty, a fair bit faster,' the officer interjected.

'I'm sorry, I hadn't realised, mate.'

'Do you have your license on you?' The officer had decided to take on an officious tone with Karen.

Seth was less than confident that the situation was going to unfold well. The blue lights pulsated while the officer engaged Karen in conversation, noting down her date of birth and running her details over the radio.

Seth slid across to the driver's seat and slowly dropped himself out of the open door, careful not to make a sound. He looked under the van to check the exact position of the two officers. The first officer was standing at the front with Karen, and the second officer about halfway along the side of the van, facing his colleague, so intent on watching his pal and the passenger door that he had not given a thought to Seth getting out of the driver's side.

Seth moved quietly; each step he took was purposefully slow and measured. The van was parked half up on the verge, and the patrol car was in the road. As he reached the back of the van, he looked underneath again – all three were still in the same places. He stayed crouched, regulating his breathing as he planned his move to the police car. Four more steps, and he was at the driver's door, still out of view of the officers with Karen. Next, he took hold of the door handle and pulled it as slowly as he could. The lock released its hold with a quiet click. Seth held himself low and still for five seconds. There was no response from the officers; the sound had not reached their ears. As he opened the door a couple of inches, the interior light came on. *Hold your nerve, Seth.* He took another step so that he was on the inside of the open door. As he peered through the car's window and out of the windscreen, he could just see the back of the supporting officer, still facing his mate and Karen. Seth slid his hand into the car, reaching up to take the keys from the ignition. There were no keys, just an empty ignition barrel. *Bollocks, all the best made plans and all that.*

He turned his body, ready to get back to the van after his failed mission. As he lifted his head one more time to check on the officers and Karen, he saw a blue plastic card-wallet hanging from the sun visor. *That's the fuel card on the key fob.* He opened the door a little wider, and half got into the car, just far enough in, to grab the fob and pull it clear. Bingo, he had the car keys. As he moved to get out, he heard the car's police radio.

'Charlie Oscar two-two, re Karen Marshall, are you one-two? Over.'

One-two was the code for out of earshot. The control room was about to send a confidential message, it would be transmitted to the car radio as well as the officers personal radio's earpiece.

Seth waited; he needed to hear what was about to be said to the officer.

'Affirmative, earpiece in, go ahead, over.'

'She's all-in-order but has a marker as an associate of a man called Tony Spiller. He has markers for violence, carries a firearm and is currently wanted on a failure to appear court warrant for causing grievous bodily harm, over.'

'All received, many thanks, out.'

Seth slunk back to the rear of the van, listening for the officer's next move. As he passed an open drain, he dropped the gun through the grate. *If they decide to search us, I can't afford to get nicked for possession of a firearm. Better to get to Emelia without it than not get to her at all.*

'Who's in the van with you, Karen?' asked the officer.

There was enough of a pause for Seth to speed his step. The van shook as he got back in.

'Seth someone,' Karen didn't even try to make up a name.

'Out, now,' came the call.

The passenger door opened just as Seth had reached his seat.

'Out, I said mate.'

Seth got out of the van, trying to hide the fact that his adrenalin had reached peak flow, beads of sweat forming on his forehead.

'What's your name, pal?' asked the closer of the two officers.

'Seth Hannen,' replied Seth, deciding to give his real details and hope that the officers had not heard of him. Patrol officers had a pretty quick turn over, and he certainly did not recognise them from his days working at Slough.

'And your date of birth, mate?'

Seth gave the officer his date of birth, knowing that there would be no trace of him on the Police National Computer. The officer wrote down the details before then calling up and passing them to the radio operator.

Seth heard him say something about Tony Spiller, but the officer's head was turned, and he had lowered the volume of his voice. *Shit, they think I'm Tony bloody Spiller,* thought Seth.

'Okay, mate, can you show me your left forearm, please?'

said the officer.

Seth was not sure if they were checking for a tattoo or if he was about to be tricked into being handcuffed. Either way, he could not risk being mistaken for Tony Spiller and arrested. He moved as if to undo the cuff of his shirt. The officer's eyes were down, looking at Seth's arm. *These guys really are off the ball.* As soon as he had pulled his arm back, he let his fist fly, aiming about a foot beyond the officer's head so as not to slow the blow too early. As his knuckles contacted the officer's nose, Seth felt a crack, the bridge of the nose separating from the skull. The officer was caught off guard, and instead of reaching for his pepper spray, he went for his nose as the pain shot into his head. Seth followed up with a double palm blow to the chest, a classic police defence move. He pushed both hands as hard as he could at a forty-five-degree upward angle, lifting the officer upward as he still held his nose. The officer left the ground, falling backwards towards his colleague, who was now moving forward, fumbling to release his pepper spray from his belt. His colleague's flailing body took him off balance, and the pair found themselves in a heap on the ground.

'In the van, get in now,' Seth shouted at Karen, who was watching, impressed at Seth's moves.

Truth be told, Seth had been lucky. He had expected to have needed to tackle the second officer separately. He ran past the pile of cops, leaning in and grabbing the pepper spray and pulling hard. The canister came out of its holder, sending the coiled elastic recoiling and the plastic tub into the officer's groin. He ran around the van and jumped into the driver seat, turning the ignition and spinning away.

The officers untangled themselves and got back to their car. Seth saw the doors close and imagined the panicked search for the keys now unfolding.

'Direct me to the farm, and don't fuck me around,' Seth

raised his voice at Karen, the spray now replacing the gun in his right hand.

* * *

Seth drove the van into the entrance to the farm. Ahead of him, he saw three barns off to the right and an old farmhouse to the left. Everywhere was in darkness.

'Park in the second barn; that's where we normally chuck the van,' said Karen.

Karen was still in self-preservation mode. She would just do as she was told until the opportunity to run presented itself. Seth gave her a glance, wondering how much trust to put in her words. He drove the van through the open barn doors, pulled up next to two cars and another van, and killed the engine.

'Out of the van,' ordered Seth.

She accommodated his request and moved to the front of the van awaiting Seth's next instruction. Seth turned his phone back off again, then walked up behind her as he pushed the pepper spray into his jean pocket. Then he removed his belt from his trousers.

'Hands behind your back,' he said.

Karen did as she was asked. Seth looped his belt through its buckle to form a noose and pulled it tight around Karen's wrists before then wrapping the loose end around the middle, tighter and tighter, then a knot to hold it in place. He grabbed hold of her tied wrists and pushed her forward.

'Where will they be holding Emelia?' asked Seth.

'I don't know, in the big barn, in the house, out in the fields, your guess is as good as mine.'

Seth did not believe her. If Karen had been to Larry's farm, she would surely know what went on where. She was far too compliant.

'Take me to the big barn,' he said.

Although dark, it was a light night. The skies were clear, and the moon and stars provided enough light for Seth to find his way without the need for a torch.

Karen led Seth from the small barn and out into the yard and then into a much larger barn. Seth could see what looked like a noose at the end of a long rope that went up and over the roof's main beam. Under the noose was an empty wooden chair standing in a puddle of water with a hessian sack on the seat. In front of the chair was a large battery and what looked to Seth like a cattle prod. A second chair lay on its side against the wall of the barn. As he stood there, he heard voices coming toward the barn. He grabbed Karen by her tied wrists and dragged her back into the corner of the barn behind a pile of old machinery.

'A single word and you become my shield. Do you understand what I'm saying?' Seth whispered to Karen.

'Yeah,' she replied.

There was a loud clunk as the power was switched on. Seth expected a flood of light, but instead, a couple of dim bulkhead lights flickered into life at each end of the barn, hardly making much difference to the light at all. He watched as two men dragged an almost naked Emelia into the barn, followed by Tony Spiller. She was still only dressed in her knickers.

Every muscle in Seth's body was trying to fire up, to propel him out from his cover and take on Emelia's assailants. But he sat still watching, his pent-up energy simmering with anger.

Mugger pushed Emelia back onto her familiar seat, and she slumped down, offering no resistance. Spiller threw an empty beer bottle aside before dropping a bag of cable ties next to her.

'Tie her back on,' he said.

Mugger tied her ankles and wrists to the chair. The raw patches of skin smarted as the ties were pulled tight. Then on went the hessian sack before the noose was placed around her neck again. Mugger nodded to Thug, who threw his half-finished beer aside and took hold of the rope, waiting for Spiller to give the word.

Seth watched hopelessly, knowing that if he broke cover, Karen would be back on her own side, and it would be only him versus the four of them. Now was not the time to affect the rescue. He needed to wait for the right moment.

Spiller hooked up the picana and dialled in the voltage, straight to the highest setting. Then without warning, he pressed the copper tip into Emelia's abdomen as Thug took up the tension in the rope. She screamed and writhed in the chair until the rope prevented her from breathing. It was the first sound that Seth had heard Emelia make. He felt her pain entering his body as he vicariously experienced her torture.

'We'll be back in a moment bitch, take some time to think about talking. This is your last chance. Don't go wandering off now,' said Spiller.

Then the three of them left the barn, pushing the doors closed as they did. This was Seth's moment. He pulled Karen out into the open and dragged her toward Emelia. As he reached the chair, he pushed Karen to the ground, she was unable to put her hands out to prevent herself from falling, and she landed in the mud with a gloopy slap.

Seth pulled the rope and the hessian sack from Emelia's head. She looked up at him. It took a few seconds before she showed any sign of recognition, still suffering the effects of her torture. As Seth's face came into focus, the recognition followed, and Emelia managed half a smile.

Seth looked for something to cut the cable ties from her arms and legs. There was nothing. He sat on the ground behind the chair and took a firm grip of one of the back legs, then pushed his foot hard against the other. As the legs gave way, Emelia fell backwards. Karen saw her moment and got to her feet, ready to run to the barn door and sound the alarm. Seth gave chase, catching her fast and pulling her back.

'Don't even think about it,' he said as he pushed to the floor.

With the chair in pieces, he unhooked Emelia's feet and threw the broken wood over to the pile of machinery. Then he moved to Karen and untied the belt from her wrists.

'Get undressed, now,' said Seth.

'Fuck off, you bastard,' replied Karen.

He picked up the picana and aimed it at her.

'Undress, keep your knickers on, then roll in the mud.'

He lurched forward, making sure that it did not make contact; a shriek from Karen would alert Spiller and his men.

Karen removed her trainers and her clothes.

'Emmy, put these on, quickly,' he said, as he threw Karen's clothes in Emelia's direction.

Emelia just stared at the clothing, still not thinking straight. Voices approached the barn; Spiller was coming back.

'I'm done with this shit. If she doesn't talk, call Larry and get him to okay the fire pit.'

Seth pulled up the second chair, pushed Karen onto it before stuffing one of her socks into her mouth and then securing it with one of the long cable ties from the bag left on the ground by Spiller. He pulled it tightly around her head to hold the fabric firmly inside her mouth. Then he used more cable ties to hold her to the chair and pushed the hessian bag over her head. Seth ran to the bulkhead light and unscrewed the bulb far enough to break its connection to the electricity. A shadow fell across Karen. *I suppose she looks a little like Emelia*, he thought, as he rushed back and grabbed Emelia by the hand and dragged her toward the pile of machinery, picking up the clothes with his other hand as they went. They reached the cover of the darkness and crouched down in the corner of the barn just as the three men staggered in with more beer in their hands.

As Seth sat with Emelia, hidden by the machinery, he saw Karen's second muddy sock on the ground near the chair, *Fuck...*

CHAPTER 32

Breakout

'How did you get your fucking head out of that rope,' shouted Spiller as he put it back around Karen's neck. Karen tried to speak, only managing a strange groan through a mouth full of sock.

'Mugger, Thug, get your fat arses over here,' he shouted.

They sauntered over to Spiller from the barn doors. Mugger was holding a mobile phone to his ear but not speaking.

'Still no answer from Big-Gun,' he said.

Seth was quietly trying to get Emelia dressed. He had managed to pull the tracksuit bottoms on to her legs and get the trainers onto her feet. He pulled the hoodie over her head and poked her arms through.

'That'll do Emmy.' he whispered. 'We'll be away soon enough.'

Spiller thrust the picana into Karen's abdomen. She let out a muffled groan through her fabric filled mouth.

'You're sounding a bit livelier gorgeous, I'm glad, it makes it even more fun,' said Spiller, then he shouted. 'Pull…'

Thug gave a heave on the rope, launching Karen upward, the rope tight around her neck, she was unable to make the slightest of sounds.

'And hold it there,' called Spiller.

As Karen swung from the beam, the barn started to be illuminated by a pulsating blue light.

'Fuck, it's the rozzers,' shouted Spiller.

'This should see us out of here, Emmy,' Seth whispered to Emelia as he felt his spirit rise.

Thug let go of the rope. Karen fell, still attached to the chair, hitting the mud below and then toppling onto her side. The three men ran for the door, but there was no time to flee.

'Fuck, there's loads of them, bloody six van loads, and some,' shouted Mugger.

Seth kept still, trying to work out a plan of escape that would enable them to get out without being picked up by the local police and become officially mixed up in this. He needed to get back to Glen in Ascot and get the three of them away.

'Bring the bitch here, quickly,' called Spiller, indicating to Mugger.

'Yes, boss,' replied Mugger, as he ran over to Karen, followed by Thug.

Mugger pulled a knife from his jeans and cut the cable ties from Karen's arms and legs, then he removed the noose and dragged her to her feet. He put one arm around her neck and the other on her waist. She felt different, not as toned as before and not as strong either. As Mugger pulled her towards Spiller, he saw the sock on the ground, poking out from under Thug's boot.

'What's that? Under your boot mate,' said Mugger.

'I don't know,' replied Thug.

'Well lift your fucking boot up, what is it?'

'It's just a sock, what's up with you?' said Thug, his brain not able to piece anything together.

'It can't be just a fucking sock, can it,' shouted Mugger, as he pulled the hessian sack from Karen's head.

'Shit, it's Karen, Tony, it's Karen, for fuck's sake,' shouted

Mugger.

'What are you on about,' replied Spiller.

'You're much better looking with no clothes on than I imagined Karen, babe,' said Thug smirking, as Mugger cut the cable tie that held the sock in Karen's mouth.

Karen spat the sock to the floor and glared at Thug.

'Yeah, well, you're still as ugly as you've ever been, you fucking twat,' she replied tartly.

Spiller turned around, now in a complete rage.

'Put the fucking bag back on her head and stop pissing around. The police don't need to know who the fuck she is. Karen, you just do as you're told, and we'll all get out of here.'

He slammed the barn doors shut and flicked the light switch. Then the three of them stood listening to the commotion outside, waiting for the police to come barging through the doors.

Tony had been right. Six police riot vans had parked up on the farm, with grilles down over the windscreens. Behind them were two dog vans and a couple of CID cars; the police had sent a whole army. In command was the Bronze Commander, Chief Inspector Brian Hannigan.

The two officers that Seth had left with the patrol car had reported the incident back to the control room after Seth and Karen had made off. The automatic number plate recognition cameras on the road out of Slough had picked up the van, narrowing down its potential location. After a short search, the reconnaissance team had located the van at a farm and reported back.

Given the size and number of buildings, along with the fact that one of their own had been violently assaulted and another humiliated, Thames Valley Police had quickly amassed a show of force. The local police areas had pooled their resources and readied two police support units, known as PSUs. Each PSU comprised an inspector in charge of three riot vans, each van carrying a sergeant and six constables and having its own call sign.

Boots thudded on the ground outside as police officers took up positions around the farm. The sound was only broken by the odd bark dispatched by a police dog being held back by its handler.

'We search one building at a time, clear?' shouted Hannigan, his voice booming out in the early morning mist.

'Clear,' a choir of voices from the units replied in concert as they moved into position.

There are three barns and the main house to search and secure.

'Units One-Alpha and One Bravo, secure the farmhouse. Go, go, go,' said Hannigan into his radio, sending the two sergeants and twelve constables to the main farm building.

Seth lay flat on the ground in the barn, holding Emelia tight, and constantly whispering to her to keep her awake. He peered out from behind the pile of machinery. Spiller and Mugger were standing either side of Karen, and Thug stood further back. They sat her on the chair and placed it six or seven metres from the entrance to the barn, the sack over her head. They were in clear view of the barn doors, just waiting for the police to come through them.

The front door to the farmhouse gave way quickly as the steel door opener battered its way in. Spiller and Mugger listened to the shouting as the police were sent into the house.

'Police stay where you are,' the shouts were followed by muffled reports as officers checked each room.

After ten minutes or so, the house was reported as being clear and secure.

'On to the barns, One-Charlie and Two-Alpha, take one each of the smaller two. Two-Bravo and Two-Charlie, you're on the bigger barn,' said Hannigan into his radio.

Officers checked the perimeter of each barn, looking for any other exit points, before lining up at the doors to each of the buildings.

Seth lay listening to the boots plodding around the barn, unsure how he would get away from the situation other than in the back of a police car.

'One-Charlie, go, go, go,' Hannigan gave the order.

The doors of the smaller barn were pulled back on their runners. There was much more shouting and more banging as officers stormed into the barn.

'Clear, no persons seen, looks like a drug factory boss, there's gear everywhere,' came the report over the radio.

'Two-Alpha, go now,' the second of the smaller barns yielded to the search.

'Clear, no persons seen. Three vehicles, two vans and a car.'

Seth moved to gain a better view of the door. Spiller now had a gun at Karen's head, waiting to shift things to a hostage situation to try and prevent the police from entering the barn.

Seth's foot slipped on a layer of dried grain. The tinny thud too loud to hide his presence. He froze, waiting for Spiller's response.

'What the fuck was that?' said Mugger.

'Fuck it, the pigs will be through the door any moment; leave it,' replied Spiller.

Seth was unable to see what he had uncovered, but it was hollow.

Two officers grabbed hold of each of the full height barn doors. 'Go, go, go,' shouted Hannigan.

The wheels on the top runners squealed loudly as the doors started to slide open. The noise allowed Seth the opportunity to push the metal on the floor aside, revealing a pitch-black abyss. The old ventilation tunnel allowed air to be sucked in or out of the barn to dry piles of grain.

The barn doors ground to an abrupt stop, and torchlight flooded the barn.

'Hold the line,' came the shout from the officers about to storm the barn.

'Report,' called Hannigan.

'Two hostiles and one possible hostage. Firearm seen. Withdraw, withdraw.'

Seth pushed Emelia into the void.

'Crawl, quick go now, crawl as fast as you can,' he said.

She started to move slowly as he pushed her legs, then her feet into the tunnel. Then he climbed in and followed, jabbing at her feet with his hands to keep her moving as he crawled behind her. The shaft headed toward the back of the barn, away from the standoff between Spiller's crew and the police.

'Back off, or the woman dies,' shouted Spiller.

The officers moved away while Hannigan called the situation into the control room, requesting armed support to attend the farm.

The shaft was only about half a metre square. Seth and Emelia crawled along, not knowing if the end would provide a way out or simply lead to a dead end. But an escape had to be attempted, or they would end up with Spiller's gun pointing at them or the police bundling Seth into a patrol car. The shaft grew darker and darker the further along they got. Emelia spoke for the first time.

'This is going nowhere, Seth,' her voice was etched with panic.

'I'll go in front, move over,' he replied.

Seth wiggled his way over and past Emelia. 'Keep going, follow me.'

Back in the barn, Spiller and his men had pushed the barn doors closed and were waiting for the next move from the police.

'Fuck it, Mugger, go and sort her out. Emelia must be hidden over there, where that noise came from. We may need a little more bargaining power if things get shitty with the pigs,' said Spiller.

Mugger ran toward the machinery and around to where Seth and Emelia had been hiding.

'There's a bloody tunnel Tony, she's gone down a fucking tunnel,' shouted Mugger.

'I'm coming; you three stay here,' said Spiller.

Tony ran to the opening and climbed into the shaft. He could hear Seth and Emelia ahead of him and started moving faster, quickly making up ground on Emelia, who was still behind Seth.

Finally, Seth reached the end of the shaft, the only option now was up, but all looked black. He pulled the mobile phone from his pocket and turned it on, illuminating the way up. A metre above his head was a large fan unit.

Meanwhile, at the front of the barn, Hannigan was trying to talk sense through the closed doors.

'There is no way you can get out of here. I have armed officers on their way. You may as well just drop the weapon and hand yourselves in.'

He shouted his negotiations into the barn, but there was no reply. Police dogs barked, eager to be let loose.

Seth could hear the distant bark of the dogs echoing down the tin shaft. He crouched, dipping his head so that he could push his shoulders into the grate between the fan and the base of the extractor unit – Seth pushed upwards, and the metal creaked but would not move. He adjusted his angle of attack and tried again with all his might. There was more creaking, then a loud crack followed by the fan unit's sudden abrupt movement as it left its mounting. The cold morning air entered the shaft as he continued to push the fan unit upward. It fell onto its side, opening the shaft to the damp morning dew. Up and out of the shaft he went.

'Come on, Emelia, get out,' he said quietly.

'I…I can't, someone's just grabbed my leg,' she replied.

Spiller had caught up quickly and had a firm hold of Emelia's right ankle. He gave it a firm wrench. Emelia fell flat, laying on her stomach. Then she felt herself being pulled backwards, a hand now on each ankle.

'Seth…' Emelia called out.

Seth looked down and saw Emelia disappearing in the wrong direction as she was dragged back by Spiller.

'No, Emelia, I'm not losing you, not now,' said Seth as he climbed down and back into the tunnel.

Seth moved quickly to grab Emelia's hands. It was now a tug of war, with Emelia being the rope.

Tony Spiller and Seth were evenly matched physically. If Seth was going to get the upper hand, he needed to outthink Spiller. Seth could not afford to return to the barn and fight it out. Mugger and Thug were there, and taking all three of them on was not an option. He remembered the pepper spray in his back *pocket. It'll be dodgy to let that off in here. We could all get a face full, a chance I'll have to take,* he thought, as he let go of one hand and pulled the canister from his pocket, scrabbling to move as close as he could to Spiller.

'Let her go, just leave her, you've done enough,' he shouted at Spiller as he let ten seconds of peppery spray loose into the tunnel and into Spiller's face.

Spiller's response was instant. He screamed with the stinging pain in his eyes, immediately letting go of Emelia's legs. Emelia cried out as she took a dose of pepper spray as well; Seth's aim had not been perfect. Seth pulled her back toward the way out. He reached the opening again and climbed out into the morning air, followed by Emelia, her eyes shut tightly, still stinging. Once he had his bearings, they started to run.

'This way, just hold my hand, don't touch your eyes,' he said, as they headed to the corner of the barn, stopping there before going any further.

There were no police at the back of the barn; why would there be, there were no doors there. Seth and Emelia started to walk slowly along the side of the barn. He could see the shape of the smaller barn ahead of them and then the parked-up police vehicles beyond that. They inched their way along until they reached the front corner. Police officers were lined up in single file, waiting for the order to take on Spiller and his crew. They were all transfixed, concentrating on the entrance to the barn. Seth and Emelia needed to get across a ten-metre gap between the buildings, to the cover of the second barn, and then move toward the farm gates.

'Run,' he said to Emelia, grabbing her by the hand and leading the way as they broke cover.

They were halfway across the gap when a voice called out.

'Persons seen,' a young officer shouted as he pointed toward Seth and Emelia, just as they disappeared behind the second barn.

They were sprinting now, Emelia much more awake than she was earlier. The adrenalin helped her move and keep up with Seth.

'Dog unit, deploy,' shouted Hannigan.

The dog handler ran past the entrance to the large barn, giving chase with her dog on the lead. As she reached the small barn, she saw Seth and Emelia rounding the corner at the other end.

'Stand still, or I'll release the dog,' she shouted.

Seth fixed his eyes on the unmarked CID car parked at the end of the line of police vehicles. *If any of the cars had keys left*

381

in them, he thought it would be the CID car. It was ten metres away and the dog had thirty metres to cover before it would catch them.

'Come on, Emmy, faster,' he pulled at her hand as he upped the pace.

They ran toward the car, and the dog let out a bark as it was released from its leash. The German Shepherd was quickly in full flow; its only objective was to get to Seth and Emelia, trained to take down offenders on the run.

As Seth grabbed the door handle of the unmarked car, the dog rounded the end of the barn. Seth pulled at the handle as Emelia ran to the passenger door, feeling her way around the car and peering through her almost closed eyes, still stinging from the pepper spray. The door opened, and Seth threw himself into the driver seat as the dog launched itself toward him as he tried to pull the door shut, taking hold of Seth's right arm in its jaws.

'Don't touch the dog, stay still and don't resist,' shouted the dog handler.

Emelia sat in the passenger seat watching as Seth pulled the spray back out from his pocket and sprayed a burst of liquid at the dog, struggling to maintain a good aim with his left hand. The dog yelped and whined as it let go of Seth's arm. A second burst emptied the canister and sent the dog back toward its handler, yelping.

Seth slammed the door shut and checked for the key. Sure enough, the CID officer had left it in the ignition. He started the engine and threw the car into reverse just as the dog handler caught up with her dog. The wheels spun, and the clutch whined as Seth J-turned the car around and floored the accelerator. They were off down the driveway, with nothing now in their way.

'Open the window Emmy, the wind will blow the pepper

spray from your eyes,' said Seth, as they headed back to Slough.

As they sped along the lanes, the doors to the barn were pulled open, and armed police officers flooded the barn.

'Get on the floor, lie face down, do it now, came the shouts from the firearms officers.

Mugger, Thug and Karen, were quickly trussed up into handcuffs at gunpoint. Spiller was found in the air shaft by a police dog and suffered quite a mauling before being taken away.

Seth knew that with the number of resources deployed to the farm, there would only be the bare minimum left in Slough. All the same, the details of the CID car's theft would be out on the radio in no time. He drove quickly but took a less obvious back-route towards Slough.

★ ★ ★

Seth parked the car outside a small parade of shops on Stoke Road.

'Let's go, Emmy, your car is around the corner,' he said.

'What the hell happened back there, Seth?' she asked, looking at Seth. 'Who was that woman?'

'I'll explain everything later; I think we both have a lot of explaining to do,' he replied.

He wiped the steering wheel and gear knob with his untucked shirt, then shoved the car key behind the visor, then they got out of the car and set off on foot. They walked along Stoke Road and into Brunel Way, where Seth grabbed the key from on top of the rear wheel of the Mercedes and unlocked it.

'What the hell happened to the back window?' asked Emelia.

'Ah, yes, I was hoping you have windscreen cover!'

Seth smiled for the first time that he could remember as they got into the car.

Before they set off, Seth pulled the phone from his pocket, turned it back on and pressed the push to talk.

'Glen, you there, mate?'

'Yep, still… are you not done yet?' replied Glen.

'Pretty much, I've got Emelia. I'll pick you up in twenty-five minutes.'

★ ★ ★

Glen was already standing outside the gates when Seth pulled up at the entrance of Kuredo. They rearranged themselves in the car, Emelia taking the smaller back seat and laying down to get some rest.

'Looks like you two had some fun, sorry I missed it,' said Glen, smiling at Seth.

'It was certainly not your usual night in Slough,' replied Seth.

'Don't exaggerate, mate, have you ever lived there…?' said Glen, laughing.

The three of them drove back to Emelia's house in Highgate, Seth updating her about the fire at his house and his mother's death as they went. Glen called and updated Xavier Addington.

'What did you do with Larry and Michael?' asked Seth.

'Nothing, they're just a bit tied up right now. I'm sure Sandra will sort them out when she gets home later. Larry will be fine, but our cover is blown now, I reckon!' replied Glen.

CHAPTER 33

A Day at the Races

Friday the 18th of June 2021 looked like a typical day, but it wore a disguise for some people, hiding its true identity. For some people, the 18th of June had decided to gossip about the past.

Emelia parked her new white Mercedes soft-top in the allocated space in car park number one. She and Seth got out, the soft top closing with the push of a button. She had finally persuaded him to go to Royal Ascot with her, he was now able to face what he had seen as his nemesis.

'Don't forget your hat, Seth,' said Emelia, reminding him to pick up his top hat from the back seat.

'I'm on it,' he replied, grabbing it before closing the car door.

'To the racing… you ready?'

'I think so; let's have some fun Emmy, I'm feeling lucky today. It's not every day that you're forty-nine after all,' answered Seth.

They walked hand in hand, in the direction of the entrance to the Royal Enclosure.

'I love those dogs,' said Emelia, pointing at a golden retriever by the gate.

As they passed through the security check, Emelia went to stroke the dog sitting obediently at the legs of its handler.

'Don't touch the dog; he's working,' came the crabby reply from the dog handler.

Emelia looked at Seth and laughed as they walked into the beautifully manicured lawns of the Old Paddock.

'This is where it all started, back in ninety-two,' said Seth.

'I know Seth, but that's all in the past. New things lie ahead for us now. Let's just enjoy your birthday.'

She stopped to face him and kiss him tenderly on the lips, but a man's voice interrupted them.

'So good to see you, Emelia. I hope that you are well?'

Emelia broke from her embrace with Seth and turned. A handsome man in his mid-forties, dressed in top hat and tails, stood in front of them. She gave him a long hug.

'Hi Paul, so good to see you too,' she said.

Seth felt an uneasiness as he watched Emelia hugging another man, waiting to be introduced.

'Seth, this is Paul,' she said.

As she spoke, Xavier walked over, his arms wide open as he prepared to welcome Seth and Emelia.

'You found them before me, Paul,' said Xavier, laughing loudly. 'Seth, this is Paul, my husband; we've been married a couple of weeks,' said Xavier, looking at Paul affectionately.

'Wow, that is great news, congratulations Xavier,' said Seth, taking hold of Emelia's hand again.

'Is Glen not coming as well?' asked Emelia.

'I did invite him, but he was adamant that he wanted to be in the main Grandstand, not in the Royal Enclosure. Perhaps we'll get him dressed up next year, eh?' laughed Xavier.

'That's a shame. He's a good chap, and I've actually grown to like him. Maybe we can meet him for a drink later, between races or something,' replied Seth.

As the two couples walked towards one of the champagne bars, another voice called out to Seth.

'Fancy meeting you here, déjà-fuckin'-vu eh, Seth the Sleuth, and Emelia too, I'm so pleased that you are both doing so well,' said the older man, as he tipped the brim of his top hat.

Seth turned to see Larry Fowler stood with his wife and two grown-up sons.

'Larry, I've moved on. You have no hold on me now. Just leave us alone,' said Seth, refusing Larry's offer of a handshake.

'Good to hear it, Seth,' replied Larry, as Michael and Sean walked away with Sandra.

Seth reached into his pocket and pulled out the engraved battered Zippo lighter that had been among his retirement gifts.

'You can have this back too; I have no need for a reminder of the part you played in my life.'

He tossed the lighter in Larry's direction. Larry caught it and then pulled out a cigar from the inside pocket of his morning suit. He put it between his lips and flipped the lighter open before igniting the flame, then sucking on the thick brown rolled tobacco.

'Thanks, Seth, but there's something I need you to know...' he said as he blew out a plume of smoke. 'But it comes with a warning, too much knowledge eats you up from the inside Seth, it causes so much pain.'

'There's nothing you can say to me that will have any effect on me now, Larry, nothing at all,' replied Seth.

'Well, that may be, but you should know that I didn't mean Edward to die.'

'What... what do you mean,' said Seth, as an ice-cold shock wave travelled up his spine, inducing a temporary paralysis.

Emelia took hold of Seth's hand, as Larry continued to speak.

'Your father, he just came home too early, if he'd just let me run away, he'd be here today, enjoying the fuckin' racing with you. Why the fuck did he have to try and be the hero, eh?'

Seth stood looking at Larry, his mind again returning to

when he was six years old.

'You were the burglar!' exclaimed Seth.

'No, it wasn't burglary, I was screwin' your mum, I was about to leave after she'd gone to get you from school. I'd just given her a happy fuckin' birthday seeing to...'

'Come on,' said Emelia, as she tried to pull Seth away, but he was rooted to the spot.

'Your dad was a brave man, Seth. He didn't make a sound when I sank the knife in. I'm sorry it happened,' said Larry.

Seth was dumbfounded. His world had taken on a new dark appearance, and Larry had taken control of his thoughts again.

'I don't believe you; you're lying, there is no way that's true. Mum wouldn't have...' replied Seth.

'Believe what you want to fuckin' believe, Seth, that's up to you. Shit happens... You just have to deal with it so that it doesn't get any worse than it already is or let it hang around in your life for too fuckin' long.'

Then Larry turned and walked away to catch up with his wife and two sons, and he disappeared into the crowd.

THE END

EPILOGUE

'Gracious God, surround us and all who mourn this day with your continuing compassion. Do not let grief overwhelm your children, or turn them against you…'

The turn-out at Larry's funeral was quite something. As well as his family, most of his generals were there. Word of Big-Gun's demise had travelled, and finally, his army of criminals knew who he was.

Seth stood at the back of the room with Emelia and Xavier Addington. They had all been surprised to see Rebecca Langford, who was brought in flanked by a couple of security guards. She had been given leave to attend, having been moved from Peterborough Prison to an open prison in record time after her conviction for embezzlement and money laundering. Tony Spiller had not been afforded the same luxury, but he was incarcerated in a high-security prison due to his partiality to violence.

Seth had needed to attend the funeral to be sure that Larry had actually left his life. But as he stood there, he realised that Larry remained in his head. Nobody but Seth's mother was able to tell him if Larry had told the truth. Seth was sure that Larry had been the man that had murdered his father, but the circumstances now left huge questions in his mind. He knew he had to make his mind up. If he allowed himself to live with such colossal doubt, it would be his penance for the poor decision he had made all those years ago when he first met Larry. He needed to decide whether to trust the word of an out-and-out dishonest criminal, or to put his faith in the woman that nurtured and protected him unconditionally.

Michael and Sean Fowler glared at Seth and Emelia as they walked out, comforting their mother, one son on either side of Sandra. They had picked up Larry's business activity, exactly where he had left it.

Seth and Emelia walked out of the crematorium with Xavier Addington.

'So, I have your next assignment Seth, it looks fascinating. I think you'll enjoy it,' said Xavier, as he passed a plastic, security sealed folder to Seth, you might want to have Glen in on this one with you. I'd imagine that he'd be pretty useful.'

'Oh, you've decided to stay with Section Three then Seth?' said Emelia, giving him a wry smile.

'Ah…yes, I hadn't quite found the right moment to tell you, Emmy,' replied Seth.

AFTERTHOUGHTS

Writing my first book has been a welcome release during the coronavirus lockdown of January 2021. Getting lost in the story of Seth's life and his first adventure has taken my mind away from other concerns and worries.

I have taken liberties with some police tactics as well as setting part five in 2020 with no coronavirus. I enjoyed escaping the pandemic, and Seth had enough to contend with, without having to wear a face mask, and carry anti-bacterial hand gel.

HIDDEN BY THE LAW is a prologue to what is yet to come for Seth Hannen. He and I have more escapades up our sleeves, and the next one has already been started. You will be able to pick up any of his subsequent adventures and read them in any order you like.

For me, this book is about leaving a legacy for my family and the future generations to enjoy, and while this book is unlikely to be a best seller, I really hope you lose yourself in the story.

Until our next encounter.

Simon Bowden
Hampshire, England

ACKNOWLEDGEMENTS

To my former police service colleagues, I am eternally grateful for your commitment; the thin blue line is a special place. Thank you for your encouragement and for allowing me some artistic license.

Particular thanks go to my wife Elizabeth for her support and listening ear as I developed the storyline and Seth's character.

To Mum and Dad, thank you for your love and support. You are amazing parents, and I am proud to be your son. Enjoy the read.

To Mark Rivett and Ian Jones, thank you for agreeing to your cameo appearances. You are slightly away from your actual postings, but I hope you feel part of the story.

Thank you, Chris Evans and Graham Norton, for challenging your listeners to do something meaningful during the coronavirus lockdown. Your radio shows helped to kick me into action. I hope you read the book.

Thank you to my wonderful reviewers and proofreaders, Lianne Roberts, Lizzy Robey, Simon Morris, and Usha Choli. Your help was invaluable.

Well done to Philippa Parker from Berkshire for winning the competition to have her name used in the book.

Finally, thank you, Pete Davies and Frank Castle, for writing your books and for your support and encouragement.

ABOUT THE AUTHOR

Simon Bowden worked for thirty years as a police officer in the British police service in various roles and ranks. In his early career, he worked on response teams, the CID, and the drug squad before being promoted. As a senior police officer, he was the area commander for Bracknell, Windsor and Maidenhead, and lastly, Slough, as well as a public order commander and a firearms commander.

Having worked his way up the ranks, he finished his career in London as a chief superintendent attached to the National Police Chiefs' Council, based in the Home Office. Simon has a master's degree in criminology awarded by Cambridge University.

Towards the end of 2020 two of Simon's friends published their debut novels, inspiring him to finish the first of the Seth Hannen stories.

Simon first conceptualised **HIDDEN BY THE LAW** in 2013 but he was never able to find the time to write, only occasionally revisiting the story to add the odd note or idea over the years.

His debut novel is finally here. Simon takes his knowledge of crime and policing and combines it with storytelling.

Simon has now taken up writing full time, working on more adventures for Seth. Seth will soon return in **BOUGHT TO DIE**.

FIND OUT MORE

You can find out more about Simon's writing by visiting Simon's Facebook page; Simon Bowden - Author. Simon blogs about writing his books and engages with his readers, considering their ideas when inventing new characters and storylines. Each book has a competition to have a reader's name used for one of the book's characters.

www.obeluspublishing.com